crazy about you

unrestrained desire

told by Mia

erotic romance

author
Hartmut Hoffmann

Ground floor of Joschua's house

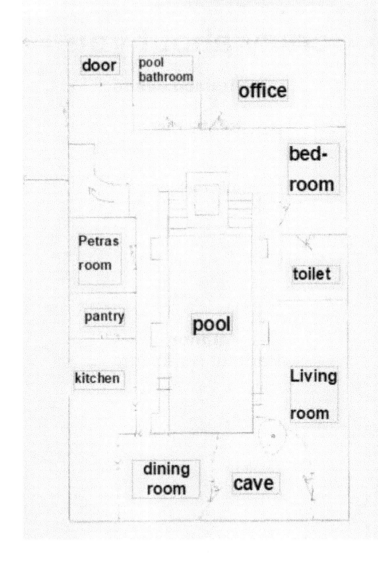

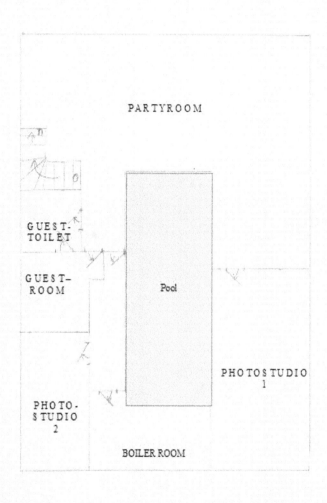

PARTYROOM

GUEST-
TOILET

GUEST-
ROOM

Pool

PHOTOSTUDIO
1

PHOTO-
STUDIO
2

BOILER ROOM

crazy about you

Oh, if you are so alone in the world in life, so completely without male protection and what else you could expect from a lovely man, you start to fantasize. To put together a man in a dream, as one imagines to be happy with him. Yes, I have just turned forty years old and already have a marriage behind me. My feeling and my inner clock tell me, if I do not slowly look for me men now, many different ones, not only of the appearance but also of the character and each test and try out, until I suddenly notice with a man it is, one of it is because my heart is screaming and my mind can not remember. If I do not find the courage to do that, then life will pass me by without it shining in on me. How should he know that I'm waiting for him?

Thoughts about thoughts that make you think about me as a man that suits me, the others about whether there is more than I have experienced in sex so far. When I watch some couples on television and then hear them scream and look happy afterwards and where you can make sex everywhere, I have to say from my experience that I have experienced next to nothing. But I think that does not exist, these are just movies or. Oh, I do not just want to know it, but also try it out, sometimes feel a man from behind in me or on the table or in nature. Sometimes a man who also takes care of me, that I also get a climax. My husband always wanted to lie on me and came so fast that I often did not feel anything at all and in order not to get in trouble I moaned softly. More was not in it, it could have heard the neighbours and that would have been bad. What would they have thought? And never cuddle or talk with each other afterwards, no, never. He always turned to the side and fell asleep immediately. What I did never interested him. That could not have been it. No impossible. I want more, a man with feelings. Hahaha I still have my sense of humor, is indeed hidden deep in me but I find him already when the right man sits opposite me. Oh, hopefully I will not jam and can not say anything. Well, if the man is good, he will realize it and will pull the conversation to him. That will certainly solve me inside and I will become freer. Yes, so I go day in day out the thoughts through my head and I am more and more urged to the certainty, I miss everything if I do not finally come to a man, a man who complements me and clear, I also him but he must. But at the very least, where to take it and not steal it. Oh, I would be far enough to steal him. What if he lived in a relationship. Oh Mia, man, if he would like you then and make with you things from your dreams, then he would have to be unhappy in his relationship right? Otherwise he would not cheat on his wife? Oh man, what have I thought again. No, it must be a man who is free, no matter what a past, for me, only the present and the future and how he enchants me. I want to be able to say something at the end of my life, since I was with him, I have lived and would like it again and again with-out ifs and buts. Mia you have wishes but how can I reach them. Oh I can not buy the man, do not bake and do not conjure. At work there are no such copies and when do I go out and if there was never one of the I liked and I must say, Schwerin is not exactly small. So go on vacation. No there can be no serious relationship, this is holiday feeling and at home it looks different. Would also be a coincidence if I met a man on Grand Canaria, who lives near me. So how?

Hello good morning dear day. Was that the solution that I dreamed or you can only vaguely remember. I was sitting at the computer and looked at ads, then my chair was extremely humid under me, so wet that I almost ran out. What have I done? Human Mia remind you please, mmm true I've read an ad and thought, if I answer, then my life changed from scratch. But the dream did not show me where to find it. Well, first get up and have breakfast and then turn on the computer. Lets see what happens. I'm very excited about the thought of the man who could turn my life upside down. Well I want to believe my dream, do not read a newspaper ad, but search the Internet. Good that it is Sunday, I have free. During the week I have lunch already. But on Sundays I also enjoy sleeping longer and have breakfast in peace. So finished with everything and the kitchen is again spark-ling, I always do it immediately when visiting un-expectedly comes, how would that look. Hahaha visit, suddenly it rings and the dream man is in front of the door as in the television commercial, but the previously sent away a few frightened. You have ideas. So dream man you could always come, with me it is always clean and tidy. Mmm thought silently for now I want to hear … . I thought so, no man rings the front door. Mia what are you thinking about again? So butter at the fish, where do I find such an ad. At a dating agency. Yes or no, I do not want to marry right away. The first man is never the one I want to spend my life with, it does not exist. Since there would be a what's that still, I saw yes-terday in the television advertising, oh yes, escapade portal. Anyone signing up will certainly not marry imme-diately but want to try something. So the chance for changing men with changing interests. Well, I take the pill, but Mia nothing without a condom when you change the partners, you never know. That comes only when it is the one I am looking for, with which I sleep without anything. I'll enjoy that, to finally feel a man in me and to be able to look him in the eye and not such a vibrator. Well, as a bridge, he is not bad, but really only as a bridge. Ah, there's an escaped portal, now or never. Mia take all your courage and sign up. Yes, but it worked quickly and then on listings - men search - clicked. Uiii, you would not have thought that's hun-dreds of advertisements. Whether they are all real. One has already heard from so many that behind it are angry people. Oh no matter what. Man, what does he want, he falls into the house with the door. No not my case. Oh no, I do not want to, he writes the same always his pref-erences only anal. No, what are they for men. Next try. Mmm sounds pretty good, but he lives too far away and the text is so normal saying nothing. This can be a long

Sunday afternoon. What they all write. Boy here are only listings of supermen. It can not exist at all, certainly not in this quantity. Oh, what's that for an ad.

He is looking for you to experience hot erotic games where almost no limits can be found and where we both can try everything, everything can do, nothing has to! If you feel like it and are between 30 and 45 years young, then get in touch with me!

Mmm in the profile, I would fit so yes and that sounds very normal but experienced happy. Let's call the guy about how his profile is.

Gray haired 35 year old, studying and now desiring to study life with you. I everything to try from A - Z, everything you can experience together and where the goal is to bring the feelings of the heart into the seventh heaven and maybe even higher, but you will see that! What do you mean, do you want to experience the fire works of emotions with me, maybe for just an hour or even a day, a week, a month or even ...?! Well that's worth a try from your point of view, then mail me and I'll definitely get in touch and try to win you over for us, so you can start the emotional fireworks.

Ohhh ... ohhh ... ohhh ... Mia what happens to you? My heart is up to my neck. I get very sweaty hands. Read again.

Gray haired 35 year old, studying and now desiring to study life with you. I everything to try from A - Z, everything you can experience together and where the goal is to bring the feelings of the heart into the seventh heaven and maybe even higher, but you will see that! What do you mean, do you want to experience the fire works of emotions with me, maybe for just an

8

hour or even a day, a week, a month or even ...?! Well that is worth a try from your point of view, then mail me and I will definitely report and try to win you for us, so you can start the emotional fireworks.

I feel it, if I answer that now, then my life changes. Mia are you crazy in your head? That is impossible. Oh my heart is racing. I answer that now but what should I e-mail. My God, if I'm the wrong maile, then he does not answer me or thinks what a stupid cow. Mia full concentration. Just be it, you can do it.

I read your ad and I almost saw myself in it again. I also have a lot of dreams but you can not experience them alone. What are you dreaming about?

Oh Mia, where did you just take the courage? I do not know that at all. What now. I'll just wait until he answers. Let's see I'll give it until tonight 22.00. Oops, what is that?

Ping

As he already answers, is he sitting at the computer right now? What is he writing?

- Hello unknown mailer, I am totally taken with your lines and the many words you put between the lines, oops do you have? Best wishes! By the way, my name is Joschua!

Without a few words but a lot of content. The man can handle words and does not fall right into the house with the door. Oh maybe my heart was right and he is. Mia you are crazy. I'll answer him and see what happens.

- Hello Joschua! What did you read between my words and lines?

- *Oh my gosh, I hope you have a lot of time to sit in front of your PC, because if I maile everything between your lines is, then it takes sooo and a little longer! But first, there was a certain amount of curiosity, something that you still want to experience in life and that you are looking for longingly and have not found yet and ...!!!*

- Sounds exciting, yes you are right, how can you read all this from the few words?

- *I do not know exactly how to e-mail you, when I read your words, it was as if they were swinging, transmitting something, something like feelings, so desires and longings. I just did not read your words with my mind, but my heart immediately switched on and the heart reads differently than the mind, which is often so terribly sober and realistic.*

- Yes!!! What kind of feelings do you mean your heart felt?

- *Oh, oh, now we have been e-mailing for only a few minutes and you are already reaching deep into me, where is that supposed to end? Or will you perhaps, the woman with whom I can experience, feel and enjoy all your and my dreams uninhibited and can?*

- Who knows, let's see what's coming, but sounds good! What do you have for dreams?

- *May I send in advance, these are all just dreams and you can only really experience if you have a partner who is totally trusted and I can trust 100%, the goal is simply to experience a lot of emotions and I believe you can only do that if you are a person who has a heart, what he can show, and then you can drop 100% with and with your partner, because only then you can fully enjoy and experience feelings. I hope that does not sound too difficult?*

10

- No, I know what you want out. You use almost the same words as I think and my heart speaks to it, ah, you've been pushing to mail some of your dreams again, so what are they?

- *It's just dreams, but they seem to be desires that you want deep down and want to experience. But do not worry, I'm not in pain, just a lot of emotions and all sorts of variations.*

- Well, no pain, but very light strokes before a climax, that can strengthen him tremendously!

- *Wow, now I'm flat, you have the same feelings like me! Say, what is sex for you or better, how would you like to experience it? Alone with a partner or with many people together?*

- That depends, but first I think it is important to experience something only with a human, a togetherness, what then results must be seen.

- *Oh that sounds as if we are already meeting in thought and the first careful approaches approach! You seem somehow familiar to me after the few sentences, even if that sounds stupid to you, my heart is already speaking and the mind holds back elegantly!*

- You can also play with words that can mess you up!

- *Thanks for the kind words, but words are one of the most important tools for people to express themselves, and how should I do it differently, I do not even know where to find you and how far you are from with. I live in Hamburg.*

- Well, we are not that far away, I live in Schwerin.

- *Almost a stone's throw! On the highway, accelerate once and brake once and I'm here! Smile!*

- Well, who knows, sounds like a fast car. By the

way my name is Mia, so now you know it!

- Sounds good Mia from Schwerin, the woman with the very big and yearning heart for a lot of feelings and love!!!

- Right! Somehow we always come back from your dreams! Take your time I just go offline for a short break and when I'm back, I'm hot to hear about your dreams!

- Oops, well then take a break! Smile!

But I need the break urgently. You know what that is. The guy can read my mind or misunderstand me he has the same thoughts as me. What should I do now. Continue writing? I feel like something is happening inside me. Mmm is a super good feeling I feel and a mad excitement. Let's see what he continues to e-mail.

- Yes, my dreams I have many, but they always play with only one woman, the woman who wants to try everything with me and who I can trust a hundred percent, because that's the most important requirement, if that's what you want and want, then read on now, otherwise just stop ...!

- Well, are you there again?

No or yes. No, I'm not ready yet. He will definitely write an e-mail again and I'll read it before I sign up again. That's as exciting as having your first date. Good that I dared. Hey, make it easy for me. There's another e-mail from him, what's he writing?

- Oh my dreams how should I say it are often captivating - smile - I have written a book, a textbook for bondage for everyone, it is written, but not all photos finished, 105 I have already but it still lacks about 200 pieces When you write you

12

have so many ideas and always new ones are added. Do not get it wrong, Bondage is for couples who want to try something, who have been together for a long time and who want to make sex exciting, or make the emotions explode, all without pain! Yes, I also listed all the legal and medical facts and then it starts. Can you imagine, I have written a book, also with testimonials from other people and could not try it yet, because I never had a partner who wanted it or who I could trust 100%. Just imagine, you would be lying on your hands and feet lying naked on the bed, all fours widespread and then your partner comes and is very, very tender doll and also determined to you and your fee lings rise, always rising and, to be honest, it of ten happened when you came to orgasm, you closed your legs or moved you to compensate for your feelings, and now imagine you can not move your body freely. You're tied down and the emotions want to go out after orgasm, where in the hands or feet in motion and it's not, so what are they doing, they slosh like waves back to the body center, like waves on the sea, over and over and over they are getting weaker and weaker, but through the waves the phase of the climax does not last longer - yeah ohhh - and al ready the feelings of the climax are gone, but - yeah ohhh yeah oh yes oh yeah - that would be the feelings you are not with can resist by a movement. You see, they take longer and that is a goal of captivating games among lovers! There's more to that, of course, but ... oh, did I shock you now? I'm so excited about your ans wer! I hope not, just gotten used to e-mailing with you, is kind of something special what I feel.

- When are you back - hallooo break is over !!!

- Have kept the break very short but want to know what you have written, I'm already curious, you make it somehow exciting to mail with you, so now I'll read your mail, oh that's long but the same.

So time wasted, what should I do? Cancel here? But if I only maile with him is also good, nothing can happen. So continue to e-mail. Mia let alone the mail in peace, because nothing can happen. Oh dear, what does he want from me? Tie me up. No, that's not possible. Well, I have not experienced something like that yet. I wanted to try everything and he said yes, he loves no pain, then he does not want me to have any. What can you get by tying for more feelings. Now I have more questions than before. I want to know more about him. Do not want to keep him waiting. I'm excited, how crazy is that?

- Sorry it took a little longer, I've read it at least ten times and already had a short dream in which I imagine how I lie there in front of you and you touch me tenderly everywhere.
- *Where exactly?*
- Now you want to make me speechless, do not go, we e-mail!!! Smile!!!
- *That does not even apply, you're already at my heart switch of the feelings rum, I already have pictures in front of me as you are lying there so completely without textiles and trying to say something, but not so, but our lips are very slow in a dialogue and deeper and deeper, oh your answer, I feel it, your tongue as she slowly, slowly moves into strange territory and pushes forward through my lips to mine, it tingles so violently throughout my body and I feel, whatever your arousal - my longest kiss took 35 minutes when I was in a disco in England at the tender age of eighteen ... oh, those feelings, your tip of the tongue feels like it's being*

14

charged with 1.000.000 small electrical particles and my lips are slowly getting moister, nestling around them and touching them, no, now it has happened, my tongue can not control itself, it thunders at yours he passes, tenderly but firmly pushes her aside and explores the space behind your hot lips, ohhh these feelings, triggered only by our lips and, of course, the tongues, just continue to speak to you, please please do not stop, it's just like that so so terribly beautiful, so exciting, with nothing to compare, soft, tender, warm but so demanding ... can not write anymore, close your eyes and enjoy.

— Madness I can almost feel you. It is as if we know each other forever, quite familiar that you write something like that, but the madness that you can also feel something, I feel your tongue, your lips, your moisture, your heart beat! I have closed my eyes and feel my outstretched arms and legs, they tingle! How would that be if you were really above me now?

— *That would be the greatest, you naked under me and I would lie on you and we would touch all over, you feel it, even with your eyes closed, also I am without clothes, as we were born naked and innocent! I am now also naked and integer innocent! Smile! To the tongue feelings come now also the whole touch points on my and your body to it. I feel your heart beating and your blood flowing in your veins. I feel your bare breasts, ohhh how is that because your nipples are so very stiff, wow, hey your pelvis pushes up, there I am, you feel my pelvis how it squeezes on yours and how do you like that, if your legs are closed and pressed together by my*
affectionately strong. Yes with every pressure I feel a twitch in your body and a hot breath blows over your lips and spreads over my face, you have feelings!!! Did you keep them all for me?

15

- Yes, on, on ...!
- *You, I have to break our lips talk just times and say goodbye to your nipples and introduce myself! Oh the way there is so soft and tender, this neck, you just have to kiss it over and over again and my tongue goes over your skin burning off a little fireworks ending up in a light goose bumps - oops I'm just redesigning you - and now my tongue tip reaches the ascent to the summit of pleasure, slowly. Very slowly, my tongue struggles up the mountain and then, ... Then she feels that hard lusting nipple in the sky and my lips enclose her, while my tongue flirts with her insistently and asks her where she's been hiding all these last few years. Where were you emotional being?*
- I was here, but you did not find me! Continue ...!
- *But now found and arrested!*
- You I have two nipples, how can you neglect the second?
- *Oh, I have no upbringing, excuse me, I come, climb a plane and fly my mouth to her - flup - landed and jumped with open lips on the nipple, cushioned by the tongue pressing on her and immediately started the dialogue. So that the first one is not sad, I immediately put my hand on her and stroke it soft and sometimes a little firmer and press lightly and then a little tighter the nipple between my fingers and .... Yes, I hear an increasing groan from your mouth, well you will not yet, mouth and hand dissolve and wait about 10 cm distance, your eyes open and look at me questioningly as our eyes meet, a short pause - It feels like a little eternity - and already fall mouth and hand again over your breasts ....*
- Please, please do not be angry with me, I'm dead tired and have to get out tomorrow at 6:00 and I would like to take these feelings with me in my

16

dream, so something I have not experienced, it's as if we were together, so strong, Hope you experience that as well and I look forward to tomorrow evening, will you be back?

– *Yes I am looking forward to it like a little school-boy, is not it already tomorrow evening?*
– Unfortunately not and thanks for the experience, I would not have believed that there is anything, good night until tomorrow - and do not go stranger!
– *Dreams, no, I'll be 100% loyal to you until tomorrow evening!!! LG Joschua!*
– Good night my dream prince!

Oh my body is totally of the character. Did that really happen? I had mail sex with a strange man. I really think I'm crazy. Had someone told me a few hours ago that there was such a thing, I would have called him crazy and now it happened. What did Joschua do? If I had stood opposite him, I would say he hypnotized me. Mmm does he have that through his words? Is that possible? But now I'm still clear mind? Have to pinch me. Au, hurts. Oh Mia you are really awake. Then that's just happened. I have to test that with my hand between my thighs. Yes, oh my hand is very wet. I had a climax. I had not had that for years. Incredible. Mia go to bed immediately and enjoy these feelings. They are still raging in my body. I also do not go showering as usual, I want to take everything, the remaining feelings and the moisture between my legs. I was right earlier, the mail changed everything in my life, the beginning was an exploding climax like a firework of emotions. Oh please, please Joschua let us e-mail tomorrow night. Will I sit naked in front of the computer? We just e-mail and did not name. Wow, what are those thoughts. Good night Mia is sleeping now you have to get out tomorrow morning. And already the dreams have reached me. I think Joschua is buzzing around in them.

Monday 02.09.2013

Brrrr - Brrrr - Brrrr - Brrrr

You can not do that, the alarm clock is already six o'clock? I just fell asleep and what did I dream? I can not remember but this Joschua was there. Oh, I'm wet again. For years down there was a desert and now something like that. Whether Joschua will be happy if he

receives an unexpected mail from me. He certainly will not get up as early as me. Well just then just go to the bathroom and no first write the mail otherwise I'm wet again afterwards. So to the computer and turned on. Oh, it takes until he starts up. Human Mia what has happened to you, can not wait to write to him. What should that be? And everything open. Man, what am I writing for now? Will try it with full honesty so get started typing.

> Hello Joschua I dreamed. Dreamed of you and I really felt you and more ... for years!!! I live since almost ten years alone, did not fit and I have I didnot really believe that can feel. Unimaginable, it was only yours written words. I can not imagine what happens when we meet and would touch! First of all, I have to go to work. I am looking forward to you this evening. Thank you for the beautiful night! LG Joschua

Oh Mia I can e-mail that. Yes, the first thought is often the best. And pressed and sent. So now off to the bathroom and get ready. Breakfast is only at work. Well that I have such a dear boss, was not so in the past, but today. I've always enjoyed going to work, I'm retrained to be a florist but today I would like to stay home and e-mail Joschua. All day and night. Hey Mia, did you just think that? That is impossible. Well, first off to work and flowers, groom and sell. Oh, I'd rather not sell today, if I just work with the flowers, I can certainly dream of

18

Joschua and what he says tonight to my good morning mail. Oh Mia, can not you stop thinking about him? Oh hell, nothing can happen and if it does, it can only get better. And then it happens, I catch myself thinking about him at work. Somehow I do until lunch break, oh I remember that I did not have breakfast, how automatic my work. Again and again the question he has already retrieved the mail or waiting for it or he has already responded. I have to go to the office and look at the computer. I just can not stand it anymore. My boss just tells me that she has to make an extra and I should stay in the office because of the calls. Well, if that does not fit like a fist on the eye.

"Then I'll make lunch here. No problem."

And she drives away and I bring the computer to see if there is an e-mail for me. I could smooch the computer, he says mail for you. Now I am so excited again. Start Mia open it. There she is, come on Mia to read there will be nothing bad inside. So I definitely appreciate Joschua. It is estimated after only one mail evening, but what a highly erotic e-mail evening.

- *Good beautiful morning! Oh, this night with you!!! And if she was just thinking. It was as intense as I have not felt it for years, you touched my heart, no swept away in the storm and my body felt an experience ... . Words are too pale to describe! I am looking forward to this evening like a little boy, take good care of you and 1000 thanks for your lovely morning mail! LG Joschua*
- I'm counting the hours, but I just had to e-mail you, just had lunch break and have read your sweet mail. It's like when my body immediately jumps into feeling mode and just feels the words you're writing. Here the sun is shining and I'm sitting on the garden bench in front of the company and let the sun shine on me, feels so warm

19

and then your feelings, the lunch break is expected to last tonight, but unfortunately it's over
again until tonight, I'm really happy, I'll have
something to eat on the PC, because then I can
e-mail you! Bye your Mia -

— *Yes, I know there are still 4.5 hours until you*
mail me again, I wish the 270 minutes were just
around, but now I have 15 already seconds from
the 16.200 seconds ...

I knew it. I feel feelings in my body again. Again just
because he only e-mailed me. That's not normal. I can
not tell that to anybody. They would all think I'm totally
crazy. I would have thought that yesterday morning, but
she did here in me. My heart is beating faster, no, it's
even racing and I feel like I'm getting wet down in my
pussy. I do not know that. How many times have I been
together with my exhusband and even I was often dry in
my pussy. It was therefore sometimes uncomfortable
and now I'm just reading something of this Joschua, not
even a love letter as before, in which perhaps a flower
inside had lain or which would have smelt after him. No,
I only read one e-mail on the computer. An e-mail that
consists of only a few words, which makes no further
emotional recordings possible and I react already. Am I
really that? Yes, it is my body that gets wet and sweats
down. My body has never reacted like this. When I saw a
horny guy on the street, my head thought, it's a hot guy
with a cool butt, but my pussy left it cold. How did the
feeling come to me yesterday that something happens
when I reply to this mail. He is so far away. Hamburg are
over one hundred and fifty kilometers and still this
reaction. I do not understand myself anymore. Hopefully
that will be fine. I wanted to experience something in life
that's what I decided to do, but if you fly so high then
the crash can be really deep and hard. Oh, I have to get
into the business because a customer calls. Oje Mia
now once again sort your thoughts a little bit. Not that
your arousal is considered. And I'm on the way forward.
Turn off Joschua's thoughts first.

20

"Oh, hello Mrs. Fischer. What can I bind them for a bouquet today? "

"Hello Mrs. Black. They always know what I want and know my taste well. "

"Well, you are a very dear regular customer and people who love flowers and enjoy a different bouquet every week are not so often sown."

"Yes flowers are for me a piece of nature that I like in my small apartment. Not only the reputation but also the smell is what I like about it."

"They are like me. When I get to work in the morning, the fragrance of the flowers, a composition of all, first of all receives me. But what kind of bouquet can it be?"

"I'm invited tonight, not to a man, unfortunately my husband died so long ago. I'm going to an old school friend I met by chance a few days ago and she invited me."

"And they need flowers for that."

"Yes, what would you recommend for this event?"

"I would not take a potted flower. A bound bouquet with the colors of the fall, no rather something colorful that looks much more positive on the mind at this time of year."

"Oh yes, Mrs. Schwarz that's right. Please give me a funny bouquet with which I can really say."

"What is he allowed to taste?"

"It's the first time I've seen Claudia for thirty-five years. What do you mean Mrs. Black. They have always hit the right mark."

"If I could make a suggestion and they are not mad about the money, then I would say thirty-five euros. One Euro for every missed year."

"Oh that's an idea. You are right with the missed years. They always say that time is racing, but you never stop them and always this saying comes from me, you do that tomorrow and tomorrow again and suddenly the year is over again. You are right Mrs. Black you should grab the luck, with my deceased husband, I also accessed immediately. You know, we knew each other for a short time, but back then I was more willing to make decisions, with age you get calmer and that's just wrong. You should enjoy life and I will do it again

21

from today. Thank you Frau Schwarz, just this sentence from you, for every missed year, it has fallen from my eyes like a dandruff. I have to enjoy my life again. Please make me such a bouquet. Very colorful and crazy. He should express what I feel right now in my heart, a renaissance of feelings. Oh, excuse me, I did not want to talk them full."

"No, they did not do that. On the contrary, they helped me with a very important personal decision."

"Oh yes, how, that makes me happy. I'm totally excited. I always knew flowers meant something to me and today it has been shown again and again. Today they have awakened me again. Again, just because of the flowers, otherwise I would not have come to them in the business and would have received this wake up call from them, dear Mrs. Black. I love flowers."

And I see how Frau Fischer shines all over her face. I've never seen her like that before. A bright face.

"Ms. Fischer, you suddenly radiate something wonderful. Her aura is glowing."

"Yes, I have the feeling that I have just lost a thousand tons of load from the heart and I am happy again. I have not felt that for years, nonsense for decades. Oh, life is nice when you let it into your heart."

And I just leave this radiant woman alone and put the bouquet together. Not so easy, it has to match the rays and reflect the joie de vivre. But the words she said, the words that hit me too, and my decision to risk it with Joschua abruptly influenced her. Joschua I will experience something with you. If you want, I'm ready for whatever you do, but only if you see Mia you're restraining. These are not restrictions, these are limits. I do not know him, maybe a bad person stands behind the lines or has desperate cravings. Then I brake immediately and have disappeared. But if he is really as sweet as he came over in the e-mail last night and maybe can make me as happy as last night, then you have Joschua already on my neck. On the neck like that sounds. Oh

yes, the flower neck, uhh on the stems must also ran something autumnal. During my wild thoughts, I automatically put together a bouquet and show it to Mrs. Fischer.

"Mrs Fischer, that would be my suggestion, but you can change it now. I have not tied him yet. do not know if such a blooming woman like them at the moment really appeals."

"Oh, Mrs. Schwarz, you are so nice, the man you get is a real lucky guy."

"Do you mean?"

"Frau Schwarz, you are suddenly beaming like that, have you already targeted a man?"

"May I talk about it openly with you?"

"But you know, you could be my daughter."

"That would be good. Yes I have, they have to imagine, had a day yesterday as no longer since eternity."

"Met a man?"

"Yes and no. I read an ad on the internet and then I wrote with him. It was as familiar as if I had known him forever and that after the first few lines and tonight, yes I am looking forward to it, we will write again."

"Oh my child, if I old woman can give them some advice, today it is the same as it was then, only letters are mails and go faster. If your heart has been hit by words, then the words come from a man who also has a heart. Men who have no heart, use words that are colder and the dear ones even write something between the lines with invisible words and you think while reading these unwritten words just with and feel the most beautiful things."

"Yes, that's exactly how it happened. Only a few neutral or sweet words and I thought I read a novel."

"Little ones, get them and do not wait until someone else does, then it's too late. I speak from experience, a very sad experience. Dear men are very rare and hard to find."

"Do you really think so?"

"Think of my words tonight and if they write or hear his voice soon, their heart will say it. The heart is almost always right when they let it."

"Thank you Mrs. Fischer. They were so understanding to me and their words have hit what my heart means and felt with him. I take care but I give him a fair chance."

"Yes, that's right, my child. Oh, what did they put together for a fun loving bouquet? He shines."

"I've taken autumnal colors, sunflowers, alstromeries, dahlias, hydrangeas, goldenrod, and snapdragon, plus some blue cornflower and columbine."

"Very nice, he should stay that way."

"Well, then I'll tie him up. Should he be in glass paper or opaque paper?"

"Glass paper, because I'll put it with me until tonight I'll go into the vase so it gets water and then I can enjoy it all day and think of the kind words that have opened my heart."

"But they also helped me with my difficult decision."

"Well, if that's not a great day, we've given each other life again."

I do not say anything, just shine it on and tie a matching raffia around the stems so that they retain their assigned position. Then everything comes in glass foil, I bind two sachets of fertilizer me a rubber band and put it on the sales counter.

"Mrs. Fischer I have made two bags of fertilizer for the water. You can use one right away, then it keeps you fresh longer. That's what makes thirty-five euros."

And Mrs. Fischer puts two twenty Euro notes on the table.

"The rest is for the coffee and my thanks for the life coaching. The man is really lucky tonight if he is nice."

"Oh, thank you, but the coffee will be happy and I hope the man too. Thank you for your words, they helped me a lot and I have already decided. Stupid only that it takes so long to write again."

"Oh, a letter would take even longer, believe me. It's time to leave soon."

"Yes, I count the hours until it is again, they have an

e-mail."
"Well then, much success and thank you for the wonderful bouquet."
"Please and see you next time."
"But then tell me what happened to her husband."
"Promised."

I put Ms. Fischer's shop door open and she leaves. At this moment my boss arrives and I let her in too.

"What was that, Mrs. Fischer has never blasted so."
"Oh, we had a nice conversation at flower sale."
"Yes I knew you could deal with customers. I already felt that during the first conversation with you."
"I also like to work here. With such a great boss. Who has his girlfriend as boss?"
"Thank you! I have brought the cake for coffee but already before for us, because you are this morning, I noticed immediately when you came in the door are very different. Somehow more alive and as you know, I'm terribly curious."
"Oh, and that's why you want to take a cake break with me to find out what's in it with the rays?"
"I knew you understand me, so in an hour in the office."
"Yes, I like to go back to the greenhouse and do my work."
"I'll call you for coffee then."

And already I'm swirling backwards, shaking my head slightly. What is happening. I have the same stuff as always and I did not change the make up. That can not come from last night? One stands on my forehead I had sex? Oje that was no real sex right? I was alone. Mmm but it felt so awesome. As good as not for a long time. No in itself like never before. Yes it was something special and only because of the writing. If this is really true, what happens to me when I see this guy and he gets me right to the point, then I flash like a star in the sky? With so many thoughts I do not even notice how time goes by and a voice screams from the back ...

"The coffee is ready. Mia the coffee is ready."
"I'm coming, I'm on my way."

Then I enter the office and on the desk are two cups, two plates of cake and a full, delicious coffee scented pot.

"So Mia now take a seat and right, coffee?"
"Yes please."

And I am served, the coffee is poured and the cake, an apple piece automatically finds its way onto my plate.

"Well, you know, I'm not curious about it, but when you came in through the door this morning, it was like a light around you blasting in like a thousand watt pear."
"One does not exist, Mrs. Fischer has also discovered something like that in me. I can not see that myself."
"You can not see that yourself, but you should feel it."
"Yes and no, but I decided to enjoy it. Mrs. Fischer gave me a stomp with the right words. "
"Sososo and where did she put you in?"
"Oh Sonja, I somehow did something crazy for me yesterday."
"Come tell me, do not let anything get out of your nose. That must have been something great after the beamman's face."
"I want to experience something else and it can not be the way it is now. Since I have read ads at an affiliate agency times and at one is almost stopped reading the heart."
"How with picture?"
"No just a few sentences and then I have looked into the profile of the man and then my heart has almost stopped beating. I have never witnessed anything like this."
"And go on, do not make it so exciting."
"Then I e-mailed him. I wanted to see what comes back and say and write, he must also have sat at the computer, because promptly came an answer. And at that

26

moment, if I did not stop now, then my life would change completely."

"And did you stop?"

"Normally I would have been too cowardly and would have switched off immediately, but there was something and we got mailed. For a while and it was sooo beautiful. He writes phrases and one thinks one reads a romance novel. In a few words he wrote novels in my head. That went off."

"How?"

"Well, you can not imagine that."

"How filthy pigs?"

"No, not at all, but then I have one … ."

"How did you get an orgasm?"

"Yes, and without me touching it, just as if by magic."

"Can you lend me that man? Get an orgasm and then I'll give it back to you. An idea. And further?"

"Nothing else, we've agreed to mail again for tonight, and I dreamed about him all night, and I do not even have a picture of him."

"And did you e-mail him again?"

"Yes, very early this morning and he answered during the lunch break."

"Oh, when you were in the office."

"Yes you want to see the mail, then you can also tell me what you think about him."

"Show me. Man myself, I'm excited, as you describe it. You can be really jealous. An orgasm only with words. My friend did not even make it with his best piece back then. Very rarely, anyway."

"look here, here's the mail from today, mine and his."

- Hello Joschua I dreamed. Dreamed of you and I really have you felt and more ... for years! I've been living alone for ten years, did not fit and I did not think that I could really feel anything like that, unimaginable, it was just your written words, I do not even want to imagine what happens if we look at each other and touch! First I have to go to work, maile you tonight, I'm

27

looking forward to it, thanks for the beautiful night! LG Joschua

"That's the morning mail from me to him."
"Yeah sure I can read and what came back?"

— *Good beautiful morning! Oh, this night, you!!! And if she was just thinking, she was as intense as I have not felt it for years, you touched my heart, no swept away in the storm and my body felt an experience ... . Words are too pale to describe! I am looking forward to this evening like a little boy, take good care of you and 1000 thanks for your lovely morning mail! LG Joschua*

— I'm counting the hours, but I just had to e-mail you, just had lunch break and have read your sweet mail. It's like when my body immediately jumps into feeling mode and just feels the words you're writing. Here the sun is shining and I'm sitting on the garden bench in front of the company and let the sun shine on me, feels so warm and then your feelings, the lunch break is expected to last tonight, but unfortunately it's over again Until tonight, I'm really happy, I'll have something to eat on the PC, because then I can e-mail you! Bye your Mia -

— *Yes, I know there are still 4.5 hours until you mail me again, alas, if the 270 minutes were just around, but now I've already made 15 seconds of the 16.200 seconds ....*

"One counts the seconds. Really great guy."
"And would you e-mail him again tonight and if he wants more?"
"Are you stupid, you do not let such a guy off the hook. Ran to him, maybe you'll get an orgasm again today."
"Oh Sonja do not make me so embarrassed."
"Oh, among friends you can say that quietly. We always talk

28

openly about everything."
"I know, that helped me in difficult times."
"Man, I can not believe an orgasm just with words."
"Yes and what kind of one. I really had the feeling I had never had one. Feelings that just exploded in me and my head."
"Class. When will you mail again? Eight o'clock?"
"Yes, he said then I could freshen up after work and put on some clothes and food. He did not want to disturb before."
"Did he really say that? Then it will be another hot night for you today, I know who said that, he will bring you joy again. Did he bring himself down?"
"I do not know, I did not tell him what happened to me."
"How not? Well the man is lucky, if you had said that to him he would have gone crazy that he was not with you."
"Do you think so? But I can not say that he brought me to climax with his words."
"Why not. You either he understands it and maybe he's happy about it very much or he's not worth it like that and just thinks of himself, then he does not care. Whenever there is more to come, remember the truth often hurts but is the safest way to grow a love. Is like fertilizer for the earth."
"If I think about it, then you're right. I would not like to lie."
"You know what, it's almost four. Now finish work and enjoy everything afterwards to the fullest."
"I have not finished my job in the greenhouse yet."
"Never mind, do not go away, you can do something later. No horny man is waiting for me, not even a normal man. But I want to know every detail of you tomorrow."
"Thank you, Sonja, that's nice of you. Then I'm on my way. See you tomorrow. Bye."
"And enjoy it, every second he gives you."

I smile at Sonja and then I take my bag and I'm out of the flower shop, on the bike and home. I feel like I'm not cycling at all, but it's being pulled home like magic. Pulled as fast as I do not drive otherwise. I walk like a savage, yet it is still so early. The wind blows around my

29

face and it shivers all over my body. A thought shoots in my head. How would it be if Joschua is touching me for the first time, then I will be so shivering and it will run down my back cold or I have no reaction. Mia what are you thinking about? He's a strange man you know very little about. Yes, but it could be the right man for longer. Oh, maybe forever. Can I love a man forever, does that not end sometime? Oh maybe he has quirks I can not stand or he looks so ugly that it disgusts me. No, a man who can only bring me to the climax on the first day with words, that can not be bad. Or? Mia you can still cycle for hours and your thoughts will raise new questions over time. Just let it be easy and listen to your heart. Here's the heart up there in the head. Just stop the thought and let me do it. I will provide pure enjoyment tonight when she e-mails again with the hot, soulful guy. Oh my heart, how I would like that but remember, you have often had the wrong sensations. But with me the whole body can feel something for some time, you can not give it to him. Yes I know. What do you think if we just enjoy it tonight, nothing can happen, the guy is far away and not physically present. That sounds good, so let's do it. Mia, were you talking to yourself right now? Hey, what's up with me?

"Hey, you're dreaming, stupid cow! Can not you watch where you're going?"
"Excuse me."

Oh Mia watch now, you almost touched the man. Joschua you totally distract me. Oh, hopefully, Joschua is not like this guy, just quick tempered and insulting. No I do not think, who can write such mails is certainly nots so poisonous. I knew it, I knew it, when I respond to the ad, my life changes and it starts. Is that good? Mmm you wanted a change. Well my life has not changed, only my body has finally felt hot again. Well that's something, but my life has not changed. No. Mmm i got freed earlier today and i have experienced i have a glowing aura around me. Mmm has already changed a bit. Not my life but something in me, otherwise I would not be so happy for him afterwards. To him, how dumb I am, to his mails. Yes, but the words he e-mails are a piece of him. So look forward to it. Today I will try cau- tiously to find out more about him. Always incorporate such small questions. Mmm that he will definitely re- member and then? Of course I can then make a de- cision, if he does not answer or gives stupid answers, he is not for me. Mmm but if he replies like he e-mailed yesterday, then no, then he could be something, no, then I could con-ider that he might be something. Oh God this Joschua is already making me crazy in the head. But you have to admit to Mia that you have not spent so much time with a man for years. Mmm and the climax yesterday only with words. It was really nice. Oh, if it was already eight o'clock. So now I arrived home. Wheel in the hallway and up to the second floor. Oh, it's only 4.30pm. Oh, I am totally by the wind. This morning I still remembered, on the way home I have to buy some- thing to eat. Crap. One of these Joschua even distracts me from it. But it's nice, yes, I have butterflies in my stomach, and as many as I have not felt since my schooling at my first great love. Mia, that does not exist, let's feel it. Yeah, when I think of him, as we'll e-mail you right now, they're flying wildly through my stomach. Uiii that's exciting. I have to shop yet. 17.12 is still time, so just the shopping basket and then I need only for after shopping, is not a weekend. What should one eat while being pampered by a man with butterflies in his stom- ach? Of course nothing, but then I'm always hungry. Yesterday too, that was so intense, because then I could have eaten the whole refrigerator empty. Oh I'll get a little sparkling wine, a Piccolo, then maybe I'll relax or you'll realize it. Well, I'm not going to start laughing at a piccolo. I'm stupid, he hears and does not see me, we just e-mail. Will I ever hear his voice? Oh Mia, it's all too fast. No, why, who says you can not fall in love or kiss or go to bed immediately? I do not have anyone to ac- count to. I am an adult. At forty you can say that but right now I feel like I'm seventeen. Oh for the decision counts only the age on paper and I'm of legal age. So now for shopping. Good that the supermarket is with me around the corner. Since I get everything I need for tonight and otherwise so. Now I almost forgot the shopping basket again. I also take all the returnable bottles with me to the vending machine. It's worth it again. And I already hear how the apartment door behind me falls into the lock, I sped down the stairs and hurry to the supermarket. Oops Mia, you still have time. Almost two and a half hours. Oh too long, why could not we date earlier? Yes I know, then it would not have worked out again and you would have been disappointed. What does he do well, whether he is looking forward to the mailing. If I still have his midday mail in my head then it was read between the lines. When will it finally happen? Oh, I'm going crazy. Mia, but now only the bottles in the automatic paver and then with the shopping cart through the store. Today everything is empty, vending machine, shopping cart and loading it goes like in the air and already I stand in front of the fruit department. I need strength and endurance, the night can be long, so two no rather three bananas and two apples, oh and there a few grapes. Oh, a couple of freshly baked rolls yes and a cheese roll oh, I'm already eating with jam. I have just the brainwave of a thought in my mind's eye. Joschua drips honey on my nipple and it runs slowly down to her. Then comes his tongue. Oh Mia stops you are here in the shop and are already very wet. That's never happened to me in my life. Los bread sex piece, one six pieces. Thought stops. If we are not, that is the heart. Am I not coming from the stomach. I'm also innocent, these are funny butterflies. No matter first I have to be at home then you can make me crazy. But you also do not hold anything good. But I'm not used to that. True, totally starved for sex and love. Rest now down there. And my brain is already trying to gain the upper hand and I push the cart on through the shop. Butter? No, I have two more pieces, oh, a piece of middle ages Gouda would not be bad. And some ham. That's enough, no more a herring salad and egg salad. Mia stop. Good on. Now to the drinks, orange juice and in front of the Piccolo. No, rather two pieces. I really like chocolate, nougat and then checkout. Crazy shopping is stupid. Well you should buy what you like right now. Stop, I have to have negro kisses. So now everything on the cash register, it's already my turn. Put in the basket and then pay, get out of the store and put the cart back on. Then the basket under his arm and home. I feel really real I am already a bit wet in the step. These were just the crazy thoughts of this Joschua. How is this supposed to continue. Oh, how that feels on the stairs between my legs again. I just do it. Yes go Mia do it. And then I arrived at home in front of the door and went in. Just cleared the basket and put away shopping, then into the bedroom, pants quickly out, the slip behind and placed on the bed. Close your eyes and Joschua where are you? Ah, here he comes from the back thoughts and smiles at me. This creates a further excitement between my legs and now my right hand helps a bit, I'm already really wet what can be this evening. I feel like going out on Friday night, as we have always used to preheat, but with drinks, now I'm doing that with highlights. Of course I'm not going out, I expect something as beautiful as last night and so that it does not happen immediately, I will now get my body down a bit, uh I get my one down. With my left hand something played on my nipples and you Mia oh what, it's just beautiful. Come on let me down and do it. It's such a wonderful feeling, but I imagine Joschua. He is a whole man, tall, slim, white haired and very nice. Very sweet, I feel his hands on my body. I just imagine it's his hands. Ohhh ... yeah ... Joschua ... what are you going to do with me ... I'm coming ... Joschua ... ohhh ... ohhh. Is the thought, it was him, penetrated into my feelings, it was beautiful. Ohhh I can still feel my feelings floating in me. It was always short and gone. Ohhh Joschua I can still feel myself. How can that be, just a few e-mails and you're in seventh heaven. I do not understand what's happening to me right now. Did he hypnotize me? No he can not, we did not see each other and did not speak. But he somehow enchanted my heart and that is slowly gaining the upper hand. Is that reasonable? Oh Mia you were alone for so long and no one was there who gave you a little luck. Mia enjoy it. Yes, I will enjoy that to the fullest. Alone to the first mails from yesterday I will think as long as I live and now my highlight. So horny and as long as I have him forever, no as I have not felt him at all. Oh, I could hug Joschua. Maybe we'll get together. Oops what time is it because I have not overslept. It's already ten minutes past seven. Must have dreamed something. Well, that I woke up I had set no alarm. Wanted to be happy only once but that lasts so long and then I fall asleep. Well then I'm the same fitter and hold on longer. Will he have to leave tomorrow morning and have little time? Just take a quick shower and eat something, no, I can not do that anymore. Well then just take a shower and take the food to the computer. Showering is fast, I'm already half naked. I feel as if I have my first rendezvous right away. Totally stupid but somehow beautiful the feelings. And already the water splashes, brrrr still cold from above on me. Ah, it gets warmer, it always takes a moment. Lathered, showered, dried off, dressed. It must have been a record time. Half past eight and now in the kitchen. Tray, rolls, butter, sausage, cheese and fruit, fruit, fruit. A coke and water and everything in front of the computer on the living room table. Twelve minutes to eight. Boot up the computer and let's see if something has arrived. Is not it okay or has he already e-mailed something because he is as happy as me?

Ping oh a mail from him.

— *Charming Schwerin female being, here sits a man eagerly waiting for your first words, armed with a pot of coffee, creamer, egg salad and an iceberg lettuce, I make with whipped cream sugar and lemon and then I feed him all alone! If you were here I would also give you 51% to join in – smile!*

34

Oh, there is something. My heart is about to race. The evening can begin. First of all, answer, he should not wait. I eat when I wait for his answer.

- Hallooo there I am!
- *Hallooo back, my heart and the rest of the body is happy, thanks for being there, how are you?*
- A bit exhausted, it was a hard day, but I got through it, because I almost always thought of you after every job. Could I say that?
- *Oh please keep writing this is like balm for my soul, another person, a female super thing that thinks of me, yeah ohhh that's good and at the same time it drives me crazy, I want you ... oh sorry, if I was so brisk, me would like to spend time with you!*
- Do you understand, not bad, I like how you write it!
- *Thank you, thank you, I like writing with you, it's like immersing myself in another world. Youuu you dive into another world with me, into a world where only we two can be undisturbed, a world of thoughts and feelings and ...*
- What do you mean with and ...?
- *Tell me about your nightly dream!*
- How do you want to distract you rascal?
- *Who I am not - smile!*
- Well then write something with you and .... meant, dare! I do not bite!
- *Oh biting a bit when you're excited can be awesome!!! oops, yes I have distracted again. Sorry so, but do not be angry if I write you what happened - promised?*
- What happened, do not make it so exciting I'm bursting with curiosity right now, I'm not angry with you either, unless you've flirted with another!

- *No, I received some e-mails and e-mailed everyone, I received the most sentimental e-mail of my life and immediately fell in love - oops - yes in you and wished you all luck for your further search and that was it, you are with me in my heart ran and occupied it in the storm!*
- Honestly?
- *Yes, 1.000.000 percent!!! I have a very big request to you but do not be angry, I have experienced so much negative in the past and there fore I would like to tell you that no matter what develops between us (hopefully quite a lot!!!) I will never do it lie and please promise me too, because trust is the basis for everything! Also for love! If you do not want to talk about something, then you can say it, that's not a problem, just do not lie! I promise you that!!!*
- I promise you, too, but no man has ever asked for that, though I've always wanted it inside! What are we talking about here? It's as if we've known each other forever, never would I have believed writing something like that with others and even feeling something beautiful that you promise me is something very special for me, tell you why later, that's why thanks for that, one hundred percent promise! Oh, and what about this and ...?
- *Well, I had some time this afternoon, just sucked in the house and then let it all hang out. I sat down by the pool and ... oh, look how tall are you?*
- You distractor I am 1.80 m tall and on.
- *Sorry, was important!*
- Ok and on?
- *Oh yes, so I'm sitting by the pool, water depth 160 cm (so the question of your size) and then I wondered what if you were here and would swim with me. What would I have to do to enjoy the*

water the way God created you?

- Hahaha you mean without swimsuit!
- *Yes, exactly, what should I do?*
- You also have to be naked!
- *Ok, that could be set up immediately! So you're triggering me ... what's that supposed to be?*
- Great! Stiff? Continue!
- *Yes and you are not there, you how are you feeling? Also something in an excited mood?*
- Yes, it depends what else happens!
- *So you are standing in the water, the light waves are playing around your beautiful breasts and I'm lying on your back on an air mattress. What would you do?*
- So, it shivers me how warm is the water?
- *24 degree*
- Ahh then comes the shiver of the picture I just have in mind, as you are lying there and I can look at you, ohhh how I would wish that! What would I do, well I would grab your hand and push it under your buttocks with you, then turn over the air mattress and push the other hand under your buttocks and tell you, because you leave them and eyes closed.
- *Yeah, that feels kind of arousing helpless when I do not see how you look at me and especially what you look at so closely! And then what you have in mind next, I do not see how you move, do not recognize your intentions! How do you know that this gives me so much? Oh please and what then?*
- I would stand in front of the air mattress and your feet would touch my breasts, I could feel your toes as they want to play on my breasts, but then I would miss them a light tap, turn the mattress and my hands would be your cock and your balls grab, embrace, and slowly begin to

37

squeeze harder until I hear a moan out of your mouth. Eyes remain closed, otherwise I will stop!
- *No, I obey, I'm not blinking either, promise! How may I touch you?*
- Not at all! Rest and my hands would continue to glide up to your nipples, before I would have heaved with them a lot of water on your body, frightened?
- *Yes, exciting and almost impossible to stop, what are you doing with me? Please do not stop, I've never experienced anything like that!*
- My fingers massage lightly and violently always alternating nipples and my tongue finds the way to your face where she licks everything until she finds your lips and follows a long intense kiss.
- *Ohhh, you taste like fresh, cold water and yet you are as hot as if you were burnt by the touch of your tongue on the spot. The excitement rises in me, an excitement that I thought I would never feel, since many, many years no more. May I touch you now and ...*
- No, I spoil you now, you do not move!
- *I've never experienced anything like that in life, a woman with imagination and energy, ohhh yes!*

I can almost feel my lips pressing on his. Oh, I also close my eyes and my thoughts are getting more and more intense. I can even smell the water and feel like his lips always with different pressure on my presses through the waves dragging under the air mattress. A light up and down. It's like being with him and really feeling him. That is impossible. The awakens so strong feelings in me that I think it's real.

- Do you feel like my hands tightly enclose your cock and your balls?
- *Yes! Very clear!*

- Now attention, I pull your testicles very firmly down and you moan loudly, my hand massages your cock and I feel like he is getting stiffer in my hand, yes I can rub it and he stands like a one. But you breathe hard and suddenly I feel like you stop and then you feel like the seeds in your cock shoot up. I feel it too and can see it, how you twitch and how it shoots out of you, over my hand on your stomach. Wow you spray so far, up to your nipples!

- *Ohhh yes !! But that was your fault, because at just the right time, you let go of my testicles and they shot like cannonballs up and have created pressure, well, like a tense bow!*

- I realize it also aroused me a lot!

- *Attention, I now pull my hands away under my buttocks, slide from the air mattress into the water - an icy shower envelops me, like a jump in the ice water. Wow and I stand in front of you, my hands find the way under your armpits and lift you easily out of the water and fall backwards on the air mattress. Oops, now you are lying in front of me with your legs apart and I see an excited area of you, which is usually hidden. Your legs dangle into the water and before you can say anything, my lips approach from your knees over your thighs in this warm moist area and my tongue begins to search your cave for your bliss. She leans back and forth like a snake, and your voice begins to ring in her rhythm! Hey close your eyes and let them close. Your hands are on my shoulders and it feels so good, I can make noises in you as I want, my tongue - oh it's so intense - I do not want to stop - and after a short while, a very short time, a louder sound groaning cry of liberation to my ears and my tongue is slowly retreating and the lips are still taking on a slow, careful aftermath through very cautious moves! But!!! There it is again with a short but sudden push, my tongue, as it pushes once more as a small farewell present, winds itself to then disappear again between my lips in the mouth. oops did I hear a loud loud moan running along with it?*

— Yes! It's like a miracle, I've experienced a climax, as violent as a sunray, where are you I want to feel your body on mine now and gently vanish into the land of dreams with you. Oh I think I'm dreaming, you ...!

It is really true, he has shot me with words again to a climax and what a. I only see feelings in front of me and a man appears in them again and again. I can not see it, but I guess it makes me crazy. Is it Joschua, how does he look like? What will I experience when we see each other later. Am I disappointed because my expectations are so high or will he surpass them? Oh Joschua I would like to have a picture of you. No, I will not ask him. He is the man, he must want one of me. Oh those feelings in me are raging everywhere. That's great. I really did not feel it forever. What must my body be happy and how great is my body. I am impressed by what he gets out of himself and how much I can feel. Oh, Joschua alone, I'd like to hug you, squeeze and shake you. If you knew how to make me. Do you feel the same way as me? I hope so, because the more you feel as I just now and the more you want to know me more. Just as I have the desire. When will that be? Oh Mia. It's only the second evening.

    - Youuu already back from the emotional dream world?

Oh, I'm still completely gone. It was just a too nice ex-perience that I've never felt before and immediately I have to open my eyes again, not that he thinks I'm not there or I want to know nothing more about him. So for-get feelings for a moment and take a quick look at the screen. Oh, he e-mailed. Moment. But I have to come down and answer.

- Oops, had fallen asleep, are you still there?
- *Yes and no! Me here, but my emotional world is still in seventh heaven!*
- Well then we meet, on which cloud do you dream?
- *On the pink big love cloud and there is still room for you, I have kept extra for you, but could not hope that it will be such a super, super, super emotional female being, which implanted in my heart. Since you are now sincerely welcome, I am looking forward to it, but respect, I am when you have arrived in my heart and then I have closed my heart behind you, then I am quite, how shall I say it, very loyally, lovingly and jealous, but that's not a problem if you trust a hundred percent, then it can only be nice, always nice if you feel like one and ... !!!*
- You can write it in such lovely words, I can imagine that, as I slip into your heart, cuddle up there and you come to it and the door closes behind us, everything is warm, soulful, just pink. Youuu I want to be, at least for now, although it started just yesterday, but I think it's something special! You caught my feelings in the flyby, stormy and felt honest, I feel like a magnet attracted by you! And I hope it will be more and will last forever!
- *I have the wish too. I've always dreamed of something like that and I dreamed a lot, because reality is not that rosy, quite the contrary, but it's not really clear until you make a mistake and then you can not often do not correct themselves or you do not have the courage to do so.*
- Yes, I can sing a song of that too, but that would not be right to tell, would steer the great evening

41

in the wrong direction and I would like to take this experience to bed with me and continue to dream what else could happen, not only in the pool! Are you back tomorrow night?

— *Oh yes, dream of and with you - not in the pool but after, when we come out and together throw some food and then romp in the nocturnal, summery garden and finally land in front of the garden fireplace and then ... well curious? I'm almost always online, because I work from home on the PC and in an emergency, if you can not stand it any more, you can call me at any time with your determined exciting voice under 0175/3359875. I wonder if I hear your voice soon, I'll answer too, so that you can perceive mine, but I'll tell you right away I have a voice that is not suitable for technology, everyone tells me on the phone. Often those who do not know me say Mrs. Richter. Then I always smile and play along. Fun until you realize I'm a man - so now you know that too! - then comes the apology and I had a funny call! So I'm dreaming and have a longing for me, because maybe I'll hear your voice tomorrow! You is like an angelic voice? No, I'm not curious - smile!!!*

— But you go, on the third day already on the phone!

— *Oops, I can call you back if you do not have a flatrate, but I did not want to ask directly for your number, so this nice detour! Smile!*

— Bad luck I have a flatrate!

— *Ok, then you are a woman on the current technical level! Oh, that reminds me ...? No later!*

— Ohhh are you mean, how should I concentrate on the dream, when I first have to ponder what you mean!

— *Well, I did not see it that way - smile!*

— I do not believe you!!!

- *Say I am made of glass for you?*
- Who knows, just an intuitive woman.
- *Yes, and an emotional, which feels exactly what I think and wish, as in the pool with you earlier. And what do you dream of us tonight?*
- I'll tell you tomorrow!
- *What was the hint that I can hear your voice tomorrow?*
- Well, you put every word on the gold scale.
- *Oh, only that was my interpretation of your words above and below the line!*
- So, now, dream, if you'll hear my voice tomorrow or not, who knows, I do not know it yet but you! Yeah!
- *You can really do it, my heart is running all night to 180, can you answer that, dead before the first date? Sad smile!!!*
- Hahaha, it does not die so quickly, you also want to get to know me, that would be the next step.
- *Well, now you've got my pulse at 240, the pro-spect of meeting you, seeing in nature, and then taking the next step, feeling yourself, experien-cing how hot you are doing today. But what would you do if I was not there then, you would not have a crazy partner for the hottest things in the world between two people who ...! Well, do I get a little hint for tomorrow?*
- Oh you poorest man, I can not answer for that, so a little tip, I'm able to use a mobile phone.
- *I understand and rejoice, my heart calms down and not only dreams about hot things that I experienced with you today, but also tries to build in your voice. Is she sexy or dominant?*
- Hahaha, you have to wait a few hours, good night until tomorrow! Thank you for the nice hours with your words so erotic and very sweet.

I'm looking forward to tomorrow, about 16 hours
- well something you have infected me with the
hours count ... and bye! GLG Mia!

— *Dream nice and thank you for everything until
after! Greetings and a long imaginary kiss wherever you want him - maybe see you soon
Joschua!*

Man oh man, how can I get out of the clamp again? To
phone. I'm so shy. Mmm if I think so, then I'm not so shy.
I also e-mailed him. I would not have thought that if one
told me three days ago. And then something so
nasty. Mia, what did you think? If my parents knew that,
they would punish me. But because I did that, I'm not a
bitch, right? Nonsense Mia such a nonsense. I'm just
unrestrained happy and super excited. Oh, I'm so wet
down there. Now I have to shower again or should I take
that to bed. I just dream then there. No matter. Off to
bed. It's already late tomorrow at 6:00. I will definitely
not fall asleep right away. Oh her thoughts, oh her
feelings oh ... .

Tuesday 03.09.2013

Brrrr - Brrrr - Brrrr - Brrrr

Oh, good morning, dear morning. Oh, I'm in a good
mood. Oh, no, I feel good too. Oh man, I dreamed about
him. Oh, I have to call him tonight. Oh man, if I dare. The
dream was beautiful and no, I am wet again. That is impossible. What has happened to me for two days? My
body is self reliant and has been feeling comfortable for
years, for the first time. Oh, that's a good feeling. So
now again stretch all fours of me and then get up. Ohhh
so I stand and now stretch to the ceiling. Smile up to the
ceiling, only towards the ceiling. Tiptoe and count to
ten. So now off to the bathroom and no before I go to

44

the bathroom I turn on the computer and when I get out of the bathroom, I'll surprise him with a morning mail. I think he will be happy about that. Bath clean, wash, plaster and ready, quickly put on and make the coffee. A cup of coffee in the morning dispels sorrow and worry. So computer times open the program.

Ping - What's that? Crap he was faster, that does not apply.

    — *Hello voiceless female being - oops was not an indication, was the anticipation of later! - dreamed? From us? And I know, you can hardly wait until you hear me at the other end of the line tonight! From where I know this? Well, not only that I feel it, I am also looking forward to it, the event of the century! Until then the ringtone. GLG Joschua!*

Crap and gorgeous. Heck he was faster, dreamlike he thought of me so early. That's really nice of him. Then he also dreamed of me. Most certainly. Well, at least I have to answer he will certainly see if I have thought of him.

    Thank you slept well, dreamed good and already in election mood! See you later! LG Mia

So now I've certainly made him crazy with the word election mood. I know that's mean, but now he's hoping I'll call tonight. But now to work and be diligent. Oh, while cycling, I can not dream otherwise I drive back almost an innocent pedestrian. And so I arrive again today accident free in my work in the nursery. At seven o'clock, as always, on time, I walk through the staff entrance door. No sooner have I picked up the first flower in the nursery to start the potting today, I hear Sonja's voice.

"Mia, come for breakfast."

"What like I have to work."

"Later, breakfast will be served. I also brought rolls and jam."

"How is today a special day. Do you have a birthday, no is not possible. What?"

"Well, well, I'm your girlfriend and girlfriends are curious when it comes to hot men."

"How did you meet a new man?"

"Oh Mia, what's your guy doing out of the mail."

"Oh, you want to know that."

"Yeah, did you e-mail again last night and did you come back and and and?"

"Yes! Yes! Yes!"

"Detailed version please. Bun?"

"Yes, please. Just because I want to meet a man so reringious?"

"Oh, that's nothing normal, that's the non plus ultra."

"How so?"

"Well I've never climaxed words."

"I already twice."

"Twice, then you got one again last night."

"Ohhh yes and how. I dreamed about it all night and this morning I was totally wet."

"Really amazing and do you already know what he looks like?"

"No I do not know."

"You do not have a picture of him, was not he in profile?"

"No."

"Then he's certainly small, ugly, with a big ringy and bald head."

"Oh, and two more horns on my forehead."

And both of us have to laugh out loud. Then a jam roll disappears in my mouth and in time there is silence. Then the coffee follows.

"And tonight is it going on again?"

"Yes, imagine I should call him. He gave me his phone number so that I can decide."

"He does not have yours yet?"

46

"No. Not bad either."

"And you call?"

"I do not know if I should call. It's all too fast for me is only the third day and then call on the phone?"

"But he has made you happy twice already. Do you think he does it on the phone again or is it just such a banter?"

"If I'm going to dare tonight, it's going to get hot in some way, that's what I feel. What does he have for a vote?"

"Yes, and you can ask him a few things. Mailing is not so good."

"Yeah, this morning when I got up I wanted to send him an e-mail as a little surprise."

"I think that's a great idea from you. But you are in a good mood and have you really done it?"

"Yeah, of course, I turn on my computer, well what lights up, a mail from him in which he says he is looking forward to my voice tonight and wishes me a nice day."

"That's very nice, he thought of you. I want a man like that too. If he has another brother ask him tonight."

"Oh Sonja, I do not know if he likes me at all."

"If you do not want him, I'll take him."

And again we both have to laugh.

"So now I have to do something, otherwise you will soon be broke."

"Nonsense your info about the guy is much more important. I have not enjoyed a chat for a long time. You do not begrudge me any fun either."

"Fun but why?"

"Well, what you have experienced is not commonplace."

"Do you think so? Do you really think it's that special?"

"You can answer that yourself, two orgasms by mail. I think that's something very special, just think it over for yourself!"

"That's right, thank you, you keep opening my eyes. Well then go."

And I've gotten up, take off with him and everyone goes to work, I back in the greenhouse and Sonja in the shop. That might be another morning. First the mail from

Joschua and then Sonja. I have a batty girlfriend. As my life has changed in the last two days, I have become more interesting to others and myself feel years younger. Can that really all just come from the mails. It's just a string of letters. Well, I know, words can hurt so badly. I experienced that painfully myself at my first marriage and why then should words not be terribly happy? Whether Joschua always plays with words or if it is only at the beginning. Maybe if I talk to him today I'm disappointed. Not about his voice, but maybe about the words he'll tell me. Maybe I do not get any words out on the phone and he thinks then what is that stupid turkey. Oh man, what does this man do to me? If this continues I will soon think of him and forget the world around me. Thats not Ok. I also have to work to earn a living. Good that my boss is also my best friend.

"Mia you can come to the front of the store. Customers."
"Come."

And on the way there I think as I pass by all the wonderfully fragrant flowers, how beautiful life can be by such a triviality and I am sure I have always passed by many things that can be beautiful and have never perceived them that way. Joschua changes my life into something positive. Wow what the man can do. It's stupid Mia. That's just you. He's just the opener. And then there are some customers in the shop who have bouquets tied. One customer ordered a bouquet for her wedding next week. When Sonja hears that, she smiles at me from the side.

"Soon, too?"
"So far, hahaha."
"Let's wait and see."

And then it's lunch time. I have the feeling that the hours have passed on the fly. I did not think about anything but Joschua. That made time forget. I did everything in an automatic way.

"Mia do you want to get something back from the bakery? I have to get home to the children only at four thirty. Then you can go if you want."
"Well then I'll just go over to the bakery."

When I'm back Sonja and I have lunch break with two sandwiches and a bottle of Coke. What Joschua is doing right now. How does he eat lunch or does he fail? But I'm far from my thoughts, because I forgot to close the shop door and a customer enters. Oh no matter is sales. Food is not cold, so served quickly. Has also rinsed again € 13,50 for Sonja in the cash register. You have to reckon with every euro. The times are not easy and the competition does not sleep. Tomorrow I have to transplant the remaining flowers in the greenhouse until Sonja comes back but I have to stay in the shop. I do not hear clientele behind. Speaking of listening. If he likes my voice. I have a very high voice. Now he has already penetrated my thoughts again. I will not let go of him. If I really think about it, if he is like I dream of now I do not want to get rid of him anymore. I have to be careful tonight on the phone that I do not immediately attack him. I hope I'm not doing anything wrong. Oh, if I did something wrong and he rides around then he is not the one I want. A man with whom one can steal horses and do everything together and with whom one can talk and who also listens and understands for me. My ex was an egotist. He can not be under any circumstances. And how is he in bed? He always manages to make me so happy. Take care Mia otherwise you will become an egoist. He must have gotten a little luck, at least fifty percent otherwise that would be unfair. Man again a customer. Lunch finished and off you go. Today is the complete madness, what is going on, one customer after another give the latch in the hand. Good that I can do everything here and also from the flowers have idea. It's really fun and then ...

"Hey Mia, here I am again. How was it?"
"You did not want to come back until 4.30 pm because

of the kids."
"Yes, it's already five minutes later. Excuse me."
"How I thought it was just noon."
"What's wrong? Joschua in the head?"
"No, here are the customers have the latch in the hand."
"Wow you have almost taken more than the whole last week. What did you do?"
"I do not know every customer has taken a big bouquet."
"I know why that is, you are radiating something so happy and everyone wanted a piece of it and bought it. You like the type of you better and better."
"Hahaha."
"No, you really shines that I've seen again this morning against last week in comparison extreme and the customers notice that. Wow Mia you become a star seller."
"Nonsense."
"Do you know what, go home and tomorrow you can come an hour later."
"Oh I accept the offer very much. Just get my things and bye."
"Bye and do not forget to talk on the phone."
"Yes, yes, I will do, certainly."

And then I leave the shop swinging on my bike, stop by the supermarket for a while, buy something for tonight and tomorrow morning in and out home. When I arrived at my apartment, it is already close to six. You can not do that anymore, but just take a shower and then smear a bread and answer the phone. Already 18.12 and I'm completely naked. Well he does not see it. If I dress now, it will be too late. I do not want to keep him waiting and I'm so excited. Nonsense will hopefully let me take off his words again. Everything does not matter now. Where is his number and chosen.

Ring - ring - ring

Oh, he'll take it off soon. My heart beats right up to the phone. I hope he does not hear it.

Ring - ring – ring

"Hello beautiful, interesting, desirable woman, great that you call me!"
"Yes, I think so, have not you been waiting for the call?"

Oh my ear perceives a pretty high voice. But after the first words she seems to sound really nice. There's a heart behind. You sometimes have the feeling right away that you like a voice or not. I like this one.

"Are you a fortune teller?"
"Honestly, I've been waiting the whole day for me to call you to finally hear your voice, another part of you!"
"I could not have said that better, the second part of you, which I like perfectly, is really like a fairy tale! Was your day ok?"
"Yes, like many others. Professional stress but coupled with the yearning for tonight he was very exciting and how were you?"
"Mmm hours counted, something in the house whirled around, to distract my thoughts, I was in the afternoon drove into the city and bought something and wanted to drink coffee, but my brain has said, not that it will be too late, take you with cake and home when Mia calls earlier. It's kind of silly, I always have my cell phone with me!"
"Oh, you wanted to be alone with me the first time?"
"Yes, how do you feel about that?"
"I do not know, I have the feeling that it could be an ex-tremely erotic conversation again today, just like yester-day the many exciting mails!"
"And did you like it?"
"And how, it was the experience of the last years for me. Have spent the whole day thinking how this happened, it's like a miracle what your written words had triggered on me."
"And do you think the spoken words could trigger the same?"
"Yes, I hope so, I am also alone and prepared for

everything!"

"Oh, and now shall I get the bow and make it again?"

"Yes, I'm helping too!"

"Should I tell you something?"

"Yes!"

"I love to do it with you! It was also a super beautiful, erotic adventure for me. I could get used to something like that. No, after the first time I've become addicted, what did you do?"

"Me not! That's what you did to me!"

"Ok, then I will often do such great things with you, if you let me! But please tell me immediately, if I go too far, you must also like it otherwise it is not good!"

"Yes, I promise you and you too if I make nonsense you do not want."

"Yes, ok then I'll let you know immediately!"

"Yes, unity makes you strong and happy!"

"And tell me, have you had such fantasies before, or when did you notice them?"

"I do not know exactly, since I live alone, before I had always other dreams or better said almost none and then many negative or sad. Since living alone and that's been some years now, they started slowly."

"What do you prefer, are you rather the passive or the active part?"

"I do not know exactly, I would like to be everything, but that's not possible."

"But!"

"For real?"

"Yes, it's like a longing, sometimes you have it and sometimes you do not want to let it all go and be totally spoiled and the other time you want to act and spoil another very active, to master what's happening."

"You've got it right, right?"

"Yes, I have written a book about it, a bondage textbook, what you can experience everything and must take into account and are also reviews. Some of them made me curious and then I went deeper into the matter. I found out that my desire to be the passive part has two reasons. I had a very dominant mother and then all my

life I had to make the decisions and I just want to give that responsibility, but it's not easy to drop carefree. Is tied up and if a woman then lovingly spoiled me. No pain, I find that off putting. Then you can drop yourself. Unfortunately, until today I have not found any woman I could trust and that's why I lack the experience. Unfortunately and how is it with you?"

"I do not know, maybe I'm just curious. But I have only become in recent years. I have never talked about it, you are the first and then a man."

"Cool, thanks for your confidence."

"Please, please, please, but somehow you bring that out of me, where we e-mailed yesterday, I also scared me afterwards something that I just went through something and found it so beautiful."

"Yes, unexpectedly comes unfortunately only rarely!"

"You are one!"

"And what a! A very bad one! No, a dear one!"

"I believe that with loving you!"

"Thank you, I would like to prove it to you. But I have the feeling, no, I know, it will not be too long and we will face each other face to face and our hearts will beat loudly to the neck and then … . How will we greet each other the first time we see each other?"

"Oh I do not know, I'm shy!"

"Yeah, that's what I always say!"

"But you do not notice anything!"

"Yeah I'm trying to hide it, so you want to know how I would start the first meeting?"

"Oh yes, that sounds so erotic seducing again."

"Oh, and now shall I tell you how I imagine our first meeting?"

"Yes, please, please!"

"It will be on a not distant day, we will meet and meet, with you in Schwerin."

"How do you know that I live in Schwerin?"

"Well, you're calling me from home and the area code is lit on my display, you did not suppress your number!"

"But you are a very smart one."

"Well I want you to be on the same level as me. I live in

Hamburg!"
"Yes, almost around the corner."
"Exactly one hundred and fifteen kilometers!"
"How do you know that so fast again?"
"Oh I know myself in Germany quite well and had to do more often in Schwerin, because you know something like that! Impressed?"
"Just a little bit."
"Better than not, I hear you just smirking! Me too, that makes you in a good mood to talk to you!"
"True, but I think it's great that you can hear my smile."
"Yes, if you broaden your mouth to smirk, your voice will change and the pitch will also get higher."
"But you listen carefully."
"I'm just curious to know everything that has to do with you. Is that bad?"
"Well, if you do not use that against me!"
"Use, that sounds like a lawyer."
"Yes."
"How yes?"
"It's so easy."
"Oh, you have to do with the right!"
"Yes."
"I feel like an ENT doctor."
"How so?"
"Well, I have to pull every little info out of my nose! And now you are smiling over your whole face! Right?"
"Yeah, you're good at analyzing."
"You also give the best templates."
"Oh really?"
"Yes! And how!"
"You can flicker with you all the time."
"Thank you, please give back the compliment! Do you accept it?"
"Yes!"
"So what are you doing for a living?"
"Did not you want to tell me about our first meeting?"
"Yes and our first date in my view, but without guarantee and to the exclusion of liability for damages!"
"Ok! Do not make it so exciting, I'll burst!"

"Hurry, I do not want to be guilty of the mess of the broken Mia!"

"Youuu!"

"So meet the coffee on the market square in Schwerin at 16.00 on Friday. The weather is perfect for people in love, bright blue sky, sunshine and about 28.5 degrees outside temperature. My blood temperature is then 66 degrees!"

"You are a hot guy!"

"Yes, you bring me to precook. But it will be 15.02 and I'm already there, always a little earlier my mom taught me. I sit down in front of the cafe at a table. The waitress comes and I ask her for a vase for the flowers, but should not die of thirst! What kind of flowers are there?"

"Oh maybe, I do not know?"

"What would you wish for?"

"You should surprise me!"

"Booohhh are you sent!"

"No, just completely ignorant!"

"Hahaha, well, I decide … . So you heard the silence? Now you have to wait until our first meeting, when we see each other, the secret will be revealed!"

"Common!"

"So the waitress brings a vase and I put in the beautiful flowers. It's hot and I order myself in advance a coke to not dying while waiting for the best woman under the sun. Time seems to creep, but my excitement rises and rises. 15:35 and I have the area fully in view. Which direction is she coming from? Will she approach me directly, with little or no hesitation? 15:40. There's a woman in the back, no, the voice does not suit her, the one in the front, who's just turning the corner, is not too sexually dressed, because that could be her, no the gang is too over the top. 15:50. Almost cardiac arrest, only the last sip of Coke to keep your mouth moist, drink. The forehead is hot, oh you dumbass only because of the sun. 15:55. There, a woman like an elf, a dress slightly wafting in the summer, in addition the movement wind that arises through the tight, conscious

gait. She heads for the cafe, apparently her eyes are already there. You scan all tables outside, if they notice me? And at that moment, maybe fifteen yards away, as it happens, our eyes seem to cross and magically stick together. It comes right up to me, it's like a miracle, we just talked on the phone and did not swap pictures, but it's, it has to be, everything I've pictured in my mind embodies it and that smile is coming a merry energy bomb of the highest female class toward me. I feel her eyes penetrate me, about ten meters and I get up and want to go towards her. She does not deviate an inch from her direction and I make just two more steps in her direction and she stops, spontaneous and almost standing right in front of me, looks at me and says - hey it's me - and I answer, I guessed, an angel on earth! You smile and I take a step towards you, embrace you, a kiss on the left, a kiss on the right, head back and a very, very intense look of our four eyes say more than words. Her eyes send a boiling hot look. Like an arrow, it penetrates through my eyes directly into my heart. I feel like it almost tears me inside. This angel, with whom I have e-mailed and phoned and now he is in front of me and my lips must be held back by my head so as not to storm and play at once. Hello, so you are Mia, the angel?"

"Yes and you are Joschua the heavenly devil?"

"Yes, devilishly excited and enthusiastic. Well then we can play angels and devils soon, but please take some space. I'll adjust the chair for you and you'll take a seat. I put my body in front of you in position, of course, in a chair. And?"

"How and?"

"Well, am I exaggerating?"

"Exaggerated!"

"Hahaha, you probably want to embarrass me?"

"How so?"

"Ok, how do you like me, I know stupid question!"

"Well, I do not know, what do you look like? The way you sound?"

"You, how do you like my voice?"

"Very erotic and also male, although sometimes a bit crazy childish!"

"Wow, I take that as a compliment!"

"Yes, that's the way it should be!"

"Thank you! Keep talking!"

"No, you wanted to go on, we just sat down."

"Yes, and we're sitting opposite each other, both of us appreciate each other and - I can simply describe you - the female dream of my sleepless nights, that's all there is to it. Outside and inside, I have already experienced the inside in word and voice and now the outside to you, I can not let you disappoint, you have to be! I give everything and more! Somehow you guess my thoughts and smile so wonderfully refreshing. Well, have my thoughts made you smile?"

"Yes!"

"Why, did I think too loud?"

"Yes!"

"And what did I think?"

"You judged me and loved it."

"Well, you think well. No, I did not think so, I thought much, much better!"

"More beautiful?"

"Yes, even more beautiful and erotic! And we sit opposite each other and laugh and do not even notice that the waitress has come and would like to take our order. How long she had been there. Well, what is it allowed to be Mia? Coffee, tea or chocolate, plus a great cake?"

"Ostfriesentea with cream and what do you have for cake?"

"The waitress counts and Mia chooses plum cake and I join in completely, but with cream the cake! Satisfied, the waitress pulls off with her order."

"What did the waitress think about us?"

"She has certainly seen us sitting under a dome of luck!"

"That is also a description of my feelings, oh man, what did I say!"

"Well the truth and at the same time my feeling fully hit!"

"So, you're so happy when you're sitting opposite me?"
"Yes, but only for starters!"
"How about sitting longer is happiness gone?"
"No, then my heart calms down a bit and then the next level can come."
"The next stage? Which?"
"Well that's like a rocket, the first stage is burned down, then comes the second and then the third. Then you are in seventh heaven and if it is as high as an orbit around the earth, then it will take forever happiness, no love! Do you want to fly into orbit with me?"
"Let's see if we can take off together!"
"What do I have to do to take off? To take off together?"
"Oh, I remember so much!"
"Well, then I have a chance, because with many things there is definitely something I can do. Define what is much."
"Oh, that can be things in everyday life or even in private life."
"Which one do you want me to fulfill first?"
"Now you want to know for sure. You have to find out for yourself!"
"Oh, you've always been particularly bad at guessing, can not you give me such a tiny hint? If I know what you want, you can get there much sooner!"
"No, first you have to guess three times."
"Ok, first of all, you want a wonderful dinner with candlelight, bubbly and my company!"
"Mmm."
"Second, you want to dance with me in romantic music and feel my closeness."
"Mmm, Mmm, and third?"
"Well, here comes the nice, naked cuddling, two attracting people who can not suppress their feelings for each other finally show and feel and ...! Which order of suggestions should it be?"
"Oh this is terribly difficult, in itself 1 2 3 would be the right order, but that would be kind of boring, right?"
"But if you start with 3, you would not be strong enough for 2 and 1!"

"Oh, is 3 so exhausting?"

"Yes, you can not imagine that, pure sporty deposits churning!"

"What deposits?"

"Well, starting with the catch (running training), then the mutual textile relief program (sporting wrestling), followed by the many kisses (muscle training) and the subsequent ... (pushups), then the recovery phase, the tender stroking afterwards (yoga). You see, athletic excellence when you see the time factor (1 2 3 or 4 hours) and then after the short recovery period, the repetition! This gives special endorphin liberation!"

"Oh, that sounds exhausting!"

"Yes, love can be terribly stressful! Yes, you can not get into seventh heaven orbit of love without effort, but this is the most beautiful effort in the world and if I imagine being able to experience these efforts with you, then I am already getting hot and cold. Only the thought of it makes me tickle!"

"That's how you imagine that?"

"What ago?"

"Well, our common sports experiences!"

"Yeah, but that's just a variation, for one night, the next night the exercise would be different, otherwise it would be boring, because I do not know the actions you are doing. Maybe I like doing an exercise so good of you that I would like to see a repetition more often!"

"I have to smile, if I imagine such sports exercises with you!"

"How do I make a ridiculous figure?"

"No, not, but as you describe it, I think that's kind of sporty, and sports and sex are a hot combination, a bit strange for me and therefore the smile."

"Oh sooo!" Cool!"

"You have unusual descriptions for it."

"Yes, for the greatest thing in the world, but only if you have the greatest woman in the world or as an angel as you are, by his side! Yes you are the angel who flies with me through the clouds into the seventh heaven of love, side by side!"

"Flatterer!"

"Oh, but what a!"

"You can say that!"

"But since I'll carry you on my hands, you can not slip on the slime trail."

"Can you carry me on hands?"

"Yes and how, I'm athletic!"

"Oh, from the many sex sports?"

"Hahaha, what you think of the poor slime."

"I do not think so, I just combined."

"Missing combination!"

"How so?"

"Alas, lately I have not had much opportunity for these sports exercises, the business, and some women's relationship deficiencies."

"How sad experiences?"

"Yes, all I can say is that as a sensitive person, when you come upon an unfavorable partner and you do not notice it immediately, but develop it a little later, then you always lose your heart and that's what I've often been lately."

"I can promise you one thing, I have an open heart too!"

"Maybe for me?"

"Could be! Feels like that and I'm curious for more!"

"Fantastic, that would be, oh heaven, I want to hug you now and just push and never let go. Just squeeze and feel your warmth and if I pressed you to me, I would hear your heart beating, alas, that would be wonderful."

"Sounds good! Try out!"

"Yes! Absolutely!"

"Why are you getting up now?"

"Well you tried saying that and now I wanted to push you."

"What, what here?"

"Yes! Why not? Or are you shy?"

"No, but the people!"

"What people, I only see you!"

"You are totally crazy!"

"Who I?"

"Yes, you!"

"Oh, that makes your wonderful presence here near me, I'm completely innocent!"

"Who believes it."

"Like, you do not believe me?"

"You play fantastic with words."

"These are not just words, these are the verbal feelings that you have awakened in me, because I just can not do anything about it. My heart feels it when it thinks of you, and then my brain translates those feelings into words and lets them pass through your lips to your ears."

"Charmer!"

"Is not it true that when one likes to hear nice words from one person and especially when they are the truth? Words go to the heart and who would not like to be caressed by a person he likes, I already and you?"

"An honest YES."

"Now I have to think, was my heart already caressed by you? Or not? If not, is that a sign that you do not like me at all?"

"Hey, there's someone looking for a compliment. I do not want to be like that! Since we e-mailed each other yesterday and even talk on the phone today, you have lit a flame in me and I have since had such a strong desire that you should trigger a blazing inferno in me. Funny thing I've never said to a man. I have never felt such desire so extreme in a man. But it is suddenly there, the desire to burn with you together, the glow of love is kindled and now wants to be stoked."

"Are you there? You do not say anything, hello!"

"I'm sorry, but ... but what you just said, those were the favorite words my ears have received in the life of a female being. Thank you! Oh, they did so well after the many years of deprivation. I even have to wipe a little tear off. Yes, men can cry too, but this was a tear of pure joy, thank you!"

"But you are sensitive, I think that's great with a man!"

"Thank you. Yes sensitive when it comes to the heart, but in life or rather I have learned to hide my feelings,

61

because in business life feelings are often interpreted as weakness. Now you could see with your razor sharp mind that I'm honest and open with you, why only, but it feels so incredibly light and relieving, just to say and do what you really feel and do."

"Yes, now that I think about it, I would agree with your words 1000%, it's good, very good, it's free."

"Yes and you can feel with what you are inside, a person who is always buried under the pressures of everyday life and sometimes I wondered, where is this person and who wants to see him at all. No one wanted that yet!"

"I feel similar."

"It's amazing what you trigger in me and somehow I have no inhibitions, it's like a liberation to chat with you about it and I have the feeling it depends on you as I send it."

"Yes, you speak from my heart. Now I want to tell you, when I saw your ad, it was somehow hot and cold on my back. I got up and stalked through the room, knowing that when I answered, my life changed fundamentally. It was a crazy feeling, but it was so positive inside me and so I just had to e-mail and you see what happened?"

"What?"

"I wake up with the thoughts of you, go to work with it, during the break I dream of us and then can not wait to e-mail or make phone calls. That's you guilty! Only you alone, no man has ever made it!"

"Wow, sounds good, then maybe I'm the right one for you, but unfortunately I have to tell you, it's the other way round for me. Can you feel my inward happy smile. Are you the right lid for me as a pot?"

"Let's see the beginning is promising, but if I pass, you can only see if we can see each other and super-impose."

"Oops, how do you mean lying on top of each other, with or without textiles?"

"Well, how can you tell if the lid fits on the pot? Do you always put paper or a towel between them when you put a lid on the pot while cooking?"

"Danger!!!"
"What!"
"On now! Now comes the question: When is fitting!"
"How fitting?"
"Well, cover on pot fitting?"
"Yeah, I already understood you!"
"Good and? Now it's your turn!"
"Yes, now I have put myself under pressure."
"Oh! Yes, you can see it that way!"
"Planning is your specialty."
"Do not distract and put everything to me, because if I should plan that, then you must not say no! Do you want it?"
"Mmm, how dangerous is that?"
"Well, that's the big question mark! Now you have to show your colours, but I can tell you, we make the following deal, we agree on a codeword now."
"A codeword, like the bank?"
"No, not one, that's just for us both. No matter what we do in the future, also and above all things between woman and man, you can, for example, say anything you want when we're together, help, no, I do not want, stop right now, no, do not let that, no matter what you say, I will not stop, but as soon as you say our code-word, it's all over, stop! This is something that can give complete trust and also gives you the opportunity to let go. So, if you agree, there's some reason for it, which you'll learn later, we'll take the word - RED! So when you say "red" I'll stop everything we're doing right now and you'll say something you do not like."
"Give me an example."
"Mmm, so we drive on the highway, you sit next to me and it's getting dark, but our goal is still far and I want to arrive quickly, because then we ... well you know what ... will do, so I press the tube, 180, 200, 220 and you look at the speedometer and you do not want to drive so fast, so you say RED and I ask why and you say it's too fast for you right now and then I drive slower immediately. Ok?"

"Hey, you are silent too loud! What is? Confused?"

"Hey, what did you imagine?"
"I?"
"Yes, you!"
"Something more erotic."
"Hahaha, I guessed that and now it came out."
"What?"
"Well, your deepest wishes!"
"Which one?"
"Ohhh, how am I supposed to get out of this situation now?"
"How so?"
"Well, what you want to hear now is - well ... ."
"Hahaha prude?"
"No, now you have challenged me. You wish you a medium fried rump steak served with baked potato, a roasted corn on the cob and a glass of beer."
"How?"
"Yes, that's how it should start and then after this culinary treat, should I ask you, did you like it and how about dessert? And then you say, yeah yummy and what do you recommend for dessert and now we come to the exhausting, but super sexy erotic dessert of the evening and we can not shirk it here in the pub, but you have to come to my house to see him there to enjoy. But the enjoyment of the dessert will carry you into other spheres and make you addicted to it!"
"Ohhh, do you think that I think so?"
"No, I do not think so, I know that!"
"How so?"
"Well that almost literally stood between your lines, which you always cling so beautifully, but my heart can decipher them. Correct?"
"Now I have the feeling I am a glass book for you!"
"No, certainly not, but we have the same kind of deciphering."
"Which type of deciphering?"
"Our feelings, since we seem to have the same feelings, I can decipher between the lines what you have encrypted inserted there. That's why I know it, I feel it, please

say yes now, then I'll tell you about the dessert pre-
paration!"
"Well, that sounds like a wannabe threat!"
"No, just a lovingly packed challenge of certain words!"
"Word juggler, but a very sweetie!"
"Ok, I can live with that."
"So we arrived at you and then?"
*"Oh, but we were fast, must lie to you! Do you have
such a desire?"*
"Desire? What?"
"Well, after dessert of the sweet kind."
"Oh, that must be up to you. Otherwise I did not have
that special desire."
*"Oh, these are so nice words, I just can not get enough
of that, thank you, my heart is always so warm. Now I
also know why for years I only felt cool around the
heart, but two days ago that changed abruptly.
Conclusion! It must be up to you!!!"*
"A direct hit, a great treat these words, but what about
the dessert with you?"
*"Look in a mailbox, please, there you will find some-
thing and study it, then I would like an answer what you
have chosen!"*
"Ok, I'll call you right now, hang up the phone."

Oh, I'm going crazy with this man. He makes me so hot
and wet between my legs. I can not stop it. One word
gives the other, and so on. My thoughts are really fast, a
small impetus from Joschua and they think fast like a
racing car from the full program. They have never done
that either. Clear and my heart interferes with it immediately. Oh Joschua you light me everywhere. Have a
quick drink of cola. I will not be back for dinner. Do not
feel hungry. Well at least not on the food, only the hot
words of Joschua. The Mia first words. Oh I'm crazy, I
did not know about me yet. Learn something again. Yes
Joschua is a great teacher. Oops Mia mind stop and
read the mail. Oh in my mailbox, it has already arrived.
The guy keeps his promise. Whether that will be so if I
give him the chance that we meet. Oh Mia what do you

mean your heart says yes and your mind says try it you have nothing to lose and you want to give your heart but also something great. Oh finish both of you I now want to read the mail in peace.

Love menu

**Gourmet restaurant
"Romance"**

**Valid daily until
end of our common
love**

Love menu

**A good woman, that's fine,
wants to be treated with reason.
Your will, females, notice it fine,
should also be the man's will.**

**All meals are served in a candlelit, comfortably warm
and well-scented room. All dishes are lovingly prepared
and served with a lot of heart.**

**Such a five star menu that is lovingly celebrated, one
locks firmly in the heart and you will never forget in your
life!**

**Please choose from your extensive food offer and con-
sider in advance whether you also have the time to eat a
complete menu or just enjoy a small selection of food.**

The prices include the service tax.

Bon Appetit!

Cold Appetizers

price

"Pure eye contact"
(Eye-to-eye talk with the caterer for a minute)
.... M 2.00

"look of sensuality"
(looking at the giver when this one with the tongue sen-
sually goes over his lips)
.... M 4.00

"look of the feelings"
(looking at the giver when this one loving each other
with both hands the face and the hair strokes)
.... M 5.00

Warm appetizers

"Caress tender hands"
(Lying hand on hand on the table)
.... M 2.00

"Tender kiss both hands"
(Palms tenderly with the lips touch)
.... M 5.50

"One-tailed nibble" .... M 3.00

"Lip smocks on both eyebrows" .... M 4.00

"Tender lip whispering" (4 lips) .... M 6.50

main menu

Standard menus:

"Eyes menu"

The opposite bares the upper body and may be for two minutes with your eyes to be devoured
.... **M 18,00**

"Fondle menu"

The opponent may over the upper body over the stuff for two minutes lovingly be stroked by the passer behind the one to be stroked
.... **M 19.50**

"Kiss menu"

The opposite can be without defoliate everywhere kiss on the body
.... **M 22,50**

How beautiful it is when the rays of the candles are gently reflected on the body of your counterpart and with their shadows let the contours of the beloved person shine again and again in a new erotic light. So we always serve with each menu a five armed candelabrum with burning, to the clothing of the female guest, matching, twenty- five inch high candles.

Pampering menus:

The passive pampering menu for the connoisseur

Starter:

A smile followed by two tender hands lovingly surrounding the purchaser's face and followed by two wet lips that initiate a fierce dialogue with the customer's lips

Main course:

A tender peeling of the customer from the entire shell followed by two determining hands on bare skin with subsequent contact of two wet lips on the flaking skin. Consumption time according to personal need

Dessert:

A warming main potpourri by a loving cuddling together of two naked bodies.

For passive pampering, we serve as a drink a well tempered champagne in two glasses with the option of refill the glasses.

.... M 56,00

The active pampering menu for the connoisseur

Starter:

Two hands tenderly embrace the other's face, caress it and caress it with the moisture of four indulgent lips.

Main course:

It is enjoyed when the counterpart is slowly scrolled completely out of its shell and now unprotected the eager hands felt everywhere and calls for the lecherous lips of the pamper. Consumption time according to personal need.

Dessert:

A romantic main potpourri by a loving cuddling together of two naked bodies and the mutual feeling of emerging happiness.

To the active pampering menu we serve as a drink a tart sparkling in the glasses sparkling wine, the good taste tempered the taste buds in the mouth.

.... M 58,00

General restaurant conditions

Who ordered paid the bill, i. the eaten M's are added and converted into minutes of love.
1 M = 1 minute time that the non-purchaser can choose at the next love session.

"Hello are you still there?"

"Sure, I'm waiting for your order. Was the menu clear?"

"Well, you're prepared for hungry lady visits!"

"No, this menu has not got a wife in front of you. She was once an idea of me how to be love life can add value to everyday life to counteract, but has never been used. It just occurred to me when we were on the phone chatted."

"And if I now have the active pampering menu for the enjoy your meal, how long will it take to deliver?"

"Since we have changed the place in the meantime and you sit down at the dining room table with me I can immediately give you the starter of the pampering menu serve."

"Well, then I order the complete menu."

"Before you tell me, what are you wearing while we are start talking so erotic here?"

"Ohhh well, after work I'm home and took a quick shower, a day is in business but often exhausting and then the faster back home - because of you - because I had to take a shower and then I really thought it was great, if I could move freely and have me dressed, red and relatively short."

"Mini?"

"No, rather midi."

"Bright red, dull or shiny?"

"You want to know for sure!"

"Well please feed my imagination a bit more."

"Ok it's midi, waisted, and almost mid red, dull and plain."

"But that sounds sexy and red pumps too?"

"Hahaha, no barefoot, have a fluffy rug in I cuddle my feet a bit."

"And what are you sitting on? Chair, armchair, sofa?"

"On a chair and before you ask, he is colourful though bluish as the main colour."

"Thanks, now I can dream something more and you have surely already your legs pulled up and you in the armchair a little snuggled."

"Yes!"

"Ok then I want to deliver the appetizer, through our little talk is certainly the kitchen with it finished."
"Grrr I'm hungry, feed me finally!"
"Yes, now we have to go to the appetizer places with the appropriate attitude."
"As?"
"You stay in your chair and I'll come your beautiful face, with the expectant sparkling eyes getting closer to mine. Slowly, very slowly, as in slow motion ours are approaching lips for the appetizer and our eyes are looking it feels as if everyone is in the heart of the other wanted to see. You have such dreamy mysterious, brown eyes, with an unimaginably strong luminosity, a sparkle, like a star. It starts slowly in me to tingle and my heart beats faster and faster. With this appetizer I, the woman, will feel that is the right thing for a shared life adventure, touch for the first time, with my lips open meet her lips, which are easily hidden under one bright pink shiny lipstick. There is a tension in the air, like an electrical voltage, always gets fiercer the closer our lips come. But respect at that moment touch my hands your cheeks, both hands are on your cheeks on and it tingles in me, a warmth flows into mine Hands, are you cooking?"
"No, I'm just so loaded, you're cooking!"
"It may be, as if it were the first time in life is the first time you kiss your first time love, that's what it feels like right now, but the thoughts do not have time to spend more time it's about time. My hands are light your face, as if to say it, just now do not be cowardly and your lips from my kiss direction turn away. Only a few inches and me feel your breath already, it's hot, burning hot, like a Sahara wind and he touches my face and touches over my lips and cheeks past my face rear. It's such a power-ful breath he has with me pulls in the neck of the shirt at the back of the neck and there with its tender warmth putting up all my body hairs causes. I shake my shoulders and you ask me with your eyes, what hap-pened. You have my neck and shoulder hair through your hot I had to shake myself slightly."

73

"And what do you mean, when you first feel everything of me as you then go off!"

"Well, that's a hot promise, come let action follow, wait!"

"Attention now!"

"And suddenly, against the resistance, she pushes her hands on her cheeks forward with her lips as fast as an arrow and they strike mine with tremendous force, our lips become deformed and the moisture attached to them is thrown into the room. Immediately, she moves her lips and she clasps my upper lip, pulls her head back and plumps my upper lip vigorously forward to then let go again. Vibrantly, she hurries back to her starting point. A short pause and then my lips rush on hers. It's like a wrestling match, but very tender, the touches are like a touch and all four lips touch and wedge, squeeze and release and what is that, as her tongue pops out and splits my lips to meet mine. A dance of our tongues begins and curiously they try to prevent each other from exploring the oral cavity of the other and they are shielded from the environment by our pressing lips. It feels so warm and humid, very intimate and yet so cuddly exciting. My thoughts begin to work, and after every single tip of the tongue, I get a picture of your interior. Exciting and that gentle wrestling match with your defense system, called a tongue. It feels so warm and slightly rough. My also?"

"Yeah, go on!"

"Time seems to stand still and you enjoy every single touch of our tongues and there is still the contact of our lips, which try hard to press each other, but by the movements of the tongues repeatedly slipping and new from the inside out moisture get slippery. Every now and then, a whole drop goes off in the direction of the chin, but that does not matter, it's wow and uiii again, it's as if a long awaited dream becomes reality, a unity arises and one can notice how two individuals become very slowly one come together. A unity of two souls in two bodies, but one. A whole new feeling, a feeling that makes one hope that it should never stop. It feels so good and you can forget the whole world around you,

even my thoughts just start to cease to exist, you just feel the two of us, our tongues and lips and the feelings are so strong, as I mean Have eyes and they can not send any new stimuli to the brain. Also, I have the feeling that the sounds are heard from my ears as if they are in the fog and you no longer perceive. Everything is turned inside and nothing seems to get inside us anymore. Simply a unity, just a unity and this indescribably great feeling, only triggered by our first kiss. Madness!!! If we can top that. Think away, heart to power and just enjoy, enjoy, enjoy!"

"Oops, did you ever look at the clock?"

"No, how come?"

"Well, the starter took as long as usual a three course meal."

"Really, it felt like it was just a second and I was just wondering if you could take the appetizer again."

"Yes please, once again the appetizer!"

"And may I lure you out of your chair for the second appetizer and ask you on the sofa?"

"How so?"

"It may be better for our backs, the second appetizer may take even longer if it tastes as good as the first."

"Who lies down?"

"I'm a gentleman, so I'm lying down and you can lie softly on me, is that ok for the most beautiful woman in my heart?"

"Yesss."

"Oh, you know, just the thought that you will put on me, so I finally feel the whole Mia, all over the body and the slight pressure you will then directly on me exercise, everywhere and then the appetizer, I feel I'm almost in seventh heaven now. What a meal. So I hand you my hands and slowly pull you out of your chair and on and on until you are right in front of me and I can again feel your erotic breath right in front of me. This time you will not blow past my neck, but your breath hits me briefly above my first button from my shirt and spreads evenly under him with a plump warmth that re-introduces a hair experience and a slight tingling sensa-

75

tion. Man oh man, you, I close my eyes briefly and let this sublime feeling act on me slowly. It's as if it's coming in from the outside in, slowly, and has my heart as its target, and your erotic brown eyes look at me and say I'm hot and continue to eat, I'm crazy about it. I take your hand and lead you to the sofa, let go of your hand and put me back on the sofa. You dominate in front of me, in full size I see you from the bottom up to the top, you have wonderful swirling brown hair, the long so loose around your shoulders and give your being a lightness. If now a bright spotlight would stand behind you, then you would look like an angel! Simply heavenly! Come slowly down to me my angel and let me feel you completely. Let me feel your warmth and wonderful body, enjoy your scent and finally take the second appetizer."

"I have never dined so luxuriously, on a man and even with the appetizer. Sorry the second appetizer."

"Your left knee is squeezed between me and the sofa, the right hugs very tight against my left thigh, so it does not slip down and you're kneeling on me."

"Olala, what's that, is that in the way if I want to lay flat on you now?"

"Well, I think it will press on you with me and then have space between us, but of course it will feel you very close and probably drive me insane, I can not just turn it off until dessert."

"So you can not turn it on and off?"

"No, it's not being done by my brain, it's by my heart, and that's not going to be easy to stop, once it's on fire, like now with you!"

"Fire and flame? I did not do anything."

"Oh the appetizer did not you experience, that was another?"

"You would like that?"

"For heaven's sake, I would not have served this appetizer to any other woman. And no other woman could have triggered these appetite feelings with me."

"Really not?"

"No, not 100%!"

"That's very nice of you! Let's finally eat, I'm hungry!"
"Good, let me slide on you and finally bring your lips to mine."
"Do you really think so, and I'm not too heavy for you?"
"The 50 kilograms spread over 180 centimeters, I hold out."
"Thanks for the weight assessment, but I love you, put it another 22.5 kilograms on it, then it fits."
"Oh those few grams, all pure love that I feel and that can not be enough!"
"Yes, that sounds good. Huuunger!"
"But you are starving."
"Yes, for years!"
"Oh, you poor female creature. Come I feed you."

Slowly his head approaches mine and the lips are pressed together. It's like when I was my neck muscle would have released, my head pushes my lips with such a weight that they almost complete with its airtight. I try mine lips to spread and his at the same time. It's a totally different feeling than the first appetizer, again another feeling, a feeling as if you do not make the decision yourself, but another one meets her for one. Oh man, he pushes like automatic his whole body from below against mine and the heat he transmits, as if we only are one and now his tongue presses against mine and demands admission and I let them, I feel like that moisture of mine slowly trickles into his mouth, it feels so unusually good, very good and those touches his tongue tip on mine, like small electric shocks, it makes me tickle so much, but I have the feelings, I can not move, although I'm on top. His hands are coming up my back to rest, now he feels through mine blouse the prints of my bra. He will be determined now through my thin silk blouse my warm, tender feel skin and my feminine scent will be in his nose penetrate, a warm female fragrance, so pleasant, as if he were intoxicated by it. And our re tongues continue to play. Oh man, how can a man like that? Be sensitive, that I have never felt before allowed. And again he does something that I do have not experienced. I feel his hand on the blouse directly over my bra closure. He will do not open my cap through the blouse? It tingles at the thought. How will it feel if my bra so undocked under my blouse waiting for something more happens. Oh, we are only with the appetizer and getting more violent my tongue activity and saliva trickles. Damp warm and so very intimate it feels on. So familiar, as if you have been together for hundreds of years experienced and yet, as if it were only a second lasts. Your own feelings can be, if you can really kicked, uh be tongued, but totally confuse. It is surprising what feelings in one body can trigger everything and how beautiful positive feelings can bring the whole body up. Everyone part in the body feels calm and balanced and but activated. Gorgeous! And the second appetizer is one of the very long kind with infinitely intense enjoyment. When our lips talk to each other so intensely and the tongues play together. I feel yet, like Joschua with his hands over my whole back strokes, tender, as if he wanted to explore everything exactly and absorb. From my waistline started stroking slowly upwards until both are his hands in my hair frolicking and rummaging around there. It's already tingling my neck again, what is he doing with me? Feelings about feelings arise and alternate faster and faster, so I do barely come and my excitement begins to rise steeply. He knows exactly how he puts me in the shooting position brings to the cloud seven.

„I could enjoy it for hours, but who knows how long she still likes the appetizer. Gently, both of my hands slide down slowly, letting a thin bubble of air between her and her body go down. The way to the bra closure is already known, but painted in the other direction again as new territory. Linger briefly as they approach the bra wearer, hooking a strip of overstrip with a small, short, so that the wearer is slightly raised and then immediately goes back into the depths, hitting the skin quickly. This makes her body tremble again, so much that I can feel it on my lips. I feel the tension transform into a

78

small, icy chill and run over her back and her tongue reacts immediately, this time by pausing briefly in her play and then instantly injecting the saved power of inner being back into a more violent tongue exploration movement. Now it's time for my hands to continue down the path in these unexplored areas, and I can already feel their beautifully shaped back, which describes a small valley before it starts slowly to lift up again. There they are, oh now I'm getting very warm, I've reached them, their buttocks on both sides at the same time. I press harder and feel a soft resistance. Oh no, the resistance is going to be tough. You, I've noticed, you play with your behind muscles and make a total strain. So you realize where I am on a journey of discovery. That's great, we talk with our bodies and even get along. It fits! Well, if that succeeds again, I'll try that and my hands will move away from her body, let's say ten centimeters to hit her like a flash. On her so hot buttocks, sexually charged like her whole body and the reaction is huge, she jerks up her head and part of the upper body, our lips are torn apart so fast that her tongue is still out, she has a soft pink color and is tailored very sharp. She jumps back, her lips close at once, shortly afterwards, reopening and letting a faint but certain moan through.

"I have a better idea not to open the bra clasp, but I explore with my hands everything on their backs, as far as they are enough and already they set in motion only up to the neck and caress their hair. She reacts immediately with a small movement of her body lying on top of me and a slightly more violent tongue whisperer. Her hair feels so soft and the movement of her hair through my hands lets her wonderful scent blow into my nose, I was right, she must be an angel."
"Ahhh, ahhh! Continue! Continue!"
"Yes, the light blow has so excited her, no, the blow only increased her existing excitement and made her start forgetting something, opening something and dropping it. And another, light beat with echo, i. two in a row, but always on both buttocks at the same time, our

79

lips can be separated, groaning and immediately lead to the next lip union, followed by their curious tongue on exploration tour."

"Yes, please move on, you're driving me crazy already!"

"Oops, there should be some madness left over for the main course."

"Do not worry, I saved a long time and waived, for the main course and the dessert is still enough there."

"Well, then I'm not worried. Well, for a change now no punches pop, but my hands are pressed firmly on your buttocks and I feel like you are already on an expectancy tension in the whole body. Already preparing yourself for the next loving stroke. Wrong, this time I press my fingers firmly into your buttocks, as if they want to hold on, so I cling to me, which elicits a sound from your mouth, whose lips have separated from mine briefly."

"Ohhh!"

"Unlike the punches, let's try out if that's always the case, and that's why I'll let you have a loving double whack, done with both hands, and listen."

"Ahhh! Ahhh! "

"Oho, that was just like before. Beats make other sounds than claws, if I can probably elicit another sound from you, let's see and I draw my hands very slowly again a little higher, until I am with them over the belt away and I am stuck there. Once again, I can feel the rising tension in your body and you're already reacting. Our tongues separate, because you bring back yours, then our lips say goodbye, because you raise your head very slowly and you open your eyes, which I already have one open while our eyes meet. You can talk with your eyes, I have the feeling and it's a miracle. I seem to understand this language. Your eyes look at me questioningly and now, what is coming now. And now I start a new attempt to explore unknown areas and push my hands, which are firmly pressed against your body, slowly downwards. What a miracle the fingertips do not push over the belt but under him. Well Joschua, how can you, but why not, push on, says my heart and I

push, but when my hands have reached the end of the finger, it is too tight and I just want to pull out a hand, because I feel like your almost not existing abdomen, by moving muscle initially einzubst to allow my hands the way to further depths and whoosh the hands are completely disappeared in your pants. I feel your thin panties under my hands and your pants over it. It's warm and tight, plump warm, but I want more and your eyes tell me - yes, go ahead. I hear your heart starting to beat faster already in the direction of exciting frenzy. My fingers begin to move slowly and up your slip to grope to reach its edge and then slowly around this and push down. Yes, full of success, there it is, the first piece of delicate, naked body skin of yours. My fingers feel it, how soft, how warm and slightly damp. A feeling like touching an angel for the first time. How emotional she is. She not only noticed and wanted me to explore her, but she immediately felt it when I touched her skin, like a little shock, of course positively. It is a very special moment again, just like the first kiss, the first contact skin to skin on the body. These moments are just the icing on the cake, because you can only experience them once. Poor are people who simply go away through these experience points. These moments can feel so extreme only people with a lot of emotions that can also be dropped. Then you notice the difference, it is not just a quickie and not a one night stand, but it is a start of something very special, a relationship of two people, an emerging love relationship of the very emotional kind. Who has not been in the everyday life felt something, where upon the body reacted with a tingling sensation. If you then imagine and realize that a limited number of these feelings can be triggered by another human being you can approach, then you are so excited about it and when it happens then it is just heavenly, totally erotic and also sexually arousing. The second and third touch triggers feelings other than the very first gentle touch explosion. It had happened, the first skin on body skin explosion was experienced and she looked me in the eyes, these brown, meaningful eyes

that have spoken to me and accompanied me on this experience, first the looks were wishing, then demanding and then. Well, I could not see her, those eyes, because she dropped her eyelids and went into a complete epicure to fully enjoy this special moment. It's like a little kind of relaxation and she enjoys it until she opens her eyes again and they look relaxed. She raises her eyelids again and I intend to finish this appetizer with an unexpected climax. Somehow she seemed to feel it again, so say her eyes and wait. My eyes betray nothing, just a slight pull up of the corner of my mouth, which spreads to my cheeks in a tiny, mischievous laugh, followed by a brief flash of my eyes and the questioning eye contact that comes from it. I quickly pull my hands out of her pants, they gain about ten inches in height and then fall down violently on their two buttocks and their eyes light up briefly, as if I had torn her from a deep sleep, accompanied at the same time by a loud cry."
"Auauau!"
"Now the second appetizer is over. Did she like it?"

I am already breathing heavily and I also hear that Joschua is breathing heavily and relatively quickly, although with his voice he works so hard to emphasize everything he tells me.

"Wow, wait a minute, I have to enjoy something and let it sink first, such an appetizer I have never served in my life. A one plus plus!"
"Thanks a million, I will pass the compliment to the kitchen."
"Please, the cook deserves too."
"But now I have to say, I have never had such an enjoyable female guest at my table! Emotional tip, what does that make of the main course?"
"Thanks for the compliment, it's so good!"
"Only the compliment?"
"Of course not, the food was the trigger for compliment!"
"Ok, I can only give that back to you. Thank you for

dining with me. What would be the best menu, if not such a great guest had ordered and experienced with the chef?"
"Yes you are right."
"How does it look? Any room for the main course?"
"Yes, of course, but please first a little glass and a little rest, then I can look forward to the main course with you, because when can you experience such excitingly beautiful. I have to fully enjoy that."
"Let's sit here at the table for a while, with a glass of champagne, would you like it pure or with juice?"
"Pure today!"
"Cheers for an even hotter main course!"
"Yes, so hot that I can burn myself, that's what I wish for."
"Burn, well I have to tell the cook when ordering. But you make high demands, whether the kitchen can fulfil that?"
"Yes, I think so, after the starter level."
"So, did you like the appetizer so much? But I have to say, it was the hottest, most erotic, most exciting and loving appetizer I've ever had."
"You have certainly already served many appetizers of this kind."
"Well, you can see that either way."
"How so?"
"Honestly, I've sent this gourmet menu of love a few times, but you're the first female being I'm allowed to experience and I could not imagine another woman, above all, it's almost like a miracle, a like minded person and be allowed to entertain the feelings at the table."
"What do these words do to my soul?"
"And what do your feelings of my soul and my body and mind do quite well."
"Ok, let's agree, we'll do each other good."
"Sounds good and I totally agree with you."
"How nice, let's toast again."
"What?"
"To the experience of our joint main course."
"On the speedy madness. Cheers!"

"Cheers!"

"I think the main course can be done. Do you remember anything served?"

"Yes, it's a cold served main course which is heated directly by eating."

"Hello, but you have described that, it is not better. You have hit the head of the main course on the head completely and think of your desire earlier."

"What wish?"

"Well, that he should be served so hot that you can burn yourself."

"Yes, I can just remember that."

"Well, if this wish of you is a coincidence?"

"How so?"

"Now you can heat it up so hot that we both can burn it and guess what I want?"

"Do you burn at the main course?"

"No."

"What?"

"I want to fall with you into the flames of the hot serving love, to roll around in them and watch you start to glow and burn. It's supposed to get so hot that we melt together in the flames and feel like one for this indulgence time."

"Is there another course like the starter?"

"But now I have the feeling that your eyes are bigger than your stomach or better that your desires receive great feelings, are greater than your physical options, because you have to remember, there is also a dessert or do you want to give it up?"

"Ohhh."

"I can offer you a solution to this problem."

"Yes which?"

"We just go to such menus more often. If you still like me after this main course."

"What do you like?"

"It may be that I burn or salt the main course."

"Salted, I have to think about it, if a cook salted a dish, then he is in love. So I apologize in advance."

"Yes why?"

84

"It's clear, since I'll be the prepared food, then the cook, so you have to be in love with me and then I can just apologize, but only because I might want to over simmer the cook."

"Oops means that you've liked me so much so far that your heart wants to see a sequel?"

"Yes!"

"Oh, that goes down like oil. Well then that will be a slippery main course."

"Yes main course, when is it served?"

"Ok, may I ask, because the main course will be served in a different location."

"Where, then?"

"Take my hand, I'll guide you."

"But you have a hot hand."

"Yes, that's because of this super hot double appetizer with you!"

"Extremely hot and hot. Where are you taking me?"

"We'll be right there, the main course must be served with the right atmosphere. I lead you into the living room in front of the fireplace, in which the wooden sheath is gaily twisted by the flames and throw many facets of light variations on the lounger in front of it. The fireplace radiates not only friendly light, but also a cozy warmth, which is for the success of the main course of immense importance. The room is also illuminated by fifty yellow candles in various sizes and thicknesses. Candles whose flames move easily in the rising warmth of the fireplace, resulting in an ever changing picture of light in the room. Not only the crackling chimney fire, but also a hint of soft sounds from all corners, which form into romantic ways and round off the atmosphere. We enter and I look in her face. I'm glad to be able to take the skin with you here."

"How romantic!"

"Yes, sweets have to be served romantically."

"All the things you know."

"Well, that's what you meant ironically, I noticed exactly and above all saw your mischievous smile. But that looks so angelic in the candlelight, that makes me warm

all over again. Do you see the double bed in front of the fireplace?"

"Yes."

"We feed like the ancient Romans lying down. How would you like the main course served?"

"Which choices are there?"

"There are several food preparation variations.

1. You stand in front of the fireplace with your back and I strip you piece by piece

2. You stand in front of the fireplace with your stomach and I strip you piece by piece

3. I stand in front of the fireplace with my back and you steal me piece by piece

4. I stand in front of the fireplace with my stomach and you desteal me piece by piece

5. We stand sideways in front of the fireplace and defoliate and alternate each other bit by bit."

"Cool possibilities!"

"No matter what you choose, it is only defoliated and fed by the eyes, and when all the leaves have fallen on both, you or I may begin a full body lip and tongue massage, discovering each other's body, with their hands touching and moving allowed."

"Move?"

"Yes, turn around to make contact with the lip massage."

"And may I make an additional order?"

"Which?"

"May I touch the defoliants during the defoliation, that would be like salt in the soup!"

"Well, there you have a very hot ulterior motive!"

"I, no, not not!"

"I do not believe you. But why not, sounds good. Agreed."

"And when we are completely stripped, we lie down on the couch and enjoy the main course, as if we were lying on a plate."

"A good comparison, yes start! Oh, you have to choose the variation first."

"I take ... mmm ... I can not decide that badly, No. 3 or

No. 5."
"That's a really tough decision."
"Hey are you laughing at me right?"
"Who, I would never laugh at you, really. I'm just so excited what you choose."
"Yes, mmm I choose No. 5 no better No. 3."
"So may I give you a little help?"
"Yes gladly."
"Are you shy, then choose No. 3. Do you have courage then choose the number 5?"
"If I am shy, the No. 3 is difficult."
"If you do not want to, then the main course will go back to the kitchen before it gets cold."
"No, I do not think so."
"How do you want to hold me?"
"Yeah, you also want to enjoy the main course with me."
"You're right, but that's right!"
"Well then I dial the number."
"Watch out, if you take No. 3, you'll have to do the lip massage, all by yourself, only at No. 5, I can help you."
"Oh, you make it so hard for me."
"Well then choose No. 1 or No. 2, then I will spoil you, but you have to endure it."
"It's like eating a romantic meal by yourself, no, always for two."
"Then you take the No. 5?"
"What would you take?"
"Today?"
"Yes, tomorrow you can choose something else. Oh, tomorrow I can dine with you again?"
"If you want!"
"Okay, then I'll take No. 5 today."
"Great, I'm glad, I would have chosen that, I'm so shy, if I imagine I'm so completely defoliated in front of you and the first time, I would be red on the whole body."
"Hahaha, I do not think so."
"But standing still and being pampered sounds good, but there would be nothing left to stand still in such an angelic treatment of you. I know explosions would follow unceasingly."

"Do you think that I am so good?"

"No, I do not think so! I ... ."

"As?"

"No I do not think so, I know that one hundred percent!!!"

"Oh, I thought you did not trust me like that."

"Yeah, if I told you now, what my heart dare you all, then the main dish will be cold."

"You always smile a smile on my face, no one has done it yet."

"That's nice, that's the way it has to be, so No. 5."

"Yes, No. 5!"

"Good that we have finally clarified, then we can start now to dine!"

"Yes"

"Please stand in front of the fireplace and I face you, do you notice?"

"That beats my heart and yours faster? Yes I realize it."

"I serve the first part! Do not twitch. Slowly, I move my hands over to her and begin to feel the top, yet closed button of her blouse and with both hands very slowly push the button through the buttonhole, with my hands touched by chance her breasts. Oh, how warm, how soft, how erotic, how quickly to make out the next blouse button, and the shapes of her breasts have come into my momentary angle, as the skin slowly begins to increase in size on the right and left, to the tops that are still hers blouse are covered. You see me all the time during the button conquest with your fawn eyes in mine and of course you notice immediately, as my eyes follow the more and more freed parts of the body and how strained to hang on them. My thoughts do hard work, because they can curiosity, what are your breasts, like the nipples, how are they or are they sagging breasts, what shape do they have, apple or pear shape, do you have a colour separation there, well you are seamless there brown or you can see bra imprints. You seem to be able to guess my thoughts somehow, chuckle and say to me."

"Let yourself be surprised!"

"What do you mean by that?"

"Do I hear a tremor in your voice?"

"No trembling, just pure excitement. It is so terribly exciting to exterminate you, it has never been this way. I know why, the heart is full of it, it was not like that in the past, that's what I thought, but from what I'm experiencing here and now, it was not like that in the past. So for me it's like a first time experience with you and you see I'm not hiding anything from you, otherwise I would have had my voice under control, but I enjoy it that way and then that just happens."

"You are sweet!"

"How sweet? We are not yet at the dessert! Yes, there you smile again, a beautiful smile you put on the day. But please do not be angry, my hands want to further unbutton!"

"Go on!"

"I'm on it, good that you do not have a blouse with a hundred buttons on."

"It's only eight pieces."

"If I'm all eight, then I'll finally be able to see your wonderfully shaped breasts."

"No, it's not true, it's just the bra in the way."

"I can do that too."

"No, then it's my turn."

"Ok, you're right, you chose No. 5. You look at the main course start do you confuse me, how can that go on?"

"Well, very emotional."

"Yeah, oops that was too tight, now I've torn off the sixth button of your blouse."

"You're just a wild tiger, keep moving."

"You've never had a woman say that to me, although I've often imagined how to open a blouse with a powerful jerk and now you're calling me to do it, I can not resist it. My two hands grasp your blouse button laces, grasp them tightly, my muscles tighten, nothing can go wrong, and a short, violent jolt makes the last two buttons fly away, and with that powerful jerk, it happens, and the blouse slips in one go torn out of his pants and now flutters loose around you."

"Ohhh, yeah, go on!"

"My ears receive your words, and immediately my brain transmits this invitation against the objections of my heart, and my hands gently and slowly brush the now open blouse over your shoulders. You take your hands back and the blouse falls over your arms, just falling to the ground. There you stand in the light of the flickering open fire almost without, only a black lace bra still covers your femininity. Now not only does the warmth of the log fire reach me, but also the body heat of you. It's starting to tingle in me."

"And?"

"I can not leave it and put both of my hands flat on your breasts still covered by the brassiere. Through the tip you feel the very stiff nipples and somehow it seems to transfer to me, but not only my nipples are hard, but also in the depth, my pants are very tight, ohhh what will now even more in me happen if you claim No. 5."

"You, now it's my turn, let go of my breasts and keep your arms and hands on your back!"

"Wow, how your voice sounds dominant."

"Do you like it?"

"Yes, I like to be an observer, because an excitement can also be carried into the air. Do you want it?"

"Is not it the goal to achieve the highest possible excitement at the partner? I want that with you."

"A woman has never said that to me, let alone tried, well my hands are on my back and I stand very still. But may I shrug if you trigger it with me?"

"No, then you will be punished."

"Real, eh?"

"You will then see or feel even better!"

"Oops, sounds tempting."

"Attention, now my hands are coming and hahaha, I'll do it too."

"To do something?"

"The tearing. Yes, your shirt is near death, it will not survive the next moment."

"As"

"Can you feel my hands clasping him tightly and my fin-

90

gers piercing through the hemiplegics at your front and clenching into fists over your undershirt, my elbows bending and taking care, I will soon."
"No you will not."
"But! Now! A kind of violent jerk to the left, right and back in the other direction shake your upper body and it gets drafty, your undershirt has seen the daylight on the front and I push your shirt over your shoulders to the rear. It slips down your arms over your back clasped hands and drops to the floor, but that's not it yet, my hands have hefted your undershirt at your sides, I throw a hot sparking look at you with my brown eyes rock back and forth again, a sudden darkening of your eyes and you get heavy air for an almost infinite time and then you feel her as my lips bother with your right nipple. How she gets sucked in and how my teeth pick her up and hold her. "
"Auauau, what's your hot breath and those powerful muscles of massaging your teeth into my nipple? I see nothing and breathe hard, what are you doing?"
"Stop, or my teeth will punish you. Stand still!"
"Yes, I do, please, please do not bite stronger!"
"Rest and feel!"
"I do. I feel your right hand as she starts to play with my left nipple. You move with your fingertips very tenderly, as if you do not touch them, always in a circle around and I feel your fingers, as if a magical current penetrates through her into my skin, wherever you make a fingertip with the fingertips. I do not know what to feel, the feelings always seem to jump back and forth, between the right and left nipples and the breath that is heavier, that can see nothing and the wind, your breath that you blow on my stomach. It is indescribable, it is as if your words have made me stiff, yes there and in the whole body, I just stand there and let it happen, no I seem to be totally selfish at the moment, because I like what I experience, What you do to me, I've never felt that way and it should never stop please. I hope you enjoy it too. Of course, otherwise you would not do it and how you do it, because you realize, if you're honest, you have fun

and I feel it and enjoy it to the fullest. Why do not you pull my undershirt over my head or no it is so exciting when you get less air and the air you breathe harder is so warm, also a reason that the feelings rose and that it turned my eyes off, a sense organ is missing and that apparently increases the other feelings many times over. Have you done this often or how do you know it feels so exciting what you do to me?"
"Oh, secret. Why are you breathing so hard? I do not excite you? Or?"
"Yes, more than you think!"
"Well, yes, after all, I am finally the master of your feelings at the moment, I steer her and I determine the level of her tension."
"Yes, you do it with perfection!"
"Should I continue?"
"Yes, please, my lady!"
"I like it that way and I'll be rewarded now."
"What?"
"Feel it yourself!"

I'm one, Joschua just wanted to dine with me, but I got him off the mark. I used to just go through it and now I take the initiative. How can that be possible? That can only be Joschua. He triggers something in me that was there but never on the surface. I just want that he gets feelings through me and the phone call for him is unforgettable. Yes, if he says afterwards he is happy, then we are both. Being happy together is the biggest thing ever. In the past, only my husband was always happy, so often faked it. But the last two days I was really happy and now playing so verbally with Joschua and to remember it makes him happy, has also made me quite wet again. Of course not in panties, I'm naked. But I could not say that to him just now. What would happen if we did not only experience this on the phone but in real life and I could really touch it and also feel his hands on my skin. I want to continue to experience, so I let my voice once again penetrate his ear and come out of his dream world, in which he is also immersed as I just come out again.

"Attention, attention now begins a roller coaster ride of your feelings, one of the largest roller coasters of the whole emotional world and I will launch it now!"
"As?"
"Well, attention now! And my lips part from your pressed nipple, my fingers from the other and my breath stops blowing on your abdominal wall. Now relax your feelings for a moment?"
"Yes, as if you had initiated a resting phase, but why, just my thoughts, which conquer my brain again, what are you planning to do, what will you do, how will I react and when will I feel you again. Oh yes. It is as if my stomach is being pinched by the belt on the pants that you are starting to pull tightly. I pull him in and all of a sudden this deadlock suddenly dissolves. You opened the belt buckle. I feel like both hands of you press on my trouser button. But he fiercely resists, which you will then bring to your feet by more force of your hands. A cool pleasant breeze penetrates through my waistband and pulls up to the thigh. It's not just a cool breeze, it's also the silence of the excitement that happens when you pull the zipper down and then touch my cock and testicles. Although the boxershort is still in between, but that's just thin fabric, so thin that you can feel your hand through it."
"Man Joschua, it's my turn to do that. You take the lead. Have you become so hot that you are not fast enough?"
"No, no, but I'm so hot."
"And then you just introduced yourself and felt it."
"Yes, and as if I really felt your hand down there with me. So intense were my feelings."
"It's great, I felt my hand down there with you as well. What is, you are so quiet and stiff."
"Stiff?"
"Oh, not what you think again, not down there, ohhh whoops, feels good, but is not it a bit too tight in there?"
"Uhhh, yeah, uh, if that's what you mean, then ... ."
"So, do you want to strip me completely?"

"Well that would not be bad to drive the excitement to orgasm, but there is still something missing."

"What?"

"Well, imagine, we would both be like God created us, and then ... ."

"Oh, you want to combine the main course with the dessert?"

"I did not think of that, but you had a brilliant idea, why not."

"You wish?"

"If you could say that, what is currently building in my brain for pictures, yes!"

"No, no, no, I like the menu as it is and there are main course and dessert separately. And now no argument."

"Otherwise?"

"Will you see me kneel in front of you, pull your pants down with your hands, and pause at the height of your strong male part? You do not know what I'm going to do, you do not see anything and you can only guess. Cool so I only see your undershirt over your face. What are you doing behind a grotesque?"

"No, I'm just curious how it goes on. I can not hear everything. The undershirt also covers my ears and it sounds like something from afar."

"Oh, poor Joschua."

"What do you do? I could swear I hear you inhaling deeply and again and again. Hey, you're at the height of my cock."

"You smell very erotic and masculine here!"

"You just lost my speech, something that happens very rarely, did you just say that? It is in me, at least it feels so, yes, everything seems to stand still and time, it seems to me like an eternity, when it suddenly shines out from the center like a flash and spreads."

"Attention, now comes my left hand and will embrace your eggs firmly."

"Wow, yes, you, yes, oh that's nice, please do not let go, this heat. It gets warmer and warmer at the point where you include me, as if you had turned up the heating, I feel the blood as it flows, no it rushes through my testicles in a breathtaking speed and brings them to a boil. But you seem to be very interested in these things of mine, because hardly this experience is burned into my brain and I would like to enjoy it a bit, because I feel more activities at my boxershort. What are you going to do now, if you want to pull me down this too, to be able to look at all my maleness in front of your eyes and breathe in peace while standing in front of you and still can not look at you. Yes, what have you done to me, I have been condemned to doing nothing while you enjoy the first unpacking and exploring the partner in full rest and lenght. That was always my part with the women and I enjoyed it so much, but now you've just turned the tables, even though the staging is mine. What a woman and the stupid thing is still there, I enjoy it to the fullest so nibbled by you. It's just exciting, no, it's almost more exciting than if I had you undressed first. You have seen me and I have not seen you yet. I have never experienced it that way and I could not imagine it either. What kind of woman are you! A woman who knows what she wants and sometimes takes the helm in her hand and not only makes it but sometimes does it herself. I have dreamed of this so often, but that you also have similar ideas, as with the undershirt instead undress it just put it over my head, so I get less air and you can not see you and then me one more command give, I should stand still. Are you also a woman in everyday life who determines everything and leads others or."

"No, I'm happy when others decide. You're somehow to blame that I behave this way. You just seem to get that out of me. But it's a whole new and exciting feeling for me."

"I do not know but the courage has to come from somewhere else, otherwise you would not have been able to discover or expose it. Or is it only the courage, because you do not see me, but the whole thing takes place in our minds only in our brains. Do you feel safe between us through the phone, or would you have acted that way if you'd been right for me for the first time?"

"I can not tell you that with the best will."

"Well, then we come back to this question after our first realistic meeting."

"Oh, I've fallen into wild thoughts, Joschua just said realistic meeting. But one does not go on thinking, because I want more, so now I demand reactions from you again, because while I have made guesses in my mind, it has really managed my other hand, the only button, the front of your boxershort holding the slot open. I like what I feel and see, but I want to see more!"

"What are you doing? And already your hand gets my already very stiff and big cock out of the shorts. You are definitely trying, but he is already mightier and harder than you thought and it is not easy with one hand to feel him out of the shorts. Now your other hand leaves my testicles and you fumble with both hands, pulling hard on my cock around to bring it to the spotlight. Ahhh, careful, he's not that small!"

"Yes, I realized that, he has a great size and why is he so hard now?"

"Well you can ask questions, if you do something so affectionate, affectionate and erotic with me and then touched him so hard, if he would not then hard, then what would I be disappointed then and you! Or?"

"Mmm you may be right, but he feels so warm!"

"Yes, normal hot 36 degrees."

"Hahaha, he's a lot hotter!"

"Then that's just up to you!"

"For real?"

"Yes, one hundred percent, just to you and the crazy stuff you do with your main course."

"How should I not do that?"

"Yes, it is beautifully erotic, better than any of my plans. You're just the part of me that I was so lucky to miss!"

"You said that nicely! Not only does it feel good, it smells good too and now I want to see it, that damn slit, finally come out. So there he is in all his splendor and greatness. Wow! You look good, right to bite!"

"No, not!"

"Hahaha, it was just a joke!"

"I do not know that, I'm not sure about you anymore."

"How do you no longer like me?"

"No, I mean it differently, I just do not know what to expect with you, you do things that I could not guess in my wildest dreams. That's so wonderful. Hey what are you doing now it's getting so hot, no, not that tickles."

"Will you stay calm!"

"How am I supposed to do that when your tongue is playing on my glans. You trigger terribly beautiful and violent feelings and they have to go somewhere!"

"Nice feelings?"

"Yes, wonderful feelings!"

"It's a good idea, because what I see, smell and feel like that I like so much, maybe I do not want to give it away anymore."

"Oh, that could be talked about, would certainly agree with a capture. Just ask my heart what that says. Oh-ohoh that screams loudly, do not let them go away! Well, there you get a compliment! And what does my brain say to you at this stage? That's better than every six in the lottery. A woman with heart, feelings, and intellect and sexual ambitions, you can fully surrender and you will be driven crazy by her. oops did i just think or say that?"

"Yeah, and those were nice words from your heart as well as from your brain. Really nice words, but sorry I have to go further here, that's so exciting."

"What's so exciting about that?"

"I have never knelt in front of a man and had the opportunity to be able to view his masculinity in peace and full size in natura and I now want to enjoy it in peace! So stay calm!"

"I try. You can take your time exploring! And what do you want to research everything?"

"Thanks, I'll take my time! So it was in your menu, the main course depends on my personal needs. look, it will not stay that way, I'll look at everything, but also everything about your masculinity and, above all, touch it, lick it, taste it, smell it and of course try it out."

"Yes, that's right and I'm holding what's on the map. And I'm terribly sorry, I'll see your threats to you to

touch, touch, lick, taste, smell and try it out enjoy more than any other sexual related experience in my entire life together."

"I want to hope so, otherwise I would have to punish you, you do not bother a lady in the enjoyment, but that you want to enjoy it and because you are so happy, that gives me somehow even more energy to have fun and courage to do. I always question everything too much and that almost always took the courage to do it. It has never been this way in my life, I often did not enjoy it, just pretended and the guy with me did not even notice. I was so happy many times when he let go of me and turned away. I never had the courage to tell him that. He was always happy and did not really care about me. I know it's stupid, but you weigh so many thoughts, what's going on, how would it go, what would happen and oh well, what would the others in the family, relatives and acquaintances say if I just split up because that would happen if I had told my husband that he did not satisfy me and almost never managed to satisfy me and that I often did things he wanted but not me. Imagine that, I would have made to separate myself, if I had had the courage, but I am just so educated and I see today, many attitudes to life and society have changed compared to earlier and you just have the courage just have to do it."

"You speak to me from the heart, because I have such an experience behind me and it has taken me a very, many years of life and health, but also I had not the courage to initiate a separation, until I just headed because fate has taken everything in hand and taken me another way, very hard, very sad, but if I had not been gone, then I would not stand almost naked now, with my undershirt over my head, so you totally delivered, in front of you. I have to say, I like it sooo!!!"

"Yes, that makes me happy, too!"

"Now have the courage and start, I can hardly bear what you will do with me."

"So, I'll start!"

"Yes, I ask for it. Yikes, not! Your hands tickle me,

behind my testicles I'm so terribly ticklish, especially because you've touched me so tenderly there, I'm sorry that my hands have come so fast from back to front to hold your head lightly. Admit you just wanted to tenderly let your breath dance on this spot. Right?"

"Yes, but I can not let it go if you disobey me. Turn around immediately and hands behind your back, now I'll have to punish you, sorry I'm sorry."

"Ok, punish me, but do not be sad, it was worth it to get your hair in my hands and feel this delicate, curly, your belonging parts so in disarray."

"Well wait, you feel like I'm holding your hands behind your back. Can you feel what I tie around your wrists? What is it, soft and long."

"There was nothing like it. Oh, my shirt off."

"What do you do if I tighten it even more?"

"Then I can not free myself without your help."

"That's how it should be! I'm your mistress and you know what I want, I want you all and all and alone and forever long and now stay, if you do something again, then you know, I'll get you, even if I'm so sorry have to punish, so stand still!"

"Yes, I have understood. Will try to listen to you."

"I wanted to hear that, fine."

"I'm glad that I can please you."

"That's how it should be! I'm your mistress and you know what I want, I want you all and all and alone and forever long and now stay, if you do something again, then you know, I'll get you, even if I'm so sorry have to punish, so stand still!"

"Yes, I have understood. Will try to listen to you."

"I wanted to hear that, fine."

"Please, please, very carefully, I can not fight back now and if I think how I'm at your mercy, madness. My happiness is in your hands."

"Or mouth."

"No, you will not be around."

"Oh, who knows, just let yourself fall, shut off your thoughts and enjoy this unexpected adventure."

"This is going to be the adventure of my life and some-

how there is a feeling involved. I can not explain. I never felt it."

"What a feeling?"

"Yes, I think that comes from the fact that I'm totally at your mercy. I can not move my hands and then the undershirt over my head, less air and that is even warmer than normal and in addition the darkness, the eyes can do not see what comes to me or what you just want to do. Guess is also somehow not, so I am at your mercy and that is the feeling that mixes with the others. It's a feeling as if it's a turbo for the other feelings. You just feel more when you touch one, you do not only feel how cold or warm your hands are, but it feels like I can feel electricity whenever you are about to touch me. It is as if the last millimeters of this tension are bridged, so first comes the tension, then comes your hand and then I feel the violence of your touch."

"Yes you have described that well, but respect the tension will come soon, I will torture you with it, I will not touch you, but only almost, so respect full tension."

"I feel pure excitement. Where are your hands when they finally come to touch my cock and my testicles? Ahhh there she is, the tension, but not where I would have thought, I feel your hands on my knees. They cling tightly to them lying flat. They are pushed backwards by their firm pressure, it is as if they were stiff. Just do not fall over, but your hands are starting to move upwards at the same time, but not on my skin, but with the notorious, small tension building up distance. Your hands brush against the front of my thighs. Now it will happen soon, they will reach my masculinity and take in the hands. Yeah, please take it! I'll go crazy!"

"Whom should I take in my hands?"

"My ... ."

"No, think!"

"No, not. Your hands slide past them without touching them, slowly, tense and looking for their way with a short stopover and in my navel, which I pull it jerkily with ringy backwards. I'm taking a frightened step backwards."

100

"Youuu, if you take another step back, you know what to expect. Punishment!"

"I was so scared when your index finger hit my ringy button like a cannonball."

"I do not care, you have to stand it!"

"It was just so unexpected."

"What do you expect, I did not tell you, turn off your thoughts and let you fall into the realms of enjoyment."

"Easier said than done."

"Watch out now, my hands now want to take care of your nipples."

"Thanks for the advance notice."

"Oh please, please!"

"Hey, hey, that's the wrong direction, my nipples, because you have to move your hands up and not down!"

"Assaulted."

"Man and how, I feel your hands not on my nipples, which you have longed for, but on my hips and they continue to turn backwards. Auauau you're pinch me in my buttocks. Hey why are you pulling me so close to you. I like that. Still further, please. No, not, your lips are so hot and your tongue is piercing my navel. Do not push from behind, I can not get away. That's the pure torture. Hello tongue, stop tickling."

"Be a man and bear it. You can yelp later when I'm in bed and do not hear that."

"In itself, that's wonderfully erotic, not able to fight back, you are simply doomed to enjoy. Whether you know that, at least your actions seem to want that. Huuu your tongue is quite wild, warm and humid, boring with a lot of pressure and now your lips are freeing the way out and it meanders higher and higher, leaving a wet trail that feels cold through your breath that you feel through your lips squeezed out violently. It shivers down my spine and your tongue goes higher and higher. Soon you have reached my right nipple, but my feelings are ever broken."

"Attention it claps!"

"Wow a loud bludger on my butt is left to feel and one more and another and now on the right side, it claps

more violently and alternately. My body is repeatedly pressed to the rhythm of gossiping to your lips and pressed your tongue through my body. My feelings jump wildly between the clapping hands and the lips that pressed against each other. Auauau, your lips, no, your teeth bite into my nipple!"

"Enjoy!"

"Oh, the blows that hit my buttocks stop, your teeth loosen the bite, and your tongue moves gently around my right nipple. It tingles everywhere, on my buttocks, in the nipple and now also on where your tongue draws circles. Man a variety of emotions and I start to drop something and enjoy."

"Well, are you still alive?"

"Yes, just now. I'm just so quiet because I'm starting to enjoy, I've followed your advice and I'm just trying to drop it and it works a bit. It's just indescribable feelings that you have awakened in me and whirled in confusion."

"I'm glad, because you will not believe it, it has also done something in me. I'm really excited and not only are you feeling unfamiliar, but it was so much fun for me. I would never have thought that, because I've never felt anything like this, let alone done anything to any man. What you get out of me is unimaginable. Anyway, I could not imagine it before our phone call and in my dreams it was not so exciting and interesting."

"Ohhh, if it's so nice for you, please keep it up!"

"Well, I could be persuaded on one condition."

"How condition, what condition?"

"That you let me experience such things sometimes."

"That's clear, I also want to experience the other side of feeling. One hundred percent promised! But please continue now."

"Do not be so impatient."

"Yes, it's so exciting and ... ."

"Well, I do not want to be like that, I do it anyway more than just fun. I am completely myself damp."

"I wanted to hear that. I also have something in mine acorn. The harbingers of the soon to be exploded happi-

ness."

"Really, that's how our telephone call made you hot. What that looks like in natura. I can only do it myself but it is very different with every man."

"Of course, always different. I hope if you do it can really take it in your hands, that you like it."

"What we are thinking right now and again at our first conversation. What should become of us?"

"If everything goes the way I dreamed it last night have ... ."

"Oh, you dreamed something about it?"

"Yes, I once risked a dream into the future."

"And what does she bring us?"

"Should I really tell you that?"

"Oh, please, otherwise I'll burst out with curiosity."

"So my dream image of the future was that we grew old hand in hand."

"Hey hello, are you still alive? One may but dream his desires and hope, right? I did not say anything wrong? Hello Mia you!"

"Sorry it just shut my fingers. The thought was a wonderful one. Maybe you do not like me when you see me or you can not smell me."

"Wait, but be honest. Did not you wish something while falling asleep?"

"Yes, but let's not continue to make erotic phone calls, I really want to touch you now."

"Agreed. Sorry if I have wished for such a thing. I've been lonely for so long and I've never seen anything like that in the mails and today on the phone call."

"True, me neither. I'm not mad at you either. I'm just totally, but really taken by surprise, because my feelings felt similar. Not now."

"Ok, I'm not talking about this now. I know you want to touch me."

"Yes, I want to and now you feel my hand that suddenly tightly encloses your eggs?"

"Oh yes, you have both in your hands. Now they are at your mercy."

"Yes, you have to be very nice to me, otherwise I can easily crush them."

"Oh careful, they are very sensitive. Mia what are you doing with it. Not like knicker rolling back and forth. It feels really weird, but it does not get arousal, but now that you start to pull it down, it tightens the skin and the foreskin of my cock goes on and on, the more you pull it down the glans withdraws, my excitement shoots up in a flash. Ohhh and I'm going crazy slightly and in addition you blow your breath very carefully and gently on my glans. He envelops her with a soft warmth, as if a desert wind was blowing over him. I let myself fall and enjoy these feelings. They want to get deeper and deeper into me, I feel like they are also gaining in intensity. It's for a brief moment as if time stood still."

"Oh, what are you going to prepare for the launch? Oh no answer, then I want to pull your eggs down a little harder. look, now your foreskin has slipped back completely and before my eyes a gleaming glans can be seen. Man, what a drunkard."

"Oh you, I can not fight back, I'm going crazy. I feel like I'm totally at your mercy. One hundred percent delivered and that feels so awfully good. For a long time, I will not be able to enjoy this moment anymore, my emotions are beginning to gather to explode. My whole body starts to tingle and vibrate slowly."

"Attention now I put one more on top. Watch out for my tongue, she will now dance on your cockhead and touch her."

"Oh, now the rocket launch of my feelings is initiated. Do you know that this is my most sensitive place on the body?"

"I know and may I feel, it is as exciting as I can get you into other spheres and you just can not do anything. This is an experience that I have never done before and enjoy to the fullest."

"Me too! And how. If you go on I feel like the lights will go out in my head, then it will only be the heart and work!"

"Cool! Then lick and again and again I licked with my

104

tongue around your glans and I feel also how your excitement rises. But that would not be your Mia, if I did not put a mood on it. I let the tongue continue to slide along your cock while he comes my lips closer and closer, until the glans touched my lips and then completely encased in them. It gets warm around your glans and wet. She keeps pushing herself into my mouth."

"How deep is your mouth, I have the feelings you want to devour me completely and already I feel your lips on my sharm hair and cock end. Your tongue is still snaking around the cock and it just makes me feel incredible. I have to breathe so fast that it gets a bit dull in my eyes and then I feel like you start to close your teeth and as if you want to bite into a sausage, the teeth press into my cock and push the blood even further forward. The glans is filled to bursting with blood and with superlative feelings and a burst of fireworks every time your tongue touches the glans. It seems as if the touches of your tongue on my glans are directly coupled with my puffs of air, no air entrapment and you realize that. Smart as you seem to be, you change the rhythm of your tongue touches on my glans and seem to listen to my inhalations also change with it. You seem to really enjoy it. In addition, you can vary the pressure of your teeth pressing on my cock and I no longer know how to stand, it's as if my legs are sagging with happiness. As fast as it all started, it ends so fast, you let go of my testicles almost jerky, rushing up like bullets and lure me a loud groan releases your tooth pressure and drive, the lips very strong pressed on my cock along to acorn. Here you stop and once again release a firework of touch with your tongue, until your mouth separates jerkily from me and takes the lips and tongue. I stand in the cold, it seems to me as if you pulled the plug. Now I will come down slowly. That was an orgasm. It's quiet for a few moments and you seem to watch me. As my body moves and slowly calms down. Or, no, you seem to have to shut yourself down a little bit from this action as well, I have the feeling that you have aroused a lot of excitement, which is something very special, when both partners can catapult each other in excitement levels, real and not just feigned excitement."

"Oh man, that was an adventure with you. Thank you that I was allowed to experience it that way. I have not felt that in life. Madness."

"You Mia, it was so unbelievably beautiful, why did you do that?"

"I do not know, when I saw you in my mind's eye and was allowed to play so freely with it, it just came over me and I had to make it steer like remote. That you also liked it was a pure collateral damage."

"Hahaha, I'm a collateral damage, really great, so I want to do more damage, please!"

"Ok, I would like to have it!"

"When?"

"Right now, I want to make my feelings go up again, so you do what I want, understood."

"Yes mistress!"

"I'll take you to the sofa now."

"Ok. But slowly, with my pants and panties around my legs. I can not run fast or take big steps."

"I know that, but on the way to the sofa, I can beat you vigorously on your beautifully formed butt every single step, the more steps, the more gossips."

"Auauau, I'll do it, not so impatient."

"So, turn 180 degrees and sit down."

"I do. Will you take my undershirt off my head?"

"No!!! And because you wanted something stupid, I have to punish you."

"Oh no, I did not want that."

"Bad luck, dear. Do you hear me walking around the sofa and standing behind you?"

"No. I do not hear anything anymore, no movement no breathing, what are you doing now? Minutes seem to pass. I can not hear you, Mia where are you?"

"Hello where are you?"

"Mia why do not you give an answer? Then I have to try to transfer all my feelings into my hearing to catch any

sounds from you. No matter what I do, I do not hear any-
thing and then suddenly ... ."
"Yes, suddenly my hands come slipping from behind
and they both press firmly over your mouth and nose.
Hahaha, now you are totally scared, gasping. Only very,
very little you can still breathe and I press a little harder.
The air is gone. But do not worry, the punishment lasts
only five seconds. One two three four five. So hands off
and you can breathe freely again. So watch out, if I do
not like something you'll always be punished like that."
"Do I always have to say mistress to you now?"
"That's the way it is and if you want something I do not
want, I'll take your breath away, first for five seconds
and then a second longer each time, until you learn to
obey me and everything I do want to let happen. Do you
understand me, then nod!"
"And I nod very carefully. I try to breathe a lot and
quickly, and the warm air flowing through my over the
top undershirt lets me return to normal. That was a
crazy feeling, I have often imagined it and if I'm honest, I
have often even held my mouth and nose, but that was
not in the least the feeling, what you just triggered with
me have. It makes a huge difference if you do it your-
self, if someone else just does it or how it was with you,
unexpectedly and you could not fight back. My hands
were tied behind my back and your hands pulled me
deep into the back of the sofa. In this position, you
could have pulled me back with all your physical
strength and you could totally take my breath away. An
absolutely crazy feeling, I would not have thought, I
even felt like my cock has greatly enlarged at this
moment as it did before, as you have edited and car-
essed him. A completely different kind of excitement
and if I always imagine now, I can get this excitement
again and again when I contradict you and this ex-
citement mingles with the other feelings that you have
raised in me, what is to become only me from poor
ailing man?"
"Probably the luckiest man in the world, nonsense of
the whole universe."

"Oh Mia are you a cannon, do you know that already?"
"No, a man has never said that to me, but I've never had such a phone call."
"I have to tell you the truth, you are the very best, most sentimental, feminine being I have ever felt. You are an angel who can only play with the feelings of me. I hope you are happy about it and especially what made me very proud, you also felt such feelings, because what is it, if you are together later and know, you do it only for me and have nothing of it yourself. That would be a great pity, because you must also be able to feel such or similar feelings, because that is the icing on the cake of everyday life, that is with the meaning of life, because the purpose of life for me is just to enjoy the moment, hahaha is harder than expected and has almost never worked, but with you Mia I have the feeling that I will experience the meaning of life more often, no, much more. You are a woman!! An absolute dream woman!!!"
"Good that you can not see me now. Your words have made me totally red. How can you say such wonderful words about me?"
"We agreed that we will never lie to each other. That's just the truth. Oh, what will become of us in the future?"
"No, do not think about the future, because then you expect too much when we see each other for the first time. Eye to eye, hopefully it will be like that."
"No, it gets even better. Much nicer, that's what I feel. When you face each other then you have completely different ways to spoil the partner, not only on the mental level, then the physical comes to it."
"Hey, where are you?"
"Hahaha, here."
"No, I've heard you thinking out loud, what did you think?"
"Oops, almost nothing."
"If I ask you something, you have to answer properly, otherwise ... ."
"I know, you have to punish me."
"Exactly, do you want that?"
"Yes!"

"Then I have to put my two hands on your mouth and nose again immediately."

"Oops I did not expect it so soon, I wanted to take another deep breath, but you surprised me again and I hear you counting out loud."

"One two three four five six. Mouth and nose free. Satisfied with the punishment?"

"Yes, mistress, I am."

"You think I'm forgetful."

"No."

"Then tell me your thoughts about your silence right away."

"I just thought what you are for a loving mistress."

"So, shall I believe you?"

"Yes, mistress it is the truth."

"Since we talk about it later, now I want to have fun with you again."

"Oh dear."

"How do you want no more?"

"But, I'm very curious, I'm curious what you come up with now to present to me unknown feelings of my body."

"Just wait."

"Mistress you do not tell me what you do, then I can only guess what you want to do. You come around the sofa. Oh you raise my left foot, take off my shoe, let my pants and pants slip over the foot, drive with your index finger in the back of my socks and press it over the heel and my left leg is completely exposed. Now I expect you to do the same on the right side."

"Totally wrong. Do you think I'm so easy to calculate as your mistress?"

"No, of course not, my lady."

"First, with my left hand, I want your left bare foot firmly and I hold my tight. So you feel my hard, certain grip?"

"Yes, and like my mistress."

"That's good, you learn fast, I like it that way."

"What have you with my foot before mistress. Why are you picking him up?"

"Do you notice it now? And I start with tender touches

with my other hand, you can call it tickling, under your foot on the sole of your foot. Are you ticklish."

"No, but if you make it so tender and decisive. Hahaha please mistress, I ask for mercy."

"Rejected, I like that!"

"Ohhh, ohhh ...!"

"No problem running into your undershirt. Good that I did not take it off completely. Do you see as a tear catcher, it now proves itself."

"No, not that tickles so terribly, hahaha, no, please stop!"

"Do not you want to pull your leg up, because then I really have to, though reluctantly, punish you."

"Stop that I can not stand anymore, you are too tender, damn, that tickles me all over."

"Fidget not like that!"

"I do not do that, it's automatic because you're so tickling, that's probably because of your fingernails."

"So, well then I'll give you a break. Are you still ticklish?"

"Yes, but I will not tell you."

"Then I'll tickle you until you say so."

"But if I say so, do not you promise to tickle me there?"

"You demand the impossible from me! So you want to let it happen that I have to search you completely? Imagine that I'm looking everywhere, at you, on you, in you, ohhh yes in you."

"Like me?"

"Well, for example, I could treat your nasal hair tenderly in your nose."

"Hahaha does not work!"

"Why?"

"Well, my undershirt is over there for protection."

"But you're pretty cheeky, you probably want to be punished again, then it's already seven seconds."

"No, I only told the truth."

"Well, there's just a little way back in the curve."

"Good thank you."

"Well, then your next fate is starting now. I take your left foot in my hand and pull it towards the left foot of the sofa. What am I planning to do? Can you feel that? I take something into my hand and now do you feel how your lower leg, directly above your foot on the sofa foot pulls and feels him very firmly?"

"Yes. What did you take for it again? Oh, sure, your scarf, the sheer, colourful patterned scarf that you have worn around your magnificent neck. Mistress, have you already planned to tie me up or did it occur to you spontaneousl?"

"But you are curious again. Just enjoy it or do not you enjoy it?"

"Oh, very much, I'm just completely surprised by your actions. Are totally unexpected and therefore extremely exciting. If you knew what's going on in me right now."

"No, I was spontaneous, just inspired by you. I've never thought of such a thing, I always thought it's something that somehow does not pay or hurts, but I'm learning so much today and above all, I'm experiencing feelings I did not know."

"Me too."

"Is not it too tight?"

"No, then I'll say it."

"Ok, then get ready for more."

"Oh dear. I know you're going to do the same procedure on your right leg now. Oops!"

"Hahaha I surprised and scared you."

"You can not be assessed. You pinch me with both hands in my two nipples and roll it back and forth between your fingers. I'm really scared and bang my legs together. oops the left leg does not work it is stuck on the sofa foot and stays there."

"Hey what's up? I have not allowed you that, you probably want to pinch my body with your legs."

"No, it was just so scared and your hands were so cold and tight."

"I will not accept this excuse, so what happens now?"

"You do not want to punish me?"

"But! For seven seconds!"

"Can I ask for mercy?"

"Grace does not exist with me, after all I'm your mistress and you have to respect me and obey."

"No, do you really do that? I can not see anything but I feel like you got up. Are you standing behind me again? Oh, you're still on the way. Hahaha you let your finger-nails wander over me. Iiii that tickles and scrapes. So my mistress is a little wildcat. Auauau! "

"Something to complain again?"

"No, just scared. You always think of something new! Very exciting but always so surprising."

"But now nothing new comes, now you will be punished and you already know that. Only this time seven seconds and I put my two hands on nose and mouth and pull you back, then you get no chance to breathe and to breathe. That's what you get from it if you disobey your mistress or move and pinch your mistress."

"Oh, it starts but again differently than expected. Man oh man I can not adjust to something for you. And already I feel like you put your hands very easily on my mouth and nose, but why do you press as announced not tight. And then you separate your hands too. Oh, one hand pinches my nose, the other presses firmly on my mouth and you pull my head backwards. I can hardly breathe, I can feel the smell of your hands through my undershirt. It drives me crazy and the seven seconds seem to be passing by in flight. What I felt most was the smell of your hands, it was so exciting. I'm fucking crazy, the smell of you alone makes me crazy. It's incredible."

"Well, punished enough now? I think so, otherwise it will take next time how long?"

"Eight seconds mistress!"

"Well, watch out and now give me your right foot."

"And I feel you have come from behind the sofa, standing next to the sofa and grab my, as ordered, you stretched right foot and you already press your nails into my sole. Even through the not yet undressed stock-ing tickles awful. But I want to show it to you, I control myself and do not react at all. I'm just holding my breath, but you seem to notice."

"Will you breathe, otherwise."

"Yes, I breathe, but then it tickles again so much."

"Exactly. You want to see where you're tickler, right or left."

"Hahaha, stop, I'm also very nice."

"Ok, I do not want to be like that then."

"Oh thanks, thank you for stopping your fingernails circling under my right foot. Oh, you're putting him down on the floor again. Oh so you let my underpants and pants slip over him again, press with your fingers in the back stocking over my heel and take it off. Well, now, what are you doing now, no more scarf and I have to smile inside, but damn, can you read my mind?"

"Think, I have another cloth, the scarf was slightly twisted from two towels. And? Can you feel how I tighten your foot on the right sofa leg?"

"Yes, I feel, I can not move anymore. Help please be nice to me, I'm totally at your mercy."

"That's how I imagined it, and I'm so excited when I see you sitting in front of me, legs apart, completely naked. This is really a totally exciting sight, as your cock is already cheeky high, thick and hard. As your glans rises above everything. How tall and fat is he? If you do not know, I'll have to punish you."

"I've never measured it, but it gets on my back when I think of how you see me now. Never has a woman ever seen me like that and now your eyes meet me and I can not even look into your face."

"If you could see me now, I would certainly be red and you would see how excited I am, but then I certainly would not be able to see your masculinity that way, then your glare out of your blue eyes would surely totally unsettle me."

"Thank you for seeing that I have blue eyes. But my eyes, if you saw him, would not distract you."

"Oh, yes, I have always been a bit shy."

"Well, I can not confirm that, what you have done with me today and certainly will do, is anything but shy."

"That was never so, you have to do that and then you can not see me makes me safer and also crazy and courageous!"

"Then I should never see you and would always have to be blindfolded at our meetings and that would be terrible."

"Why terrible?"

"Well, because I imagine how you would look like without everything and blindfolded, your beauty can never reach my eyes and I enjoy it."

"Maybe that's better."

"No, when we met today, I've got that, you can imagine that, you certainly did that too, introduced me to you completely naked."

"Nope, I do not have it."

"Ha, you've blushed, you're scowling."

"You can not see that."

"But intuitively, that's the way it is. Be honest, am I right?"

"Well, you're right."

"And how did I cut off?"

"Not bad."

"Like, not bad at all."

"Fine, I liked what I saw there, but I did not unpack it in my mind's eye."

"Oh, I do and what I have guessed, I find more than successful, even more, more great and how I look forward to receiving a real confirmation, you can not imagine."

"Honestly, are you so looking forward to it?"

"Yes!!!"

"Why?"

"Because I know that what I suspect is exceeded a thousand times. I am curious about you."

"You are as nice as you say. Now I am afraid to disappoint you."

"Why scared? You are not only a shell, but also inside! I've already got to know the interior a bit and it's already a hundred percent more than I had hoped, so there would not even need to be one percent outside and all my wishes would be exceeded. And I also know the outside come one hundred percent to me!"

114

"Thank you, just thanks, you can say such sweet words and formulate sentences with a lot of hope. I feel so close to you!"

"Hahaha, but only because I can not fight it right?"

"No, I do not think so, but that reminds me, I wanted you."

"What? Continue watching?"

"Think, now it gets serious, you should get to know me correctly."

"Oh, you're up to something again. Attention Joschua, it will start again soon, it's like waiting for the Christ child earlier when I was still very small, only there there were gifts, here there are emotional explosions."

"Yes, good comparison. I kneel down in front of you, between your legs. This time, you can not spontaneously close and pinch me. Oh, I'm fine. Can you imagine my excitement starting to rise again?"

"Yes, because I feel like your eyes rest on my masculinity again. Of course that excites you, me too. Never has a woman looked so intensely and directly at it and I can not defend myself. A really new and crazy erotic feeling. Thank you my mistress for that."

"You did not answer my question earlier. How long, how fat?"

"I do not know, I've never measured it."

"Really, men always do that and admit it."

"Not me. Never really talked to other guys about it."

"You are really different than other men."

"Maybe, but hopefully in a good way."

"So far I have to agree with you, you are really different and really exciting."

"Thank you."

"I want to measure now, where can I find a tape measure."

"Really, then you have to ... ."

"I know, before getting really upset."

"Yes, that's what I wanted to say."

"I know, where is a tape measure?"

"Hahaha, I'm sure you want to lure me out of the reserve and you mean I take a measuring tape now and measure

115

it. No, that's only when we see each other and you do it personally, not on the phone, hahaha, you're one."
"Oh, that's mean!"
"Oh, something must still be secret, are you really allowed to unpack everything in reality? If you were here now, then you should unpack that."
"Well that is, if we see each other I can unpack you, right!"
"Ok, but only when we are alone or you would ask for it in public and I'm still a prude."
"Hahaha, but agree."
"And now, can we keep playing or do you need a break?"
"Yes, five minute break, I have to go somewhere."
"Good, but do not hang up the phone, just miss it, I do too. See you soon!"
"See you soon, I'm looking forward to the sequel."
"Me too."

Oh man, the man makes me crazy and wet. If he knew that I was sitting here completely naked then he would definitely redden and turn off completely crazy. Oh I have the feeling he turns off already. Cute the comparison with Christmas. Certainly a romantic man. I've never had one like that. I'm really looking forward to seeing him completely, dressed and clearly naked. So now I have to hurry. One was on the toilet but my arousal is still in my body. What am I experiencing with this man? It's just like a lottery in the lottery, a six in one for the heart.

"Are you there again?"

So now everything is done in the bathroom. Will I have something to drink with me? Tea or coffee, no, I prefer Sunkist in the fridge. It's cold, with the hot words and feelings he sends to me, that's exactly right. So now all thoughts switched off again and only the heart form my words and let them receive from Joschua.
"Hello, are you there yet?"

"Yes, I've been waiting for hours, were you shopping?"
"Hahaha, just on the toilet and wanted to make a tea, but then I thought, the games with you make me so hot, something cold would be better and I have taken a Sunkist from the fridge. I like to drink and always have it in the fridge, at least in summer."
"Also something to nibble brought?"
"Yes, how do you know, some cookies. They always taste so delicious for tea, now for the Sunkist."
"I know, when I drink something I always eat something. When I was a kid I used to drink Sunkist Orange when we were on vacation on the beach and if I do that sometimes I think about my beautiful childhood."
"We have one thing in common again."
"Let's keep playing, I'm so excited, you're kneeling between my legs."
"Yes I know. I can see your unmeasured virility."
"Well, you can imagine everything now, how long would you like him?"
"Oh, I've never thought about it. Is twenty centimeters too much?"
"You would like to know that now?"
"You'll be rude, will you finally tell your mistress the truth about your length, otherwise … ."
"I know, otherwise you'll punish me for eight seconds, then I'll have to endure that, poor man."
"You wanted it that way, then I'll stand behind you, I'm sorry. Do you think I can count to eight?"
"Yes, you are very smart, you can make it to eight. It's just a second longer than it was before."
"Right."
"How will you do it, nose and mouth again with single hands or both with both hands?"
"No, otherwise it would be boring."
"How different?"
"You still have not learned, I choose, do not be so curious, you'll feel it right away. I get up, but I do not go around the sofa. I stay here and kneel next to your thighs. Can you feel me on your thighs?"
"Yes I feel you left and right of my thighs. You knelt

down on the sofa next to me. Why?"

"What am I going to do now? Oh, I wanted to punish you. Poor Joschua, I have to punish you for eight seconds now. Do you already feel like I'm going to do this time?"

"No, I just feel it is getting harder to inhale air and it is already much warmer. What do you do?"

"Oh, I'm just getting close, but not with my hands, but with my entire upper body and in particular, my breasts will wrap around your nose and I'll press your head from behind quite firmly."

"I feel your excitement through my undershirt and body scent, a scent of vanilla, what you take for a perfume, and how much have you done before we meet?"

"You'll see for yourself at our first meeting, stay secret until then."

"But the thought was apparently so long that the eight seconds are over again, before I have noticed correctly. Whenever you take my breath away, I have some thoughts about you and I'm totally distracted. And it's all over again."

"If I have to punish you next time, remember it will be a nine second penalty. Poor you."

"Yes mistress I know. man oh man you have soft and yet so effective breasts. You totally confused me, what perfume do you take?"

"Oops, what's that question?"

"In itself a very simple one."

"Will you be cheeky again?"

"No, just honest. When you pressed your breasts into my face indirectly ... ."

"Indirectly?"

"Well my undershirt and your blouse and bra were in the way."

"Oh, that's it."

"Yeah, so when you pushed your breasts indirectly into my face, I got a vanilla smell in my nose. What was that?"

"My perfume, did you like it?"

"Yes, I love vanilla and this vanilla was mixed with your

own body scent, that distracted me so much that I did not even notice how you took my breath away. The eight seconds were gone. Will you do it again at the next punishment?"

"Let yourself be surprised and do not be so curious, you know the next time it will be nine seconds."

"I know, I will try to be nice, but your scent was so appealing and the way you transferred it even more."

"I have to say, I really like what you like about me and I like you too and I like the things I'm going to do now. I hope you like it too!"

"Think definitely, oops you're already kneeling between my legs again. Damn it, I can not close it, the scarves keep me from it."

"Watch, the more you pull, the tighter the knots get."

"Yes, I already noticed."

"Do you know what I am doing now?"

"I think I suspect you are starting to look at me and slowly excite my cock."

"Slowly, no fast, it's such an erotic, great sight and how you keep it so in front of me."

"Well, you were responsible for arranging the exhibits yourself."

"But that was only possible with your help and it was so inspiring."

"You want to start over again?"

"What do you mean?"

"Well, by letting your tongue play ... yes, just sooo!"

"What you like so much."

"And how, the head cinema starts again, not all over, because I'm very excited. I feel like you take my cock all the way into your mouth, your tongue starts to lick it again around him and your hands, no I only feel a hand that covers both of my testicles and begins again to pull down. It builds up a tremendous tension in me, more than before. That's because of the wide spread legs, the complete nudity and the inability to close my legs."

"That's right, it makes me horny to see you that way and to be able to work unhindered. Really cool, I was so un-disturbed with no man. Thank you for that. But now I'll put it back in my mouth and go."

"I feel like you are slowly moving your head to and from me and I can barely regulate the blood flow in my cock. I notice how he gets more and more tense and harder and at the same time my heart seems to have switched gears faster to increase the blood pressure. My forehead forms small beads of sweat and I hear an ever louder groan from my own mouth. What are you doing there, you do not want to let me explode in your mouth? I know you can not answer, you have your mouth full. Hahaha. You can not stand this any longer, your tongue games and the lip movements, the roughness of your lip pressure and the pulling on my testicles, I can not stand that anymore."

"Then let it shoot!"

"How to shoot?"

"Well, try not to prevent it anymore, please let yourself fall completely."

"Really! I can understand you very badly, you have your mouth too full!"

"Stop talking and think, do it."

"Well I try to turn off all my thoughts and the entire brain and just follow the heart that feels somehow like it's gone in the cock and when that's not enough, I feel like the explosion is about to happen, but you also notice it through my louder groaning and the shorter distances between them and ... no, not at all."

"I only pressed one finger with you against your mouth."

"And at this moment, it's all too late, it's like, no, it starts to turn in my head, I have the feeling it is black in my eyes and then suddenly like electric shock. One by one hunts like a cannonball through my cock and shoots out of the glans directly into your mouth and your tongue just keeps playing, a very weird feeling that somehow makes everything even longer and your mouth around my cock feels fuller and warmer. Suddenly I feel like a suction on the glans. What do you do? You have swallowed everything down and very slowly the lights go on again. Sweat bathing, I sit in front of you, now you can

certainly perceive my own body odor. It is as if I would collapse into myself, but I can not bring my legs and arms into a relaxed position and it seems as if the feelings bounce off their ends and waves are thrown back into the middle of the body and back and forth, always a bit weaker. It seems like an eternity to get the emotions back to the one hundred percent level, they were way over it, maybe two hundred percent, compared to my previous experiences. And suddenly a violent coolness spreads around my cock. You pulled your mouth off and seem to look at me. Then you give me a kiss on my ringy button, go higher on my nipples, first one then the other."

"That made me wet down there just because I was allowed to do it with you the way I wanted it, thanks for that, that was really the ultimate experience for me and I hope for you too."

"And how, and how. I think I have not even had such intense feelings with a woman I was with. The head cinema you lit was just as indescribably beautiful and as intense as if you had been here with me."

"Yes, that's how I felt it. We were really together."

"Now I feel your hands on my head and you finally pull my undershirt over your head over backwards. Two sparkling, demanding brown eyes flash in front of me and your lips approach mine, meet and it begins in peace, a dialogue between our tongues. It's intoxicating, because it feels like I feel the moisture in your mouth that I knew from earlier on. Now a little different. Yes, my seeds that you picked up during my semen shootings have mixed up and now you give them back to me, at least the taste and it's wonderful, a very different kiss feeling than before and I see you closing your eyes slowly and apparently your brain turns off and only the heart is there. Heart to heart connected by our gently rolling tongues. An intimacy that I have never felt before. The most violent, most soulful experience of my entire life."

"I can feel it too. Feel it the way you do."

"You Mia hear my thoughts, you have changed me and I

121

never want to experience this without you again, I fell in love with you. And our tongues talk to each other for a very long time. They have a lot to say and their thoughts are silent and enjoy our hearts."

Oh dear, what have I done there, he never believes that I've never done anything like this. My heart just answered what Joschua told me to do. But it was the experience of my life.

"Hello, may I wake you from your dreams, I hope they were beautiful."
"Yes, and how! Perfectly."
"What do you think if we stop the phone call now and go to our cots, then maybe I can hold those incredible feelings even longer and continue to feel."
"Yes, that would be great, you have nice ideas. I was on the phone, it was the experience of my life and we call tomorrow again. Thank you for everything and dream of me!"
"I'll do that and tomorrow morning I'll stay in bed longer, to make the dream even longer. Just want to feel more and if it's just that I think about you. See you tomorrow, so is 19.00 right?"
"Yes, gladly and I'm really happy. Sleep tight and pleasant dreams."

Quickly hang up the phone and go to bed. I no longer need to take off my clothes, I am already completely naked and so wet between my legs, but I experienced this moisture through the greatest experience in my life with Joschua. That was pure erotic madness. I can not tell Sonja tomorrow if she asks me. I am embarrassed for that. But why in itself? I am single and grown up. I am not accountable to anyone, so what the hell. It was just amazing and that's what I take with me in my dreams. Quick as wet and nude cuddled in my cot and eyes closed. Hello, there I am.

Wednesday 04.09.2013

Brrrr - Brrrr - Brrrr - Brrrr

Oh, six o'clock again. Man, I'm not really well rested. Joschua disturbs my normal bedtime and it has to my poor finally get used again between the legs of wet body. Joschua was pampered and exploded with words yesterday. Well, I was not bad when I think so. Where was my courage? But now get up otherwise I'm late in the business. After all, there are still some things left over from yesterday. The work is not less and again, new work is added. Well, if you had no work, that would be terribly boring. Just set up the coffee and then off to the bathroom. Funny I'm still wet down there. No, that can not be wet again it's better. Well, the dream was probably erotic, even if I can not remember it anymore. So water and ground coffee in the machine, Mia calls the shower. And so I do my necessary work on me in the bathroom to fully occupy myself in the bedroom. Can not go to work as I was yesterday on Joschua phone call. But was really erotically spoiled I think. So now in the kitchen, ready coffee, toast in, two equal and then eat in peace today. Had to come an hour later. Really great if you have such a girlfriend and boss as Sonja. Whether Joschua is still hanging around in his dreams or is just turning around in his bed? What does he have for a bed in the bedroom? A single bed or a double bed. I bet he has a double bed. Oh, poor man, he lies lonely and alone in it. If I ever manage to lie there as well and fall asleep next to it and wake up in the morning. Man Mia what are you thinking about that again? I have never had such thoughts. These desires have just arisen since I met Joschua. Well know is too much said, no do not know but already kind of loving. What should become of you Mia. You already dream with your eyes open. Good that the coffee did not run on your blouse or you would have had to change your clothes. Oh 6:45 am must go. At 7.30 it starts. You have to supply all the flowers in the store before the customers come and take out the old, withered ones. The clientele should always have a fresh impression, otherwise we would not sell anything. So enough food, dishes just washed off, then it does dry by itself. Take a small bag and get to the bike, unlock it, get up and leave. Attention Mia please with open eyes and thoughts on the way and traffic. Oh, Joschua, twelve more hours until I can hear your voice again in my ears. I miss you now. Mia stop dreaming. That's hard since I met you. Yes, you Joschua. Watching the way Mia. I do man and shortly thereafter at 7.25 I stand with the bike in front of the shop. I'm on time. When Sonja comes immediately, we first ask again how it went last night and if I dare. If she knew what I dare. Here she comes.

"Hello Sonja, good morning."
"Hello Mia. Got late last night? "
"How so?"
"Did you dare to talk on the phone?"
"I can tell you that in the breakfast break we have to do something first."
"Hey who is the boss. Well, you're right, so we'll have break-fast at ten, I'll bring the bread after delivery."
"Sausage and jam we still have in the fridge."
"Okay, but I'll make a coffee first."
"I'm starting."

I thought so. If it had gone to Sonja, we would not have left the business today and I would have had to tell Joschua everything right away. So I can but once until they come back from the delivery comes in peace to do my job. I did not think what a man can bring a disturb-ance in my life and Sonja my best friend apparently also. She also wants to experience it. She really has to see that I shine all over her face. She can not under-stand that. Has never experienced it with me, but neither am I and the work goes by quickly, and shortly after ten o'clock the shop door opens and Sonja waves the bag in her hand.

"Breakfast and report."

We go back to the office. When a customer enters the store we hear the ring and then someone has to go there and wait, but otherwise they have breakfast and chat.

"Everything on the table. Tell me how was it last night with Joschua. As you hoped? More beautiful? Do not let anything get out of your nose."
"Everything in order."
"How was it so beautiful how you beam? I could go down to the cellar with you and read the newspaper without light, so you're blissful. Man, I'm curious, tell me finally."
"Sonja, Sonja, Sonja let me have a say. You're so excited."
"Of course I have never experienced anything like this, let alone experience it myself."
"Me neither. I never thought that there could be such a thing at all. That's too good to be true at all. When I think of him everything changes in me. My heart beats faster and I can only think of him what I have already experienced with him. I do not even have the time to think about the future experiences."
"As you experienced, did you come on the phone with him last night?"
"Come, no I have experienced something that can not be described as that. I just exploded like a rocket. But very slowly, and not by him, but by the things I have done verbally on the phone with him."
"How did you do it? You're always so shy with men."
"That's just it, I've done things with him, stripped him, tied him, punished, loved, blown and I do not know what else and he is not only verbal but also correct and me too. Man, imagine, was so late yesterday, had to go shopping and at home I then took a shower and because the time was so tight I put the food on the phone and put on nothing."
"How did you talk to him naked?"
"Yes, but I told him I have a fitted red short dress on."

"White lie, but you have not chatted video, right?"

"Are you crazy. I also do not have a webcam on my computer."

"So you were naked and whispered bad erotic things in the phone."

"Yes and I do not know how it started. One gave the other and then he sent me an e-mail with a homemade food menu and I chose a menu and then we lived together. I often thought in the time he was right on or in me or I had his cock in my mouth. I could often feel that right. It was like real, how real."

"Sure and then your feelings have become so intense and exploded."

"Yes, can you imagine that?"

"No, but I see it happened, you already tremble when you talk about him."

"Yes and he had such a sexy voice and he always played with very different pitches. I felt like I was in the middle of the sex adventure. Yes that was an absolute sex adventure. I've never experienced that before."

"And then?"

"Well, then when we had finished eating, I mean erotic way, then I was so wet and just went to bed and made it myself when falling asleep."

"Then you did not come to him."

"But even so, there was still so much feeling inside of me, I went to bed naked without taking a shower before and there were the feelings, then one hand just let me grab between my legs and the other had to I lay on my chest."

"As?"

"It was like a compulsion. It just happened and then I fell asleep."

"Did you dream about him?"

"Can not I tell you. But when I woke up, I was totally wet again. So it must have been an erotic taro, right?"

"I think that's great. Enjoy every second with the man who must be awesome. When will you hear him again?"

"Today at 19.00 we want to call again. Introduce yourself. Just when I came into the living room after shower-

ing, the food was still from yesterday evening next to the computer. I was so busy with Joschua that I did not eat or drink anything."

"Hahaha then me he the perfect diet."

"Yes, you just do your jokes but I'm completely happy, totally lifted, I float in luck. What will that be?"

"Does not matter, just enjoy. Man, I'm already excited about listening to you."

"Sorry I did not mean to upset you."

"It does not matter, I just think it's so amazing that you've met such a guy and that on the internet. That such men still exist."

"There you are a customer in the business."

"I'm already leaving."

"I'll cover and go to the greenhouse. See you later."

"Yes you happy."

And off to work. Oh, the greenhouse is beautiful today and it smells so intense. Man the colours of the flowers. They were always so beautiful. Mia hello, come down to the floor. No, somehow not, I'm floating. Did he feel that way? How he is doing now. He is looking forward to to-night as I am. Oh his voice, I can still hear her in my ear. What do I put on tonight? No naked was so beautiful and imagine he does not know. No today I will tell him I have nothing but my skin. That will certainly make him very hot. What he will probably say. Oh Mia how can my thoughts change when one is happy. I've never experienced that before. Not even with my first love. Oh, I had butterflies in my stomach where are they now? Not only in the stomach, flying all over me. Wow, if we have e-mailed two days what happens if we have two days on the phone?

"Mia are you still alive, it's 13.00 I have to go home to the kids. I close the front. Have lunch first, you're almost done with the putty action."

"Like noon, oh, I did not notice."

"No, you dreamed, and Joschua certainly helped you repot."

"Hahaha, can be. See you later."

And no sooner has Sonja gone I go to the office, let's see if I got an e-mail. Oh yes, actually a mail from him and what a long with many questions. If I answer him now. Whether he waits for it, certainly, I would do so.

- *Hello you female being from another star, yesterday's phone conversation has catapulted me into space and there I am now floating and trying to get to you with all my strength, so please read this mail today. You I want to ask you something:*
  1. Did you sleep well?
  2. Did you dream about us?
  3. If so, how?
  4. If not, why not?
  5. Did you think about falling asleep to our experience?
  6. Was it as nice for you as it was for me?
  7. Are you looking forward to this evening like me?
  8. Do you still want to hear me?
  9. Do you want to see me?
  10. Yes I want!!!
- *Oops were too many questions, you just made me curious and the questions are also there to remind you of me, while you certainly have to work a lot. Hello it's me, the crazy man who is looking for his mistress! Smile!*
- *If you are reading this mail before we leave at 19.00 - do not forget! - telephone you can answer these questions like and if you prefer to mail something else, also ok, because only a sign of life to catch you is the purpose of this mail.*
-
  Until tonight, my heart beats faster as the time comes when your wonderful voice reaches my ear. Think about who should have the lead, my left or right ear ... smile. See you. GLG Joschua -

128

He really makes me smile. It is as if a positive arrow penetrates my soul and he does so many times. How many times I have smiled and laughed in the last few days. That's right, as often as in years and no more, and whenever I've heard or thought of him, even while e-mailing, I often had to smile when I read his or sent my answers. So Mia laughs so well, then send him an e-mail. Or be crazy spontaneously. You are alone now and then you could call. Oh no, if I hear the erotic voice, I'm sure again very wet in panties and ... oh Mia, no one is here, besides, you have something on and no one can see anyway. Yes call first and then e-mail. Let me see where I disturb him. Oh, Mia, he will not be with another woman or another with him? That's men. Oh you are stupid he made you happy yesterday and I him too, there will be no other. No Joschua is solo as he said. I have the feeling deep down inside that he is telling the truth and is just right for me. Stupid why am I so afraid? Because of the bad experience I have made. If I get dis-appointed with Joschua, then my life is over. I will never find such a man again. I want that. Miaaa, you want that, you've got yourself shot. No, not only that, it was not just me, he just mesmerized me like a whirlpool, a big whirlpool, no, a huge whirlpool, like a black hole that attracts everyone. Hey presto now I'm inside him. Oh wake up Mia otherwise the lunch break is over and you have not even heard his voice. So pick up the phone, dial the number, breathe deeply three times and then pick up the phone. Rest oh this rest, ahhh there is finally a sign. Yes the dial tone. Immediately he picks up the phone, already the second dial tone ...

"Hello, who is there?"
"Hey, did you sleep well, how are you?"
"Mia, what a great surprise! Wow I'm totally blown away, I never expected that would make my day a very special day!"
"Why that?"
"Well, you can ask questions - oh, you fish for compli-ments. So so! But it is a highlight to hear your voice and

then so unexpected, I never thought. Thank you for this successful surprise!"

"I'm glad, but I wanted to reward myself after a busy morning."

"How to reward?"

"Well, your voice and your words do me so well. Brighten my heart. You see, I'm quite selfish to call you, but if I made you happy with that, that's twice as good."

"Yes, have you and I have been hoping I get a mail from you and I was looking forward to it and now I can even hear your voice. Excellent! And an idea what awaits you today on our evening phone call?"

"No. Give me a hint, then I can prepare for it."

"Well, you've seen so much of me yesterday and I've felt so much more through this than anything else in my life, you've given me so much and today I want to try to give you back some of it. Do not give it back, keep it up! I'll try to make you feel what you've made me feel yesterday."

"That sounds good and how?"

"Well, who is so curious, you, you, you, if you continue to be so curious, I have to punish you!"

"You can not do that, I'm a lady and you a gentleman."

"Hahaha, do you know the definition of gentleman?"

"No, which do you mean?"

"A gentleman is a man who makes it easy for a woman."

"Is it good or is it bad?"

"It depends."

"What for?"

"Well, whether you want it easy or not."

"What do you mean by easy?"

"Well it will be easy if you get involved with it and let yourself fall, to give you the greatest ecstasy."

"Sounds more than good and conjures me a light goose bumps. I have to keep working, I'm looking forward to 19.00."

"Thank you for your dear call, hit my heart. See you soon, well in approximately seven hours. Bye."

"See you then dear Joschua."

My heart is racing, as if I had run a thousand one hundred and fifty feet. Hahaha, I'm stupid. Hardly heard his voice, I'm already blown away again. Nobody believes me. Thought stop or I'll be sitting here tonight and not coming to the phone. Oh to distract myself I'll answer the questions in his mail, in a nutshell, that will certainly make him more crazy than when I talk around long. So tell me how I was pleased to hear him.

- Hi Joschua, it was just nice to hear your voice on the phone, reminded me of last night and played the most beautiful pictures very briefly in my mind's eye. I'm looking forward to tonight, oh have to quit a customer is at the shop door. Bye-

I do not need to open the door, Sonja has closed it. Let's see. Oh, there are really two women looking through the glass. Let's see what they want. Door open minded and the two elderly ladies come in and I can each of them a bouquet of flowers as a gift, they have told they are invited to dinner, sell. I always make sales during the lunch break. That's already noticed Sonja yesterday. Well, no problem, because I'm here anyway. But now again briefly to the office and his curious mail answered.

— There I am again, there were only two older ladies that I could make happy with flowers. For you I need something more. Smile! I just want to answer your questions. Hope you are happy, no I know you will be sitting at the computer and feverishly against this mail. Right? Yes, I slept very deeply, but I do not know what I dreamed, but I woke up and first saw your picture in my mind's eye. I hardly lay awake. I just tried to relive the experience with you once again and I fell asleep and you know what, when I woke up this morning. I was down very wet. Do you know what that means? Well think about it! Yes, I'm already eager for 19:00 the whole time but it's

131

still almost six hours, unfortunately. I never want to give up on your voice, your words and your stories, but I would like to experience them not only through the phone, but with you, sitting opposite me or lying in my arms. So now I have to do something, but I find it particularly difficult today, because you are constantly distracting my thoughts, always catching me. Have you dearly closed in my heart. Greetings Mia.

And pressing the button, I wrote too much with my heart closed after this ultra-short time? I know I'm out of whack. Oh we are both grown and I want to enjoy it as long as he wants it. Hopefully the guy wants it for a very long time, from me even longer. Oh, Mia is nice to be able to think like that. In the past people only thought of their empty home or how well other people are and how modest their own past was. Now I'm living through Joschua for the first time in the present and thinking about the future. Horny, really cool! So sent and I go back to the store, unlock the door and wait for customers. Hahaha waiting for customers, I still have so much to do. In addition, I wanted to tie up ten bouquets for our flower campaign tomorrow, the special offer for five euros a piece. So the time passes and when I have finished the ten bouquets, interrupted by three dear buying customers, Sonja comes back again. She has to look after a family and then the business. Think often how much she does. When I go home, I can sometimes put my feet up. She has two children and one man who works for a very long time.

"What would I do without you? You are absolutely reliable and make sales on the side."
"Is not that good?"
"But even more, and then, above all, that we have become friends and I can witness your love adventure. It's better than any television eleven."
"Hahaha. But I really enjoy working here in comparison to my previous job, it's like paradise and I have the

dearest boss in the world."
"Mia, you want to make me as red as the roses, right?"
"No, you have to face the truth."

And we both have to smile and then go back to work until Sonja reappears much later.

"When did you make a phone call today?"
"At seven o'clock. How so?"
"It's half past five, finish tomorrow."
"That's great, then I can prepare for it."
"Prepare, how is that? You only telephone."
"This is not a normal phone call, this is an extraordinary erotic adventure and today he wants to pamper me."
"Well then let's go tomorrow, we have breakfast together again and I can experience your telephone experience then?"
"Of course I'll tell you everything at breakfast. See you. Bye."
"And do not dream to ride a bike, or you will not arrive home safely."
"Thank you, I turn my mind off and pay attention."
"I wanted to hear that. Bye."

And then I disappeared in the office, grabbed my things, got on the bike and went home. Oh, I'm looking forward to his voice. Why only, what will he whisper in my ear today? I am already so excited and excited. Oh, I'll shower again and then sit down on the phone naked. Today I'll tell him, mmm or not. Oh, I'll decide it over the phone, if I can decide before he puts me under his spell. So finally home, once again take a shower, stay naked and then lubricate a bread and a small bottle of coke with on the bedside table and then I will cuddle up in my cot and talk to him. Oh, how that sounds good and tempting in the run up.

"Hello little angel, I've been waiting for you like that, how are you?"
"Now alright, where I hear your voice. Hello Joschua!"

"You, it has happened again, I have had to deal with such an immense yearning for you all day long and now your voice gives me salvation."

"I felt the same way, that's why I called you this afternoon, I missed you. Is not that funny, we have not even seen each other just e-mailed and talked on the phone and that's only the third conversation."

"But what was the first conversation for one! One that I will never forget again in my life. Definitely not."

"Yes, that's the way to express it. You spoke to me from the heart."

"Tell me, how are you sitting there now?"

"It starts again, you are curious, but it has never been so interested in me. I think it's great, but do you really want to know that?"

"Yes, absolutely or do not you want to tell me how erotic you are dressed?"

"What do you mean, dressed erotically?"

"Well, that would be if, for example, I knew you were lying on your sofa, completely relaxed and only lightly clothed, waiting to get wet and then experience the climax, lying down and completely relaxed."

"Where are you, behind the curtain?"

"Ne, just felt a feeling through the phone and I felt right?"

"Yes and what do I have?"

"What do you want to hear, what you have on or what I believe in and wish for what you would wear?"

"Both!"

"But you have wishes. Ok, I would like to, and so you lie today while we chat in my mind's eye, on your sofa. You have a black lace bra that enhances your beautifully shaped breasts even more, but unfortunately protects me from my greedy looks."

"So, greedy looks."

"Yes, you know I'm curious and it's understandable. I am only a man and you are the angel of my heart, because you want to know everything and always."

"Okay, if you think so, I'll allow you and what do I have downstairs?"

134

"Down there you have a cuddly woolen blanket, in which you have cuddled your feet and not only your beautifully shaped feet, but this beige woolen blanket nestles up to your bra, light but warm to your soft skin. I could be really jealous of your rug right now. Well, down around you have a black panties, with a slight lace edge, matching your top, a little casual cut, so that a certain freedom arises."

"I do not have that and more?"

"No, you are almost completely covered by the plump blanket."

"Hello, are you falling asleep under your warm blanket?"

"Hello, youuu!"

"Sorry, I just got distracted a bit by your words and imagined you're lying on me and there instead of the woolen blanket ... ."

"That's how you developed that kind of goosebumps of the positive kind."

"I think I'm crazy, do you feel me so much? It's like standing here next to me and watching your blue eyes, even under the blanket. It's as if you could see through them and that has already excited me again, so the silence break."

"No problem, what would I give now to really stand next to you and then I would not just strip you with my eyes, but after my hands gently stroked your cheeks, they would go down the exciting path, reaching along your neck and then the tops of your bra. Very light, with some distance, my palms inside would move over your nipples protruding through your bra. So tender, that these magically dressed, want to rub against my hands, but they can not reach and therefore develop more and more. They look as if they stand up like very strong strong nipples. This is the moment that immediately puts my hands on your stomach by squeezing under the plump wool blanket and your standing breast nipples the impact of my lips, only your left nipple, but this must

135

intercept the impact and prevent it from bouncing back, my teeth are lovingly biting into her. "

"Ohhh, auauau, yes, what are you doing?"

"Ha, I would have succeeded in the surprise. Unexpectedly, I would have released many feelings in you that would now be floating around in your body."

"They would not do it, they always manage to arouse me in just a few words."

"That really is a very big and loving compliment for me, but what you awoke in me yesterday is equal. Could it be that we are sparking at the same heart wavelength?"

"Yes, certainly. My heart receives your heart waves as if it were right next to mine. And they come so violently and unencrypted for me that they get right into my body and there trigger these terribly violent erotic waves."

"Cool!"

"Hello, here writes my right nipple, I'm neglected."

"Maybe I'm a dolt. Sorry, I did not want that, your other nipple was just closer and I screamed louder, but now I'll put my lips around you and edit your nipple with my biter. And do not complain of left nipple, my hand will keep you warm while massaging."

"Ohhh the excitement is already rising. Say, can you get a climax from a breast massage, a hot erotic breast massage?"

"Now if you put your hands under your panties and lightly stroke your clit, then yes."

"Oh, you're right, it's already rising, ohhh push harder, please, please. Even harder, yeah, oh, it, beware, I'm about to explode, yes, yes, yes, oh yes, ohhh, ohhh!"

"You drive me crazy. You are so loud when you come, it's like being allowed to experience everything exactly, how it rises and rises and then the calm at the peak and then falling into the comfort phase. I love it when you let me experience through your volume everything. Thanks for that."

"How do you like it when I get loud?"

"Yes, I think that's great, it excites me and you can also act great, because if you always know exactly where your excitement is currently, then I can fine-tune my

actions. *Whether you want to explode immediately or later, and where to invoke which level of arousal on your body."*

"It's really like that, you as a man pay attention to how it starts and where it works. No one of my men has done that yet, they all only meant that when they have fun, I have that too, and when they reach a climax, then I auto-matically have a climax."

"Yes, I've heard, men can be stupid, but women too."

"Really."

"Yeah, imagine I'm with a woman and she's lying on her back, and if you caress her, she will not show any reactions."

"There is not."

"But I have already experienced and once she says to me, can stop, I'm done."

"What?"

"Yes, because you think you get hit with a hammer into your emotional world."

"That's a joke on the woman."

"It's even better, the TV was on and we were in the middle of sexual intercourse when she said, hurry up the movie starts. What you feel then you can not ima-gine. You're like a hundred to zero in a second and you feel like the last ass. Simply sad to have ever started something sexual with the woman. That really hurts. And you feel so used, so helpless when the feelings are pounded against the wall."

"Yes, I have experienced something similar, because men often come rather than women and most men then do not pay attention to us. How many times have I faked my former partner a climax."

"Honestly, I do not like that!"

"You're right, but I've never talked to a man like you. No man has ever asked me anything like you."

"That's the problem, all over the world, people do not talk to each other. As well as when two people are not open to each other. "

"Yes."

"Do you remember what I said in our first conversation

as a prerequisite for a working relationship?"
"Sure, trust, that was like a door opener for you."
"How do you mean?"
"Well, when you put that so vehemently into the fore-ground, you flew through an open door with me and opened many other doors, including those to my heart."
"How only open?"
"Well, later in the conversation, you went with blowing flags through the slightly open door into my heart and have you stuck there."
"Fixed sounds good, may I stay there?"
"If you are always honest, you are welcome forever."
"You've just shot a heat packet into my heart. Thanks for that, it's more than I expected. I hoped that, of course!"
"But you are one, are you always like that?"
"In my private life I want to be happy, always honest and straight, but in business life that's not always possible."
"I can only confirm that and I have no problem with that."
"I hope that you have no problem with me and never will have, will do everything to keep it that way and I can do a lot!"
"Sounds like we want to have a long relationship of our hearts!"
"Yesss, yesss and still yesss, yesss and ...!"
"I know, yes. You make me laugh so often."
"Laughing is healthy! You know, when you laugh for ten minutes a day, a laugh that makes your stomach vibrate, then you consume as many calories as half an hour of jogging."
"And that's not so exhausting!"
"But it's really rare to laugh heartily. I do not remember when it was the last time with me. In business life things are not like that, but in private life. Only there I really had nothing to laugh in recent years."
"Had bad luck, too?"
"That's more than mild, downright unlucky, and when-ever it would have been enough to win the next step, I've been hit by sticks, stumbled and had to get up

138

again. That worked several times, but you lose strength and eventually the desire and just wondering why and why."

"Yes, who are you saying that?"

"Well maybe later I'll tell you about it, if you have a lot of handkerchiefs next to you to dry your tears."

"Hahaha, do you want to make me laugh now?"

"No, I just want to tell you, your season is over."

"How my season?"

"I think you have rested enough, I have told you other things about me and your body has relaxed in the meantime. Right?"

"Yes and now you want to arouse me sexually again?"

"How do you know that?"

"Well, I'm not serious! But good bad!"

"Oh yes, there was something. Something that looks like an angel and feels like an angel and speaks like an angel, so it has to be an angel. The Miaangel, in which her heart I feel so good and that I will tickle now on the stomach. Tickle, tickle, tickle!"

"Hahaha not."

"And oops I was too deep, but felt smooth on your soft skin textiles, so what, they do not want to prevent you from an erotic experience?"

"Should I remove it?"

"Yes with both hands and very, very slowly pull down until you can take them in the hand and then."

"Slow, what and then?"

"Then you put them on your nose and eyes. Yes, exactly on your nose and eyes."

"Ok. I have made."

"Do you now perceive the scent of angel Mia?"

"Yes, I smell it, it's right in front of my nose, I've never felt that way, that's me."

"Well, now you know how beautiful an angel can smell. Close your eyes and please do not open it anymore."

"Yes."

"I'm sorry, but the plump woolen blanket will say good-bye to your knees and not warm up further up. Ohhh, what does she release for a wonderful look, an angelic

body that lustfully lies before me and just waiting to be lovingly but definitely spoiled with caresses and touches."

"Yes, exactly and ...?"

"Do you remember how it felt when my hands and teeth on your breasts were engaged in the use of pleasure?"

"Yes."

"Well, then we start again and my teeth caress your right nipple, a little less pressure and strong sucking and she darts in my mouth. Ohhh how your breast feels soft and tasty."

"Yes and I feel the heat and moisture in your mouth. Completely pleasant and so moving."

"And the left nipple is now pressed by my free hand, always firm, loose, firm, loose and then suddenly a slight pinch in the nipple."

"Au au au!"

"That's what I wanted to hear. I lift my head, leaving your chest, which is slipping out of my mouth again, as I squeeze my lips and approach your face. I see how your panties are on your nose and eyes and I bring my lips to yours and start plucking at them. Well you will not interfere with your tongue? Oh well, well then I have to use mine to keep the upper hand. I want to nibble your lips, but your cheeky tongue, lick, push, oh it's all wet, really wet and slippery and then I press my lips firmly on yours, open them with pressure and immerse my tongue in your mouth. As my tongue holds your mouth, I carefully slide my left hand to your navel, so far I have not had time to explore it and I want to catch up now. Whether you're as ticklish in my ringy button as I am. Let's see and my fingers touch your ringy button very tenderly, because only tender can bring about the tickle effect and tickle ... tickle ... tickle ...! I only hear a dull huhuhu. Yes, you want to laugh, but nothing can come out of your mouth, I'm messing with your tongue your words totally confused. You realize that words can not stop my tickling and throw your hands into the game to grab mine and push it aside. You are strong, yes the tickled develops strong forces and now I dis-

solve from your mouth, take distance and see how you make your mouth a sweet smile and laughs loud, because my hand pushed away has further awakened the tickling on your flank. Yes, tickle until you laugh properly, so that you can feel it in the stomach. You, your laugh is beautiful and sexy! I want more!"

"Oh yeah, that's good, laughing is doing so well."

"Yes, and already my second hand continues the tickling on your other flank."

"Grace, stop, hahaha, please, hahaha no, please, I can not anymore, hahaha."

"I'm not letting up, I think it's as great as you laugh and now it's getting more, you're reacting all over, your legs are kicking the blanket all the way out and if I did not stand in front of the couch, you'd be sure of it roll down to escape me. Your whole body is laughing now and you are gasping for air. Well, I stop, one, two, three. You look at me questioningly and at four my hands are putting on tickling. Since you are already starting to squirm and roll, your panties will fall off your face and I can see these wonderful brown eyes laughing. They radiate like two suns and out of your mouth sounds again and again and only interrupted by deep inhalation, a loud laugh."

"Hahaha, oh hahaha, no, stop hahaha ...!"

"Well, laugh enough? Should I stop?"

"Yes, yes, yes, hahaha ...!"

"Ok. End of the tingling hour!"

"Oops, I'm totally out of breath, hahaha! No, not again!"

"But! A little bit more!"

"No, stop I surrender!"

"You surrender?"

"Yes, yes, I surrender!"

"You're really a great tickling object, well out of breath."

"No one ever tickled me like that forever."

"Did I really enjoy it, I hope you have something to eat on your couch to recharge your batteries?"

"Yeah, I'm smart, I knew it would be an exhausting, very long conversation."

"Well, I'm really impressed. Fit again?"

"Of course, what do you want to do to me now? To conjure up a climax?"

"No, now I want to go on a journey of discovery."

"Like a journey of discovery?"

"Well, I want to discover all, even the most hidden corners of you."

"What do you think you discover?"

"Yes, I should have said better."

"What do you think you experience?"

"So I've just got to know and love your wet mouth, your lively tongue and your grippy lips, now comes the rest. I look into your eyes and my lips approach your chin, reach it, taste it with the tongue and the lips crawl over your mouth to the nose. My lips wrap around your nostrils, I feel in my mouth as you inhale and exhale, very quiet, no, a little faster than normal. It's like waiting for my next nickeliness and there it is. I press my lips tight, but without my teeth touching your nose and the next breath you open your lips and blow the air over my chin. Tenderly your breath caresses my neck and my shoulders twitch with something that has triggered that breath. My lips open and want to move on after your nose has restored its beautiful old form. Mia close your eyes. And after they are closed, I give a tender kiss to each eyelid then drop off a lot of it on your forehead, while my hands caress through your soft hair and seek out your ears, once again there to squeeze them violently at the cartilaginous outer edges driving up and down. Do you like it?"

"Yes, go ahead."

"After the head, of course, it goes down, but different than you think. Please turn around and lie on your stomach, put your hands on your sides and stay that way, understand?"

"Yes, my lord."

"Sounds good so turn around, slowly."

"Right?"

"Yes, really great and now rest and lie down. I let my gaze glide from top to bottom on this excellent figure and up and down again and again, I feel that you feel my

eyes as they look at your body from above. Your fine body hairs stand up and you twitch with your shoulders. Stay calm, no movement!"

"This is easier done than I said when your eyes glide down and up. I can literally feel them, your looks that estimate me and examine. Do you like what you see?"

"Oh man, you can say that. You attract me, which should I treat first, the left or challenges me the rights more out. Ok, I'll take your left buttock and already my lips are moving towards her. When they open up, it's as if your buttock continues that impact pressure in waves. My lips feel it very clearly. They dig into your buttock and the area around my lips, as well as my nose gently caressed by your delicate skin. Rrrr I want to bite into it and when I can't hold myself back and do it ...!"

"Auauau, what do you have for teeth."

"Oops, I could not resist, she looked so appetizing. I could feed you now, would you always be with me ...?"

"Better in you. But then you can not devour me so greedy with your eyes."

"I'm right again and I'd like to see this enchanting sight forever, even though I have to unpack you every day to experience it."

"Every day?"

"Well, I probably cheated on that. I would see you naked in the morning in the shower, dressing in the bedroom if you came home from work and you would put on something more comfortable, if you would swim naked with me and of course completely naked during sex and then lovelocking and imagine the day, day off. Great. However, you often have to endure being naked."

"Oh, I could bear that, if I think about our phone call yesterday, not bad."

"Cool then we agree, a lot of bare skin and greedy eyes when we get together."

"Will we get together?"

"When, how and where do you want to meet me for the first time?"

"But now you have fired directly at the target."

"I should always be honest and that's what I would want

more than anything else right now. That would be like Christmas and what do you do Christmas?"

"What do you mean now?"

"First you are looking forward to the special moment. In my childhood, no until today, when I can go into the Christmas room and enjoy the Christmas tree with the candles and the shine he spreads, it's the most beautiful moment of the year. In our case we would experience this together, hand in hand, looking at the tree, then our eyes would meet, our lips and tongues and then I would unpack my present - you - under the Christmas tree in the flickering candlelight with Christmas music in the background."

"That sounds very romantic."

"Yes, I like to be romantic, that suits my feelings and you as such a great emotional man are certainly also romantic. Could you imagine a romantic Christmas together?"

"Would you be happy if I said yes?"

"One hundred percent yes and a little more. That would be the most romantic Christmas for many years. Have you ever noticed what we are talking about?"

"Yes, we jump from one topic to another, you can not do that with every human being, you're in good spirits right away. You know how I mean that, a lot of positive."

"Yes, I'll gladly give that back to you. It's fun to talk to you, have fun."

"Auauau, again."

"Yeah, do you still remember how you lie on your stomach in front of me, without any textiles, so I had to nibble on your right, cheekily upright buttock again."

"Nibbling is allowed, but please do not eat, then you have nothing left of me."

"But kneading with your hands is allowed?"

"Oh yes that's nice, no not between the buttocks in the slot."

"How so?"

"That tickles so awful again, you make it so tender."

"How should I be more brutal?"

"No, no, that's not what I meant, but you can also turn

144

the words in your mouth."

"Not me, not really."

"But you, oops, where is your finger?"

"Down to your wet cave. Is she already wet? Attention I am the moisture controller."

"Hahaha, who? The Humidity Controller?"

"Yes. But that's not how it works. You sit down normally on your couch and spread your legs."

"And if not?"

"Then I will examine the first accessible opening from behind."

"No, no, just not that, they turn me around. Is it right?"

"Wow, yes, what a sight, it can really stay away from the spit. I was right, like an angel, and then that long, curly hair hanging from your head. If they keep growing for another two weeks, you can cover your breasts with it. Madness."

"Good that I like you so much, I'm so happy about it."

"Please spread your legs, I want to kneel in between. Yeah, just like that and now put your legs on my shoulders."

"Right?"

"Yes. I knelt in front of you and when you put your legs on my shoulders, you slid so far into the sofa until your knees came to rest on my shoulders. As a result, I slid with my face relatively far between your thighs. Oh, you smell good erotically, very good."

"No, I just took a shower."

"No, not so, that's the humidity of your now erotic longing."

"Erotic desire?"

"Yes, I feel like you're getting hot, you want me to get closer to you, touch you or even better spoil my tongue."

"Oh yeah!"

"Your scent, you can say, the chemistry is right, it makes me animal, I have to get closer to you and my tongue is already licking along your thighs further towards the source of the scent and you are pursuing this with ever more violent groaning and breathing. An

145

increase until I finally arrived where you probably like it. My tongue touches your labia and tries to penetrate deeper. It hits the tip of the tongue fully on your clit, which in turn elicits you a loud groan. It also goes through and through, it tingles in my whole body, it demands more and my tongue begins to indulge your clitoris in a steady rhythm. From further back penetrates more and more fragrant moisture to me and very intense, because my nose is already almost touching your labia, I can almost feel it and Mia puts her two hands on my head and starts to scratch him. You can almost just scratch my head, because my hair is no more than six millimeters long. It's a really hot feeling, I can not remember when a woman last did that. Darn, stop, Mia is almost on the cusp and now, not yet trigger, you'll have to suffer for some time. Hahaha, suffering is good, you enjoy it to the fullest, because whenever a wave of emotions, triggered by my tongue, chases through your body, you press your fingernails more on my head while scratching. After the dance stop my tongue on your clitoris and the slow decay of your excitement, my tongue wants to continue and strengthen the fragrance again. I push my tongue between my lips and after a renewed, brief touch of your clitoris, I press my tongue close to this past, further into the depths there to lick unrestrained. Oh, I'm so sorry for how you have to suffer and it will take so long."

"Hahaha, you may be funny, ohhh, yeah, go on."

"I want to increase your feelings even more and put my hands over my head and put them on your breasts and then take the hard nipples between my fingers and whenever my tongue touches your clitoris. I squeeze my fingers together and your nipples deform. I pull my hands slightly forward and your breasts have to follow, which causes an ever louder moan and faster breathing. It sounds compliant with my actions and yes it is so unimaginably great that I can fully control your agitation. I feel directly how your blood shoots faster and faster through your body. My ears are now firmly on your thighs, because you squeeze them together more and more, but does not quite work, my head is in between. Result, I can hear almost nothing more and therefore I hear your blood throb and somehow, through this pressure, your slight, increasingly violent twitching goes straight into my body. It's amazing, as if we were just one person, so I feel close to being one, and I can really feel how you keep heading for the climax and yes, it's about to be almost all of your muscles, we have yes 656 pieces of it, start to twitch and my tongue dances on your clitoris, press my finder and pull on your nipples, everything is violent and faster and there, suddenly a total silence, almost unbearably much peace, it seems as if this phase takes a long time. Once again a tongue touch your clitoris, a firm press of the nipples and a violent, vigorous twitching goes through your rearing body, holding briefly tense to then very slowly followed by a relieved groan to slide back into the old position. Then suddenly the pressure on my head goes away, I pull my tongue in, close my lips and raise my head between your thighs to see in two bright brown eyes, where the happiness, what you have just experienced reflects. You lovingly stroke my head, over the cheeks and our hands meet, lie down together and stay. The breath is always screwed back to normal, but that still takes some time. A time when I just have to watch Mia, you are beaming with happiness, radiating a contentment and then falling into a complete calm, like a rigor. Yes, I know it has been a peak performance for your body, lie down on the sofa, I'll cover you. Enjoy the still raging feelings in you. I like to watch you, you are like an angel, radiating peace and quiet, to me. You do that well!"

"And for the first time. With you, I feel like a complete woman again."

"Yes, that is you, absolutely desirable. Well, the other men are all blind and have not recognized your female talents."

"Yes, you are the only one and I am so glad to have found you."

"Just fall asleep and enjoy, we'll call again tomorrow

and then I'll have a surprise for you if you want. Kiss on both cheeks, your eyelids and your lips."

I'm so blown away from the experience and I just hang up the phone as he said and I'm already in my bed. I just turn around and the dreams have enveloped me.

Thursday, 05.09.2013

Brrrr - Brrrr - Brrrr - Brrrr

I just dreamed so much. Always this alarm clock. Why does he always tear you when it is the dream in the most beautiful out. Sometimes I feel like he does it on purpose. He somehow knows exactly when I would reach the hot spot in the dream and then he fancies before. Oh well then let's go to the normal routine. Oh, I have a goal in mind that makes my day totally different and beautiful. At noon today I will make Joschua happy again with a telephone call. Hahaha, if he knew how that always makes me happy when I hear his voice. Then it will always be very warm to my heart. Alas that I may experience this is like a miracle. Oh, I'm really curious if we'll meet and I'll be so happy, or if the shine falls off the moment I see him. Oh Mia the shine is even greater than now. Does it work? Heart to brain I am still able to expand. Well, then I let myself be surprised. These thoughts are so intense, I've already done my morning toilet during that and no coffee is not there to wake up. I'll definitely have to have breakfast with Sonja again to tell how it was yesterday on the phone call. You are always so curious friends. Funny it is, when I'm with Joschua, hahaha together, but somehow it feels like that. Or should I rather think since I have grasped Joschua in my feelings and like. Yes, since the day on, Sunday, everything has changed. Sonja discovered my radiant aura and immediately gutted it. How that sounds gutted. No, she pulled all my feelings out of my nose and had to tell. But I also realize that the feelings have become much more aware of me and I realize how I look forward to the next contact with Joschua. I fever right to the time when his voice on the phone reaches my ear and is immediately forwarded to my heart without mental testing. I have not experienced that. This Joschua really makes me crazy from far away. How will it be when I'm standing next to him, will I go crazy? Oops arrived already. Somehow this happened again in auto run today. I was thinking of him all the time and what if. Madness as it distracts me in my real life in the direction of happiness. Oh that's nice. Mailing and talking on the phone for a few days was like a miracle to me. Please, please let it go further and become an infinitely great superwonder. I do everything for it. Certainly and I will love you very well Joschua. Will you take me then too? Mia what are those thoughts. You first have to get to know him in natura. Maybe he is very different.

"Hey, do not you want to come in? You've been standing motionless for almost a minute. Are you here or anywhere else?"

Oh that was Sonja, where am I? Oh, I'm standing in front of the flower shop. These thoughts are so real in me. I'll go crazy. Could I tell him this tonight on the phone? Or rather not. At breakfast Sonja ask for advice.

"That must have been something even crazier last night than the day before?"
"Yes until 1.30, then I was happy in the bed. I'll tell you at breakfast."
"Good at ten o'clock breakfast break as always in my office."

Well then to work, if there my thoughts are back with him. Oh Mia, that's not possible, you also have to be careful. Everything is not automatic and flowers need love. Hahaha, my thoughts of the beloved flowers on the already closed in the heart Joschua want to skip. Is it a

149

man you could love forever or just a wonderful, erotic adventure? When I think about it in peace, then I am adult and completely independent. No children and no one needs to be considered. So why not get involved in an erotic adventure? What I have experienced so far is more than what I experienced in my erotic life in my whole life, and a man who is so sweet inside can really be very angry. Where should I suggest a meeting? On neutral ground, maybe somewhere meeting at a dinner and then. Oh Mia are you crazy? You do not know him, but as a dessert then a sweet Joschua in any hotel room? It sounds hot, but is it really romantic? In a hotel room you have no relation to the real own life. But I want that at the first meeting? Oh Mia what should it be because you have to be clear about it first. Pure sex or maybe more. If I think so, then it must not be pure sex, because I have already let him slide into my heart something. Good pure sex is also great if you have some heart, but oh no, Mia does not matter. Anything you plan now does not happen anyway. It always comes differently than you plan. That's how it has been in my life.

"Mia ten o'clock the coffee is waiting for you."
"How nice? I'm coming."

And I'm on my way to the office. In the last days I have the feeling that I do not have a boss but a curious friend. I'm sure that a lot of people want that job and I have it. Oh, I'm really lucky, if I think so after so many years of real pitch. Everything seems to be on the way up with me and now also a man, apparently not only for the needed sex but for the heart. Could it be a life? Already I take a seat opposite Sonja.

"You want to spoil me, coffee, rolls, sausage and cheese, jam."
"Just as you like it. Just for my best friend."
"Hahaha, it's like home with mom."
"Should it be. If you feel comfortable then chat you more and I'm getting very nervous. Such a man of Doing this crazy

150

drives you indirectly too. Ask him if he wants to do a three-some."

"You would like that?"

"Oh, it could be funny, but I have in the field no experience."

"Me neither and it will stay that way. Sex is always something between a man and a woman for me. I want to be the focal point of the man and do not share with another."

"Man, you're completely selfish."

"Yes, and also jealous"

"Now you have betrayed you are in love up to your ears."

"Why are you on it?"

"Because you did not want to share with me. Was only a trap but now I know it. My best friend Mia is in love."

"You may be stupid."

"I know. But it's really fun and to see you in love is not bad. Love has become so rare in this world."

"Whom do you say that? But I do not know if it's love yet. Maybe in love."

"And last night."

"Oh Joschua has seduced me with the hottest words and I was lying naked in bed and then I really came. It was an explosion like I did not know. Simply indescribable. Then we ended the call and I fell asleep immediately. The only unpleasant thing this morning was the alarm clock at six o'clock. I had the feeling I just fell asleep."

"Yes, and you have dreamed of cycling again."

"Hahaha but you are really right. You let us just look in my mail, maybe he has already e-mailed a good morning mail to me."

"Yes, but only if you let her read me too."

"It's clear. Come let me sit in front of the table."

"You sound like a fairy tale."

"I hope so much that it ends well."

"Fairy tales almost always do that, so it will end well for you and you will find your happiness."

"Oh look, I was right. He e-mailed me. Hot."

— Hello you wonderful Angel of the emotional world! You were suddenly gone yesterday and apparently you are immediately fell asleep on the sofa. Did you spend the whole night there or got up at night and cuddled up in bed. Oh yes I know, I always ask questions, but you make me so curious and there I am can not see what you do, I have to ask to introduce myself. I have slept great and that's your fault. See, there is also a positive debt – smile. Do we make a call tonight at 19.00? Of course, you can also choose an earlier one at any time Take time, you will not be angry. his. So dear Mia, I await your answer - You can imagine in what textile condition I send you this mail? GLG Joschua -

"Of course he wants you to think that he was completely naked while writing."
"I know. It's cute, is not it?"
"Yes, really erotic without much to say. He is clever. Do not you want to answer him immediately?"
"Should I, may I?"
"Sure, write something and do not forget to send it."

And so an e-mail to my dear Joschua, which he is sure to be happy. As I suspect he sits on the computer and sees from time to time if something has been received.

— Good morning you women spoilers! Thank you for your dear mail, I have just read. I slept well and really did move into bed at 1.30 at night, as you guessed. Was with you again a top hot, erotic telephone chatter. You make me really hot and somehow I become dependent on it, I hardly wake up, you're my first thought. I had never experienced that before. Nice that there is still something like you. Do you know what I'm thinking right now? I'm sure you know it, I wonder what you want to offer me this evening in the daily phone call for a surprise. I'm not calling

you at 19.00, not even 18.55, but 18.47. I am very happy. Express yourself vigorously and give you a kiss, such a great long lip whisper kiss. Now I almost write with your words. It is up to then. Have a nice day. Love Mia.

"Well about such a hot mail, he will certainly be happy. If you write like that I understand that you both are burning for each other."

"Really, are they written so erotically?"

"Yes, I have never received such an e-mail, but I have not e-mailed yet."

"Yeah, I do not either, but since I'm with Joschua, well, by mail and by phone I mean, I'm experiencing some-thing like that. That is absolute madness."

"Good that you are my friend, then I can experience it firsthand. If one thing had told me, I think I would not have believed her. This is something unlikely, but in the lottery, there is often a winner. You're the winner of the love lottery this week, no, this year!"

Ping - Ping

"Did you hear that too?"

"Yes, there's another mail coming. Let's see. Oh yes, from him. Do you want to see her."

"There you may ask? Open at last."

— *Hey, you're a lot of boiled, no, that's wrong, you beloved female angel. Thank you for your kind words in your sweet mail. You are just a dear angel and I love you already, something more, very much already!!! Man how that probably arrives with you? So thank you a thousand times that you call thirteen minutes earlier. I am glad that you can not stand it until 19.00. To your surprise for tonight I can only tell you, you can not use it alone! So more only when you call me. Do not work so much, yes I know a stupid wish. What needs to be done needs to be done.*

153

So do not use all your energy, please pick something up for tonight. I could go on writing page by page, but you do not have time to enjoy these lines. So from me to you a very, very, very big kiss on your cheek, the rights!!! Ok, one more on the left. Well, you insatiable, even on your wonderfully wet wild lips. Your Joschua, who misses you so much. -

"You can get real tears in your eyes. As he can write so nice, but he has to feel something for you."
"Do you really mean?"
"Yes, I really mean that. That's amazing. I'd like to invite you tonight and talk to you on the phone oh listening to the speaker, no listening is not the right expression, it would be experienced."
"Sososo."
"No need not be afraid, I know you experience with him intimacies and pure eroticism, because I would only bother. Full understanding for you. When did my husband in reality turn me on like Joschua did with words. You are and will remain a lucky child. Enjoy it. Then tonight you can go half an hour early so you can focus on him and not be in stress."
"Man Joschua not only gives me luck, a friend who enhances my feelings, but also more free time. Where should that end?"

And we both look at each other and have to laugh hard.

"Yes, you are right, this is a man. Tilt him and do not let him off the hook."
"If you say so, but carefully, otherwise he'll break away again."
"That was a great breakfast with you. Then we want to go again. Now we have to have breakfast together every morning, then I get the erotic livestory that I was never allowed to experience."
"Yes, we do. Hopefully it lasts longer, then I always get breakfast here and can sleep ten minutes longer."
"Yes, that's how I am."

And then we both go back to work. I have a cool job. Many would envy me for that. Oh right now, I'm feeling better than I've ever done in life.

Ring – ring - ring

Oh my phone. Will Joschua give me a surprise now and send me a nice kiss through my cell phone? Well, let's see.

"Hello, who is there?"
"Mia is it you? This is dad."
"Papa, you usually only call in the evening. Did something happen?"
"Yes, Mom came to the hospital. She suddenly had stomach ache and I immediately called an ambulance. He took her. I have arrived at the hospital now and they do not know what it is yet. I am totally dissolved. Can not you come? Please, come on, I'm so worried about mom."
"You know what, I ask my boss if I get free immediately and then I'm just going home and then by car I'll be with you in two hours. I'm coming straight to the hospital."
"Oh thanks, Mia, I'm so worried about mom. Do you call me when you're in the parking lot, then I'll tell you which station she's on. We'll meet there then."
"Well, I do. I'll call you if I can not get away. Otherwise until after. I hurry up. Bye dad's going to be all right, mom's tough."

When I tell Sonja of the sad call, I can go immediately and I take the whole next week my vacation. Sonja is such a dear boss that she gives me immediately without ifs and buts. Immediately I cycle home at top speed, I just put a few things in a travel bag and I see that nothing in the apartment is on and off in the car and in the direction of Rostock to my parents. Are only about one hundred kilometers. On the highway Joschua remembers us, we wanted to call tonight and experience sex on the phone. That is not possible right now. I have my mom in her head how she is doing. But I can not wait to

155

let Joschua. I just call him to tell him what's going on and that I drive to Rostock. Nice that we can always tell the truth. Now it is important and liberating for me to have no excuses for tonight. Good that I have a speaker-phone in my beetle, so choose and wait until Joschua decreases.

Ring - ring - ring

"Hello darling Mia, that's great to hear your voice now."
"How did you know that it was me?"
"Well I just thought of you, funny you did not happen something? Just had such an indefinable feeling."
"No, nothing happened to me. Beloved Mia, that's good for the message I've just received. I'm so sorry and I'm sad too, but I just received a phone call that my mother came to the hospital with pain in her stomach. I do not know exactly, but at her age you never know and I drive to her. My boss immediately released me and I just rode home, packed my bags and got into the car. I'm already on the highway and there you came to me. Thanks, now it has helped me that I can always be honest with you. I do not need to lie for tonight if I do not have time to make phone calls. I can just tell you, that has really done my soul good. Honesty. My mom is in hospital in Rostock. I'll stay overnight with my parents and I do not know if I can call you."
"Do not worry, I'm surviving, it's more important now how your mother is doing, you only have one, and I'll credit you for the fact that you're going to her right now, unfortunately I do not have a mom anymore. If you know how she is, just call, then I know and you have arrived well. Please drive, please carefully and not think so much so that you arrive safely and not in the thought of making an accident, because I need you for a very, very long time!"
"You need me?"
"Yes, I need you to breathe like the air, I need you to live. For that you are responsible through your phone calls with me! Only you!!!"

156

"Thank you, that's nice of you, nice of a person you like to hear, he needs you, but that makes life meaningful again. Thank you for caring for my mother as well."
"She is also a part of you."
"As you say, yes, I have not thought about it that way."
"We can talk about it later, I can tell a lot about my life experience. Please be careful and if I can help you in any way, I will do that, even if I have to drive to Rostock, no problem. Even if we know each other so briefly, I feel with you and if you need a shoulder to lean on in a difficult time, I always come to you. For you I have 24 hours to help!"
"You are nice, thank you. I can do it, I almost always had to do everything in my life, even during my marriage, but thanks again. Gotta continue now, but promise you, I'll call you tonight, if I know what's going on and then you know that I've arrived well. Kiss."
"Have a good trip and I'll hit you very hard. Until tonight, in my mind I drive with you, but do not sit in the passenger seat, but in your heart. Bye"
"Bye and thanks."

Joschua is a nice guy. Not that he immediately understood for me, but that he offered me his help. He even wanted to come to Rostock when I needed him and we know him and not even personally. It's great. I have to thank you for that. Good that one can send an SMS so fast with the mobile phone. What am I writing, let's see ....

- Hello Joschua, thank you for your kind words on the phone. Nobody ever said that to me and never offered it. Thanks again and see you this evening. A very long and thick pusher Mia.

So and sent off and now just watch out for the road and gas. I want to arrive quickly. Good that the road is clear. daddy is so worried about that, otherwise he would never have asked if I could come. Well, if you're together as long as the two, then you suffer when one partner gets sick. My parents have always been nice to me and also to each other. From whom else did I get the feelings that were already wrong with my first husband, but that they made it possible for Joschua and me to invade his heart. As sad as it may seem now, this situation has just shown me that Joschua will certainly be with me in times of need and that I would not stand alone. Yes, I think that is also a very important side of a person, when you stand together not only in good but also in bad times. Because it really shows if you love yourself or just has sex and lives side by side. Oh I think, no, my heart says with Joschua the great happiness and the true love could enter my heart. Man Mia you should not put so much expectations in such a guy. Who knows what this human being really is. He started with sexual things the first time. Oh, he's just as starved as I am and he's longing for love. That was just love on the first mail. I have to smile again and again when I think of such things. That never happened before. There just was not that much to laugh about. Oh I fall again my thoughts and they are busy with Joschua. Yes, it always draws my thoughts. Why is this happening? Am I really so curious to meet him in person? Maybe then I will be totally disappointed. No, I will not be and besides, I finally have the certainty, in one direction or the other. So the journey time flies by in a flash, yes the thoughts of him let the time shrink. Unfortunately, the time we e-mailed or phoned always flew by. Oh, I would like to be with him now. What he's doing right now. Oh Mia wake up, it happened again. I arrived here as automatically on the hospital parking lot. Call dad quickly where to go.

"Hello Dad, it's Mia. Get down in the parking lot and where are you?"
"I'm still in front of the emergency room, I do not know anything yet."
"I'll be right there and hug you and then we'll both wait for Mom. See you soon."

And then I got out, pushed the legs completely after the

long ride and then immediately to dad. The road is well signposted and I come through the door and see him sitting there back like a small pile of misery. Good that I drove here. Both of my parents love them so much and I need them for a very long time. Nothing should happen to anyone.

"Hi Papa."

And I rush to him and take him in his arms. I see tears running down his cheeks and push him very hard and long. And after a really long period of sedation comes a sister who tells us that mom had a rotten stomach and they pumped him out and she has to stay another one or two nights in the hospital for observation. We can visit her right in the room, she's just driven upstairs. Oh man, we are both totally relieved.

"Dad have you eaten today? Definitely not right?"
"No, but we can eat something when we get home. Are you staying with me overnight?"
"Of course I will stay with you as long as mom in the hospital is with you. Someone has to take care of you."
"You mean I can not stay alone. Well, I was not any more for ages. I've been around for almost fifty years, so happy years with your mother and when I get home afterwards it would be totally empty there. Thank you for staying."
"That goes without saying. But we are a family to always hold together. Well then let's go up to mom first."
"Good we do. Oh, it's nice that we have you, my child."
"Oh dad. You have always been so kind to me. I like being part of the family."

And then we go up to the room where mom is. Oh she can even talk again right and the pain seems to be almost gone. She is so happy and beamed when she saw me and was happy as bolle. What were we talking about? How nice it is when you see yourself again after weeks, although you have often phoned. I always feel good when I'm near her. Yes my youth was beautiful and

159

I always had mom and dad as a contact person. Of course I was next to the track and it was sometimes needled, but always worn again and I have never received blows. Oh it was an often difficult but incredibly nice time. And when they asked me how I am, I started to shine. That immediately struck my mom and she immediately gave a tip.

"My child you have fallen in love with us and have not told us about it."
"How am I supposed to call you every Sunday morning, and it only happened last Sunday evening."

And it is as if a mother reads a bedtime story to both of her children, both are sitting, no, mom is lying there and listening with wide eyes. The eyes are getting bigger. Of course I leave off many erotic highlights, that would be a bit too much but the thread of the story I have made quite clear.

"Mia I think that's great but you have to promise us when it gets serious, then … ."
"Sure Dad, I'll introduce him to you, but first I have to meet him personally and then I'll keep you up to date."

We chatted for so long that we did not notice that it is already dark outside. The nurse comes in and tells us that mom desperately needs rest. She wonders why she can laugh again and brings that back to us. The sister is not stupid, we had so much fun together that mom was distracted by it and has really mentally recovered already. Something only, but at least.

"So mom, we'll go soon and I'll stay with dad in my nursery and tomorrow we'll meet again. Dad, you can stay here for a few more minutes. I just want to tell Joschua and that I arrived well."
"Yes, do that, my child. Thanks for coming. I have the dearest daughter in the world."
"Is that a miracle with mom?"

"Order Joschua of us times, dear greetings."
"Do you like very much."

Laughing, I go out of the room and I see how she looks after me with a smile. In the door I turn around again and throw her a kiss. Then I go downstairs, in the hospital you should not talk on the phone and in the car I take my phone and call him, if he is already waiting for my call?

Ring – ring - ring

"Hello Joschua, sorry that I call so late, but I wanted to let you know. I arrived safely and my mother only has one or two more days left to watch and then she can go home. I'm glad I had expected the worst. I was quick here, no traffic jams, but then I talked so much with my parents until the nurse came and said mom needs rest. Oh, I am to greet you, unknown, from my parents, mom and dad. You also realized I would radiate when I talked about you. Now I'm really tired. Drive home with my dad and sleep in my old nursery. I took off tomorrow in the business and then drive back tomorrow afternoon. Do not be sad, when I'm back home in Schwerin tomorrow we can again make such a great phone call as yesterday and the day before yesterday. I'm looking forward to it and think on the way back to what you'll whisper back in my ear."
"But do not think too much, watch out for the other drivers, still need you, more than you might think now."
"So what do you need me for?"
"That reminds me of something, are you a spontaneous person?"
"It depends."
"May I suggest something to you, it just came to my mind. But you have to promise me something in advance, whether you like it or not, please do not be angry with me, that I might be like an elephant in a china shop. If you say no, just forget it. Is that promised?"
"That sounds exciting, yes, I promise you, great word of

honor. What do you want to tell me, you make me very nervous and ... ."

"No, no harm."

"Okay, tell me."

"I just came to mind, if you go back tomorrow after-noon, it could not be great if you ... do you really want to hear it?"

"Yes, go on, dare!"

"Well, it's Friday tomorrow and you do not have to work Saturday and Sunday, then you would not be able to take the highway exit Schwerin when you go back, but drive a bit further and drive off in Hamburg. Can you guess who would expect you with so much heartbeat?"

"Hello, I shocked you, I said something wrong, please say something, Mia are you still there?"

"Yes, excuse the silence, I was just so flashed, I imagined a lot what you wanted to say, but that's really ... really interesting, but we have not known each other that long."

"You can change that in these two and a half days and I promise you, you can leave any time if you do not like it with me. But guess, you had a hard week, not only because of our phone calls and if you came to visit me, I could pamper you and give you new energy for the next week."

"Sounds good, may I sleep over it one more night?"

"Of course, but please do not see you in any way forced to do anything."

"No, are not you angry with me if I give you an answer already?"

"No, of course not, that only proves that you are spontaneous. I find it good."

"Well I do not know why and I never thought that I would ever do that."

"What are you doing?"

"Say yes, I'm coming! Hello, now you are shocked."

"No, did not you hear it, I jumped under the blanket and it is 2.80 high with me and my heart beats somersaults, I just miss the words. I wanted so many arguments why

162

you have to come and you just say - yes."
"I did not want to let you fidget any longer, I already wished for our telephone calls that we were together."
"You take my breath away, I'm so happy, thank you, and you responded to my ad."
"Well maybe you do not like me anymore after the two days and you do not want to see me again."
"I do not think so, I know, I'll never let you go again if you want it."
"It's been a beautiful day today and I feel like my life is going to change, forever!"
"I know something, my life will change then, but for the better, I will finally be allowed to be with an angel."
"I have to stop now, we call tomorrow, have a nice dream and I'm looking forward to our first long term meeting."
"And I first. Good night dream something beautiful, if it goes from me. I love you!"
"I also you!"

Oh, I can not really have said that. What is wrong with me. I have never heard of the brave people. And now I want to visit him, at his home. But at the moment I can not think dad is coming. I will not tell him about it. He would think me crazy, but that's me too. Crazy about the guy who addressed these kind words to me and whose voice made me so happy like no other man personally.

"Dad get in or are you there by car?"
"No, I came here in the ambulance."
"Should we stop at the supermarket before, then I can cook you something nice tonight and we can chat all the time."
"Oh, yes, that's a good idea. But should not we take something from the snack quickly? You've been up since this morning and the day was exhausting enough."
"Yes, well, we all want to take half a broiler with us as before."
"Oh that sounds delicious, I'm hungry for that. Well then we stop at the snack bar on the corner with us at the settlement.

163

He always has some on the spit and they are really delicious."

"Yes, I can remember that well. Although it has been some time."

"I know, some things are not forgotten. Do you remember when we used to be in the snack bar and ate there and you wanted to tear the bag with the ketchup."

"Oh yes, I was about ten years old. I've done it all."

"Yeah, and I was full of ketchup everywhere, you had pressed full on the bag and then it shot straight at me."

"Right, but where I remember it then. You both were silent and then you laughed. You both have not scolded."

"Why, too, was really an accident. There had been no intention."

"Right, there was no intention. Oh papa, you have always been so kind to me. Lately, I've often thought of how nice you two have to have you. I have never really gotten any stress from any of you and you have always had understanding for me. That was certainly not easy."

"No, it was not always easy, but it was a lot of fun to educate you, you know why?"

"No, I'm really excited about that now."

"You have a lot of your mother and some of me, but only the positive things. You are essentially a very sweet and emotional being."

"Oh dad, that's good. So good."

"Now you can understand why we did not like your first husband. He was not nice at heart."

"I know he hurt me too many times."

"And you could not resist because we did not teach you that. Often Mom and I have thought about whether we should have educated you differently. Prepare harder for life."

"Dad, do not worry about it. You did everything and what you did was great. I would not have changed my education myself."

And although I drive I see my dad looking at me from the side and smiles. He takes his hand and strokes my right cheek. I have the dearest parents in the world and

164

we have arrived at the snack bar after a short while of silence.

"Stay seated daddy, I'll get the broilers. Do you want something more?"
"No, only half a broiler and your company while eating."
"I can do that. I'm even looking forward to that."

And already I got out of my beetle and hurried into the snack. Oh the chicken are still turning on the spit and I get a very fresh, what takes the snack man just for me from the skewer, cuts and packs in two heat bags. Then I pay and I'm in the car with Dad. Dad keeps the bags and I drive the few meters. There it is again. My parents' house. How nice it is to come home. I park in front of the house and we get out. Dad closes and a warm feeling goes through my whole body as I enter and close the door behind me again. I'm home. Now only mom is missing and everything would be perfect again. Oh, I'm glad that you're feeling better tomorrow. I was so worried this morning when dad called so sadly. Oh, what luck. Whenever I think so, since I responded to the ad of Joschua, everything worked in my area and turned to the positive. Dad has already brought two plates from the kitchen and placed on the dining room table, plus two glasses, water, bionade, cola and knife and fork. He knows exactly how I like to handle the fat. I put the bags on the plates and both of us go to the bathroom and wash our hands. Learning is learned. Wash hands before eating. And before I sit down at the table with dad, I take him in my arms and press him close to me.

"Dad, I love you so much and Mom too. You have to live another hundred years."
"Oh Mia how beautiful you say that. Let's try, but today that was really so terrible for me. Now it works, but if you do not know what she has, I'm really so terrible. We still love each other so much, and if one person suffers, the other will suffer as well."
"I can understand that well. That's how I feel when you

have something."

And now we are shutting our broilers and empty the glasses several times. We still talk so much, because when you sit opposite each other there is always something to report. The narrative jam, if you live alone like me is reduced by it and that is so good for the soul. Then we just clear the dishes and go to sleep.

"Your nursery is done sleep. Mom has always moved into the beds, if you come unexpectedly."
"I know. You are the best parents in the whole wide world and I like to come. Every time I come, I feel like I'm coming home and my beautiful childhood is instantly rekindled inside me."
"That's nice Mia. Then sleep out tomorrow. I'll wake you up at eight if you're right. Then we can have breakfast together and drive to mom."
"Thanks dad, good night and sleep well. If what is you just come over to me."
"I'll do it, good night."

Very quickly out of the clothes and off to bed. Oh that's cuddly. Oops, who is there? Joschua in my thoughts, there you are again. Oh well then I will fall asleep with you in my thoughts and I'm already gone.

Friday 06.09.2013

And at eight o'clock there's a knock on my door. I call in and my dad comes in the door with a freshly brewed cup of coffee in his hand.

"The coffee is ready. I thought if I bring the fragrance, he'll wake you up."
"That's a service like in a first class hotel."
"Yes, today Hotel dad."

166

"Thanks, I'll get ready soon, then we can have breakfast."
*"Take your time, I've got everything ready and read until you
get the paper."*
"Thank you daddy right away."

And he is gone and I go to the bathroom and get ready.
Then down the stairs and I can already see how dad
peeks out from behind the newspaper and beams at me.

*"I have already talked to the hospital. Could not wait any-
more. Mom is doing very well and she comes out at noon
today. If we go to breakfast after breakfast. I take our car
with you and then you can drive straight back home after the
hospital. I'm sure you have a lot to do."*

And we have breakfast in peace with baked rolls and
jam and honey. Dad has set the table so nicely. I enjoy
being so spoiled. With me I have to do everything alone.
Since I can sit down only after work. But even the most
beautiful breakfast comes to an end and I cover with
and pack a few things from me into the car. Then we
drive in a row to the hospital and to the parking lot.
Together we go up to mom in a good mood. She has
already had breakfast and is sitting in bed waiting for
us. She shines as we enter the room.

*"Hello you two. I'm fine again, I can come home im-
mediately."*
"Oh that's the best news. Good morning mom."
*"You will not believe it Mia, it helped me so that you came
immediately and I knew you would take care of dad. He's always worried about me, and if he had been home alone
tonight, I would not have slept so well and quietly here."*
"I am so glad that you are fine. Schwerin is just a
stone's throw away. You just have to call and I'll come.
My boss is so nice, she gave me when she heard it was
released immediately."
"Thank her for it when you come back."
"Of course I like doing that. It was nice to sleep in my

cot again. And we had broilers last night."

"If you come next time, I'll cook for you again."

"That's great. Should I buy you something else?"

"No, you do not need to be able to do dad later. But I get medication and have already received a prescription, if you could just go to the pharmacy and get me the drugs for home could get, that would be nice of you."

"I'm clear. See you soon."

"We are still here."

And already I have the recipe plugged in and go down to the pharmacy. Is one in the hospital. Great thing. Oh, just outside the door and Joschua call. I could bet he's already sitting on hot coals if it really works or if I'm backing out.

Ring - ring – ring

"Hello, good morning, are you awake Joschua?"

"Haaaaaallo Mia, nice to hear your voice. Of course, I'm already awake and could not sleep any longer."

"Why not, badly dreamed?"

"No, I get the most important visit of my life tonight and I'm so excited, can you understand that?"

"Something like that, I visit a strange person tonight, but I have already closed in my heart and because we see each other for the first time, I am also sooo excited. Even more excited."

"So why, if you already have the man in your heart."

"Well, you're excited too, if you see your female angel tonight, right?"

"No, just totally, because it is the most special angel in my life and I feel it, when we see each other, my abrupt life will totally turn upside down, one hundred percent."

"Funny, I have that feeling and that's why I really want to see him! Finally, it's good, after five days."

"I also you! How are you doing for your mother and father?"

"Thanks for asking, I just went to the hospital with my dad and he's with my mom. looks good, comes home

168

today, then I start driving. Just get drugs from the pharmacy."

"Good that your mother is doing better."

"Yes, better a false alarm than if it had been really serious."

"Do not be angry, but the false alarm also has something good."

"Something good?"

"Yes, be honest, otherwise we would have met tonight?"

"I do not know, you're right. Yes, what my parents are all good for, right? I have not seen it that way either."

"Yes, you can say that."

"I'm breaking up now, shopping for my parents and calling you when I leave here. Is that ok for you?"

"Yes, very nice of you. I was already shopping this morning and guess who?"

"Mmm are you going to visit?"

"Yes, exactly, I have bought something for my upcoming angel. See you later and take good care of yourself, I need you too."

"What for?"

"Well, to change my life."

"Let's see, see you later, bye."

"Bye."

So now brought to the pharmacy and the recipe. Then back to my dear parents and into the hospital room. In the door I meet the doctor with attachment. The visit is just over and the doctor smiles at me. Thanks for the quick and good help with my mom and the doctor nods and smiles at me. Then he disappeared with the entire appendix. I give mom the medicines and she looks at me. Somehow asking.

"You have something in mind. I feel it. Does that have anything to do with this Joschua?"

"Oh mom. I did not mean to tell you that. But yesterday, when I called him and told him that you were feeling better and I'm driving home today, he made a crazy

proposal to me. I should just drive past Schwerin and come to Hamburg. Although we only e-mailed and talked on the phone."

"Take care, you do not know what kind of man this is. But I see such radiance radiate from your eyes when you speak of him. If your heart says yes, then do it. But you have to promise me that you call us if everything is ok. How long are you staying?"

"He said until Sunday evening if I want. But I could leave at any time before."

"Oh, kid. We wish you the big draw now, as I with your dad."

"Yes and me with your mother."

"Just be careful and do what your heart tells you. If you do not try it, you'll worry about it for a lifetime and always wonder what would have happened if."

"I did not want to tell you anything, but now I'm glad that I did it and that you give me such a good feeling."

"Oh Mia, be just like you, do not pretend and do not think about your stupid first husband. As you talk about Joschua, you never used to think about him. So he must have aroused something else in you. Maybe even love. That would be such a great thing. We wish you that with all your heart."

"So and now you can drive. It takes almost three hours to get to Hamburg, and if I were him, I'd be up for it."

"I just called him and he's so happy. He was already shopping because he expected to visit later. He said that was a visit that could probably change his whole life."

"He meant you that. Sounds very sweet and romantic."

"Yes, I have never felt such feelings in my life and that only while I was talking to him on the phone. What happens to me when I see him?"

"I can give you a very good tip."

"Which mom?"

"Just enjoy everything as it comes, but watch out, but other-wise drop and enjoy. Who knows if you'll shine like you do now?"

"Your mom got it right back to the point. I wish you too and now hiss off. We can do everything here alone."

"You are the dearest parents in the world. I call when I

170

am there and when it becomes something, I introduce it to you. Promised."

"Well, we'll take you at our word. He may come with us any-time you like him."

"Thank you."

I push both very doll, give them a kiss on the cheeks and then I turn in the door again.

"I love you very much. You are the best parents in the world for me."

And I go down to the car and sit down. A little teardrop rolls over my cheek. I would be totally sad if I went to Schwerin. I would be even sadder then. Loneliness is often hard to bear. Good that I have such a great job. Oh, but now I'm not going home but to a man. An un-known man. A man who has excited me as sexually as no one before him, even though we have just phoned. A man I have already closed in my heart. A man that I'm really looking forward to. So given his address in my sat navigation system and the clock indicates three and a half hours. Then I would be at 17.20. I could call him and tell you my arrival time. He's probably waiting for such a call. I would certainly do that in his place. So go on handsfree, connect me ...

Ring - ring - ring

"Hello, who wants to talk to me?"
"I want to see you and see you!"
"Mia, you already, that's great. Your voice sounds so happy, what happened, did you have a nice experience?"
"Yes, my parents are both back home afterwards. I also got medication. A lot of chatting and I even told where I'm going now. My mom thought that when I said it, it started to glow, even my dad noticed."
"So you have already talked about me, but hopefully only good."

171

"I only know good of you."

"Oh, then it should stay that way, I think that's really good."

"I believe you about that. I'm already lost and on the highway."

"As! You call me while driving a car?"

"Do not worry, I have a hands free system and also navigation system, everything already entered and it separate us only 156 kilometers and I am according to the announcement at 17:20 with you."

"Wow at 17.20 I'll stand in front of the house on the street and wait until your car comes around the corner, then I'll see you for the first time in your beautiful brown eyes and my heart will melt away."

"You flatterer!"

"No, I'm just honest, I promised you."

"I know, I think so, too."

"What kind of car colour do I have to pay attention to when you turn the corner, not that I wink at the wrong woman and then come to me. Imagine that and then you come around the corner, what would you think of me at the first sight?"

"I understand what you want, I drive a white VW Beetle with Schwerin number."

"I know with SN."

"Did you google?"

"No, I just happened to know."

"What else I should believe you so much."

"Oh, there are certainly many."

"I can imagine that."

"But almost only positive."

"You just do not tell me the negative, right?"

"Hahaha, there is not so much of it and you have to spare your angel."

"I like it when you call my angel, no man has done that yet."

"Nice that you like it, then may I still call you my angel?"

"Yes, may you. Please give me a hint, in itself I would have to make a stopover at home with me, but then I would come about two hours later."

"No, please drive through, I think I have everything you need as a woman for hygiene and with fashion, we can help a little bit on Saturday in the city."

"How to help."

"Buy something."

"Nonsense, I do not need it, thanks anyway."

"I have a washing machine and in the meantime I could provide you with a fluffy bathrobe, of course freshly washed."

"Sounds very good, but only if you wash your things too."

"Hahaha, I know what you wanted, but I also have a second fluffy bathrobe."

"Pity."

"Oh, if you please, please say, I can do without the bathrobe, but only if you really want it."

"Let's see."

"Ok, so you go through please."

"Yes, I do, I can hardly wait to take you in the arm."

"Wow, are you stormy."

"I'm sorry, my horses went through with me."

"No, it was just so unexpected and that you take the initiative, unfamiliar but full of cool. Finally, I may get to know a superwoman. But then you have to be prepared for the answer."

"Which answer?"

"Well, if you hug me stormily, then I'll look into your brown eyes and then kiss you stormily."

"Sounds great, I'm so happy, but it's still 141 kilometers."

"Do not drive so fast, you have to arrive safely because of my selfishness."

"What self interest?"

"Well, soon to experience everything with the greatest female in the world and if something happens to you, I can not do that anymore and then I sink into depression."

"No I do not want this. My GPS says I arrive at 17.18. Do you know what, I call five minutes before I turn around the corner with you, then you can prepare mentally for

me, hahaha."
"Okay, then I'm starting to prepare, hahaha. See you soon and thanks for the call. Kiss."
"Yeah, see you soon, kisses."

This guy makes me totally confused. Car drive already I want to finally see him and take in his arms and feel his kiss on my lips. Oh I get one on the lips or just on the cheek quite shy. Let's see if he does not, I will then see him with my brown eyes in his blue eyes and kiss properly. Mia right means with tongue. And the first time. Oh nonsense, you already had intimate contact with him. He has already licked you too. But only in the thought of the phone. Oh that was so nice as if it was reality and this time the kiss with tongue is just real, in reality. I will do it. Mia since when do you have so much courage. Alas, since I feel so many butterflies in my stomach that I could shake myself from tingling. Watch out for the street. Good that my navigation system tells me where to go. I'm already there in the thought and would certainly not find the way. Oh, I am happy, like a toddler on the Christmas room. Funny it is, but before I knew something about Joschua, I have always so normal thoughts, everyday thoughts what do I have to do, what would people say. I forgot something and then the stupid worried thoughts, everything works you have earned enough and so on thought. But now the thoughts are only near this heartbreaker Joschua. Whether he has had many women and has all captured and nibbled in the same words. Mia he said that he has never experienced anything like that and you should believe him now. You were not like you used to be now. Then he can experience it for the first time. That's right, I have not seen that yet. Oh, I'm getting on well, hardly any traffic on the train. Traffic, Mia where that reminds you again. Mia stop thinking, that distracts too much. Oh. I'll be with him a few minutes earlier. Oh, I have to refuel again, otherwise I'm running out of gas in front of his hut. There's a gas station at the back. And I drive to her and make brimfull once. Sure, if I have to flee quickly. Would be stupid if the car would be empty then. Stop thinking. Pay and continue the rapid ride towards my hardly to be expected almost love Joschua. Almost love, oh Mia you are really stupid. Let mom say it has surprised you and just enjoy it. Yes, that's a good tip. Oh, what does the navi say? I'll be there in ten minutes. Then I have to call him. But before I call home at home if they arrived well and I'm right there.

Ring - ring – ring

"Hello, here's Schwarz."
"Dad, it's me, just wanted to ask if you came home well."
"Yes we are and mom is fine. Where are you?"
"I'll be with him in ten minutes. I am as excited as ever in life. I feel it changes my life right away when I see it completely."
"Oh, kid, enjoy these feelings, you can not buy them, you get them for free and only once in a lifetime. Report tomorrow or the day after tomorrow if you can. Greetings, mom calls from behind. See you then and enjoy it is announced."
"Greetings back to mom and thanks for everything you have given me more than you could think. Thank you until then I'll contact you, promise!"
"Bye, have fun."

And already the line is dead and now I have to call Joschua.

Ring - ring - ring

"Hello it's me, the excited angel!"
"Hello here I am, the more excited Joschua, I'm coming outside."
"Lasts nine minutes after my navigation system."
"Ok, I'll make it to the property entrance."
"How is that big?"
"No, but through the front door, then open the gate and out and wave, let yourself be surprised! See you soon, I'm shaking with excitement!"

175

Did I hear that right, he is trembling with excitement to see me for the first time. What does he mean because what I do. I'm as excited as my first kiss, no, much more excited. As excited as Joschua's first mail. No, even more excited than the first phone call with Joschua. Take a deep breath and then Mia. The Navi says he can be seen after the curve. Take another deep breath and turn the steering wheel slightly to the left. Oh the car goes into the curve, he's almost through and I'll see him for the first time. He is probably already outside and beckons to me. He can already see me, because he knows that I drive a white beetle. Oh, there's a tall, tall person in the back. He has to be. He waves with both arms. You also seem to be as happy as I am. Let's have a quick welcome with the flasher. He's sure to be happy. Oh Mia I'm so excited, my hands are shaking slightly, no my whole body is shaking. Oh he has to be. Immediately I'm closer then I can see more than just the outlines. Oh Mia, that could be your luck, I've never been so excited in life. I hope I'll get a sentence out and not just stand there. How will he greet me? Does he shake my hand or does he hug me or even kiss me on the cheek? He will not do it on his mouth. No not that. Oh one is the tall and slim, a real man with white hair, I can already see that. And he seems to radiate all over his face. This is even more beautiful than Christmas. Oh he waves that I should go straight to the property. I do. Oh man, I'm so excited. Now I'm getting close to him. He smiles no, he grins all over his face. You look great. I also put on my best smile and I have to wave to him. Right hand away from the steering wheel, left you can do it alone and command to right hand waving. And I drove past him and stop in front of the garage. In the rearview mirror, I see him approaching me very quickly. I have to get out, I can not wait anymore. As soon as I opened the car door a bit, the rest goes by itself. He pulls her up and there he is. Joschua the man to the hot phone voice and the crazy mail words. Yes, he looks good. You even look very good. This is my man. And I've already switched off the engine and turn to him to get out. He reaches out his hand and my right hand grasps it. He pulls me out with ease. It is a man, like the man I have always imagined in my dreams, no hotter. So now I have to build up in his full size in front of him, so he sees what he gets. Hahaha gets. Who knows if he wants what he sees there. Me with my red pumps. Good idea Mia, now I have the right size. Oh, his eyes are on me, in my eyes. No not in my eyes they go deeper, much deeper. They drill directly into my heart. I'm totally gone. Mia now just do not faint. This is my man. The poor man will not let me go. But his head is getting closer. What does he do the same for me? I almost can not control him anymore, oh those lips that come to me. Oh, Mia, you can not stand it any longer and I close my eyes and already I feel his lips on my hot lips and they begin to flirt with each other as I dreamed. Affectionate and yet determined. Just a man on the other lips. A man who knows what he wants. Oh Mia does not faint. Mia are you still alive or already in heaven? How it tastes. How the kisses. Madness. I will not forget this moment in life. Oh he is restrained his tongue, where is that. But I have to look for them now, they are part of it. Lips attention I push now through to his tongue and then I feel it. Soft and moist. Oh man, I'm through and through. Now I'm definitely lifting my foot again. I always do that with a hot kiss. Oh he has noticed and holds me by my hips. You are a very tender man. I almost can not feel his hands just as little as he thinks I need it so I do not fall over. Oh, I could always stay that way. Oh, Mia, you've never been greeted in your life. But now I want to see, smell and feel more of him. I pull my tongue back, but his lips are still flirting tenderly with mine. Stop now Mia and I separate her. Then a quick look in his eyes, which he had closed like me and I want to whisper something in his ear.

"Hello, I'm finally here, I've been looking forward to such a greeting for almost a lifetime."

After a short break for pleasure he puts his mouth to my ear and whispers.

177

"Wow, an angel on earth has just touched me and reversed my emotional world. Nice that you are there, the best decision of your life."

"Well, I only came because you invited me so nicely."

"Well then that was a masterpiece of mine."

"Yes, really an extreme masterpiece!"

"If you want to drive your beautiful beetle into the garage, it will be safe and dry, who knows if we'll get to it tonight?"

"Oh, what are you going to do with me?"

"Well, I almost do nothing."

"Why do not I believe you now?"

"Mmm, I'm not sure, please drive in first."

"Ok, I like to do it for you."

"Oh, you like to do it for me."

"That's not what I meant."

"How come?"

"Well maneuver the animal into the garage."

"Oh ok."

As if in a trance, I sit smiling in my bug and engine and driven into the garage. Now my beetle is next to his car. When I want to get out he is already back and helps me. Man the same spectacle as just. I am outside, standing in front of him and the welcome ceremony begins again. How automatically. He has deliberately planned to kiss me so hot again. My thoughts are racing and my heart is doing that too. He has to remember that my whole body shakes slightly. But this kiss. He walks me through my thighs, even into the tip of my little toe. Mia, I have to laugh like that inside. Oh, I really landed on a cloud in the sky. Oh, now he is parting our lips, what he wants now? I think at the moment he could want everything from me, the first look at him and I locked him in my heart. To the mail and phone Joschua the superlative is now also the real Joschua. My heart is full, there is no other man fits in more. Finally. And I look him in the eye. It's the eyes that let me see in his soul. Blue and clear and they radiate a warmth. Ohhh!

"You, come in."
"Where in?"
"Not that, with me in the house, we can safely leave our cars alone, there will not happen much."
"Hahaha."

And he radiates so much, then he presses a button and the garage door moves automatically. Now I'm locked up with him for the first time. But I feel well, not afraid, not a bit scared. Oh, this man.

"Please come with me to the house."

He holds my hand and walks. It feels good, I never want to let him go, so I follow him into his house. Oh Mia with a strange man I've never gone to a house like this. Right the first time. Oh Mia is not right you already had sex. Nonsense only on the phone. Well, always do not be cowardly with you. So far, you have dared to do so. do not know how I could muster the courage. But for the two kisses it has been worth it, no matter what will come now.

"Wow, what's that, I've never seen anything like it."

A swimming pool in the middle of the house and huge palm trees around it. Did I land in the tropics? The sheer madness. Well that suits Joschua, he is also different than any other men I've ever met. Oh Joschua, you're driving me crazy now.

"No, that's overwhelming, I've never seen anything like it."
"What a pool as a home center?"
"Yes and the huge palm trees, like in a holiday paradise."
"Yes, this is our holiday paradise, I have only created for you, do you believe me?"

Oh, how I would like to believe that. I would be totally

flattered. But I would never have come up with such an idea while building. I would be really solid, I mean uncomplicated how to build just like that.

"No, I do not believe you, but I think it's great that you said that. No one has ever done such a thing for me."
"Yes, the men are all stupid and no one has seen the angel in you."
"Let's just say, no one was able to recognize the angel within me, let alone activate it."
"That's the way to say it. Nice that you trust me so much, gives me real courage."
"Courage for what?"
"Well, for all that is coming now, our conversations and above all our feelings. Oh, when I think about how they can explode, and now with you, with you, where I can touch, smell, taste, feel. It will be extremely nice. In any case, I'll do my very best to do that."
"I like to believe that and I'm really looking forward to it. It is overwhelming how you received and kissed me. Do we always kiss like this when I get out of the car?"
"Of course, also in the middle of a crowd. Everyone should know, I'm the happiest man in the world with you by my side."
"You always say such heartfelt words, they really do my heart good and it always screams, me too!"
"You, what can I do for you now? You have been traveling for a long time, would you like to freshen up? Should we get something out of your car? Would you like something to drink and a cake or would you like dinner or what would you like to eat? I can offer you something else too."
"You all sound good, but how should I decide if I do not know what it means?"
"Well, we could cuddle up on the sofa in front of the fireplace and have a drink and play with a lot of words or with our hands to greet you. But we can do something else as well."
"Oh, but you make it exciting, with fireplace cuddling sounds great. What else?"

"Well, we could visit the house and kiss each room. Or something else."

Now he makes me crazy again on the phone. I'll get him to the left side first. So now he has to confuse me so much. So much at once. How should I decide? I would love to hug and kiss him again. Oh that was just nice, I can still feel it inside me. Oh that's not wet again with me. Oh Mia you are not alone in your apartment on the phone, he is standing next to you when he realizes that.

"What else? Do you have a note and pencil?"
"Yes, for what?"
"You offer me so much, I have to write that down, otherwise I'll forget it. It's such great stuff you want to do with me, so I'd like to do it all with you, one at a time."
"Everyone and those I have not told you yet?"
"Yes! But I think I'll freshen up, I'll get my things out of the car."
"Good, let's get your things and then comes the question of conscience."
"Oops, what question of conscience?"
"No, first get your things and come back here."
"Oh, you make it exciting. Ok, let's get my bag."

And off to the car, I take out my bag and already we are back in the same place as I just with my travel bag in hand.

"Now please the question of conscience."

Now he definitely wants to lead me astray. Attention Mia, Joschua is a slap ear! Watch out. But a darling jerk. Oh, I've never been with a rascal.

"So the question of conscience. There are four ways to freshen up.
1. In the bathroom for the pool,
2. In the pool itself, because you can jump in naked and refresh yourself,

3. In the bathroom from the guest room or
4. In my bathroom! Now please choose or should I show you all bathrooms before?"
"You surprise me more and more. Which bath should I take in your opinion?"
"But you are also really clever, I should decide."
"Yes, exactly, please."
"Good, then come to my bathroom."
"In your bathroom? Why this?"
"Well then you might not have that far up after getting up tomorrow morning."
"Hahaha, if another man had said that, I would have fled, but I'm glad for you. Can not understand myself, what are you doing with me?"
"I have loved you and I would like to show you that!"
"Yes, you do that perfectly."
"Thanks, come with me, I'll show you my bath and then I'll go out again."
"With pleasure."

He goes ahead. One has the one crisp butt. Really cool if I can hold it in my hand. Oh Mia, your thoughts should not be heard now. Nonsense I'm an adult. That's his bedroom. It is something cool and set up as a man himself. Mmm. As I thought, a double bed.

"Wow what a bed and you are sleeping alone?"
"Tonight maybe not, otherwise unfortunately yes."

But you always find the right words. Not angry but always so that then form in my mind thoughts of the erotic kind. How he always does that is unique. Oh Mia and how you always react to it is even more unique. Hahaha Mia this is a hot game, but so beautiful. I've never been able to talk to a man like that, and I've never experienced such hidden allusions. The men I knew so far were always a lot heavier, often so clumsy that it was off putting. But Joschua is always antagonistic. Mia follow him further into the bathroom otherwise he notices what you are thinking or he thinks you are thinking of the super large bed. He stops in the bathroom door and my heart wins over my mind at that moment, because my left hand grasps around his neck and my lips start a conversation with his lips. Then automatically my right hand releases the travel bag and lays down behind my neck on my left hand. He is now standing right in front of the door frame and I take my leg up to his waist and pull up my second leg too. Now I clasp him like a monkey and we kiss each other violently. Our tongues are clawing wildly and I have done something that I have always dreamed of, hanging on a man kissing. My legs fit perfectly around him. He is perfect for me. Whether he enjoys it or whether he is happy when he gets rid of me and longs for the time when it's time? Mia no that can not be, otherwise he would not kiss you so intense. Oh what is that I get extra stop from below. How can that be. I feel his pants through the pants. Is Joschua so hot? Sure, there is only one man, but what a man and a man who may soon be there for me. Oh, what a tempting thought. I want to see his cock naked and feel inside me. Mia, that's too fast. Oh, I'm an adult, and so is he. Besides, we both heard each other during sex. Yes, but not heard. Mind, let the heart rule. Well that just wants to feel his cock. Not everything else is wrong with the man. If I do not get off him now, then my moisture will still come through my pants and he'll see them. It would be embarrassing. So still it was so awesome. Finish kiss and legs back to the floor. So thought done.

"I think I'll just freshen up and then, let's go."
"What do you want to do then?"
"Oh I would like to see all the rooms of your dream house with you and ...!"
"So, and so ...!"
"Yes, exactly and at the same time ...!"
"Ok, I put everything you need on the cabinet next to the sink, I hope it's all there for you."
"How did you buy it for me?"
"Yeah, I did not know if you had everything with you, now you're away from home longer than planned and

*with me by your side, you certainly want to feel different
from your parents in the hospital or at home."*
"Did you have a female counselor?"
"No, just my intuition and your image in my mind's eye."

And then Joschua leaves the bedroom, I close the bathroom door and make myself fresh. What he has put everything from shower gel on shampoo for the hair to eyeshadow and lipstick. Everything in three colors completely. You can not be a man, it must be a covert angel. All this for me. I almost do not believe it. As in a fairy tale. Well then I'm definitely the enchanted princess for him. Let's see how it goes on and already I'm back in the bedroom. I just have to try and I sink, what is that. Oh, a waterbed and very warm. I've never felt that before. Horny and these movements when I press with my pelvis. Oops Joschua is already waiting for me, get up quickly and strip the bed smoothly. Not that he gets angry when he sees it. But I do not think so, he'll throw me in right away and then take me hard from behind and in front and I would have to ride him. Mia stop, stop thinking. Man oh man I'm going crazy in his area. And out the door. Oops, where is he? Oh the water rushes. Oh a waterfall from the roof in the pool. What's that, it's getting crazier. The man has ideas.

"Wow even more dream, where did you hide? Juhu, shall I seek you, little prince?"
"Small?"
"Hahaha, fallen for it, just felt it already and he is not small!"

The small came to my left ear, so from the back. Let's go in the direction. If I do not find him, I'll call something crazy again. It's like in my youth. I always liked to play hide and seek. We were four girls who used to play around in the garden, but when we played hide and seek I always thought that was great. Is that nice here, the waterfall is rushing and there is oh, a fire, how cool he has turned it on and the fire is reflected it is beautiful and ...

"Yeah, I found you!"
"Yes, thank God, what would I do if you had not found me, then I would have to sit here alone on the sofa all weekend and could only dream."
"Now I'm really there!"
"Yes, that's more than just great!"
"I agree. May I sit next to you?"
"I ask, here to my side."
"So, how close to your side?"
"Well, so close that I can feel your heart."
"You want to feel my heart, why?"
"Because it gives me the feeling that there is a being, what I can feel and if you voluntarily slipping so close to me, then you want that too."
"Yes I want, but I also want to feel your heart"
"Why do not you put your ear on my chest then?"
"May I?"
"And how! Come closer. Oh, your hair smells good. Oops, it tickles my nose."
"I'm innocent, just wanted to put my ear on your strong chest."
"Yes, yes, that's what I would have said. You knew very well that your hair could tickle me!"
"Nope!"
"Well, that sounds like you wanted it."
"What did you want?"
"Well tickle me."
"Nope, I just wanted to hear your heart and look down."
"How to look down?"
"I wanted to see if something is happening in your pants when I'm lying on your chest."
"And?"
"Something, too little, I guess I have to ... ."

Oh Mia where do you just take the courage. And zack my hand lies on his pants, where his masculinity is reflected and I try to embrace them. One hand is hardly enough.

"Ohhh, you rascal. What are you doing here?"
"Well, I check if everything works, it is needed more often today."
"More often?"
"Of course, this will be the hottest weekend of your life."
"I'm really looking forward to it, when will it start?"
"First enjoy something, you have this beautiful here. First of all, I have to let the atmosphere affect me. Perfectly."
"Really, do you like it?"
"Yes, I've never seen anything like it. I could not have imagined that either. Surely many women have already told you that you invited them here and then ... ."
"How about her, then what?"
"Well, then to seduce her."
"Honestly, no, I finished the house just over a year ago and you're one of the very few female beings who have been here and they were not here for what you're here for."
"What am I here for?"
"Well that's obvious."
"How do you want to make sex with me?"
"Also, but you are here because you opened my heart and implanted yourself in it."
"Oh, I have settled in your heart?"
"Yes, one hundred percent!"
"And you like that?"
"And how!"
"Hahaha and me first. Well, then I'm the first heart waving woman here, so called maiden wife."
"Yes exactly! Absolute premiere."
"That's a very nice feeling, as you put it that way, that makes me feel very special."
"That's you too. Something very special. My heartbeat!"
"I want to be more, too."
"What?"
"I want to occupy your pants content."
"You have it firmly in your hand."
"But there are still so many textiles in between."
"Then remove her."

"I'll go smoothly."

Well, that will be surprising. Such a permit has never been granted to me. I am allowed to do what I want with him. So get on your knees between his legs. One is the one hot position is still all hidden but you can already guess it. Oh, I put my head first on his masculinity. Gorgeous and now the zipper. What he thinks of me. Whether he can stay so calm or whether he wants me to do the laundry and see me naked and feel. No, I'll put a stop to that. I want to be the first of us both to experience the others in natura.

"I spoil you, please just enjoy it and drop yourself. It is really nice and exciting for me, if I may spoil you so. In addition, I'm the first of us and that's so hot for me! "
"A woman has never said that to me, I've never had the feeling that one really wants to pamper me, only to spoil me and to do it, and that I also feel something about it. My angel is the first. Well, I close my eyes and start dropping."

Does he really do that, he closes his eyes and I can play on and with him. How cool is that? One already this situation and the thought to hold his cock in my hand makes me quite tingling and wet down. I feel my own moisture and how it gets hot between my legs. Well, Joschua, what are you doing with me? You heat me up indirectly. Well there you were on the phone and a mas-ter inside. So now the zipper is down. Oh what's that? He wears, yes, looks like a boxer's shorts. Thank god no white ribbed pants. Then I would have fallen backwards. I hate them like the plague. Bad memories of my ex. Your boxershort is striped blue. Get a little closer with your nose. I need to know how my future, hahaha not man, but smelling erotic game partner. You can not smell him. He also sprayed deodorant down here before. Oh man, the smell of the sea. Oh, that's exciting to un-pack for the first time. I want to finally see him. Feel his skin and how his cock feels in my hand. Oh, I can not

187

get the button on the boxershort. Do I have to use more power? Finally. Man now stuck his cock. But he is already big. Start Mia shoves your hand through the slit and finally seizes him. Oh yes Mia you are going crazy. One leaves me one immediately. Is that insane, oh how soft and yet firm he feels. Oh, I put the whole hand full, that's cool. Oh, what is that, if I press him then he always breathes heavily. So again and again. Oh, I can control his breathing. Is that cool. So beautiful and exciting I would have never imagined that I could unpack a man and conquer. Joschua is amazing. How can I get this wonderfully big, stiff cock out of the narrow slot?

"You have a strong voice, I like it when you hear something from the partner during sex. Oh, you know that, I told you on our hot phone calls too. Now I can try it out directly and that makes me very fuzzy. I'm already a bit wet in my panties, but you can not do that now. Later."
"That's mean, but I enjoy the warmth of your hand."
"You can enjoy even more!"
"Yes, what?"
"You, if you continue to be so curious, do you know what happened?"
"Yes, just like on the phone, the five-second fine. But you do not really do that?"
"Well, guess what, or do you want to try it?"
"Mmm, I'm very nice."
"I wanted to have advised you too!"

I have to get the cock through the slot. Damn it. Press and tighten. Does not work, repetition and again one way it does not work. Joschua will probably laugh half dead inwardly.

"Man oh man, I have never known a man who can make his cock so stiff. But there is another solution, that must be now, you make me crazy. I want to finally see him pure, smell and taste!"
"Oh, yes take it, but how?"

"Quite simple, stand up for a moment."
"How so?"
"Do not ask, do!"

Oh, the man obeys me and really gets up. It's like a dream. I think I am on a drug. Pure Joschuadroge. I feel like I'll be right there. Oh Mia you can not get a climax now. Why not continue. Oh man now he is in front of me. Oh, you can see at the long high. No, now he's wallowing my hands through my hair, touching my scalp. Joschua I'll come right away. I do not want to yet.

"Hey, stop that or do you want me to come now?"
"Like, you still can not get by, that I stroke you through your hair."
"The situation is so tingling hot, I've never done anything like that. Only when we were talking on the phone the other day did I think of something like that. Otherwise, the man has always taken the first step and I was always naked first, before I, well I must say, I often did not have the desire to see him first. I just wanted him to make me happy and he does not always have to be naked. But for the first time, this is completely different. It just makes me crazy to think of pulling down your pants and boxer shorts right now. You say, will your cock pop out immediately or slowly?"
"Hahaha, I will not tell you!"
"My fault, now I'll try it."

Oh Mia, let's go and get his pants off. It does not work. Mia not so excited, you have to first open his belt, then his head on the waistband and then she can fall. If you did that, then it will fall by itself. Where should she get stuck, on the front of his hot cock. No, the pants are open at the front. So thought, done and gravity has done the job. His pants are down but his boxershorts are still on him. You look hot in it. Male and how big the bump is in front. Good that he is not so tight, otherwise his cock would not have so much space. Oh Mia, you have to put it in his mouth as far as he goes. With boxer shorts around it. Hahaha like sausage in casing. Oh one feels the horny and bulging. Joschua is totally hot, I think if I have him naked and touch it immediately. How cool and that only because of me. I did that and I got wet too. Is that a nice get together. The game of my life.

"What are you doing there?"

Now I have to answer him why I put it in my mouth and inhaled so often. He certainly heard that. It was also the violent execution. But with a full mouth I can not answer him. Well then just released his gorgeous cock back to freedom.

"As"
"You breathe in so much."
"Mmm, you smell so manly."
"Like, uh, and."
"Do not worry, you just smell scary erotic, I like that, I smell a scent like that for the first time, wow, it turns me on! Grab your nose again!"

Oh Mia how are you talking. Oops, the words just slip out of me. Is that the way my heart gushes and my brain says nothing. It's like being in another world, a world where there's only feelings. A world in which I am alone with Joschua and only feelings guide us. Oh that's cool, I sit in the height of his cock in front of him, can see him and smell. The scent is so masculine. I like it. But there is still something missing, taste and feel. So now the boxershort must fall. Pull the collar with both hands. Yes, it works. Oops he is hanging on the tail. What now? Inside, Joschua is probably already laughing halfway over my clumsy handbag. Nonsense Mia, who does not laugh, is fully in the enjoyment phase and how. I feel that exactly. Even if I put some more pressure down, then I hear ...

"Did I feel your powerful glans there?"
"Yes, and how. Please again, it was like an explosion,

no like a tickling explosion, no like an erotic electric shock, yes erotic electric shock. It was like when the blood shoots into the glans and has no room there."
"I also felt that and a warm light humidity."
"It's your fault alone."
"Oh, I want to take that blame. You!"
"Yes?"
"You, I'm even more guilty now!"

Oh, I'm not stupid or awkward. Now grab a little further forward, the boxershorts can just slip down on his backside and I get space to get his cock out in the front and I pull. He bends down a bit with the boxer waistband and then, after a few more inches of pull towards the floor, he jerks out of the shorts with a jerk and stands out from Joschua's body in my direction with his glans shiny. It's a sight. The glans shines so beautifully, almost shines. And the boxer shorts automatically go on their way to the ground and lie down on Joschua's pants down.

"Danger!"
"Why respect?"

Well, now you are finally naked in front of my eyes, you a horny sight and the hair around the eggs, then the shiny glans. Oh, that's great to look at. I have never done that. Thanks Joschua for allowing me this.

"Wow, ohhh, yes, what are you going to do with me?"

And already I put my mouth over his cock and my lips press firmly on him. My teeth are not used and my tongue begins to get acquainted with his glans. That seems to please him, his whole body reacts. His thighs twitch and push against me at the level of my shoulders. They squeeze me hard together Joschua shrugs.

"What's happening?"
"You, you, you trigger such violent feelings, sorry, these

191

are just reflexes, but incredibly beautiful and intense."
"Lovely?"
"Yes, indescribably beautiful and ticklish at the same time, so violent that it comes to uncontrolled convulsions. You make me crazy, I have not felt that for a hundred years."
"Hahaha, you are not that old yet."
"Well, you're right again. But it feels so erotic."
"I think it's great how I can conquer you and live so closely, how it goes in you. On the phone you could only guess it and that was nice."
"And is that bad?"
"But on the contrary. It makes me feel like I'm really the trigger and it's so much fun to experience it that way. I've never had that feeling before."
"Which feeling?"
"How should I describe this. Simply to have erotic fun and be able to shape it yourself. At the same time, I feel the full erotic load of you."
"Wow, that's exciting. I'm already dropping, that's certainly the reason why I'm so excited."
"Me too!"

It gets more intense as I can watch it. His masculinity, his thighs and knees, his stomach and his sweet ringy button. He is still dressed upstairs. I will also change that and then look at this hot specimen of man in peace. From all sides. Oh, I'm so excited. I'm already swimming between my legs. Oh that's cool, Joschua is also exactly right on the sofa edge and everything hangs freely in front of it. I take his eggs in one hand and his cock in the other hand. Oh, I can slide his eggs through my fingers like eggs. Hey, that's cool and hold on and pull something down. Oh Joschua reacts immediately with a slight moan. I can really use it and he allows it. I've never been able to, the men were always against or did not want this or that. I am also very careful, but playing with his masculinity is driving me crazy now. I'm coming to the same myself. How cool is that? This is unbelievable, I never thought that there was such a thing but on the phone and even by mail, Joschua has not only managed to make me hot, but to give me the most beautiful highlights of my life and now that he is directly and naked down sitting in front of my face and I can not only touch it but also smell it, Mia that is more than in any dream, that is simply unimaginable, just oh Mia thoughts stop and just enjoy. Mia drop, immediately.

"Tell me, can your little eggs break off?"
"You'll notice that!"
"But you first."
"You're right!"

But I want to savor it fully, who knows if he granted me such a situation once again. It is like a dream. I have so much fun playing around here, like a little kid getting a new toy. It is a marvelous unit, its two little eggs, separated and yet together and then the tail to it. Everything can be played on individually but it is firmly connected together. If I pull down his eggs floor, then the tail is always pulled along and the foreskin has already completely exposed the glans. It is when I pull exactly at the level of my mouth. Even this animal smell, he has already become a little wet on the glans, which makes me totally. Never before have I been able to absorb this fragrance in such a direct and unhindered way. It must be, I want to feel this wonderfully stiff cock in my mouth now and oh how he reacts when my lips touch his glans. Oh, that is the madness, Joschua is so sensitive there, hard to believe that a man can be like that. I can see it directly not only through the twitching of the glans, no through his moaning, what he feels. This is an experience and my whole body is already starting to burn inside. I press my lips firmly on his cock and now I move my head slowly back and forth. Wow his tail skin goes along. That's so exciting. Well, I'll fill my hands with his eggs, squeeze and pull down. Never thought that you can pull that down so far. I feel every time the attack of his glans when I push his head completely to him.

"I can not stand this anymore. I'm just a man too. Ohhh, no, no, I can not anymore, I'll explode right now, please do not."

That's wonderful, he's telling me exactly how far he is. At the moment I really feel like I'm one with him. I feel him and he me and I can control him with my mouth and my hands. If I'm right, I let his little eggs go when his seeds are ready to launch.

"I'll be right, attention!"

Oh, if I just pull my mouth away now and if I notice it let him cum somewhere. That's what I did to my ex, but I've never had an experience like this. I'm on the verge of a climax and I'm going crazy in my head. No, Mia you are doing exactly what Joschua is doing. I feel he just drops and has turned off all thoughts and will just enjoy this climax emotionally. I have risked so much in the last few days and it has always been more than worth it. I closed my eyes and I will do it now for the first time in my life. I'll keep his cock in my mouth and feel for the first time how it is when his seeds hit my mouth. As it is, they just fall out dripping or no they will pop into me energetically. How will they taste? Do I like her or do I disgust me right away. Mmm its scent alone has turned me on properly. Oh, Mia, it will certainly make his seeds. Thoughts on zero. Oh what is that, I have the feeling in me, a complete emptiness spreads. A calm as before a climax. One does not exist and I do not feel Joschua at this moment. My head pushes once more to Joschua and I press my lips hard on his cock and then, I see colorful lights in front of my eyes and then feel my lips as Joschua does something on his cock. After the first violent jerking I let go of his little eggs and they shoot automatically back up to the starting position on the tail. It's as if I can feel something moving backwards and forwards in an insane speed, but it seems like I'm experiencing it in slow motion. These are his seeds. He shot her down and had just climaxed. My tongue pushes in this moment against

194

his glans on top and I feel like a hot point. They are them, they are and with me the lights go out for a moment. I really have ohhh, one i have even come. Joschua I came and I saw your climax in slow motion. Slowly I pull my head back a bit. Oh I can taste Joschua, its seeds that taste exciting. I can not say what but they are wet and hot. They squeeze my tongue all over. You have a pressure. Now Joschua is in me. Hahaha not down there, but it was like he was in me. I got a climax just because Joschua came in my mouth. No this can not be. But it is so I am seduced by this man in emotional worlds I have never experienced. I believe him through me too. That's nice. You could say we fit like a lid on a pot. Oh, that's wonderful in me. It is as if everywhere in the whole body small explosions take place and do not stop. Oh Joschua gets stiff again and some seeds come to me like a small extra shot. Come all, I love you already now. Whether it tastes so interesting every time or whether the taste always changes something. Oh Mia what you think again. Maybe the dream is over on Sunday or earlier. No, he is not by my side I have more than just fallen in love with this man. I hope he feels something too, if only a little something. I would do anything to make him happy. Oh, I came here. It's a very different feeling than when I felt it on the phone. Also a different feeling than when I slept with a man. Oh, how will it be when I feel Joschua in my cave for the first time? If he shoots like that, then I would have to feel if his seeds break. I have never. Oh Joschua. How long have I been thinking again? Oh, he's retreating already. Of course, after such a conclusion, he needs recovery. Then I want to let him slide very slowly through my lips into freedom.

"Wow you shot sharply. I thought you wanted to get out the back of my mouth."
"Sorry for the strength, your excitement art was responsible and it was gorgeous."
"So, did you like it as much as I did?"
"Liked? Can I tell you something?"

"Yes always!"

"You Mia, that was the most violent explosion in a mouth I've ever encountered. You were great with what you did. Your tongue, which pressed at the right moment on my mouth, your solid lips that have pushed me to orgasm, by your head movements and then, that has not done, while my testicles pulled down so strong. I even went to orgasm, the light really went out, everything stood still, absolute calm and then an explosion like in a thousand colours, whose way I could feel exactly and then the thought to be in your mouth. A dream. I think that was so exhausting and beautiful at the same time, I even have sweat on my forehead."

"Yes, you see! I also did not know why I did that, you have animated me in our phone calls. After that I just wanted to do it, if we see each other. But that it would be today, I would never have thought and then this experience. It was so beautiful when you came. As your cock jerked in my mouth and then came as the seeds, they taste good, I think. I just could not pull my head away, it was so exciting. I'm still completely gone. Take me in your arms, please."

And he helps me up, pulls me towards him and our lips fall into a wild gimmick. He also wants to taste how his seeds taste. I still have some in my mouth. Whether he knows how delicious he tastes. Oh, what's he up to now? Only the lips do not release the kiss is so beautiful and lets my feelings swell once again. Oh, he pulls me but cleverly on the sofa. Joschua has certainly done that many times with many women. Oh Mia no jealousy. It was just one of the most beautiful experiences of your life and what has been before has been before and will no longer count. Ok Mia cut. It counts only from the first mail from me to him and there he certainly had no other woman here. So I can be happy as his first wife here and it is so nice, because he lies flat on the sofa and I lie on him, only lift my feet. So and now Mia do not think so much. Just enjoy his tongue and lips for a while and everything else you can feel from his body. But I have so many feelings in me, after some time it just has to come out of me and to his ears.

"I love you!"

And I look at him. I see how these words are absorbed by him and he gets a serious look. Oops, I did not say anything wrong. It is a moment where I can not describe my feelings. They are totally confused. But then his mouth turns into a smile and I hear the words from him ...

"I love you too!"

I looked him in the eye and deep inside. The words came out of him in such a wonderfully deep and serious voice that came straight from his heart. I rest my head on his right shoulder and let her work. I think those were the most beautiful words I've ever heard in my life, not just the words I've heard many times, but how they came out of it, and then the tone, it was so much heart that enveloped the words. It was words that were so heavy, that they are right in my heart, and yes, I immediately locked them in. I want to keep her there forever. So lost in thought, we simply lie motionless on each other for some time.

"Oh, did I fall asleep?"
"Yes, and I enjoyed it, that peace and quiet, the feelings you send when you lie on me. They go straight into my heart. Beautiful."
"Am I not too heavy?"
"You are an angel, it weighs nothing, I only feel your presence, not your weight."
"You always say such sweet emotional words. I have not heard them for ages and many never. They do so well for the soul. I could always hear you."
"Sounds good, but then I must not have word technical failures."
"Hahaha, I have not experienced it with you, but you

197

often have such funny word formulations."

"Hahaha, that's up to you, you're just getting the best out of me, even what has been totally hidden in me."

"Well, I can do it. Not bad. What else do I trigger with you?"

"Well, if you ask me so, after such wonderful feelings and a soulful rest, big hunger!"

"Hungry for me?"

"You're the dessert, then I'll enjoy it hot and very slowly."

"Sounds good, I the dessert. Oh, am I so cute?"

"So appetizing, so sexy and so hot, that's why you are today's perfect dessert."

"How only today?"

"See you tomorrow, the hot, sexy, sweet appetizer, so the appetizer."

"Ohhh and the day after tomorrow?"

"Well, there you are the insatiable, hot, very sexy main course."

"Oh, nobody has seen that in me, I'm so versatile!"

"And even more."

"What more?"

"You are the drink of life for me. You are the air to breathe for me!"

"Well, now I seem to be the complete menu if I've been paying close attention."

"Almost, because a very important part is still missing."

"Oh, which one?"

"Well, the most important part you can portray, I have not told you yet."

"The most important?"

"Yes, important is also meant by the longest part you can imagine."

"The longest?"

"Yes, do not we want to change the subject now? Is not the fire cozy, warm?"

"Yes, but do not distract. What is still missing?"

"Oh, I can not tell you that yet, you know I'm so shy."

"Hahaha, you and shy. Say it or I'll never get up from you!"

"What a charming thought, let's try it? You do not have to stay long, I'm starving!"

"Oh, you poor Joschua. Starvation is so unpleasant and takes almost two whole weeks."

"Oh, do you hear my stomach growling?"

"And I thought it was the guilty conscience that rattled there."

"Guilty conscience?"

"Well, because you do not tell me what you thought, what's missing."

"Well, since you want to know it so much and smile at me so much, I can not resist. There is still that certain something missing. The something that you are and what you can experience in nocturnal sessions, from unpacking to experiencing to resting. How should I say, you are the special bedhop, you are the most important part of feeling, to taste, to see, for the heart and ... ."

"That's all you can do, stop it, I'm going completely red."

"Red is particularly good for you and it emphasizes the smile of your mouth, it makes your cheeks shine with a red glow and it makes your brown eyes shine."

"Sycophant"

"No, I just can not lie!"

"Hahaha, men!"

"Like men?"

"No, I have to say, you're a bit different from other men I've met."

"How different?"

"Very different. I can not say it right yet, but I have a feeling that something special is coming out of our common understanding, as I felt on my first phone call. If I talked to other men earlier, it was just a conversation or, as they say, a banter. For us, the words were always not only squeezed to my ear, but my ear directly into the heart. You have opened the direct ear - heart canal with me right away when I first heard you on the phone. I got goosebumps all of a sudden and you only knew this once in a lifetime and so far I have not had it!"

"Thank you."

199

"Thanks for what?"
"Well, for telling me so directly your most intimate feelings and for that you the dearest words, well, I've heard something like that before, but you've been almost like me, I felt right away, you're different, something special and that came right over. Like a magnet, you pulled me into your area and I did not feel the slightest inclination to fight back. I have and I enjoy being able to be in your area to the fullest and of course not only in the vicinity, but inside it!"
"How, inside? Oh, now I understand what you mean. Cool, that was the first time for me in this way. Premiere!"
"As? Did not you do that to another guy like that?"
"No, somehow I did not want that, I always pulled my mouth away before. I do not know why."
"And how was it with you, please tell me, I'm really curious."
"It was unusual. Feeling something alive in me, what you really can feel, that you can loll about, what you can squeeze, where you can feel the warmth of the other partner in it, and above all, your feelings. Your cock has always told me exactly how excited you were and then when you came, I just felt like your sperm shot up in your cock. How they came against my tongue and then swelled at her sides. It was a damp heat and then the taste came. I do not know anything like that, it was so warm, velvety and slightly sweet. The taste was full, full of pleasure. I never thought that I say something to a man. You really get everything out of me and I do not even feel bad about it."
"Thou shalt and may never feel bad in my presence. Bad is delivered before the house entrance."
"That's good, I'll do it with you."

That's the hell of madness. I look at Joschua and he not only shines on his whole face, there it is the aura that surrounds him shining like a sun in all the colours of the rainbow. I am happy. Do I shine like Joschua? I have a complete butterfly farm in my stomach. That has never

200

happened before. On the phone with Joschua, I have already felt some butterflies, but now my stomach is full of them. I feel close to him as if we've always been together and I just do not want to leave. To look at him is such a great thing for me and that alone makes me happy. Touching it makes me happy to smell, taste, lick it makes me happy. I think, no, I know I did not fall in love with just this man. I love him from the heart. Mia what happened only to you. I'm like in another world just because I'm in his arms. If I look at him like that, maybe he thinks the same as me?

"You what do you think? Something nice or crazy about me?"
"How can I say that, I've been thinking about the past, about the present and the future."
"What past and present and future?"
"But you want to know exactly. But it is really crazy. I have always been a bit different in my life, but what I experience now is totally crazy and it was only triggered by you. You have opened a door in my heart, no not open, you shot like a rocket and then stopped in the middle and have awakened feelings that I have sometimes felt and also some of whose existence I did not even know and are now they have become a part of me. I do not want to lose you anymore and will not be able to forget you for a lifetime. This is now youuu and that for ... ."
"Always? Well, let's see, maybe you'll have me over this weekend."
"Oh, I do not think so, I feel like I'm going crazy on Sunday night."
"Go crazy, why?"
"Well, if you sit in your car and I can not see you anymore, because you've turned the corner again, then you've taken a lot of my heart with you and what do I do with a third of my heart?"
"Hahaha, how am I supposed to take your heart with you?"
"It's easy, inside your heart!"

"Oh, but there is another way."
"But I'm curious which ones?"
"I'm not leaving on Sunday and chained to a palm tree here. So you will not let me go."
"If you are chained, dressed or naked?"
"What do you think again? How would you like it? Oh, I can imagine."
"Why do you think I wanted you to stay dressed, otherwise you might feel cold after days."
"Hahaha, I would have said that too."
"So if you did not leave on Sunday, not only could I keep my heart close, but I would be the luckiest man in the world."

Wow, what come to my ear for words, that's the hell of madness. Joschua is expressing what I just thought. How should that end? But what could be better than having the same feelings for each other? At the moment I am the happiest woman in the world. That's what Joschua made of me. Just because. I do not even know how he is in bed. Mia what you think again. He'll be as emotional as he is now. Oh man Mia, I would so much like to feel more of him in me. Mia you're crazy, no just totally in love.

"Yes, I feel so close to you too."
"Oops did I just say that aloud?"
"No, but your thoughts were so loud that my thoughts could receive them."
"Totally crazy."
"Yes, I think we fit like a pot on the lid."
"Yes! You it's weird, I could talk to you for hours now, but do you hear him growling?"
"Yes, your poor stomach, totally empty. I hear him growling. Very masculine. Should I get up now?"
"Yes, please. I just scurry into the bathroom and then we go to the kitchen together and prepare the dinner or do you want to sit by the fireplace and I make the dinner?"
"No, I would like to be with you … ."

202

"You but the washing machine is not in the kitchen with me."

"Oh, why washing machine?"

"Why, the women always want her when she hurls ... ."

"Hahaha!"

"Was a good joke right? Or have you ever been to the washing machine?"

"You, you did not want to go to the bathroom, or else I starve to death."

"Yes well the subject changed. I'm already gone, oh just lay a few logs on the fireplace, then the fire stays on."

"Yes, it's such a nice heat. I enjoy it until you come back from the bathroom."

"Hurry up, dream something nice or just look around."

I look after him as he disappears around the corner, then I lie down completely on the sofa. Aching once does so well. He certainly does not mind. I wonder what he has on when he comes back. How long does a man need to shower and get dressed? Oh, what is that nice here. If he knows that he has a paradise here. How did he get all the ideas. A swimming pool in the middle of the house and the huge palm trees around it. The waterfall and in front of the fireplace by the one can look through. Crazy glass on both sides. As the light of the flames reflects and then the light from the pool. The water moves like small waves and the underwater lights make everything appear light blue and the light breaks on the glass roof. A glass roof over the pool, there you can certainly if you are lying on your back on an air mattress and all the light is off, see the stars shine. I have to ask him if he had the ideas all alone and how he even came up with it. If he had told me on the phone, I would not have imagined and I would have thought so synonymous, such a nutmeg. You just have to experience this. Such a feeling what comes up here. A peace and contentment. With the chimney the chilly warmth if you close your eyes you could be on a ski lodge and if you then open your eyes again, then you can feel displaced on a tropical island and the waterfall. A waterfall in the house. This is like a holiday paradise with a perfect full service. Oh, that's cuddly. I have to process so many impressions. Since when am I here and what has happened? It seems to me as if I live with him forever and still like the first day. I can not tell Sonja but I have come to him and have already given him a kiss in greeting and even before the first dinner I gave him a blow job. One will think of that as long as I live. I never wanted to have a man in the mouth and now. In my ex, I had to do that often and that has often disgusted me. It was so mean and today I wanted it for the first time. Volunteer for the first time and that was so nice. I can even taste it. The seeds can be so delicious. I do not know, what happened only in me. I do not recognize myself again. It's as if Joschua conjured another Mia in me. A Mia that only consists of feelings and has nothing else in mind than to be with him. Forever and ever. Mia are you stupid. I can not help it if I feel that way. It's not like a match in me this feeling, it's like a volcanic eruption and the lava flows and spreads and will never give it back. Oh yes, that's what true love must feel like. The true love at first glance. No, not true, today was the first look when I saw him stand there, as he waved and when he then stopped me the door and I have built myself up in front of him. Oh, what a reception. It could not have been better. I think he liked it as much as I did. And that I just spoiled him without being allowed to do anything, I alone are to blame for his climax and also at my own peak. I've never felt that before either. When I used to satisfy my ex with my hand or mouth, my thoughts were always somewhere else and I was happy when he came and then turned aside. I think it's great that Joschua takes a quick shower. I hate it when it smells like sweat. If it happens right now I think it's great, but if it gets so dry and stinks then it's weird. Mmm Mia think, what is up to now to suspend your Joschua. You have to take that into account. Mmm if he, no, mmm it does not exist, I can not think of anything. So again in peace, he can write and talk I already knew and how he can do that. Then, when I saw him, my heart exploded. Tall, slender, white hair, blue eyes and a laugh as I love it, the whole person laughs and that is totally on. Then it smells so good and its seeds taste wonderful, the smell and also the taste. Oh Mia seeds eat and that also like. Yes Mia I'm sorry, so far I can not find anything I dislike about him. The man could live in a tent with me, that would be the same. Yes, if I draw such a conclusion, then it is the man of my dreams. Oh that's cuddly on the couch. Turn around. Oh why is it so cold all of a sudden? Where am I, eyes open, oh that can not be true, I fell asleep. The thoughts just were not thought, they were dreamed. Where is, oh Joschua is sitting in the chair opposite me. You look cool with your legs up. If he sits there for a long time and watches me as I sleep. Oh that was a cuddly blanket that slipped down when I turned it over. I did not have it before. Then only Joschua can have carefully covered me in my sleep. Oh this man ...

"I fell asleep, please do not be angry, but once upon a time, when you went to the bathroom, it was so cuddly and I started to dream. In the dream I really saw that again what I just experienced here with you, sooo something beautiful!"
"Yes, and I watched you breathing very slowly and deeply, and when I laid the blanket over it carefully, I felt like you were sinking even deeper from the heat of it. It was really nice to see you like that. I thought for myself, finally one is no longer alone and to be able to experience something like that, just to watch another person, whom one has closed in the heart, as he sleeps, is something very great. Surely other people will not experience it this way anymore and when you're together for twenty years, I do not know if it's so special to see your partner sleeping. But the last two hours have been for me."
"How two hours did I sleep and you watched me, all the time?"
"Almost, I just prepared dinner for us and then I sat down here and decided I do not wake you, but watch

you. I slipped into long forgotten thoughts and that was restful."
"That's nice. Thank you."
"Not for that, it was nice for me too. You."
"Yes?"
"I wanted to give you three options now, what we do now, but first you get a good-wake up kiss."

Oh, what's he up to now? He gets up and stretches, man, turning at three hundred and sixty degrees. It looks great on all sides. Now he comes to me. Oh, he kneels down in front of me. This man oh his lips are approaching, that will be another good wake up kiss the special tender, intense kind. Oh I've never enjoyed such a kiss as when Joschua lets his lips and tongue play with me. I also did not know that kissing can excite you again and actually makes me slightly wet. If he touched me down now, then he would feel, I'm pretty wet. But he keeps his hands very calm and only the tongues are playing with each other. If you close your eyes and drop you are like small electric shocks you always feel when the tongues have separated and then collide again. Over and over again. Oh that just should never stop. That's nice. Feelings that spread throughout the body, starting from the tongue. The sheer madness. Joschua you have me since the first second when I saw you and will never let me go again. Oh, poor Joschua. When I eat, I have to ask him later what he dislikes me. Hopefully the list will not be too long. No, I do not think so. Oh, now he's ending that lovely kiss, Joschua, I'm not awake yet.

"So you, oh that was nice, every kiss was nice. You are a real super kisser with everything you dream about, tenderness, moisture, violence, lip bite and tongue whisper."
"I'm going to turn red."
"Why?"
"Because you say such beautiful words and there are always showers of lust in the body and they bring the blush on my cheeks."

"You're fine, very well even, I find that shows that you have many feelings in you."
"Really?"
"Yes, but I wanted to give you three choices now."
"Let's go and concentrate."
"Well, first of all, I'm going to the kitchen and in fifteen minutes we'll meet in the dining room, as long as you can wake up slowly. Second, you go swimming, then you're fit again and I make the food."
"And thirdly?"
"Third, you come to the kitchen and watch me do the last jobs, but I always get a big kiss after every job."
"And now should I decide?"
"I ask for it."
"Well, first of all, I do not need to, I'm awake again, just as restful, real deep sleep and then the wake up kiss."
"Ok."
"Second, swimming takes too long and you alone in the kitchen can not, and I want to experience eroticism with you in the pool."
"In the pool we both experience eroticism. Cool and you then."
"Yeah, I'm naked or better off you."
"How did you know what I wanted to say?"
"It's clear what you think and want, but I want to do the same to you."
"This is really an announcement. Agreed, one hundred percent."
"So all that remains is third. Wait, I get up."

Legs on the ground and it is a cavalier, he reaches out to me his two hands, I grab her and he lifts me with. So now I'm getting on my feet. Of course the train is so strong that I almost bump into it.

"I want a kiss from you, now."

Oh, I get it. Greatly requested and already he has de-livered. That is a man. Whether he likes it that I also say what I want? Sure, otherwise he would not have liked the blow job so hard. Oh, how nice it is to kiss him. Oops his hands on my waist, how exciting, oh no he wants to hold me that I do not fall over, no I do not run away. This man olala!

"Hey, I'm ticklish too, hahaha, stop, hahaha, do not."

"Oh, it's a pity, I like to tickle you, because you laugh so wonderfully and it comes out of your mouth, how can I describe it, with your words a warmth that you can feel comes from your heart."

"Really, what you can feel everything."

"Yeah, that's because you push the right buttons with me."

"Oh, so!"

"So and now off to the kitchen."

"Are you going ahead, I'd love to see your butt when you walk in front of me, he looks really sexy."

"Now I'm blushing."

"But that's the way it is!"

"You are a crazy woman, really cool. It's like we've been around forever, and yet it's like the first time. But I've never experienced something like this before. I have never had a wife like you behind me. Hahaha."

"Go on, ohhh your butt dances with you in the corridor of your footsteps. Huuu, it looks really cool if you had no pants on now ... ."

"Then I would still have the boxershort."

"Well, he has to go away, completely naked and then I would always beat you while running with my flat hand on your buttocks alternately."

"Auauau, would I have to scream then or?"

"Ok, if you had, I'd fix you gently with my tongue and my breath."

"Sounds good, but then we would not come back to the kitchen and I'm hungry, first on Happi Happi and then as dessert for you!"

"On me, as a dessert?"

"Yes, I could nibble on your delicious tartlets, lick your sweet sauce and tickle your hands."

"Why tickle?"

"Well, then I would have all three things that belong to a

good dessert, lovely, sweet and funny. The perfect dessert and very important, finally a dessert that does not make you fat, but lean!"
"Hahaha, that's a logic."
"Yes, a logic that is tailored to your needs."
"You are one."

Oh cool I can run after him. Well two meters are good, there is everything to see. The lout wobbles deliberately more with his buttocks. Oh without clothes they would certainly be very tight. Oh, when can I sneak in there? I could now attack him from behind and knock him over and oh Mia, I'll eat you first will be eaten. What he does. A man in the kitchen. I'm curious. For me, when I think about it, never cooked a man properly. Ordered something from the Italian and put it on a plate and also made breakfast, but cooked. I am curious what is there. I eat everything he does. It will certainly taste. We go through a cave, looks like a pirate cave. Really the walls are made like a cave of rock and the lamps look like torches, how cool is that. Ah and then you come out in the dining room and then comes the kitchen. Oh he's already there, catch up quickly or I'll lose him. Oh, the buttocks are sexy from him. I can not get enough of it, he turns around in the kitchen.

"Even a glass of red wine while cooking, Mia?"
"Oh, I'm not saying no, though I'm just watching."
"Oh, you have to spoil your guests and especially if they are guests that you were looking forward to, like me. I think I have never been so looking forward to a visit. You are the guest of the guests for me and I have so many ulterior motives here!"
"Ulterior motives?"
"Yes, but only very dear and you can always say red as I have promised you or go home at any time and kill me with it."
"Kill, hahaha? You're a real blackmailer. "
"But you have to admit a dear or right?"
"Yes, more than that, more than that, and I feel so com-

fortable with you, as if I had always been here with you."
"There they are again, the words of yours with special meaning!"
"Special meaning?"
"Yes, the words that make me dream and think maybe it works and she is the angel for the rest of my life. Then we drink a sip of red wine and I want to see you in your wonderful brown eyes."

Oh he thought of everything, there are the two red wine glasses and he gives both half full. I think well, I've already experienced that a man has filled it to the brim. Not my Joschua. Oh, did you just say my Joschua? Mia, you can not know that yet. Oh, it does not matter, just enjoy as long as possible. I hope I do not wake up from this dream at all. Oh, he hands me a glass. That smile on his face, if he knew how I already love it and what it gives me for a satisfaction in me. I grab the glass.

"You make me totally embarrassed. Cheers!"
"It will soon be called only us! Cheers!"
"How attentive of you. So I always want to be pampered while cooking with you."
"That can certainly be set up. Will you promise me that it will always be so nice between us?"
"You never know, but I promise you will always try to make us both happy. Cheers!"
"Me too, in your well, cheers."

Oh, I've always seen this on TV when people cook or are in the kitchen together drinking a glass of red wine. I have never experienced it. Oh Joschua what you show me everything that I have never experienced in life. What should that be with both of us? I stand here leaning against the sink, lazy and watch you laying the meat on the grill. They are two huge pieces of meat and in the oven are baked potatoes and corn on the cob. Oh, I'm spoiled right here. When was the last time I ate a steak? Oh, that was so long ago that I can barely remember it. Oh it smells so nice in my nose and the red wine runs

210

so slowly through my throat and the aroma. I can only be in heaven. And when he turns to me and smiles on his face, those eyes when they give me a look as if they wanted to say I'll never let you down again, you're the woman I've been looking for and my gaze screams back, yes, yes, yes and also I have a big smile on my face. Not a grin as when laughing at another, but a grin of well-being, of happiness.

"Can I help you?"
"Yes, here are the matches, please light the candles on the dining room table."
"I do. It smells delicious, I'm really hungry now."
"I am glad! You Mia, what do you want to drink to your steak? Beer, malt beer or a juice?"
"Oh, I think a light beer would go well."
"Take a chilled light from the fridge, it gets a bit warmer when it is dipped in the Bunzlauer cups."
"Sounds good."

I'm just going to the dining room and lighting the candles. A silver chandelier for us for dinner as lighting, as romantic. Back to the kitchen. Oh Joschua already has everything on the plates. Oh he served on wooden plates. How original. Something very different. But I'm also absolutely spoiled at midnight. Oh, I have to lower my head a little bit if he passes by now with the plates and take a deep breath. A kind of pre enjoyment for me. One could always eat here. Whether he likes it when I cook for ourselves. Whether he will allow that at all. Mia just let everything come to you. He puts the plates already on the table. Matches just lay down and off to the dining room. Oh, how did he know that I liked this combination with the baked potato, the herb quark, the corncob and the steak. Joschua seems to be a clairvoyant.

"So Mia, please take a seat here."

You already stand behind my chair and push it forward

while sitting down. My ex never did that. How polite he is and attentive. Here I feel almost like home and so secure.

"You are a perfect gentleman."
"I am everything to you, you are also my angel."
"Oh, how that smells."
"Yes, our midnight meal, it's also 0.11."
"I never eat that late."
"I often, but when I'm alone, of course, not so opulent."
"Good appetite."
"You too."

Then there is a short break, where words in the mouth have no place, because the excellent tasting food finds room there and is transported down. One bite of pleasure after another comes in. Oh man, how that tastes.

"Mmm tastes delicious."
"Salt and pepper are also on the table and here if you still want a sauce, I still have some to select."
"No thanks, the taste is so great. What do you have because everything else for surprisingly good features?"
"Oh, you have to find out for yourself."
"Ok, then I'll start with it after dinner."
"Yes, you are rested."
"So you can say it and now this power intake, that gives power."
"Olala, I have to be prepared for something. But I still have some strength!"
"Power for what?"
"Well, to pamper you after this supper."
"Spoil me?"
"Well, you have spoiled me more than a little while ago and I'll be right there."
"No man has ever done that I knew, always thought only of themselves."
"Do not laugh, I could say the same thing about women,

212

that I knew until today and then you came!"
"And is that good or bad?"
"Neither good nor bad ... ."
"What do you mean?"
"Well, you are an angel and it is very nice to know you to be allowed and then it is almost indescribable that you are here now. If I had not dared to dream."
"I would not have believed it, I did that again to experience something beautiful in life."
"Yes, we want to enjoy that together for a very long time and disturb us by nothing and no one to let."
"Agreed."
"You, it's nice not to eat alone, I could get used to it again."
"You said it."
"May I pour you something liquid."
"Yes please, it tastes really delicious."
"Well and tired after the opulent meal?"
"No, I have just two hours to go slept deeply."
"That's right, it was nice to look at you. You are very deep slept and breathed so calmly. You can breathe always see how well or unwell the sleeping person is just feels. Whether you have a good dream or a nightmare have."
"Yeah, what you all know and where you pay attention to everything."
"That's part of the allround feel good service."
"I like to accept it, I feel very well, I honestly have to admit."
"I like to hear that, so it was meant to be with you yes, that's something special."
"That certain something?"
"Well, that you've conquered my heart, that's what you're like Person still a million times more important for me become."
"Wow, I'm a millionaire."
"How so?"
"Well, I'm important to you a million times."
"Yes, you can see that and that's the way it should be stay and maybe even more."

213

"Even more! Well I stay and wait for it!"
"Agreed."
"By which?"
"Well that you stay."
"That you interpret that now, I almost thought."
"Man, I'm so predictable."
"Yes, if it concerns your heart."
"Oops then I have to be very careful with comments his or?"
"No, please do not, it's so beautiful what you say and it's so beautiful almost always hits my heart."
"How almost?"
"Alright, always."
"Thank you thank you thank you. Then I try again to hit your heart. What does it look like, you are got fed up or you want a little more look?"
"Like a look up from you."
"No, steak or baked potato or something liquid?"
"Oh no, I'll burst, yes, it tasted so delicious and that was the cook, my great counterpart fault."
"Oh. Now it's my fault."
"Sure, it's your fault if you do not go online would have, not e-mailed with me and then phoned I would not have been here now and you would not have me to watch while sleeping and eating."
"Well, I like to blame myself for that. What about a dessert now, do you have enough place in your sto-mage?"
"Mmm, what do you have on offer?"
"Well, I could offer you hot raspberries with vanilla ice cream or a chocolate custard with whipped cream or a Danube wave or an espresso with biscuits or ... ."
"Or you completely naked on the dining room table and then I can nibble on you."
"No, I can only offer that for Sunday breakfast."
"Okay, then we keep the order for the Sunday breakfast firm, please with two eggs."
"Hahaha, how should I take them off?"
"I better not say anything about that now."
"Like nothing?"

214

"Just nothing. You, if I have an espresso now I can not sleep anymore."
"Oh, do you want to sleep? With who?"
"Well with the cook, is he still there?"
"Take a look, cook, are you still there? No answer, that has certainly gone already. Can you please me?"
"Yes, I would be one hundred percent satisfied."
"Good that I could still fulfill your wish."
"Did I almost think you want to get the stars from the sky, did you say well and you're the most desirable star for me."
"Great, that fits."
"What's up?"
"Well, I'm a star and you're an angel. Becoming a heavenly, astronomical union."
"You always make word games, I often laugh heartily."
"That's the way it should be, imagine you always have to cry with me."
"Then I would not be here."
"Well then I thank you for this praise. Oh, that's good."
"Please happen. And what's that chocolate pudding out of the fridge?"
"Well, now I'm confused. You dare offer that to me?"
"Excuse me."
"I would rush to the kitchen right away, take the place of the cook and cook you a fresh chocolate or chocolate custard. You can also ask for a vanilla pudding, and then I would like to have enough forest blueberries."
"You are really cute, what you would prepare for me."
"Well, if I may say how you have spoiled me before, there is no comparison."
"Did you like it so much?"
"Yeah, as good as I will not forget it for as long as I live."
"Me neither, tasted delicious."
"And so high in protein."
"Yes, I was almost full, but after the nap, the hunger has come back and after the smell, which was in the kitchen in my nose just rose, it was done, the stomach wanted more."

"More of what."
"Well, you know that, especially of you."
"I seem to be an appetizing bite, but you have to divide yourself, otherwise there will soon be nothing left."
"I do not want to nibble you, just suck it out."
"Sounds sparkling good."

And there it is again and now it has caught both of us, only started with a slight smile which became more and more and now degenerated into a real laugh. A laugh that gets so violent that you feel it in your stomach and you can not stop it. If this continues, then your eyes will start to get wet and you'll cry the famous laugh tears. Yes, with Joschua it is so far and now with me. Well, then you can control yourself again and slowly start to calm down. It was an action again. I have not laughed like that since childhood. Oh man. I wipe my tears with the served one. Oh Joschua does that too. Now it is getting less and we can calm down, but when we look directly at each other comes another laugh. Oh, now I laughed once. This Joschua man oh man, he does everything and again I have to laugh, but I can catch the laugh again immediately and become very calm. We look at each other.

"Your laugh makes your eyes shine as if you're exploding with happiness and your mouths, which you've pulled up so mischievously, until your teeth have turned into a hearty laugh, are ravishing. You're putting me right."
"Well, you were born to laugh with me."
"Really, a woman has never said that to me."
"Then you have not hit the right one yet! Thank God!"
"It can be! I've felt as well with no one near her as well as with you. You're just the ones I've been waiting for all my life."
"Sycophant."
"No, honestly, I never wanted to lie to you, I promised you, so that's the truth, not one!"
"Merci!"

"And again you distracted from the dessert. What do you want?"
"I take the same as you."
"Well, that's not true, I first asked, besides, I have already determined the main course."
"And I the delicious appetizer!"
"It does not count, because in between you have rested and then the meal began again, besides, I just mean the culinary meal."
"What's going faster, the ice cream or the pudding?"
"Did you have an urgent appointment?"
"How do you know this?"
"You can also lick the pot while cooking custard, I've always done as a child."
"And not today?"
"Still like and the wooden spoon too."
"So a freshly cooked chocolate custard with whipped cream and a cozy espresso with biscuits afterwards, mmm would not be bad."
"Ok, I hurry."
"I bring the dishes to the kitchen."
"That's nice of you, I'll take something with me."

Then this Joschua is actually in front of the dishwasher and puts the dishes and cutlery in the subjects. He really dares to stoop in front of my eyes and just stretch his hot, tight ass. Even if he did not do it deliberately, I just can not resist. I'm just a woman too. And already clap my two hands on his two buttocks. You are the tight.

"Auauau! Oops, I was scared."
"Your butt looked so appetizing, I just had to hit it."
"Oh, I'm no schnitzel what you have to knock flat."
"Have not knocked flat, just struck once to check the quality."
"And how is she?"
"Tight and hard, good quality."
"And now you want to tap the rest and see if everything is in the same condition."

217

"Oh, that's a tempting offer."
"Oops, what about the dessert?"
"Oh, after the beating test I can also do the wet leak test."
"And you get sick of it?"
"Yes, one could say so, is certainly better for the figure."
"Well, you really do not have to put up with your character, it's perfect as it is now."
"Hahaha, how do you want to know that?"
"My eyes are still working really well."
"But I have not shown you textile free yet."
"That's right, we have to catch up now."
"No, what about the chocolate pudding?"
"Well, would you like it now or would you prefer the replacement chef?"
"If you ask me so and I can decide freely, then I'll take the replacement chef! Please serve lukewarm, around thirty-seven degrees without much decoration, served on the dining chair."
"How do you want me sitting completely naked on the dining chair?"
"Yeah, so you could put it more easily and that's quick, so the dessert will not cool down."
"Okay, then take a seat at the table, I'll send the substitute cook over."
"Yes, it will be a feast. I'm hungry again."

He does it, then off to the dining room but I have to turn around in the door again and show him with my finger come to me, I'm waiting, come to me now. Then on my dining chair from the same. It is even slightly warm. look to the door, I do not want to miss when the replacement chef serves the dessert. Oh, where is he? What is he doing for so long, his Mia is hungry for dessert. I'm dreaming now? It goes out in the kitchen, the light. What comes for a figure. You are not naked. The lout he wants to outsmart me again. Oh he has a tray in his hand. What does he serve? Of course, he really thinks of everything. Sparkling wine with orange juice and strawberries. Where he has it all. The must have yesterday when I told him that I come over really have planned everything down to the smallest detail. What else did he buy? That is pure madness. It could not be done better in a Hollywood movie. Really this rascal, a white apron with bib up. Whether he is underneath naked or still has the boxershort on. If he turns around, the back of the apron will not be closed. Oh, then I could see his pussy slit. Mia what you think again. Oh he's getting closer. The flickering candle makes it but also damn romantic, no, something spooky. Oh, Joschua, you're just totally screwing me up. I notice I'm getting wet between my legs again. You certainly wanted to achieve that. You have the same thoughts as me, I want to feel you and you choose me. Come on closer I want to have my dessert now at last, otherwise I melt there before.

"Wow, it's going to be exciting!"
"I'm coming!"
"Oh, like now, I have not even put my hand to it."
"Not so, only spatially to you."
"Oh, yes, come on, I'm looking forward to it. Become very hot and wet."
"So so!"

Oh Joschua finally put the tray on the table. He has heard me. He does it and pours us each a glass but he still hesitates. Why? What does he want to know? Oh sure if I want it pure or with orange juice.

"Pure or sparkling, how can I pour?"
"Oh, I want pure champagne."
"Gladly madam."

Hahaha how I knew what he wanted to ask. Oh, I'm fine. What he wants now. Well, I'll get him upset, let's see if I manage that. Yes Mia does it and he gives me a champagne glass but I grab it with my hand so that he can not free his hand and his hand must come to my mouth. Before the glass reaches my lips, I tilt my head and so can reach his forearm with my lips and lick and lick it.

219

That worked, he really is frightened and hey, the sparkling wine will soon spill out of the glass. Quickly with the lips to the edge of the glass and the sip of champagne in me. Maybe that was an action of mine again and we both smile at each other.

"Oh, you are fast. You're a reaction master."
"You also ask me."

Well then I release his hand once and take my glass and we take our toes.

"On the very special, what is currently developing between us!"
"And never, never!"
"Cheers!"
"Cheers!"

Oh, I could ask him to turn around, then I see how the apron is on the back. You do not treat yourself otherwise.

"Turn around your own axis, please. Mmm the back is not bad to look at."
"That's what you wanted to see and be honest, if I stood closer to you then you'd knock on my buttocks. Yes I know, your quality check."
"Hahaha, that's what I'd like to do, but now just sit down in your chair."
"Ok, I'm sitting."
"Yes, I can see that too. Please move the chair one meter away from the table."
"Ok, is it that good?"
"Yes, perfect and now just keep quiet."

I will gracefully rise from my chair, slowly go around the table, put myself in front of him and prevent me something, so that my mouth is at his ear, lightly blow over it and then lick my tongue violently in his ear. Hahaha, I knew it. He shakes himself all over. Since I have to stop for a moment to then nibble with my lips on his earlobe. It makes me extremely happy and now I use my teeth easily. A bite and I pull his teeth violently at his ear. I have fun with it.

"Do not tear down help!"
"It will not be that bad and now take your hands and open my pants, first the zipper and then the coloured button."

This request will surely confuse him, but he will do it as soon as I judge him. Oh, now I'll leave his ear alone and I'll put his hands on his short, extremely short hair and stretch myself up in the air. I knew it, he could easily pull down my zipper and his hands are already on the collar button to create. Oh, what does his left hand do there, but I have not allowed it yet. She touches me on my panties, exactly on my triangle, you now feel how wet he has already made me. Darn now the moment comes where he me as well as I could smell him before. I'm so wet that he can already smell the moisture. His head with his nose is nearby. May he smell me? Oh please, please. If he likes me as much as I smell his scent, then he will never send me away again.

"Hey what are you doing, did I say that?"
"No, but I'm just a man too, and this still hidden area of my angel is so magically appealing that I'm not in a position to fight it."
"Liar! You only want that!"
"Oh, that's not how I thought about it. My heart is currently controlling my hand and it is really offended from your body line to your soulful inner life."
"Really? Hey, not deeper."
"Why is it too tight?"
"Also."
"Well, you can do something about that."

Now I will not be able to hold him back. Oh please, please please him, everything he now sees and feels

221

and smells of me. Oh, he has opened the waistband button with a slight jerk and now the gravity engages again
and already I'm down in front of him only in the panties
and almost at eye level. Well, he has the same right as I
did and he did not say anything. What he thought. Did
he also hope that I like him, if he knew how I like him.
Oh Joschua what are you doing now. Oh, I'm excited like
a little girl doing his first experience in the field.
Joschua hey, you know how to do it, he presses his
right hand against my stomach, which he gets when
pushing down his hand behind my panties. That's a pro.
What did I get involved with? Oh man, he touches my
clit for the first time. Oh Joschua, it's your turn. I am
totally out of my heart, full of excitement. Joschua oh
yes now, oh you have found her. Oh your fingers how
loving you are on her. You press carefully and emotionally, not brutally like others. You seem to be able to em-
pathize with me. Joschua, oh where are your fingers going now, oh, even deeper. Joschua, you drive me crazy.
You can already feel how wet I am and oh Joschua I
will ... no, I will not last long. Now he also knows that I
am completely shaved down below. He soon knows me
completely. Oh Joschua do you like me? Oh Joschua,
please penetrate with both your fingers as deep as you
can. I'll help you too, do you realize if I slightly spread
my thighs what I want to do now? Oh man Joschua, did
I just say that aloud or did you read my mind. Oh, you
have long fingers. Why are you bending her forward
now? Oh man Joschua what are you doing? That can
not be true. I'm about to explode without you moving
your fingers. Joschua oh Joschua you are the first man
in my life to have found my G-spot. Joschua please do
not stop. Oh, now his left hand is supporting him on my
right buttock. Oh he beats easily. Yes I know, he checks
how is the meat quality. Oh ... I'll be right Joschua. Crap
why do you pull your fingers out of my pussy. Want me
some crazy. Man I was already at almost ninety-nine percent, just had to press once more on my G-spot, then I
would have come and how easily exploded. Oh!

"The quality control has been good. 1 item."
"That pleases me. Thanks, it has been well maintained, just for you today, for this test."
"Hahaha, you said that nicely, I believe you right away."

Oh he turns me with both hands, I'll let it, let's see what happens. I hope he comes in again with his fingers. Now I stand at a ninety degree angle to him. He can not see much on my narrow side. Oh his left hand reaches into my buttocks and his right hand spreads very carefully my labia. How he does it with one hand. Oh, now he touches my clit again. Oh Joschua, I'll come right away.

"Ahhh, you, what are you doing again? Do you want make me crazy?"
"Yeah, that's a great idea of yours, I'll give you a temporary craze."
"Oh yeah! Please make me this madness announced by you!"

Oh, he understands. His fingers of his right hand circle over my clitoris very easily and gently. If he pressed hard now, I would explode. How does he know how I love it? Oh, I have to moan constantly at almost every touch now. He will follow closely as I did with him earlier. Since I could control him indirectly. Oh, now he's trying to push his two fingers in with me again. I am very close, he will notice that now. Oh what is he doing, he hardly has the two fingers inside me, because I feel like his thumb is on my clitoris. Oh the pressure on her makes a really exciting feeling. He hardly moves her and then he pulls everything away again. Oh, I moan aloud. Joschua, you want to kill me always these crashes I'm already so far. He does not want me to come. What is he doing now? Oh he pulls me down the panties completely until he lies on my pants. Now he too can see me unhindered. Oh, his head is coming closer. He gives me a kiss on my side flank and takes a deep breath. He tries to catch my breath. I have my eyes closed. So he can not see how I blush, but I feel it. I have to be bright red.

Good that he has his head so deep, then he does not see it. My upcoming heat is now slightly cooled by the air because the panties do not protect them anymore. Now his hands can rest on my skin undisturbed and his left hand now claps several times on my buttock and his right hand starts to drive me crazy again. His two fingers penetrate into my cave and the thumb lies down on my clit. Then he starts to move all three. Violently.

"Auauau."

Oh Joschua takes the pressure back immediately. He reacts immediately. Well I do not tell him that it did not hurt me, but I wanted to know if he continues or what happens. One is really careful, very lovingly. He really loves me otherwise he would not react that way. Oh he's attacking again and now he's not just putting pressure on my clit with his thumb, but is this the way his thumb starts circling my clit and he's always changing the pressure. Sometimes less. Oh now also his two fingers inside. He not only pushes her in and pulls her out again, he's inside with them now, bending her slightly forward. Oh, he hits my G-spot again. So many times in a row, no man has excited me yet. He really does it on purpose and pays close attention to my groans and knows how excited I am. And again, I am at over ninety percent. Groan. Oh, no Joschua I'll bury you, do not stop everything again. You make me Crazy. You crazy man you.

"You can not swallow the dessert so fast."
"How?"

Now he stops again with all the movements, but leaves his hands where they have just prepared me bliss.

"I would like to eat the dessert now but very quickly. Please, please continue!"
"So, and then you'll ask for a lookup afterwards?"
"Let's see."

I still have a fifty percent excitement and Joschua lets his hands dance again. His left hand is now clapping in tact on my buttock, a light hit again and again. It really makes me feel and excites me more and more. Oh, now he continues the orbits with his thumb on my clit. The excitement rises. He knows exactly how to do it. He increases the pressure on my clit. Oh please, Joschua please do not stop it rising so wonderfully evenly and not a thrill thin as a rope, but like a long cloth quite wide on all levels. If he continues to play on or in me, then it's about time. But it would not be Joschua if he could not add something else. Yes Joschua is right for me and my sex life. He flexes his fingers forward and hits my G-spot. His fingers are quiet but he starts to press firmly on this point. Yes that's the madness, so I have never felt it, no one has done so with me. That also works and how, one climbs, no it shoots to unexpected heights. There is already cloud seven if he keeps going I shoot far beyond. Joschua I'm coming right now, oh I'm getting dizzy, I'm starting to shake and I see ohhh colourful lights in front of my eyes closed and ...

"Ahhh, ohhh, now, yes, ...!"

A loud silence spreads. Joschua does not pull his fingers away, he leaves them in peace on the spot. My breathing and my heartbeat are slowing again and want to return to normal rhythms, the twitching in the abdomen ebbing away and the shaking of my legs subsides. Then it happens, but slowly he pulls his fingers out of my cave with pressure and my excitement makes a small ascent again and this is again hit me a bludger on my right buttock. Oh, Joschua, what are you doing? Now I'm starting to relax again, slowly, slowly, I'm coming back to the normal world. Nonsense, with Joschua I do not live in the normal world, that's a dream world somewhere. Now I let my hands slip from his head and sit on his thighs. We look at each other.

"That was the tastiest dessert I have ever been served."

"That was the heaviest dessert I was ever allowed to serve."
"What will become of us two gourmets only?"
"Well culinary sex foodies with a strong tendency to love delights of the extra class."
"You always have crazy descriptions and above all the right words."
"Do you find? You draw it out of my innermost."
"That's great. Let's see what else I can elicit everything."
"Oh, there are certainly many things over time."
"Yes, time has become totally irrelevant with this menu. Have you ever looked at the clock, it's already three o'clock."
"Class then we can cuddle something in bed before the sun rises"
"Sounds good, I'm in it."
"But you have to get up and follow me."
"Follow where?"
"Well on the warm cuddly meadow."
"Well, may I pass the bathroom before?"
"Of course, but only if you come out naked then."
"Naked?"
"Yes, completely naked, without everything. Just get naked and then cuddle up in bed next to me and take me in my arms."
"You are the man, you have to hug me."
"Ok that is alright. Come on, get up, I'll accompany you to the bathroom."

I have to get up first. Oh, I'm still really shaky on my feet. What Joschua was doing with me is incredible. I have felt so many feelings in me, I have never had, and earlier I was able to give him this luck and I have come here even the moments of happiness. If I overfly it that way. I am currently the happiest woman in the world. Oh how nice, he takes my hand and we walk along the pool to the bedroom. Oh he wants to go to the bathroom and watch. Oh man, I am so happy today, I would be able to endure everything. But all my doubts were unfounded.

He lets go of my hand in front of the bathroom door. Oh he pushes me and I get another kiss.

"See you in the cot."
"Well, I hurry."

Oh, I'm still full of feelings. So bathroom door too fast to get ready for the night. Just take a quick shower again. It's so good. Dry off, brush your teeth and then off to bed to my Joschua. I feel like I've been with him forever and everything is normal. But it's the first evening and I have had so much sex with him and not even seen him naked, at least not completely naked. But he does not hahaha me either. We'll pick that up for tomorrow morning. He'll certainly be when I'm in the room in bed. Surely he is completely naked and happy if he can feel me everywhere. Well, I'll make him happy too. I have not even unpacked my night clothes. If this continues I will certainly need hardly any stuff during my visit here with him. Oh Mia what you think again. Yes, the thought just shoots through my head. I've only been with him for almost ten hours and have experienced so much and learned about my body myself, that's just plain unimaginable. Yes, Joschua seems so familiar to me. When I arrived, my heart beat with excitement and also some fear wildly, but since the first glimpse of him only the excitement has remained. I have not been scared of anything we've done and what I've done and I've been allowed to experience it. No, Mia, that's not you, you've always been so reserved and careful. Everything was thrown over Joschua because of Joschua. That something like that happened to me would have never been thought of in my life and if I had seen that on TV as a movie, I would have smiled and thought about it. Yes but not in real life. The feeling I feel right now must be true happiness and if that is it, then I know, I was not really happy in my life before. So finished with everything and naked I am too. But he should not see me like that now. I just turn off the light in the bathroom and then he can only see my silhouette when I crawl into bed very

227

quickly. Oh Mia you creep into a strange double bed to a man you barely know. Oh thought stop now, I just want to feel my heart, as come from the most beautiful feelings I have ever experienced and that because of this man who is right next to me in a double bed and in his strong arms I cuddle me right in and into the country the dreams can migrate. So Mia light in the bathroom and attention, bathroom door on and through. I quickly go to the cot. I can only see a head lying there. So I crawl quickly under the covers and snuggle up to him. But he is warm.

"Ohhh, that's nice and warm."
"Yes, the water is 30 degrees. Now you do not need to freeze, as in the past, because you had to warm up the cot first and that took a long time. The warmth makes you tired quickly too, you will soon see."
"Not only the warmth, the whole day was amazing. Starting with the drive to you, the excitement where we met for the first time and then the many excitements that followed."
"Yes, I've never had so many erotic experiences in one day."
"Neither do I. But my body thought that was really great and just wanted to experience so much. Catching up and with you it was stunningly beautiful."
"Thanks, but you did most of that, too, with your great body, and above all, with your hot feelings and many of your own ideas. That was the best day in my life, if I may say so and I thank you from the bottom of my heart."
"Mine too! May I put my head on your chest. I would like to hear your heartbeat so much. Do not be angry, do not go to any trouble right away."
"Never mind, I'll follow you right away. Dream something exciting and thank you for the unforgettable hours."
"Good night dear Joschua."
"Good night beloved Mia."

And the thoughts of our dreams pick us up immediately.

Saturday 07.09.2013

It is the morning after. It was the night of the nights, it exceeded all expectations - oops, I hope, too, for me. The sun is already quite high in the sky and the sun rays penetrate not only in the room, but also in my heart. It is still completely open because of Joschua and that's a feeling like floating on clouds. I have not moved yet, only my eyes and thoughts are awake. He's still lying next to me and I see it's like a smile on his face. Is he still in the realm of dreams? In any case, in the realm of positive dreams, you can see it directly. It is great considering that you only need to look at your partner and can feel what is going on inside him. And it is even better that I am responsible for this positive feeling with him. No not only with, but it was me. Super, my ego, I have strengthened so indirectly also. My heart and emotions have driven Joschua to unimaginable heights. Oh, I can not even think about how long I have wished for such a thing and I thought I will not be able to experience such feelings. One often thinks, in the age of sex is less, perhaps less in number, but it is much more intense, perhaps this has to do with the experience or else with the wishes and ideas that one dares but then more and do also to find the partner who is especially compliant or who is so open to try it out and add some of his elements as well. This is like the salt in the soup, which then gives the certain icing on top and determines the length of the feelings, in the process and afterwards. Well, I know when you drink champagne for the first time in your life it's a tingling, wonderful feeling, but if you drink it all the time, even if you change the variety more often, that means not only the men change, but you having found the man where the heart says that's it, I mean to change the things you experience sexually with him, whether you're passive or active, day or night, in or out of the house. There are so many possibilities, but even these are emotionally commonplace at some point in the day and this high level of flinging out of emotions is almost always reserved for the novelty, so you can always enjoy them to the fullest. Oh Mia, what are you thinking of again? Just enjoy his smiling face and the rest, which is still covered by the blanket unfortunately. But you know, when we fell asleep last night, no, it was already this morning, he certainly had no textiles on. If I turn my head to look at him, he'll wake up. So just let his smile play in the mind's eye. When he gets up to go to the bathroom, he will walk around like God made him. Oh that will be a great sight again. Oh, how I look forward to it again. So far I have not seen him completely naked, at least not in all his beauty. Beauty is good. How can a man be beautiful? Mia clearly he can be built beautiful and harmonious and then move smoothly. If he is brown or white, he has pimples or no, how is his skin, soft or rather hard. Well, you know that, where you could see it, he had no pimples and his skin was slightly brown and very soft. Yes, everywhere she was warm and soft. What I saw was beautiful and it worked perfectly, it just can not get any better. Yes, a whole man with everything. What luck do I have? Well, you do not look so bad out of Mia. And your body has been well preserved. I also always cared for him. And now I think it's great, mine is also a bit brown. Of course I go to the solarium once a week. Whether Joschua likes that too, a slightly brown body. Well, when I'm awake and he has to go to the bathroom, I'll see him. He will not be like the bed in the movie so often the bed to cover? No, then I just tell him he wants to please leave and go to the bathroom naked. He will certainly fulfill my wish. Yes, I know he will fulfill that. Oh, these thoughts always, as if a man consists only of thoughts.

Am I awake? Did not a door move? Oh yes something open my right eye. I'm lying on my left side. Oh there Joschua is, he was in the bathroom and I did not hear it. Oh, that rascal, he's wrapped a towel around his waist. He does not know yet that I'm already awake and watching him as he tiptoes slowly to the bed goes. Oh that looks great in the light above but also great. Man a super copy. Oh, for me, a man does not have to have a six-pack. He has a very small stomach, oh there I will often cuddle up and tight skin everywhere and the arms have some muscle to offer. That has to come from a lot of swimming. If I get it too. Oh, I'll leave tomorrow. It does not work that fast with the muscles. Yes, he is slightly brown everywhere. So he goes to the solarium just like me. Another commonality. Then we can go together. No, not in a cabin but in the same studio. Oh Mia you should be able to hear yourself, just like if you want to stay here and never wanted to leave. Oh why not. Judging by my feelings that would be exactly right. He and I connected and forever as happy as yesterday and in this moment. I am really happy. In any case, my body feels so much in my little toes. Is that still from yesterday evening or again from this morning, so now. I can not figure out that and I do not have the time, because Joschua has al-most arrived at his bedside and makes ready to cuddle under the cot again.

"Good Morning Joschua!"

Oh, he jumps startled and goes down from his ten point. I really scared him. He did not expect me to be awake and he did not even notice my eyes blinking. Poor Joschua in the morning trouble with this stupid Mia.

"Oh, I did not want that."
"What not?"
"Well scare you."
"Ne did not hurry ... but totally frantic, although I almost expected it, but you were faster and better. Since when are you awake?"
"I just heard the bathroom door, but it was still so cozy in the cot and I thought, I'm just waiting for you."
"Cool, for the wait you will now be rewarded."
"How to reward?"
"First of all with a ... ."

And he bends down to me and presses my lips on his. A

gentle good morning whisper begins and I put my arms on his shoulders. Then I pull him close to me and in that moment his tongue is already in my mouth again. Hahaha, he can not get away, he feels the pressure of my hands and arms on his neck. I pull him down to me and his lips and neck follow his whole body and then he lies half on his side on his bed, his head is already with me. Crap so I can not get him to me under the down comforter. At the moment I have no way to get him directly on me. So Mia let it go, let yourself fall and enjoy the warmth of his mouth and his lips. Oh, how that works well again. I have my eyes closed and I am floating in a blue sky, surrounded by white clouds that lovingly envelop me. In addition a light cool breeze, no it becomes a warm desert wind, which blows emotionally from above over my entire skin down to the toes tips. It is as if I can follow this piece by piece and feel at each point, pausing for a moment. To experience such a thing in the morning and that a partner is so active, otherwise had only tired partners and never thought, there are others. I'm just brought up, the initiative comes from the man, but I've always wished me, it goes from me and lo and behold, here at Joschua, this desire is already partially fulfilled at the first morning awakening. I pulled him to me and he followed.

But how can I get him under my comforter now? Ahhh, I have an idea. I finish the kiss and just ask it. Will you come under my blanket to me? I have to praise myself, a cool idea. And off. My body rolls to the side and my lips tear away from his own. So fast that I can still see his tongue in front of her lips. He is quite confused and looks after me, but before he can say anything, I ask him and he smiles. Immediately he gets up again and then he crawls under his blanket, where he lets his towel fall off his hip when he crawls in and he crawls immediately to me on my bed half and under my blanket. My hands are in the way and hit his body. They touch his stomach.

"Ahhh, ohhh, you are freezing cold."

"Please, please warm me."
"Well, then come under my blanket. Ahhh do you want to catch a cold?"
"No, just refresh and bring in the day."
"Oh, that's what you call it!"
"Yes, and now come to the cold, my handmade feelings between your thighs."
"Brrr, cold."
"Not for long and then you'll be hot! Promised."

And his right hand has already opened the way between my thighs in the depth and now tries to penetrate slowly. It is still very dry and so it begins only on the surface, caressing and rubbing circling. Well, the day before yesterday I shaved down there. Mmm or would he rather have found a jungle. Oh, do not ask Mia just enjoy this wonderful hand.

"Well, still freezing?"
"No, it's getting warmer and more comfortable."
"May I continue?"
"Yes, please, it is already getting warmer."
"And moister."
"Yes and I get more excited. That's nice, not quite down from dreaming in seventh heaven, maybe only on the third cloud and now switching back up the elevator."

I feel on his right middle finger, as he slides a little deeper. Yes slide, there it is the moisture, it comes up from the depth and now wants to be whipped through properly. And his right index finger begins to move to the middle finger to hand and both manage to penetrate with a very slight pressure in deeper wetlands. Slowly, they describe a small circle that always keeps in contact with my inner side through the pressure to the outside and thus gives me growing feelings. Stop, a complete finger rotation stop and a slight withdrawal and then turn again, but not in depth, but around my clit.

"Ohhh, how nice, do not stop."

233

But the exact opposite is the case. The rascal keeps his right hand completely still, only a slight intensifying pressure flat on my clit and again sounds like automatically from my mouth ...

"Ohhh, yes, please keep going, ohhh ...!"

I know that he loves it when I say something and not lay out like a board the most beautiful thing in the world. And he slowly starts to move my clitoris between his fingers back and forth and push something. Careful, he does not want to hurt me. I am only at the beginning of the excitement and then it is sometimes painful, so let go with the pressure and again circling into the depths. How does Joschua know that just how to make a woman happy? Is that in any textbooks? He makes it so cautious, as if he could feel every feeling I experience. Anyway, he always reacts immediately. A really tender man and I found him. You poor other women. I keep it for myself now. That's why I'm going to fight.

"Ohhh, what are you going to do with me?"
"I, but nothing."
"Liar, you touch me totally."
"Oh, you mean, I can not help it."
"How can you not help it?"
"Well, your wet depth just pulls me in, I'm almost completely innocent."
"Innocent, hahaha, you're a rascal. Please do not stop and go on, deeper, deeper, deeper, faster."
"No, slowly, you do not want to come yet."
"Hahaha, come, I'm already here."
"Hahaha, I do not mean that, come with your orgasm."
"You make me crazy with your fingers, I'm pretty much ahead of it."
"Where?"
"Silly, before my climax."
"Well that can not be."
"How so?"
"Well, you can still talk too much about it."

"Oh, no, ohhh, yes, please, please push a little more, faster, faster, ohhh ... yes!"

And again he puts in a complete hand rotation and -ruckstopp and stays down there very calmly. I feel my breath slow down a bit and my moisture gets a little less. My Joschua seems to be able to determine exactly with me. The closer I get to the climax, the more moisture comes in and I feel like the moisture is getting smoother. Joschua also seems to have noticed that as another indicator of my emotional world. Now I'm a little thicker again and immediately he starts again with the movements. He just lets me down a bit in the excitement, not quite. How does he know that, if he drops me all the way down it will be harder to restart. Is then always like a reboot. But Joschua always makes a warm start. Hahaha, if he knew what thoughts of that kind come to my mind before I can drop myself completely. Oh with Joschua I can at least, in the past with my men I was often unable to do so for many different reasons but this Joschua makes it finally possible that I can experience such feelings pure without thought simply with the heart. I'm still very tight down there, he just comes in with two fingers, that's great. Some women are said to be so far down that the man can put a whole fist into it. Oh, he probably feels as much as I do now. No matter, I'm me and that's what counts now. But what is he doing now, not only that he always penetrates to the rear, no, now he is looking for my G-spot again. And he finds him. Straight in and then turn to the front and back, there he is and he seems to be waiting for his fingers and enjoy it to be finally touched and used. Oh, that's a man. A man who really looks after me when he loves me and does not just think about himself. That's great, because then I can think of him. He proved to me last night that he allows it and enjoys it. So we both have something very special about it.

"Hey, what are you doing with me, hey, not, not, ohhh, ...!"

And I feel with every touch of him at my G-spot sounds automatically with me a hot tone and my body makes a twitch. It's great how he can make sounds in just the right place with just one touch in me, just as he wants.

"I'm coming! Now!"

And all at once I stop breathing like it automatically, it gets very quiet in my body, a silence that wants to keep the excitement up longer, I feel it exactly then to come immediately as in an explosion. I feel the twitching in my whole body and my breath is heavy but slows down gradually. My heart is racing as if I had climbed Mount Everest. Hahaha, good comparison, the Mount Everest of emotions and I did not get up, Joschua catapulted me up. Oh how can a man caress one to climax. That's just great, you can follow every moment of tension in me, everywhere in the body. I did not know that I have so many muscles and other parts in me.

"Hello, good morning my angel! Are you coming back to earth, then I'll have breakfast. Do you want an oak?"
"Only your two eggs!"
"Oh no, they will come later, now we need something for the stomach, otherwise we'll lose our strength today."
"Please stay with me for a moment, is so nice."
"Yes, that has become so nice and warm through you."
"But you are also to blame for the most part."
"Okay, take that blame on me. It's such a nice debt, I can live with it."

And we cuddle for a few more minutes until the greatest excitement has subsided again and I open my eyes and he smiles at me. With this wonderful warmth under the covers, with him together I could fall asleep again. Oh, it's wonderful of a male being that you really, very sweetly love to be spoiled. And I have as much fun with him as he seems with me, because it seemed to him to have gone the same way with me last night. What a great coincidence it is to find a person who seems to think and feel just like me.

"You, little angel, when I get up in the morning I always go swimming, will you come with me?"
"That will definitely wake me up, right?"
"Yes, that makes you fit for the upcoming day."
"Ok, then I'll go to the bathroom first and then come. Are you already in the water?"
"Good, I'll wait for you in the bathroom."
"Why, can you proceed or do you think I'll fall asleep again?"
"No not that."
"What?"
"Well, let's just say, if I'm lying in bed here and you have to go to the bathroom, then ...!"
"Oh, you want to see me completely naked as I scurry into the bathroom. And then I'm sure to turn around in the door and throw you a big hand kiss."
"Can you read My mind?"
"No, but I would have done that too, so you go to the pool first."
"No, then I have my towel around, which is in front of the bed. There's nothing to see."
"Oh, what you do not say, the rest of your body is also beautiful to look at."
"Oh, thank you for the compliment! Never has a woman said so nice to me."
"Thanks, but we promised not to lie."
"Hahaha, you learn fast, you used my words from yesterday."
"Did you notice that?"
"Yes."
"I liked them so much, so I thought, I can use them sometimes."
"Sounds good and I like what you said. But you off to the bathroom!"
"How do you want me to do that?"
"Yes, little angel, duvet, get up, go to the bathroom and slowly turn around while you walk, around the whole axis."

"Yes sir. As commanded."

And I push the blanket away. Oops, it gets really cold. Get up, turn your head to him and smile at him.

"I love you, sir!"

He seems to be totally confused. What I said seems to go through him thoroughly. It's very special what my heart feels for him and I have to tell him that. I'll walk slowly and provocatively in front of foot with the bathroom and smile at him constantly. Then I suddenly turn around standing foot, look directly at him and wiggle my bare breasts back and forth. He has not seen it that way yet. Yesterday evening they were all still packed and when I crawled into bed, it was very dark. Let's see how his face changes, if he likes her? Oh dear, what do I have to see there, his gaze hangs like magic on them. Oh, but he seems to fix it exactly. He liked that, otherwise he would have long ago gone away. I like them too. Firm and firm, not hanging. Oh, what are you doing to Mia. It seems to happen to him something like automatic. Judging by his gaze, I feel the blood is pouring down on him. Then I have to stand here from his point of view anyway somehow. But he wanted to swim and then have breakfast, otherwise poor Joschua starves me, so I turn around again, wiggle my buttocks and go in the direction of the bathroom.

"Do you want make me crazy?"
"How are you getting hot?"
"Do you want it?"
"Yes! Now!"

And I take two quick steps to the foot of the bed, with a violent and very strong jerk away the blanket, drop me next to him on the bed and smile at him. Again, like last night he lies completely naked in front of me. All right, this time completely naked. I sit on his knees and he feels the pressure of me. I'm already lustful again? I lay my hands on his thighs and lead them pushing and stroking with gentle force higher and higher, my thumbs touching his testicles and he jerks violently. He stands like a one and I look at him unabashedly and ...

"Man, this morning looks almost better than last night in the fireplace light."
"Oh thanks, if you like it, then you can use it too."
"Ok."

He does not say more, just looks at me, somehow expectant. I keep sliding up. Until, until I can almost feel my pussy his cock. He looks at me smiling the whole time. He watches me intensely at every touch and my breath reacts immediately. Now he plays with me. Slowly I raise my pelvis and slide a little higher. On his glans I see very clearly he is already wet there and my pussy too. Still from now and again from this splendid sight of his masculinity. He is stiff again. Apparently also excited when he catapulted me so high. What's going on in his head? Whether he thinks as much as me and what he thinks now, but I'm not coming with my thoughts, because I feel like his cock pushes very slowly into my pussy. Wow! Wow! What a feeling. I have not been able to experience that for years. At the same time, our eyes meet and stick to each other as if firmly. No one lets the other out of his sight and the deeper he pushes him into me, the more intense his breath will be. That one can feel so much, although we hardly move. That must be because of my tight pussy. I feel its warmth, a warmth that can not be easily described. No heat as from a heater, no heat as from a chimney or the sun's rays in summer, but a heat that can only come from another creature and then my moisture. She is right to hear and I feel like his cock pushes her on further immersion and she lays around him, like an exciting warm movie. This continues until his cock docks directly on my cave wall. He is inside. Wow, but now he starts to squeeze blood into his cock. I feel that very clearly because he moves without our bodies move even a bit. What a feeling. I did not know that a man can influence that way.

"Oh, oh, oh, yes, yes, more ... ."

I feel every movement of his cock and every time he pumps in blood, I realize how he gets stiff. He is thus a little bigger and harder and I feel it on my pussy inside very clearly. His glans is so hard and firm, but also so sensitive. I feel a twitch every time he teases somewhere in my pussy. Hahaha a plump round glans that teases. Oh her thoughts do not play with the words. Feelings to power. I sit on him and his cock presses each time when pumping against my G-spot. If he does that more often, I feel like I will explode once more. Our eyes are still fixed on each other, but I notice how a slight blush forms in his face and on his forehead he begins to get wet. My Joschua starts to sweat without body movements. Well, that's not quite true, because his cock works like that is also a part of him, a very important part. This is a special moment, because it is in my hands when he comes and how. I have stretched all the way to the back and so pressed his cock ever more firmly to my G-spot. This always puts me a cloud higher. My hands are resting on his knees. What a sight I have to leave for him. He can look at my entire upper body, although our eyes are still connected. My beautiful breasts have become very tight and are now like cheeky almost in his direction. My nipples have become very hard and big. It feels like my whole body is taut like a bow. Now I have it in my hands and I will ...

"Oh, oh I'll be right over, go on, please, do not stop."

Oh, I'm close to the point of no return. Now fast. But Joschua is still on top of what he expected, instead of waiting for what I'm doing. He rips his hands up, takes my nipples between his fingers, presses and pulls hard, while he pumps blood into his cock and make with my legs a strong back and forth movement and massage his stiff cock in me. Goes perfectly because of my tightness, the friction is enormous with him and then it is so far with him and I feel it, this time not in the mouth but in my pussy. I clearly feel a huge twitch and then shoot his sperm through his cock, kick out of the glans and squirt into me. Wow that feels so gorgeous, like last night the explosion in my mouth. It is hot in me, especially hot and I move only very slowly back and forth and I distribute so his semen all over his cock. That was such a wonderful feeling that it happens now also with me ...

"Yesss, yesss, yesss, ohhh!"

And he knows what I love, how did he get that out? Exactly when I explode he lets go of my nipples, just like me his eager eggs down. That always gives such a little extra kick, with me as well as with him. Oh that's nice if you are spoiled as you like it and how to get the most out of his explosion feelings. Really Mia this is the first man that can with you but I believe and I trust him what he tells me, I am for him also the first woman who can arouse such feelings in him. When I think about it, I've had those feelings in my life for a lifetime and never did a man activate me like this. Oh how happy I am that I got to know and love Joschua.

"Auauau!"
"Oh sorry, did not want to confuse your feelings."
"But you have!"
"No, you attacked me."
"And how, I had a lot of fun doing that. You challenged me."
"How challenged?"
"Well, first you wake me, then you love me and then you want to look at me everywhere and I have to walk up and down in front of you, with all sides to look at. Do not you think that makes me sharp and then the thought of how you lie under the covers. Naked, completely naked!"
"Thanks for sharpening through me."
"Oh please, please, I really liked it."
"And now you want to go to the bathroom."

241

"Yes, I'm running out otherwise."
"Well, then I just go to the pool shower and then into the water. I'll wait for you there."
"But I do not have a bathing suit with me."
"Oh God, what are we doing there? So, with a wrapped towel, no, you can lose it in the water and I have to dive it back."
"So, how should I appear?"
"Mmm, there comes to me a thought of lightning, which I did not come there earlier."
"Lightning thought, which one?"
"Just come the way you are dressed now, uh, move out. That's the hottest disguise."
"I could have thought of that again, that you say something like that."
"Really, am I that bad?"
"No, not that, but so greedy."
"Yes, I'm eager to see you like this and feel it under water again. Everything feels totally different then on the dry land."
"No, it will not touch. I'm supposed to swim for health and fitness."
"Who says that my touch does not contribute extremely to health promotion."
Yes, you are right again. See you then. And you also get naked in the water!"
"Sure, of course."
"See you soon!"

And I'm already breaking loose from his thighs, our skin has become slightly stuck due to the super erotic experience. I really notice exactly how his cock slowly slips out of my vagina and again sees the light of day. Splash, now he is already very weak on him. Were these feelings, wow! It is empty in me without his tail. I slide a bit back to the foot of the bed and stand in front of it slowly. My legs have to sort first, well I mean my muscles in them. They were so tense and then relieved by the erotic explosion. But now I have to hold my left hand between my thighs, do not want to lay a drip track

242

here. Now turn off to the bathroom, oh now he sees me from behind and I could do everything I have, he looks at me and on my buttocks. Funny that I always want to make him happy. Now with a funny looking way to the bathroom. I myself enjoy heating it up like this. I never felt that before and therefore did not do it with my men. But no one has shown such an interest in me and told me that he finds it cool when I'm naked in his field of vision. Oh, it's just nice with Joschua. So the bathroom door to and from under the shower and everything again. Oh, I do not have to, go swimming right now. Yesterday I had no make up after showering and he said nothing this morning that I look bad. Well my skin is clean and pure even without make up. Just ask him later and hurry up now, he will certainly be waiting for me in the pool. You swim in the house that is pure luxury, I never had. Joschua goes swimming several times a day and I will. That's healthy and it's really fun to see what Joschua thought up right away. Oh please Joschua let our shared adventure never end. Never will I stay with you until the end of my life. Oh Mia good that he did not hear that he would have certainly pressed into the corner. Men do not want you to decide about them. Oh, Mia is just your personal feeling. So finished showering. Oh I do not need to dry off, I'll get wet again soon. But I could tie the towel when I go to the pool and then drop the towel very slowly and sexy. If he stands in the pool and sees that, he will certainly be happy. Again I want to give him pleasure. Mia you, nonsense I have so much fun to make him hot. From the bedroom to the pool. I knew it, he's already in the water and as soon as I open the bedroom door, he turns around and looks at me. Huii a look of him who goes through and through. He smiles, probably because I've changed the towel and I'm not completely naked.

"What have you thought again, you put your head so diagonally on your shoulder, then you've had a bad thought again."
"No, not a bad thought."

"Oh, which then?"

And I'm slowly getting closer to the water and enter the first stage, still no water contact.

"What do I have to see, you did not dry yourself off after showering, the water is still running out of your hair and down your entire body."
"Yes, do you like it?"
"It suits my just thought, you're my Eve."
"Eva?"
"Yeah, I just thought how heavenly it is here in the pool with the sun, the water and the palm trees, but it was always missing that certain something, Eva, how else to enjoy such a thing? And there I thought, Mia is my Eve, finally I found her and in that moment you appeared in the bedroom door. And then the sunbeams hit on your almost naked body, you are a revelation for my life and I hope I can give you something of what you have already given me in this short time."
"You have already given me more than all my men in front of you together and I know you have more to offer and I would like to have a bit more of that."
"A little bit, no, I will whole heartedly give you everything!"
"Really?"
"Yeah, promise!"

And I reach the water with the next step, which seems to gently wash around my right foot. I like it, it also seems to show my face. Did he think I'm doing a scared mine. No, I think it's great to be in the water. I still have my bath towel around. Now it is time to remove it immediately or should I let it get wet and put it under water, then it can not see my bare breasts. Whether that will turn it on anymore. He will certainly say nothing. Let's see. One more step and one more step and the water already flows around my knees. Oh, that's not cold at all. What did he say, it's always twenty-four degrees high. I have to say very pleasantly. Well then

244

one more step. If I dare to go one level lower, then the towel is down in the water. He still only looks at me and has not said anything.

"Cool? It's twenty-four degrees, I know, my love is hotter, but that's the way it has to be."
"Yes, you are much hotter, I can not understand why the water is still in the pool, when we are together you always cook, it should have evaporated long ago."
"Then you would be left dry now."

His greedy gaze hangs on me and I can pinpoint the destination of his looks. My breasts, well then I do not want to be like that now and I lead my two hands very slowly and looking him in the face, to the towel and let it slowly drop a bit until it lies on the breasts, then something further, so that he can now see my nipples in the neck and then with a quick jerk I pull it away completely. So now his eyes have arrived where they wanted to go. On my nipples. I really enjoy turning it on like this. He always challenges me. This is really a game between us. I have to admit that I have also seen so intensely on his masculinity, last night when I pulled down his boxer shorts and I was allowed to look at his masculinity undisturbed. Yes, he was allowed to, he has not closed his legs or held his hands protectively in front of it. It really turned on him that I could see him like that and did it and enjoyed it. Now I do not want to spoil his fun, but I could shake vigorously with my breasts again. Oh, that works. His smile on his face has intensified. And now I'm standing up to my chin in the water and I'm coming towards him. Four meters, three, two, and suddenly he pushes off and jumps up to my neck. It came so unexpectedly and with so much momentum and I fall, sticking with it to my neck, backwards and dive so deep that the water, without my permission, spreads in my nose. He releases his grip and we both get up again and stand down. When planning the pool, Joschua really did a great job. One hundred and sixty centimeters of water is perfect for swimming, standing and making nonsense.

Oh, this man surprises me with his temper and ideas again and again. I shake the water out of my nose and hair. Have long hair down to the shoulders. The flying drops clap Joschua in the face and he also starts to shake. But there is no drop avalanche for me, because he has short hair only six millimeters long. Hahaha, he can not bunker a lot of water while diving, like me. He quickly holds his hands over his face and most of the water bounces off. When we are again free of water drops, we look at each other and start loud and hearty to laugh.

"Good morning my stormy Mia, how are you?"
"Thanks for asking, as good as ever in life, thanks to you!"
"What you always say so calmly for heart touching words."
"That's the way it is, I can not help it, you literally pull it out of me."
"Hahaha, I pull, how, where? Oh!"

And he grabs my hands and runs backwards as fast as it gets in the water and I fall forward and he pulls me through the water. Also there I have a smile on my face, although I have swallowed some water in this action. What can you have fun with this man, I do everything with you. Maybe he wants to make sex with me in every room in the house. Oops maybe in the garden and elsewhere. Blubb, blubb, he stops and puts me back on his feet.

"Great, but only if you tell me what you just thought again."
"How are you coming back?"
"If you're thinking something crazy or you just think it's crazy, then your mouths always pull up a bit and your eyes start to sparkle."
"But you are watching me very closely."
"Yes, so what?"
"I had previously thought in the shower in the pool

246

room, I always like to have sex with a woman in all rooms and on the whole property, but never, no matter where I've lived, has come to it. It was never the right woman, either they did not want it or I did not need it, but with you ... ."

"What with me?"

"With you, I want to experience this in every room, on every piece of furniture, in the garden, in the garage, in the car and what you do not know about. You just make me totally crazy and I'm so crazy that I think you'd also enjoy it."

"Yes and how, but only under one condition."

"Under which condition?"

"That you only do it with me."

"Well, you really think I would leave you to another man and then I would probably have to watch. No way."

"I agree with that and would you like to have a second wife?"

"How did you come up with that? And you?"

"I asked first."

"I have often imagined being with two women at the same time, at the same time, but please tell me if you now love a woman named Mia in our case."

"You love Me?"

He looks me in the eye, long and hard. Then he take so my hands and puts them with his to my heart and he says to me ...

"Yes!!! With all my heart, yes!"

I return his gaze, squeezing his hands tighter and saying ...

"You have taken my heart by storm and it feels as com-fortable as never before in your life elsewhere. I love you too!"

I say that with such an insanely calm and determined voice in a pitch that makes my voice sound very high, which makes it crazy, because he loves higher voices. It follows, feeling like an eternity, a very deep silence in which one can hear our hearts louder than any other sounds of the environment, throbbing. It's a mood that spread throughout my entire body when he said I love you. Not only were those words spoken that way, but they came out of his mouth and heart in a very special way, in a way that I've never felt before, it was somehow significant. The words came without wasting any thought of another person. They came across so incredibly honest. I'm totally upset inside. How can three simple words do it, of course, if they are said in the right situation by the right man, a man like Joschua, who does not come out of his mouth and brain, but directly from the heart, only through his mouth in my direction brought. And there they are again.

"Mia, I love you!"

And a tingling sensation trickles down my face and back, but in any case, I've never felt that feeling in my life, listening to those words. Madness. The absolute madness. Really. Oh, how happy I am at this moment and I realize how I have pressed my hands very hard, oh ...

"Did I press too hard?"
"No, but when I pressed something really great, what did you think?"
"But you are totally sensitive that you always notice what's going on in me."
"That's not me, that's my heart, that's with yours on the same wavelength. And?"
"I felt a very special, never felt feeling when I said Mia I love you. A feeling that went through my whole body and I was somehow free of everything, only you were there, incredibly beautiful, soothing and somehow liberating. I love you!"

And again the feelings overpower us and he pulls me

close to him. I rest my head on his shoulder and we are feeling one for an eternity. It is as if in the places where our naked bodies are touching and these are not just a few, so close we cling to each other, small spikes arise again and again and transfer from one to the other. It tingles me everywhere, but a warm positive tingling sensation. Now you have to be able to stop the time and just stand there, but then I notice him again something to stir. Is that great to see a man like that? I have all feelings in me again on excitement course. Sure, if down there now was not the pool water inside, he would immediately notice how wet I am through his words. He can not see it and now I can not feel it. I can see, no, only on my body feel like his cock trying to straighten up. But my body is so close to his turn that he does not make it, so I take the pressure off his cock, which wants to be stiff, so true. You can not feel the words more directly.

"Hello you down there, I've noticed you, you're probably going to charge again?"
"Oops, I can not help it, he also wanted to see you, has felt more than just comfortable in you. But it's your fault now."
"Ok. I think it's great that your cock so much like me."

And we part, holding on to both hands, stretching out our arms and walking like children in a circle, without letting go as fast as we can.

"Oh, with me everything starts to turn. Stop!"
"Do you know what, we'll get drunk and have breakfast."
"Okay, but we're talking about you and two women. I have not forgotten that, but with you one always comes from one topic to another and then there are many answers to my questions open."
"We still have a lot of time for such conversations in life or not?"
"I have an eternally long time!"

"It sounds tempting in my ears - forever. But now out. If you go to my bathroom, I'll just come with you and dry off, then you'll have it for yourself. Is it okay?"
"Perfect."

Together we step through the water until the steps carry him out and he gives me a towel, which he had deposited at the edge before. He smiles at me.

"You really think of everything. Thank you. Oh, please rub my back. Tighter, firmer, that's like a massage. Really nice!"
"Careful, otherwise I'll push you too far forward and you'll fall over."
"Hahaha and then you can pick me up again."
"No, I would rather put myself on it."
"Oh no and then you want to do pure eroticism again."
"But no, I would like to protect you with my still wet body only from the eyes of the curious people."
"Curious people, so, where are they?"
"Oops, I thought everyone was standing around looking at you."
"Me?"
"Yes, you, where you have such a great figure and that you have this light, seamless tan, is even more challenging."
"You flatterer."
"What can I do, if you take it that way? I just say the truth."
"Your truth, that's subjective. A lot."
"True, but the others should not see you that way either. I want to have you all to myself. Sorry, but I'm a bit ... ."
"Jealous?"
"Yes, is that bad?"
"I believe there has never been a man jealous of me."
"They just did not see and experienced all that happened to me in a short time. I was allowed to experience more feelings with you than in all my life before."
"You're sweet."

He reached the dry scrubbing now deeper places on me, my buttocks and he tried with the towel covered by the hand between my legs to push forward.

"No, not, that will end badly."
"Like, I did not want to heat you, just dry it, otherwise the water will run there and then down your legs."
"But you have an excuse for everything."
"Like an excuse, is it a fact or would you want to dispute that?"

And I'll confuse him a bit and put my feet slightly apart and get a little bit down. Now there is room between my thighs for his towel covered hand. Oh, I'm messed up, I've never been that. It is clearly due to Joschua.

"So you can get better now. You do that tenderly, do you mean you catch all the drops?"
"Oh, who wants to be rubbed hot again?"
"I!"
"No, now it's over with the scratch off, come off to the bathroom. But before that, a scratch reward kiss!"

I just do not get it, every time our lips touch, it takes longer and now we're getting so close that I can feel my nipples on his chest. They press right on him and I move something my upper body to the left and right. I just want to rub against him for a moment. That invites me sexually again. Hahaha, if he does not want to rub me down, then I am now scrubbing on his upper body. Also really cool. Oh, he wants to tell me something. Crap then comes the kissing end.

"But I will not dry like that."
"But first, and then the moisture dries off."
"Hahaha, when I get so hot, I'll get wet again automatically."
"Oh. Well, let's just leave it that way."

I turn around, go to the bedroom and pull him on my

hand behind me. Go to the bedroom and continue to the bathroom door. There I let go of his hand and ...

"Up to here and not further. Make breakfast right away."
"Ok, can I wear my clothes?"
"Of course, otherwise I have nothing to undress afterwards."
"Oh, right. Well then I'm looking forward to the upcoming dressing."

Smiling, I disappear in the bathroom, close the door and now I have to hurry. I hear him getting his things out of the closet and out of the bedroom. Already I'm out of the bathroom and take my clothes out of the closet and put on my clothes. Everything is on the fly. I want to prepare the breakfast, but I also want to spoil him. So far he has done everything. It's cute of him, but if I'm so lazy, then he will not like me at some point. So Mia quickly in the clothes. No, I'm not doing any make up, it would take too long. Oh, when I have breakfast, it will be fun to see how happy he is. Alas, the left leg has hit only the right opening at the slip. This never happens to me, but when I'm in a hurry. Too stupid, leg out again and start a new attempt. Time passes, he is certainly already finished and smiles when I come with so much delay in the kitchen. Now it worked and off to the kitchen.

I catch myself, I do not run around the pool, but run. Mia, what are you doing? No, that's not me, Joschua has to answer for that. Yes, all this positive mess in me. Ah finally, I have reached the kitchen. How well I already know his house. Just forget everything and everything in the right order to make it happen quickly.

"Oh no! When did you do it all?"
"I conjured for my little angel and then there - hokus pokus - everything we needed on the table."
"Hahaha, how little table will cover you."
"Yes exactly. May I ask you to sit here then you can look at the whole garden while having breakfast."

"But I want to see you, too."
"It's mutual, so I've placed myself next to you on the front. Did not I think that well, because then I can hold your hand from time to time. Touch so much, it's always a little experience."
"Just a little experience?"
"I mean if I can touch your hand, otherwise it's an indescribable experience if I can touch and experience your nipples or vagina."
"Good, good, good, stop it, otherwise we will not be back for breakfast."
"How so?"
"Well, you know."
"Nooo. Oh yes! Exactly, you'll be boiling hot again, but that would fit the outside temperature of twenty-eight degrees."
"Youuu!"
"Mia, may I offer you a hot roll or a croissant?"

He hands me the bread basket and smiles at me. I look at him intensely with a piercing look, as if I wanted to say, well you want again. But then I reach out and catch a warm croissant.

"I hope you drink coffee, or I can make you a tea or cocoa."
"No, coffee is just the thing."
"Milk, sugar is there, although I was already entangled with you in erotic, hot experiences, but still do not know how you drink your coffee. Otherwise it's always the other way around."
"Yes, I only take milk and I found getting around really something really special. Never could have imagined, in the slightest, that one could really experience it that way. If I had seen that in a movie, I would have thought that it does not exist."
"Right."
"Do you always have breakfast so rich when you're alone?"
"Yes, I also make myself a tray, sometimes with rolls

253

and croissants or sometimes with bread. You can not always eat the same. I often take an egg, sometimes also scrambled eggs or fried eggs and jam, and often for dessert Nutella or peanut cream."

"Peanutscreme?"

"Yes this, try it, is a peanut cream from the US or do you have a nut allergy?"

"No I did not. Try a knife tip. Mmm yummy."

"Sometimes sausage and cheese, but that is very different but always fruit. Either grapes or raspberries."

"Tasty raspberries."

"Wait, now I'm so careful that nothing is missing and I have really forgotten the raspberries. Just get it."

"Do not you need it?"

"But they are part of it."

And Joschua gets up, goes to the kitchen. Shortly thereafter, he comes again with a glass plate full of raspberries. The man is really great. What all thought and bought in advance. I do not know if I would have thought of everything like him. I'm really spoiled here. This is like in a luxury hotel, no much better than in the hotel is not offered this insanely beautiful erotic.

"Please fresh raspberries, I always like to eat them. Is a reminder of earlier."

"What memory? A beautiful?"

"Yes and no. I was in a host family with a language tour group in England at the tender age of eighteen in Bouremouth on the south coast. The food was cruel and not enough, so every morning on the way to school I bought a bowl of raspberries from a fruit grocer. Since then, I have always eaten raspberries and always thinking of staying in England. Was just a nice time. Just a pity that you can not turn back."

"Yes, turn back time. What else would I do differently?"

"And I first, I would seek you immediately to never let go at the age of eighteen years. What could we have experienced together until today?"

"Wow, that sounds tempting, but would we have had so

much fun together?"

"You do not know, because you have this extreme fun out of the experience. I would have reacted differently in the first years of my sexual discoveries than today."

"Yes, we are only through our experience what we are today."

"Yes, that's ok, but are there so many negatives? I would have liked more positives in my life as well."

"Was it that bad?"

"Yes! Unfortunately, and I almost never had anything to do with it, I always got into really terrible situations and then had to suffer without being guilty, but we can talk about that later. Since I know you, I have moved these things into a very deep drawer in me. Will only enjoy the positive experiences with you. Now for a nicer topic."

"What do you want to know?"

"How do you know what I just wanted to ask."

"Well, it's quite logical."

"Either you can be clairvoyant or we are more than just something similar. Did not even know that I am in a female version."

"But I have to laugh heartily, hahaha. You in a female version, I think that would be impossible."

"True, even if I could choose my own sex, I would always want to be a man."

"But you also have many feminine facets about you."

"Female, which."

"Like, for example, your emotional way of putting yourself in my shoes yesterday and this morning."

"But that has nothing to do with female, that's just the feelings and the other liked and want to spoil him. I'm not an egotist. Although sometimes I think it would have been better."

"What do you mean by that?"

"Just think, have not you often thought, why do the good guys always die first and the bad guys live longer."

"That's right, sometimes it has made me desperate."

"That's easy to explain in itself."

"I'm really excited about that now."

"For the bad, the worries go into the left ear and come out right at the right ear again. For the good, these are the people with feelings, the worries move into the left ear, then over the heart and only then to the right ear. It is always affected with the heart and there is stress triggered and then triggers all sorts of diseases. That's why the good guys always die first."

"That's a really good and obvious explanation. You realize you've been busy."

"Let's say life experience. Another roll?"

"Oh yes and some coffee please, it really tastes like more."

"I'm glad that you like it. Please which bun do you want? Sesame, poppy seeds, sunflower seeds or spring."

"That's a choice as in the finest hotel. I take sesame."

"Well, if I think about what you used to do last night after the midnight meal and today before breakfast for calories, then you would have to eat tons."

"Hahaha, had enough calories in stock."

"Oh where, I have not seen any stockpiles."

"Flatterer, but thanks for your kind words."

"My pleasure. You, what do you want to do right away? Should I suggest something?"

"Yes, be brutal and beat."

"Why do you ask me again. I heard the ulterior motive up to me."

"What ulterior motive?"

"Well you wish that I hit you in sex, right?"

"Mmm yes, but what did you want to do with me right now?"

"Hahaha, but we made the bend very well, but then we come back later. So I do not know if you know Hamburg or the harbor. We could first drive into the city, stroll through the passages and search the windows for something special. Then eat something in the Hansa Passage, then go for a walk along the Inner Alster to the Aussenalster, and then recharge your batteries with coffee and cake. At the same time we can observe the sailboats and dream that we can glide over the water

with them."
"Oh, I have never sailed before."
"Never mind, you're safe with me and you'll have a lot of fun with it. I can promise you that. And you can swim too, I saw this morning."
"So you saw that? Did not you see something else all the time?"
"How do you mean?"
"Oh well, I think it's really hot when I'm naked and your eyes are eating me."
"And how I like it. Or do you want to make a harbor cruise with subsequent feed intake somewhere on the Elbe border?"
"Oh, you make such great suggestions, what would you recommend?"
"So if you can not decide, then you have to be surprised. Agreed?"
"Yes, okay and how! Are you ready to have breakfast, too?"
"Yeah, you still have to change or get ready, for me you're super chic, but I do not know if you want to go that way?"
"No, I'm done. Just help cover the table."
"Oh, yes, thank you."

And in no time at all we cleared the breakfast table and carried everything to the kitchen and tidied it up.

"So finished and now a thank you kiss for you."

Yes, we kiss each other and it is as beautiful as the first time our lips unite. Then he takes me by the hand, we go past the pool in the garage. There he accompanies me to the passenger door of his car, a BMW X 3 in bronze metallic with beige leather seats. Open the door for me and I'll get in. It is a service. Was he like this to all women or just to me? No matter what was important to me, not at all, only from our first mail, well, I mean my answer e-mail.

"Thank you."
"Please, please, my beautiful angel."

I sit back and just want to enjoy everything. Joschua does everything. He also gets into the car, garage door, lock house, well that everything is electronically controlled via the smartphone. Pull down the drawbridge, open the street gate, drive the car in and out. Once arrived on the street, everything is closed again. Now off to Hamburg. I am first guided by him through the city. Parking in the underground garage at the town hall, from there you can reach everything. On the way there, it will take in about thirty minutes, he tells me everything, where we come from and we chat about this and that. The journey goes by quickly and he sets off the car in the parking garage. Get off and go up. As soon as we have seen the light of the day again, I say to him ...

"You like to drive a lot of car, do not you?"
"Yes why?"
"You realize how safe you are to steer it, even though you can explain everything to anyone else that happened and could be seen outside. Driving is an automatic side issue for you."
"Thanks, but you described that cool. Yes, I have more than four million kilometers without accidents behind me and driving is still a lot of fun, but especially today, with the passenger!"
"Flatterers. Where are we now?"
"On the left you see the city hall of Hamburg, here on the forecourt is always the Christmas market for Christmas. In the evening with lighting, the class looks just great. Well, I'll show you when it's rebuilt."
"Do you think we're together at Christmas?"
"Which Christmas do you mean? 2100?"
"Hahaha, 2100 is good. Ok, I agree with that. Will be there, probably in a wheelchair and you with a stick."
"Oh yes, we will make a good pair then. Let's go over the bridge there, then we come to the passages. This is

the Rathausschleuse to the Alsterfleet."

"You are the perfect tourist guide."

"Thanks, let's go right into the Alsterarkaden. What interests you, a painting shop, a jeweler or clothes?"

"I like to look at everything. It's the prices."

"Yes, we are not only in a big city, we are here in a cosmopolitan city and everything is a bit more expensive. But just in these shops, in the outdoor areas, all prices are quite normal. You also have to remember that most millionaires in Germany live in Hamburg."

"Yes, you have to be a millionaire, I sometimes think so."

"And what would you want to buy right now?"

"Oh, I've never thought about it. Maybe some jewelry, but I do not have many wishes, only healthy I want to stay until the end."

"But you are modest, just staying healthy is a wish that you can not buy with all the money in the world."

"You're right. How many people are shopping here. The city is very busy."

"Yes, it's Saturday and families go to town with a man."

"They hope that the man then opens the wallet."

"Hahaha, you have funny ideas"

"No, not for a long time, I have to earn my own money for a long time, I can not get support from my husband."

"Being divorced means not being taken care of, but I think your husband is great."

"How are you crazy?"

"No, if it had not divorced and you were still with him, then you would never have contacted my ad and we could not stroll through town now."

"Oh, you're right. Then I'll see it that way."

"I know a divorce can plunge you into a very deep hole, but after that love can shoot you right from the bottom of the hole into seventh heaven. You definitely did that with me!"

"Really?"

"More than real, yes directly and without detours. I already felt that with your first mail, that's why I was so persistent."

259

"Stubborn?"
"Well, persistently not letting go and bringing you to me. Otherwise I would not have been able to show you that there are also very sweet and emotional men."
"Dear and emotional, yes that's you!"
"Ha and now I'll do something crazy, I've never done that spontaneously. Come in."
"Where in?"
"Well in this business."
"No, are you crazy?"
"Yeah, I just said, I'm doing something crazy!"

We stand in front of a jeweler and he pulls my hand through the door into the shop. I'm quite dumb and look at him in a puzzled whisper:

"But do not buy anything just watch."
"Yes! Yes! Yes! What would you like? A ring, a necklace or a bracelet."
"As?"

The seller welcomes us and asks what he can show.

"A necklace with pendant in gold. Or do you prefer silver?"
"I have not thought about that yet."
"Gold would stand you."

The seller will pick a selection and put it in front of us on the template board on the showcase.

"I like this necklace with very small, round links. But what kind of pendant do you want, what shape?"
"Consult me."
"Well, you are one. Do you have something in the shape of your heart?"

And after a short while the seller comes back and shows several pendants in heart shape. I immediately notice one of them. They are two intertwined hearts. Not massive but like two hollow heart shapes, but overlapping together and on each heart a small brilliant set.

"Try this one, please."
"As?"
"Turn around, please, I'll put it on you. And now look at me. Wow, that's yours right away. look in the mirror over there."

I turn around and go to the mirror, look in and smile a little.

"You got a good taste."
"You have the right neck for it, I think. Do you like her?"
"Yes but no."
"Okay, we'll take it. Please let her in immediately, your neck was just too naked, he would have caught a cold."
"Hahaha. That's not possible."
"Shhh."
"That's beautiful!"
"Well, then it suits you."

Joschua pays and we leave the shop. Outside I seem to look at him totally stupid. He looks back at me question-ingly. I tell him ...

"Are you crazy about buying such expensive things?"
"I told you before, I'm spontaneously doing something crazy."
"I can not accept that."
"Oh, you're begging for punches again, well wait until we get home."

And my face turns into a silent, strong smile.

"She is so good to you, please accept her so that we both always remember this experience. I have never given any more jewelry to a woman. I just enjoyed buy-ing them and putting them on."
"I have never received such beautiful things. Thousand

261

thanks, you'll get a very big kiss for that."

Oh Mia, that has never made a man for me, given me something outside of a holiday and I've never even received such a piece of jewelry. Of gold. Oh Joschua and already I take his head in my hands, pull him close to me and give him a first tender and then violent kiss on the mouth, oops no in the mouth. At this moment I do not even realize how many people are watching us. The gift has brought me totally off the role. Oh, that's sweet, when a person can spontaneously make another person so happy. Oh, I'm completely blown away. Except me with pleasure. My heart rejoices and my brain does not know what to say for words. Oh best still a kiss afterwards. Well that's how I reward myself. I like it so much to kiss him. He tastes so good and his inner life feels so hot. Every kiss from him excites me and it was often the starting signal to many more feelings. Oh Mia we are here in public. Oh Mia, you are already on cloud nine without having intimate sex with you. How is this supposed to continue. To buy the necklace with the pendant and to give to the woman, whom he loves to say, how cool is that? Yes, I love this man too, not because he gave me such a wonderful gold chain with hearts, but because my heart just feels it. Now I know it too, yes, there is it, love at first sight and now all I have to do is to keep that love forever. I will do everything for it. Oops, the kiss is already over, or have I thought too many thoughts again. We look at each other and it shines like the lights on a whole Christmas tree. I feel that I have made him so happy with my heartfelt joy and that was my goal. Oh, what's to become of me? Now I'm so on clouds only because he is so nice to me. I hug him again and squeeze him. Oh what do I care about the people around me. They are just jealous that they do not have a partner like me, a partner who loves you with all your heart and that you love as well. I'm so happy. What a day. What a weekend.

"Thanks, I'm overwhelmed."

"Do I always get such a kiss when I give you something?"
"You get as many kisses from me as you want, but without you having to give me something because of it. But I see the kiss was special for you as well."
"What do you think about that?"
"Well in your pants, the air is out because your cock has filled with blood. looks erotic."
"I think I'm going red."
"Just a bit."
"What you do with me. Come on, let's go to the Jungfernsteg."
"Yes."
"We just have to cross the street, there are the tour boats. Come on, we'll take a tour of the Alster and through the canals, which takes one and a half hours. Do you want?"
"Yes gladly."

We solve two maps and climb the already waiting round boat. We sit in the still free first row. Good that many guests always go backwards, but I think it's always better in the front. We sit down on the first bench and I hug him. It feels so good, it really feels like he was the part I always missed. I am so happy and already the boat leaves. We listen to the sometimes funny comments of the captain and I watch him doing so. It is as if he absorbs all the information and the boat weighs easily in the few waves. It goes over the inner Alster to the Aussenalster and then into the channels. In the meantime, we hardly talk. He only pulls me closer to him, he looks at me and takes my left hand in his hands. They lie on his right thigh, and it is as if the warmth and the feelings revolve within us, from our hands through his thigh to my left shoulder, there through my resting hand into my body, through my heart, over my hands back to him back. So a circuit and I have the feeling that the captain's voice is suddenly very far away and I hear only these circling emotions and his heart. Joschua also seems to have totally slipped his thoughts into another world. Suddenly a jolt and ...

"Oh, we're back on the jetty?"
"Yes the boat has put on again. Like, did not you know, where were you? Hello, are you still away, come back, I'm here."
"Yeah, nice that you are there. I was well in the thought."
"What thoughts?"
"Thoughts and feelings of us."

We get up and leave the boat. Man oh man, I almost did not notice anything, what is wrong with me. I enjoy Joschua's side every second. It's like being in a world of pink glasses.

"It's already 15:08 my stomach would like to feed something. Yours too?"
"Could not hurt."
"Drink coffee?"
"Yes."
"It's so nice weather, in itself I would invite you to the hotel Vierjahreszeiten in the hall. They have such delicious Petite Fleurs, but the weather is so beautiful, do we want to sit down on the terrace of the Alster Pavilion?"
"Yes understood."

We go there hand in hand and are lucky. There are just people standing up, who had a table with full Alsterblick. Joschua storms immediately, pulling me on the hand behind him on this table and won, we have conquered him.

"Please take a seat."
"Thank you!"
"Do you want coffee or tea or chocolate again? A piece of cake for that?"
"Chocolate and cake."

The waitress comes and he asks what kind of cake they

have. It counts up a lot and we decide.

"I take apple pie without whipped cream and a choco-
late."
*"I take cherry cake with whipped cream and also a
chocolate."*
"It's nice to sit here and the sun is still really warm."
"Yes, your hearts shine in the sun."
"Our!"
"And how do you find such a cosmopolitan city?"
"Exciting, but I feel safe with you by my side."
*"Yes, if we explore the city at this rate, we can do it for
another 100 days."*
"Wow, that's how big Hamburg is."
*"You have 1.8 million inhabitants and a huge area, plus
a lot of surrounding areas with great sights."*
"Then we have at least 1000 more days to mix."
*"Yes, you mean days where we are alone with us and
explore us."*
"Exactly! You understand me!"
*"I have the feeling that we could communicate without
words only with looks and gestures."*
"Yes, our hearts would control everything."

The waitress comes and delivers the ordered cake and
chocolates.

"Looks great with the cake."
"And he will certainly taste like that."

And as we start to eat the cake and drink the chocolate,
we chat nonstop.

"You wanted to answer me the question that would be
how you would find it, two women and one man."
"Oh yes, you also think of everything."
"Naturally. I'm also very interested in burning."
*"Do you think you can love two people at the same time,
I mean, could you imagine letting two men into your
heart at the same time?"*

"That is a difficult question. I do not know."
"Imagine we both love each other ... ."
"Yes, I can imagine that, I'm experiencing that right now."
"Great me too and now imagine that there would be a man to come. We would be three naked in bed. How would you decide who and how you would touch each of the men, and who would you let in first? The one you love or the other? Would you ask yourself, do I hurt the one I love when the other one sleeps with me or you first give him an orgasm?"
"Mmm, I just can not tell you, somehow I always feel guilty about the man I love."
"So you would always be somehow inhibited and never let you down properly."
"Right."
"You see, that's how I would feel about two women. Just think, for example, I would lie naked and tied up on the bed ... ."
"Wow, what a hot idea. Will you excite me now?"
"Yes and no. I just wanted to describe something or ask questions."
"Oh, please continue, so you're lying naked and tied up on the bed in front of us."
"Yes and now the other woman would touch me intimately and you are standing next to it. If that gave me feelings, what would you feel? Would you be hurt or would you be happy about it?"
"Honestly, when I think about it, only I want to touch you and only I want to experience it when you come and be happy and I just want to feel your skin and explode. Does that sound selfish?"
"Many people would definitely say you're selfish and prudish, but I think it's very special when two people only experience it together, that's very intimate and a third person, no matter if man or woman or any other couple would just go there to disturb. I could not focus on you then and not drop. No, I just want to experience it with you alone. And you?"
"You speak from my heart."

Oh these conversations, I've never been able to chat with another man about such topics and then Joschua has the same opinion as me. It is exciting and the cake is already plastered and the cups emptied. Yes, time keeps racing on and on in such conversations. It is already 17:34.

"Do you want to go for a walk?"
"Yes gladly!"

He pays and we leave the Alster Pavilion.

"You, we'll go through the Alsterhaus."
"Well, I've heard of that, a huge department store."
"Exactly, with really great things to see and buy."
"Yes, what?"
"Sex toys."
"Why did I think you would say something like that?"
"I have no idea."
"Oh no."

We cross the Jungfernstieg and go through the airlock into the Alsterhaus. Many scents rush on you and you are a bit off the hook. We stroll slowly through the house, stay on the ground floor and pass a stocking stall.

"What do you think of a hot pantyhose?"
"Now I have pictures again in my mind's eye."
"So which?"
"No, not now, otherwise you will get hot again."
"Well then we chat about it on the way home."
"Ok."
"I will not forget to remind you."
"So what do we take, a pantyhose in which colour?"
"Black or red?"
"Both colours. look here, fishnet tights."
"Yes and size 38."
"Well rated. Are you a professional or a professional?"
"No, I do not buy any tights otherwise. Well, we'll take

267

those two and they'll be in black as well."
"Well."

From the checkout and the three tights paid, in the bag and on. Oops there are still great bras.

"I want you to choose a lace bra."
"No, you spend too much for me."
"No, I'm only doing this for myself."
"Yes, I would have said that now. But I surrender to my destiny."
"Well then we'll take the black one here and the white one out of smooth fabric. The fabric feels so soft and your nipples will surely show through."
"You can see everything again in your mind's eye when choosing."
"Yes, I think what you look like and what I can experience with you then. Is that wrong?"
"No, only I have never heard that one chooses something on such criteria."
"Yes, I'm just different than others."
"Well, I can fully confirm that."
"Size 80 B."
"Right again, slowly you're getting scary."

So go to checkout and pay. Still in the bag. And now we stroll through the Alsterhaus and leave it on the back and go across the street and into the Hasenviertelpassage.

"That's really great, you can go from one passage to the other."
"Yes, and the passages have laid, in succession, nearly two kilometers in length. In the rain, you can buy almost everything by drying it and eating it everywhere. Day after day, dry shopping."
"And almost all shops are represented. Showcase, one more interesting than the other. And every passage looks different. Really great. Thank you for showing me that."

"Gladly, I often go through the passages just to watch and pick up the atmosphere."
"Of course we do not have that kind of thing in Schwerin. But we have small business streets for it."
"Also nice, but very different. Say, it's already 6:51 pm, do we want to have some food here or do we want to take something home with us?"
"Oh, just the cake, I'm still pretty full."
"Well, do you want to eat fish, for example, cold or hot tonight?"
"You can decide, I eat everything. It was really delicious what you have done so far."
"Well, then we just pass the fish shop, would be hungry for fish."
"Sounds good."

So out of the Hansaviertel and through the Postgalerie on the Rathausschleuse and the Rathausvorplatz into the underground car park. Just redeem the parking ticket and off to the car. On the way home we pass the fishmonger's shop. Stop, get off to the store. He would have been lucky in six minutes. We both storm into the shop and pick the fish together. Eel and a mackerel and 300 grams of North Sea crabs. Oh and two pegs in aspic. So that should be enough for us tonight. An almost full bag and he puts it in the back of the back seat. I can almost taste the fish and I think about it already, as we sit together at the dining table and feed these wonderful things and the talks there. It is interesting with Joschua and everything so uncomplicated. We always have something to talk about. If Christmas 2100 is still like that. I have to smile hard into myself. Christmas 2100, that's right in me now. Oh, that's a great feeling.

"Oh, what did the great fish find their way into our bag?"
"You, there are some delicious fish come in."
"How are they still living?"
"No, already ready for food."
"Good, because I do not like killing animals."
"Oh, I always say that living alone in the world would be

the hardest thing for me to get fish or meat, because I can not kill any animals."

"Yes, I feel the same. Something in common again."

"Well then, we would have to be a vegetarian or not."

"Good that we are not alone in the world."

"Well, you alone would not be bad."

"You, I remember, in the Alsterhaus we did not want to talk about it, what did you think with the tights?"

"Oh, there are many things I want to do with it or want to get it."

"How do you get, you also want to wear tights."

"No, do not wear it."

"What then?"

"I do not know if you ever thought about it, a pantyhose can also be used to regulate the air, pull it over the head, for example. Sometimes it is really exciting, if you are already aroused and the partner then a short and shut your mouth and nose. But you need absolute trust, so I could not even try that feeling myself."

"And how do you know that then?"

"Years ago, I wrote a book called bondage for everyone. A textbook, where I deal with many things, such as medical or legal requirements, knots, materials and then I have also collected reviews and what I got to read there. Partly Impossible, some interesting and there was the air reduction also there."

"And how is the pantyhose used?"

"In that case you pull them over your head and you get less air. But then you can tie down an adhesive tape, because of the tights it does not stick to the skin."

"I have not dealt with that yet, but what is not, can still be. But I've already thought of how it feels when you close your mouth just before the climax."

"It's really exciting, because it gives the feeling that you are defenseless."

"Oh, do we want to give it a try?"

"Yes, with pleasure, but with each other."

"How mutually?"

"Well, sometimes I'm passive and sometimes you're passive."

"That sounds tempting. Can I also read your book?"
"Sure, it's almost done. Everything written is ready, the book has about 200 pictures, but I have only 80 pictures ready. Model are not easy to come by and there was always something in between. But now I had an idea, instead of models I have inserted mangas and that is not available on the market yet. Will publish the book now. Well, then you can just read it and tell me if it's good or not."
"I have no idea about that."
"Even if you, as a layman, understand it, there are others. You're my guinea pig with it now."
"Sure, I do, but if I like something in it, then you have to promise me that we try it out."
"Great! I'd say I'll give you the trial copy when you go back home, which will make me totally sad, and then you have something of mine at home, something very intimate."
"Yes, I do, very much even and then I dream of all the indecent things the girls are standing in and you have to do everything in my dreams."
"You sound good, but you have to know bondage has nothing to do with SM."
"SM?"
"Sado-maso, harder and more specific, and it's also about controlling pain. But I'm not in pain and many think that bondage is about violence, but that's not true, just to increase the arousal. But both have to want that and have fun with it. I would recommend everyone to leave out the prejudices and try it very carefully. Certainly, partners would discover feelings they did not even know. You can not explain that, you have to experience it on your own body. And what you can experience and have to pay attention to, that is stated in my book."
"I did not know that, nor did anyone explain it to me and I have not heard or seen anything like it in this way."
"Yes, somehow still a taboo subject, although to experience feelings about these and other ways come on television many reports."

271

"Right."
"Oh, we are already at home, as time goes by with you."

After we drove the car into the garage, got out and wanted to go into the house I have to say something important to him.

"You, do not forget the bag, otherwise we must starve tonight."
"Right. I almost forgot. Yes, to talk to you about such things, I start somehow dreaming about what it would be like when you and I ... ."
"Yes what?"
"Let's go to the house, otherwise we'll stay in the garage and clap here for hours. Mmm being, sometimes hot sex in the garage, would be exciting too?"
"But only with you!"
"I totally agree with this condition."
"What would you do with me in the garage now?"
"Talking about it would be great only on the phone with you, here only if you do."
"Yes, now and immediately, put the bag away and come here."
"How do you want to seduce me into a quickie?"
"Yes here, today and now!"
"Wow a woman with initiative. What should I do?"
"Yeah, mmm you could just lie on your back on the workbench."
"How easy?"
"Yes, please and completely dressed."
"Dressed?"
"Yes, the way you are, dressed."

It is not easy to jump back onto the workbench. Joschua is having a hard time and I have to smile. I know that's mean, but I can not suppress it, it looks so funny. He complains that the bank is so tough. There he lies like on a board, but somehow it makes me and him that full. I can see that again on his pants. He is quite flat and his masculinity is very strong in the pants and forms a very

272

nice huckle. Oh the thoughts start to rotate with me already determined with him already or he has fixed ideas.

"Well, can you do it? High with you, that's good. Hey, you're an agitated man."
"Yeah, I get hot thoughts right away when you say you want something from me."
"How, you get hot when I command you something?"
"Well, only when I feel you want something erotic of mine."
"Oh, right. And that's something erotic when you have to lie down on the workbench."
"Sure, you're watching me and that's what makes it exciting."
"And I will do more, not just look at you."
"So what?"
"Touch you too."
"Where?"
"Now do not be so curious, otherwise."
"I know, if I'm too curious, you'll punish me."
"Yeah, you really understood what I said on the phone."
"Sure, I remember every word of you. The words have taken my heart and that's why they are firmly anchored in my mind."
"That shows me that I really mean something to you. Super!"
"Yes, you have become the most important in the world for me."
"Rest now, you'll flatter me again!"
"Only the truth!"
"Rest, otherwise!"

And before he can start the next sentence, I press my lips firmly on his, but he can not kiss with, no movement is in my lips and I do not even try to sink my tongue in his mouth. I just shut his mouth with my lips. And I press my head firmly on his. Suddenly and unexpectedly for him, I put my right hand with pressure on his pants. Then I grab him full in the eggs and the tail. I feel

273

he would have screamed if I still did not shut his mouth with my lips. I feel his breath in my face. Warm and very fast. He is really excited again. The chemistry is right, because which man would excite so fast, if a woman just does just normal things with him. Well, normal things are not quite right, because not every woman would grab him so in the step. He would certainly not put up with this by any woman. From me already and he even enjoys it, so he has to feel something positive for me. Oh Mia that is so beautiful and I feel something moistening in me again. His feelings seem to have invaded me so that I can not do otherwise. Oh, Mia, what should become of it?

I still do not loosen my mouth press, but my fingers on my right hand begin to move like a crab, all the fingers apart, open, close, close, open. I massage his manhood so tight that I think there would be no more pants in between, which does not correspond to the fact. Oh, I did not think so. Joschua has both hands free and wants to use them against me now. That will not do. Joschua is mine now, it's my playing time with him. But Joschua goes over to the attack and his right hand, still hanging down, grabs my chest and massages it tightly. Oh, it's like feeling his hand through the thin fabric of my blouse on my chest. Oh now he takes his hand to my other breast and massages it so hard. He succeeds there only three pushers, then I raise.

"Did I allow you to touch me?"
"Yes!"
"I can not remember that."
"So what, I just thought it?"
"You're getting pretty naughty. Not like that. I order you to push your hands immediately under your buttocks. Come on, do it now."
"And if not? Auauau, do not press so tight otherwise you made break eggs out of it, I obey yes!"
"It's so good, nice to put your hands under your buttocks."

And I put my left hand on his lips and press lightly. He can not contradict me anymore, only with his eyes he can communicate with mine. I approach very close to the workbench. He should feel it as if it were a piece of mine. My right hand has loosened the grip on his masculinity and my fingers are now trying to pull the zipper down. I have to say, it feels like I have a lot of experience in it, it succeeds very easily. I can not shake the feeling that I will give him great pleasure again and the poor person has to endure it. This guy really makes me a vamp and what a guy. Head, heart and grasping hands, everything present and my thoughts are fixed again on his lower part. I've loosened the button on his pants and now push me down on his ringy button to the bottom. Wow, it starts. No, I'll change my tactics and bring my hand back. He certainly counted on it, that I am massaging his masculinity. I have something else in mind. I see, his cock is already so sharp and pushes from the inside against the boxershort. If I would estimate he is on a sharp scale of 1 to 100 determined to 80. He would beg me immediately please continue. But he can not do that. My left hand still closes his mouth pressingly. Then I both take my hands away from him, prop them in my hip and take a step back from the workbench.

"Hello Joschua, how are you doing on the workbench?"
"I'm starting to cook, but why are you stopping? Was this just the appetizer? But I also want the main course and the dessert. Please please!"

I smile at him. Then I slowly open my blouse from bottom to top. Now he must be able to see my bra. What a sight for my Joschua. He reacts immediately in the lower area. Geil to be able to experience something directly. That really makes me think I would never have dreamed.

"The sight seems to please you, right?"
"And how, when I imagine the bra away, then I see clearly your tight nipples in front of me."

"That's good, burn that image into your brain, because it will not last long."
"What do you mean?"

Hahaha, now he will experience something. I take off my blouse completely. Now he sees my beautiful upper body in full splendor, only a little protected by the skin-coloured bra.

"Wow you have such a wonderful upper body, take off your bra."

He can not say more or even see more, because I folded my blouse and put it completely on his head. Hahaha, now I have turned off the light for him. He'll close his eyes under my blouse now and start dropping. For this he may now also inhale the scent of my body, which is in my blouse. I guess that will make him even more and really true, in his pants it will be even closer. Oh, maybe I'm mean, I could have just put his blouse over my head, but it's so thin it would not have prevented him from seeing and breathing. Well, since I've folded her more often, she has become opaque and he's going to get heavier too. I can already see how the blouse always rises and lowers over his nose. Also, the air he is inhaling now will bring my scent to him and it will be warmer. Oh, what my blouse can do. Yes, he has to breathe deeper through his nose and he also breathes through his open mouth. I also see the movement of my blouse lying on it. And oh, my poor Joschua, now I press my left hand again on his mouth and the breathing over the mouth is no longer available. Only the nose supplies him with air now and that is a bit handicapped. It excites him a lot, though he knows that I can control his life now. This powerlessness is what he has told me, which will increase his excitement immensely. It is not that wild, because he could free himself at any time with his hands or murmur the codeword red. I would immediately take my blouse back to me. It's all positive, much more positive than I thought and so exciting. His cock wants to blow himself up, but he is still being hindered. Now not only by the boxer's shorts, but also by my right hand crushing him. She just pushes him down on his stomach. As much as he tries to set it up, I push harder. No problem for me against his cock. I am a strong woman. I can really feel it whenever he pumps more blood into his cock as he wants to go up, get harder and bigger. Oh, how long can I do this, not that his beloved cock bursts, then Joschua would bleed out. Iii a bad idea, but he will regulate it himself. If it is too much and no longer beautiful for him, then he will stop pumping and counter fighting. Oh, it's fun to play with a guy like that. I just found the right toy in Joschua. The best living toy for me in the world. Mia what you thought again, no one should hear. Everyone would think that's crazy. But I enjoy it.

„Oh!"

Ah, he wanted to say something, but my left hand is just right and I press a little tighter. Now he is very quiet and his feelings he will see inside already in front of his closed eyes dancing around. Anyway, I hope. He could pull his arms away from him and stop me from doing what he does, but he does not, so he enjoys them and I enjoy them immensely. I have never had a man in my life so I can do everything I want. Clearly without really hurting him, I would never do that.

"What did I tell you? Rest, but you do not want to obey, now I have to teach you manners first you obey a lady, understood? How was that, five seconds? So now."

And I push my left hand a little higher and put it on his nose. Very carefully, I increase the pressure and he gets hardly any air, but something he can still breathe, I feel the draft. But the air is even more mixed with my fragrance from my blouse and now even from my hand. Yes, when inhaling heavily, my hand scent comes through the blouse. At this moment, when he gets only

277

little air, his blood flows even more into his cock. One has to increase his excitement even further. Let's see what his cock is doing now, because the five seconds are up and I take the left hand completely from his blouse covered face. He immediately takes a deep breath and lo and behold, his cock loses some strength, because the bump in his pants is wrinkled. So, when I turn off his air, he gets bigger and when I let him down, he gets smaller. Then his excitement would rise and fall in the same way. If this goes on with Joschua and I get to know more and more details of sexual possibilities with this man, then I will soon be an expert on excitation

issues with men. Hahaha Mia you and your thoughts. Now go ahead so he is not deenergized. So Mia direct attack on the zipper and immediately afterwards on the waistband button. My right hand obeys and promptly does its job. The others, his cock to maneuver through the slot of the boxer shorts succeeds easily, because Joschua moves a little with his hip and the boxershort is flexible enough to get through the tail. Oh, it's already big and bulging, and the glans is glistening, not yet quite. I have to admit some excitement.

"Well, are you nice now and obey me?"

He tries to nod his head slightly.

"Well, I understood that, that's fine. Imagine how hard my buds are now, they're standing very hard in your direction."

Oh, I'm mean. He can imagine the determined now and I increase again the pressure in his cock. But this time there is no textile in between and I feel his bare cock in my hand as I push him back towards his stomach. Oh Mia if that feels so good, try to push him in the opposite direction, towards his feet. You give that a resistance. Do not push too hard Mia, otherwise you break him off and my mom used to always say that if I break my toy, I will not get anything new. So do not break Mia's caution. Hahaha what you sometimes get back for thoughts from the depths and which connections you make so is really cool. I have not thought about that for ages. Joschua, Joschua, what you bring back to me in my life. Oh, Joschua is really delicious too. It is a pity that he is still clothed everywhere. It's exciting, I have total control over his cock and his entire body. I have it in my hand. Oh no, in both hands. Human Mia today you have but thought games of funny nature booked or? What do I have to see when I push down and the resistance becomes too big? Joschua relieves him by raising his pelvis a bit. But that is not infinite, so let go of Mia and already his cock swings back in the direction of the stomach. Oh, I will embed this wonderfully tight, warm, tender, thick, yielding cock all the way into my right hand, squeeze something and then push it slowly and with pressure up and down. Oh, when I push my hand to his stomach, the foreskin is pulled back even further and his glans shines. In the other direction, the foreskin goes back to the glans. The is really flexible and if I press it I can feel exactly when he gets a little firmer again. But now I want to bring it to a climax with all my might. My hand speed is slowly increasing, and he is reacting with ever faster breathing. I press my left hand tighter on his mouth and he breathes harder and on the right hand I feel his cock is firmer. Immediately he has reached the point where he can no longer hold it back. I increase the pressure on his mouth again. His scream is going to get stuck in his mouth in the explosion, that will make him totally mad and I guess it will push all the feelings into him. At the same time I increase the speed of my right hand again. Hahaha I realize how he tries to endure a bit, by tensing all his muscles and I see how his legs are pushed through. Now he's about to explode.

"Well, are you? Yes, let it come! Now! Come on! Now!"

He obeys my command and lets his thoughts fall. Now it

is when I close my eyes that I can look into it and feel it as at my own climax, with him now colourful lights will dance in front of his closed eyes inside and soon they will explode like fireworks. I feel his excitement both on my left hand and on my right hand, it is as if his feelings pass through his right hand on his cock through me and on the left hand on his mouth back to him. A complete cycle of emotions. That's sheer madness. I feel again, if I rub my two thighs slightly against each other, I'm really wet. Whenever I am allowed to be so nice to him, my body rewards itself as if it also takes away some of the happiness I am preparing for Joschua and spoils himself. Now his cock builds a, what shall I say, explosion pressure on which I can feel so much, before he presses his sperm in his cock to accelerate it there, accelerate like projectile bullets and I feel her shoot the whole long way through his cock and then the feeling as they reach the light of day. Oh, now I can even smell her. Oh, it was beautiful when I had it in my mouth the other day, but now they are sprayed on his shirt. Alas, poor Joschua has totally messed up. Hahaha I am one. The thoughts in my brain start again. What an experience and I can always experience it directly. It can not be more direct. Oh my right hand also got some as I have painted over his cock. Wow. And now I take both hands off him and slowly open my eyes. He has his still closed, I can see that because I have just taken my blouse from his face. He smiles and still seems to enjoy his feelings. Yes, I know that, the more beautiful the climax, the longer they last. He also has his hands under his buttocks. Real, hot workbench sex is something really cool. My right hand played pliers and my left worked as a trowel. So I used the tool and how.

"You've been shot, almost up to your neck. Has probably built up so much pressure. Why did that happen?"

Instead of bringing words of happiness to my ear, he just smiles, pulls his hands out from under his buttocks, looks at her and does finger exercises, then looks at me again, his right hand grasps behind my neck and he pulls me to it to him. So close that I can already feel his lips and he keeps pushing until my and his lips can unite. Then follows a long and intense tongue play. Oh, when I feel his tongue against mine, then it goes through me thoroughly. It is just arousing and spreads from the tongue in my whole already very excited body. Real tongue sex. Hahaha, Mia, you can not even leave your head without thoughts. No, they always come automatically. Oh, heart just push it away and tell them you just want to enjoy. I try but the thoughts are very intense. No, now I can do it and really, all at once I can clearly feel all the feelings that arise from my tongue at the touch of his and then spread further in my body. That's nice. Such a cozy warmth penetrates everywhere. Right down to my toes. I feel like electrically charged and hovering just above the ground. Here I just put my right hand on his already completely withdrawn tail, clearly the seeds are still partially off, but that does not matter to me. It's just an extra kick to feel it so small. He is so soft and warm on his cock. A really good feeling and it reinforces the other feelings in my body. Then Joschua lets go of his right hand and my head automatically stays in that position, but I feel it has set in motion on my way down. Oh she has reached my breasts and squeezes them several times and then his fingers pinch my left nipple and push and pull. These extra feelings start to drive me crazy. We both have our eyes closed and it's getting light in front of them. Oh Joschua, please, please continue and let your so horny hand slip down and touch me. Quiet on my pants. But he doesn't do it. After the pushing action on my nipple she slides deeper. From this angle he can not get close to my pussy. Will he try it with pressure over the pants. No, he does not want to, he manages to loosen my head on the waistband with his right hand and pull down the zipper. I help him immediately with a lot of small movements of my thighs and already the pants arrived at the bottom of the floor and his hand gets entrance behind my panties. He is really agile, because two of his fingers penetrate deep into my pussy and his thumb takes the standard position on my clit. Once there, she starts to move violently and I can hardly bear it anymore. All feelings now seem to be heading there to meet each other. Full concentration of feelings on these points and my moisture gives him the right gliding ability. And to enjoy that wonderful feeling. I stand on my tiptoes and my hands rest on his body so I do not fall over. But this extra tension only caught the feelings for a very short time, because Joschua's hand leans heavily, in terms of pressure. And I can not control it anymore, the automatic of the emotional processes to the cloud seven has begun and I get so violent that I go down from my toes again and my upper body is almost on his again. I am totally exhausted after a thousand meters run. He did it again. First he let me enjoy how he came and then he gave it to me to be able to reach the happiness of cloud seven and to stay there for a while. Oh this Joschua. It has never been so with a man. It's a give and take with it. We understand each other only with deeds without words and I enjoy them so much. I've never enjoyed anything like that or enjoyed it better than luck with Joschua. In all my thoughts, I did not notice, I was so busy with my excitement and the great way. Joschua has grown bigger under my right hand. Well, if I felt so appreciated, the small has already doubled again. That a man can come so fast in a row is that possible. He is still far away from the seed explosion, but he is on his way again. I am always learning new things what men you can love. Is really interesting. I've already thought I'll be a sex expert by Joschua. Another lesson to come. Oh, he moves. Of course he will not be able to lie on the hard work bench anymore. I take my hand off his cock and he looks at me. Sure it gets colder now, but he does not spoil a mine. He's still smiling at me, no, that's not a smile, that's a grin. But such a warm and positive. I take a step back from the workbench. And already he tries slowly to bring his right foot and then the left back to the ground to then straighten up. I still smile and give my hand to him. With a slight pull of it he comes to the sitting position. It was great and now it goes on. I pull him a little to me and he is back on his feet. Well, he looks a bit shaky, but that goes away quickly. In time he gives me a big kiss and take him in my arms. It feels so perfect, as I have missed something, for years. This feeling of not being alone and being liked by another person or even more, being loved, that is simply indescribably beautiful and certainly not comprehensible to people who have not yet experienced this feeling.

I do not know why, but where he stands there in an open trouser pocket, slightly excited, my feelings rise in me. That just can not be. It was only a few minutes ago that I was upstairs, but it also fell quickly. It was kind of a quickie and I have not used up my feelings yet. Funny in me it starts to sizzle otherwise I often have not even ex- perienced a climax in men and now my body wants to have one more. I feel like he wants to challenge him. I can not say that to Joschua now although I always wanted to tell the truth. He explains me as a sex addict. Oh Joschua you, hey how does he look at me. This is the look I know, the look when he wants me to the laun- dry, clearly in a positive sense. He will not want to come back again. Apparently.

But now, I can read it in his face. I can read his feelings. It is the desire for me. I feel he wants to do it to me again. My feelings about this thought make my ex- citement rise again and make me even moister down below. I stand there and he kneels down in front of me and he makes without my sayings on my pants closures to create. First the coloured button and then the zipper, open and down. It goes fast and I think if he could see my face now, it would be a bit confused. I am looking forward to what will happen to me right now.

"Hey, what are you doing? Did not we want to have dinner together?"
"Yes, we wanted, but I did not say when and now I want to have more fun. That one of you was indescribable,

now comes with me."
"I did not expect that."
"I know, but some men are just different."
"How true and you are one."
"I hope so!"

And already my trousers have landed on the garage floor, he lifts my foot, strips my shoe and removes the trouser leg completely and after he has gently put his foot down again, he does the same procedure with the other foot. He spoils my legs with his kisses and strokes them tenderly from bottom to top. At some point he hits the edge of my panties. Naughty push his hands underneath until they have reached my pussy and clitoris. Ohhh Joschua, I'm already very wet, even from now and now again. I never could have done it that fast before. Yes, it was enough again for me to undress me downstairs. These were only a few moments, he was so fast. Yes, but also so tender on my legs. Great decision by him to indulge me for the second time now. I have fun again. It really makes me happy again, although I have just come from a high altitude flight. Oh, what makes this male being only with me. Only my slip impedes him. So he pulls out his hands, reaches over the panties and anchors his fingers on the slip. Now he pulls the slip in one go with both hands to the ground. I take my feet up one after another and he's already taken off. He leads his head closer to me and with his hands, which now rest on my buttocks, my cool buttocks, he presses me, more precisely my pussy to his head. His mouth touches my pussy and he just drives out his tongue for a moment and immediately hits my clit. She responds immediately to this hit.

"Oops, what are you doing?"

He does not answer, but he removes his head from my private parts, then he gets up and his hands remain on my buttocks. We face each other now, looking at each other, and I do not know what will happen to me now, but I feel a yearning joy in it. I look at him expectantly. Oh, I hope he will not disappoint me now. I am so hot and excited, as if I would get a present. He pushes me back a step, then he takes my buttocks vigorously in his hands, lifts me up, taking me one more step and settles on the car radiator. I automatically support myself with my hands behind my back and Joschua pulls his hands away from under my buttocks. Now I feel the bare plate of the hood.

"Ohh, cool."
"Yes, that's the way it is, hot meat on a cold plate."

Now it will happen, he gets down on his knees in front of me, lifts both of my legs up with his hands at the same time and puts them on his shoulders. I seem to be as light as a feather for him, not quite, but it feels that way. Probably because I want it and really loaded, sexually back to full speed. My legs on his shoulders and with his head close, where I like it so much, on my pussy. The smell of my moisture penetrates his nose and makes him somehow and wild and he shows me with his tongue, which feels very comfortable in my pussy. His hands are on the side of my pelvis and his tongue switches between my inner pussy life and my clit. He listens carefully to my moan, because he reacts immediately with his tongue on my sex parts. My tension and my sexual excitement rise and rise and rise.

"Ohh, ohh, yes, I'll be right, what are you going to do with me?"

Joschua does not answer. How should he, his mouth is busy down there with me and that's just fine. Ohhh, ohhh and how good that is. Yeah well that's awesome He can do that. He makes me crazy. Oh, I could eat him now. Oh Joschua your tongue, yes please keep going you horny piece of man. Yes, I notice how my moisture is getting more and more and flows out of me and his mouth catches her, because he squeezes tightly between my thighs on my pussy. A feeling that I have not experienced so synonymous. Now you have to feel it as I start to shake, I press my thighs from both sides against his head. Skin contact of the oppressive kind. Hahaha Mia your thoughts are stupid. My thighs begin to vibrate with tremendous sexual tension. It has to feel like a vibrator to him and he can control it with his tongue. I am very excited, so much is pouring on me. My moisture flowing into his mouth, the taste of me his tongue picks up, the heat that comes from pressing and vibrating my thighs against his cheeks, as well as his hands catching on my pelvis and then my moaning what must sound like from far away, because my thighs press repeatedly on his ears. But this groaning, which sounds like something from another star, is guilty, which increases my feeling even further, an increase almost into ecstasy and that only because of my sexual arousal. The madness. I would now like to see if it turns on to lick me and lick me. Oh man Joschua is your cock again hard? Oh he does not just stop producing my moisture, but also eating it, just as I like his seeds. He still presses his head against my clit. I feel the heat in Joschua and the heat in me. Then I feel the brief stop of all feelings with me and I know, it is the absolute calm before the explosion. Now Joschua, if he rages his tongue once or twice over my clit, will manage to trigger the next climax with me. How I will enjoy the same again. Boom, boom, bamm. One twitch after the other, one more violent than the previous one, haunting my whole body and I am through the skin tight contact with him at this moment, like part of him. He experiences my crazy feeling explosion directly with. I'm so hot, I'm wet all over my body, as if I had done hard labor and my moan is so loud, you can certainly hear it outside. That certainly makes him so right to be allowed to experience this loud, lively Mia. What can a fortune exploding woman make a man of a pleasure with it. It used to be like that when my ex partner came, I was never or better I never felt like part of him. This has just brought me Joschua, the feeling of being really one with him. And I have not even slept with him. It makes me really happy inside that I can finally experience such a feeling so intense and may. If Joschua knew what he was doing for me through this super great climax, I think he would get himself a climax again. Or if he has become damp again in front of the glans again. I also did not know that happened to men. Since I know now always exactly how horny he is right now. I always learn from him. One of Joschua will still be my teacher. Mia you and your thoughts. Oh they are just so nice when they turn around my Joschua. My Joschua how that thinks. Is he my Joschua? Well, if he is not, I'll make sure he gets it. Oh, that poor man. Nonsense he gets me back completely for it. What can be the feelings of happiness, if you have the right partner at your side or just me, no between me. Smile. Oh well, I'm floating on cloud nine, right next to him, better half over him.

I feel like with me the voltage drops and the fast breath slows down a bit. I feel like the moisture production in me off again. I feel so good, well and human, he still has his head between my legs and his tongue just will not stop and also hits once again smooth on my clit. It elicits me a very tender groan. It's as if he wanted to thank him down there before he retracts his tongue once again for all that he was allowed to witness there. Say a goodbye, see you next time. As soon as his tongue has reached him again, I let the pressure of my thighs on his head and he slowly pulls him away. Oh man, my skin is stuck to his. The pulling away is like tearing something apart. Somehow a funny feeling and the proof, we were just as one, a soulful being, not two. I have to smile and what must I see when he has freed his head and is slowly straightening his back again, Joschua smiles too. It is not a smile from the corner of his mouth, no it is a radiance of his entire head, mouth, eyes, cheeks, everything is summed up like an intense smile and fed with 100.000 volts from the inside out. It looks like luck, then I have never seen this with a man, now for the first time with Joschua.

"Ohhh, what did you do to me?"

"I? No you with me!"

"I'm not back yet, a lot of bright lights are dancing around me with a lot of warmth around me."

"Hold her tight!"

"I'm just trying, it's so beautiful."

"That's how it should be."

"What did you do to me down there?"

"Nothing, my tongue just loved you. You just animated it."

"Animated? As?"

"Well, where you showed her a place where she was allowed to let off steam and, above all, you allowed it, and not like many others, pushed her away or pushed her away."

"Hahaha, why should I push them away, she showed me the ladder on which I could climb in cloud seven."

"But you have described that plastically. But you'll laugh, all the while I felt you climb the ladder. And if my tongue took a breather, you stopped on the steps."

"How, you could feel that?"

"Yeah, it was weird, it felt like the first time in my life, as if I had become one with another person and then you can feel your feelings climbing. And just before the jump, the complete silence and with me the feeling, if I let my tongue visit once or twice your clitoris, then it comes to the explosion. I really felt one with you and experienced everything. It also strengthened your body, it has smelt, tasted and sweat and took me so into a new, beguiling world of feelings. I would have liked to have my cock, which made it completely hard again, sunk into you, but I could just my head out of this cave of perfect pleasure, not pull away. You magically held me. It was indescribably intense and sooo beautiful. Thank you for being there and for letting me experience this with you. A lived dream. Thank you my angel."

"Thank you! I thank you! I would never have thought in life, no matter what I would have been told that I could experience something like this. On TV you often think when you see some movies, you want that or you do not exist at all, but what you just let me experience was more than I ever expected to feel. It was just indescribable, the feeling of what has also increased by the fact that I have felt your head between my thighs so intense. I could hardly move, I was always afraid I would slip off the hood."

"Yes, I sometimes noticed that in the beginning, then you always pressed your thighs tighter."

"Yeah, right, but then I forgot everything around me at some point, it just went away and I just saw heat and brightness. Brightness is not right, it was like warm sun rays in which I was embedded. Like a child in the lap of his mother. Sounds weird, but ... ."

"No I know what you mean, the warmth and security. I also felt that."

"How could you feel it? I think you're right, at that time it also felt like it was normal for your head to rest between my thighs and your tongue to be part of me. Crazy, but it was like that."

"Yes, I felt the same way. Is not that great, that can only work if you can really drop and the other just blindly familiar, otherwise that would not be possible."

"Yeah, I just let myself down and my body does the rest almost automatically ... ."

"No, not automatically, I steered it with my tongue and my breath."

"Yes, I felt that too, totally confusing. Tell me, did you even get air down there?"

"Heavy almost as hard as when you first put your blouse over my head, only there I was passive and here I could be active. With the blouse, I could smell something of you inhaling. Right here at your pleasure center, you sent out scents that I breathed in and catapulted me completely into another world of feelings and then the taste that you carried with me in your moisture. I do not even have enough words to describe exactly what I experienced between your thighs."

"Oh, you describe that really exciting."

"Really and then there was the moisture inside of you and later the moisture of your skin, you started sweat-

ing everywhere. These humidities then spread almost all over my face. And by the pressure of your thighs everything has been well mixed. That's why I felt like I was stuck to you. Was a strange, but somehow warm, positive feeling. It literally tapped me all over my body, as if a slight current charge were spreading. Simply indescribable. "

"Give me a kiss, I want to taste you!"

What follows now is really indescribable. We start kissing and I do not know how it happened, whether it's because of what's accumulating in his mouth and mixing in the adventure down with me or if it's the scent that's back in my nose penetrates or maybe the entire situation. I lie with my back on the hood of his car in the garage, a really unusual environment. I propped myself up with my hands behind my back and my breasts were full in my blouse and my bare legs hang down the radiator. He tries hard to push his head forward, against mine and the lips close our mouths almost completely, only the tongues are amused. As it happens, his cock wants to play with all violence again and has become quite stiff. Otherwise I'm not like that but I do not know how or what's happening right now and he pushes his pelvis towards me. There it is again this feeling to be one, because he does the same at the same moment and I feel like his cock hits my still super wet pussy and it runs through me like a shiver through, I passed on to him or came the shudder by him. I can not tell it anymore. I only feel like something thick pushes into my pussy. It gets warm in me and it is so wet and wet, then he pushes with a jerk of his pelvis, him completely into me. He really did push his cock inside me. Oh Joschua, how, what, ohhh how warm, how warm, how ...!!! My feelings start to roller coaster and I realized, I really noticed it, my thoughts, it's as if my thoughts are slowly on the horizon very small, tiny and insignificant. They seem to disappear completely and my feeling world starts, which starts to take over the helm and triggers also the following rhythmic counter impacts of my pelvis. Our pelvis thrust again and again, first very slowly, then a little faster, but always very intense against that of the other and I make loud noises from me, again a moan, coupled with the words ...

"Yeah, go on, yeah, faster oh Joschua, faster ...!"

And our bodies are one again, because my body or I believe it's mine, reacts immediately and I start to hit faster and more violently and it's always like a warm slap when the pelvis meet, with his cock always on my vagina rim inside docks, I mean my bang on my G-spot. Yes pop is the right expression, it splashes correctly you can hear it. My moisture is pushed aside by our clashes. Like a game of warm water, splash, splash, splash and our groaning succeeds in a consonance that gets more and more intense. And then there it is again, this calmness and silence and the short pause caused by it, as if one wants to keep the tension at its peak, the most beautiful tension in the whole world, heart tension, but unfortunately there is no time to stop and come back again violent jerk of the pelvis of both of us and both of us scream loudly ... and the tension begins to slowly dissipate with each additional cymbal stroke. It takes a while until we look exhausted, smile and recover.

"I am innocent."
"You, no you are the friend donor of my life."
"I?"
"Yes you, please stay on me for a moment. I want to hear and feel your heartbeat a little bit more."

I feel like his cock starts the retreat and slowly says goodbye to my cave. Now he lets himself hang. Yes, that's the way to complete relaxation, total happiness. And for a short while we'll stay on the hood together without saying anything. We just enjoy the just experienced and the existence of another person, of a person you just felt like yourself and who has given you

291

a feeling that you did not think you had.

"I could sleep so under you now."
"I have to be too heavy for you?"
"No, you're just intense and I think you're still in me, definitely in my feelings, they're still very confused, but in a good way."
"My also. Will we ever get it right again?"
"Oh, if they stay so confused happy, I can and want to live with that."
"Oh yeah, me too."

A while later, he lifts his head, resting on my shoulder. We look at each other and smile. I think I have never smiled at a man in my life and that he always shows his smile is just a nice feeling.

"You, I'm trying to get up to free you from me."
"Yes, please hold me, otherwise I'll slip down and fall over, my legs are not quite there yet."
"I know what you mean, they do not want to obey yet, they've got too many lucky ones."
"Yes, that's the way to say it."
"Take my hands."

I grab both hands of him with mine and he pulls me back to a normal straight position, right in front of him and I give him a kiss on the forehead, let his hands go and put my arms around his shoulders and press him firmly to me.

"Firmer, firmer."
"Yes, I'll crush you right away."
"Never mind, then I'm always close to you, a great idea."
"You, I would like to take a shower now."
"Alone?"
"Shall I rub your back on you?"
"That would be great."
"But then I can guarantee nothing."
"How to guarantee for nothing?"

"Well, in a sexual sense."
"You are so hungry."
"Now you have reminded me of something."
"To what?"
"I just wanted to take the bag of fish I bought into the house and then you seduced me and ... ."
"I should have been that?"
"Sure, of course!"
"And I thought that was you."
"Wow, I was just involved. You have done everything and now I take the helm again. You were responsible for the sexual part, me for the culinary part of the evening."
"Does that mean I have to take a shower alone?"
"Yes, you in my bath. I go to the other bathroom and then we meet afterwards fresh and happy in the kitchen again. Ok?"
"Well, I do not want to be like that. I got hungry too."
"What is it?"
"You made sure that I burned a lot of calories. But it was the most beautiful burn of my life."
"You were also the nicest sex fire of my life, in any case so far!"
"Oh, thank you, but how am I to understand that, do you want to do more experiments with other women?"
"Silly, experiments yes, but only with you. No one else will have the slightest chance anymore. Promised!"
"That's music in my ears! Well, we meet in the kitchen."
"Go ahead, now I want to see your beautiful naked butt in front of me, as they move in time as you go."
"Bad boy, see you soon."

And I go, with my buttocks extremely exaggerated wobbly into the house and disappear in the bedroom. Oh, Joschua, what an adventure of explosive feelings. Good that I have a healthy heart, otherwise I would now determined arrhythmia. And now quickly into the shower, I'm also totally sweaty. My clothes are ready for the washing machine. After that Joschua has to ask if I can wash my things. Oh the warm water is doing so well, now I could fall asleep standing here and experience the last hours over and over again in my mind. The time with him should never stop. Yeah, she's leaving right now, he's probably still planning so much, but it's already Saturday night, oops 21.23 and tomorrow evening I'm going home. Oh, Joschua is just wonderful. A man who takes a different path in every situation and takes it with him. I am a woman who also has feelings and fantasies and ... oh Mia, do not remember, finish and off to the kitchen. Shower cold set, oops but that makes clear thoughts and I still have to get into the bedroom new clothes, but can not walk around naked. So dry off and off to the bedroom. I have to hurry, Joschua is certainly back in the kitchen and prepares everything. Oh, I like watching him, I'd even rather help him, but I'd love to prepare something for him alone. If I continue to linger on my thoughts, then I will soon be starving. What an idea. I'm starving in bed but just totally happy. What a stupid thought, if I were dead I could not receive happiness from Joschua anymore.

So over to the bedroom, carefully open the door a bit to take a look inside. He is not there. So in, wardrobe on, clothes out. I'll take her to the kitchen and dress in front of Joschua. Oh Mia always such crazy thoughts. Where did they come from? You did not have them in the past. No you get dressed here otherwise it will be nothing to eat again. Better safe than sorry. You really know how to have so much sex at once. To be honest, I was really starving and when was the last time I had sex with so many feelings. My men were always different, they all thought of themselves and I was just the tool for them. Here at Joschua I have exactly the other feeling. Here I am the most important person for him. That is a truly wonderful feeling. I am his center. Too much memory Mia los hurry up. Thought, done and off to the kitchen. So now out of the bedroom. Oh how beautiful is that, everywhere light in the house, the spotlights with soft light on the palms directed, the countercurrent system, put on small waves made, in addition to the underwater lights, the water looks bright blue and sparkles. Oh, he's already lit candles on the dining room table. The atmosphere is so nice, you get real local feelings here. An absolute feel good atmosphere. When I get closer I see, he has even set the table. Oh today we are eating cold the delicious fish we bought together. Even the drinks are already in bottles on the table. Two small Schillerlocken on a plate, you can eat so. broken kipper on a board. Oh, he even skinned the eel and cut it into small pieces, and he even made warm scrambled eggs with chives. I can even smell the fresh rolls in the oven. How fast is this man? I appear in the dining room door, he sees me and smiles.

"How are you done again, I wanted to help you, can you do magic?"
"No, but the thought that exists gives me tremendous speed, because I want to give you pleasure."
"That's very nice, thank you!"
"I know how long it takes with your beautiful long hair to blow dry after a shower. You make it so extremely cool for me."
"Did you notice that? Yes, I want to make myself as beautiful as possible for you."
"Thanks, I noticed that already and you know what I noticed?"
"No!"
"Ever since you arrived here, you're starting to light up more from the inside with every passing minute. I'll write that and that's the biggest thing you can do for me."
"And love and pamper you."
"Yeah well, but now I can spoil you with something culinary just a little something."
"I find it incredible how a man can do it all. No man has really done that for me. I'm always finding out things about you, what you do to me and to me, something no one else has ever done. Thank you, you are the dearest man in the world!"
"Stop it! I'll turn red!"
"That's for you!"

"Thank you, may I take you to your place. Over here, please."
"Oh, thank you very much."
"I hope you brought really big hunger?"
"Yes, I also look delicious. I'll try everything."
"That sounds good. May I pour you a light beer or a malt beer. I can also cook you a tea or coffee."
"A light beer to the fish that would be delicious."

And he opens the bottle and gives me and a cup. Otherwise he never drinks alcohol, but to the fish tonight with me, well that's an exception he means and then I sit down in the chair opposite him.

"The big feed can start. After these nice hours and strenuous exercise together, I could beat half a pig."
"Hahaha and I'll take the other half."
"Sounds good, but would you like a starter first scrambled eggs with fresh chives and a piece of eel?"
"Oh yes please. I have never eaten eels."
"Mmm will certainly like you and the scrambled eggs."
"If you say that."
"Tell me. Why did you ask earlier that I put myself on the workbench?"
"I'm not sure. It just felt that way. I just wanted to touch you all at once and it was nice."
"I have never been with a woman who has taken the initiative and it is as if you can look into me whatever I want, or rather need."
"And I've been with men who have taken the initiative, but somehow they never knew what I was standing for and what I was feeling. Often I have not even come to a climax."
"And then you faked one to encourage the men in their selfishness, they would be the greatest."
"How do you know?"
"Well, I can imagine that. You are so emotional and you do not want to hurt anyone."
"Smart!"
"But how are the men to learn when the women tell them

296

that they were good even though they were off putting? Why are you playing something to them and not being honest?"

"Most men do not care about honesty and it's hard to be honest. To be honest, you're also vulnerable."

"Yes that's true. I always wanted to be honest with my partners and I was almost disappointed and it hurt more and more if you were honest than cheating."

"Yes, that was my experience too, but when I e-mailed you and you wrote to me trust and honesty is the basic requirement to let me down, because I felt something inside of me. An inner voice has told me, attention that's a different man than the one you've known so far."

"Honestly, did you feel that?"

"Yes, I was quite pleased and then our phone calls. If it had not been something very special, I certainly would not have come to you."

"That you already said yes, that was the sign for me."

"What sign?"

"The sign I was waiting for, because then I would meet a very special woman, a very, very special."

"And do you have?"

"Yes, you an angel!"

"I could listen to you for hours, you say such sweet words and in my heart I feel the honesty of them."

"Oh, that reminds me, do not you have to call your parents today and ask how your mother is doing?"

"Oh man, I did not think about everything I did with you."

"Do you want to call me?"

"What time are we having it?"

"Let's see it's 22:46. Are your parents still awake?"

"Yes, may I just call her?"

"That's probably clear, come to the office from there you can call undisturbed."

"Do not you really care?"

"No, in the meantime I eat all the eel."

"Oh please leave me a little bit over, that's really awfully delicious."

"Well that was just a joke. I'm not going to eat without

you."
"Love you, I hurry too."

We get up and I follow him to his office, that's the room between the bedroom and the pool changing room.

"There is the phone can stand off and dial directly. I pull the door, then you can call undisturbed. No rush."
"Do not need to close the door."
"Ok, I'm in the kitchen. See you soon."

It is nice of him that he thought of my parents. I am so happy and honestly did not even think about calling her today. Joschua really thinks of everything. And despite the late hour, my parents were happy that I called. And they recognized by my voice that I am really happy and wished me luck. They are so happy for me. Oh it's just beautiful since I know Joschua. No matter what I do, it works. I am flown by happiness. Out of the office, where is Joschua? Ah, I hear sounds from the kitchen. Since Joschua is the only one outside the house, he has to be, so Mia is off. When I stand in the kitchen door I see Joschua. Oh, what's that on the shelf, you munchies. I'm hungry again. It's also clear Mia, in the sex I consume a lot of calories and he too. I steer towards him, hug him and then I give him a kiss on each cheek and ...

"Thank you for thinking, they were really happy that I called. My mother is doing much better. And they asked me how it is with you."
"How, how do you know that you are here, you have not made a phone call."
"You know, I have a lot to tell the evening when I was sitting alone with my father at home, and he must have noticed that I was more excited than usual and then I told him about our mails and phone calls and my heart very doll beaten and that I'll drive home to you yesterday instead of yesterday."
"And what did he say I was so excited, but he was happy, right?"

298

"How are you doing on it?"

"Well, if he had not agreed that you're going to a near-strange man, then he would not have wished you luck and much fun. So you inherited the feelings from your father then."

"Yes, you're good at feeling what others mean. He said I should be happy to meet such a man and enjoy every second with you."

"Well, your daddy is great. Finally someone who wishes and gives happiness to another. And what did your mother say?"

"She said if I wanted to, I should do it, life would go by so fast."

"You have maybe cool parents."

"Yes, I was really lucky with them. They have to live a long time too!"

"I'll keep my fingers crossed for you, how old are you?"

"My mother 68 and my dad 71."

"That's not an age today. You'll have that for a long time and maybe I'll meet her sometimes."

"Like, you want to meet my parents?"

"Later, if you want, gladly. I do not have any more. My dad left when I was seven, and my mom raised me alone."

"And she did a great job."

"Thank you, that's nice of you. My mom died eight years ago and I still think about her many times. If you knew beforehand that death was so definite, you would be different sometimes or spend more time together, but you always say tomorrow, tomorrow, tomorrow, and when death comes in between, you think afterwards, I would have had one me one."

"But you speak sweetly of your mom. Sound really sad."

"Oh let's change the subject please, otherwise you'll see a man crying."

"Men are allowed to cry too, but it only makes them more human."

"There you have a very rare attitude. That's really great of you. Many say men who cry are sissies but that's not

true. The company previously did not accept crying men. The man always had to be strong and take care of everything. But I think that when you eat everything into yourself, you get sick. I can sing a song about that."
"With me you can cry and put your shoulder on."
"It's bound to happen sometime, but now that you've been here I could only cry!"
"Cry? Why did I do something wrong?"
"No, I could cry tears of joy!!! But where you ask me that, yes, you've done something seriously wrong!"
"How?"
"You should have called in twenty years earlier!"
"Surely you would not have wanted me yet. I was also immature and very jumpy."
"I would have tamed the wild instinct in you with a lot of understanding, even more feeling and astronomical love!"
"You're right, I've missed twenty years of luck. I was stupid!"

And we look each other in the eye. Joschua takes me by the hand, leads me again to the dining table, put me the chair and I sit down. Then he leans down to me and give me a kiss on the forehead.

"You're just nice, thank you for your understanding, and I have to thank your parents later, for putting them into the world, otherwise we would not be able to eat together and enjoy our lives here."
"Ok, can you then."
"Well then let's continue to feed."

There follows some time of silence while food intake continues. When we have satisfied our hunger, I look at him questioningly.

"You probably want to tell me what you want to do with me now."
"I wanted to ask you what you want to do to me now."
"Hahaha, but you have cleverly distracted from my

question. Are you full or do you want something for dessert?"

"Dessert, yes you!"

"So you think I still fit all the way into your stomach?"

"No, not in my stomach but … ."

"How did eating sit opposite me so excited again?"

"Yes!"

"Do you know strip poker?"

"I've never played, but that's with the clothes off."

"Yes."

"But I can not play poker."

"Well, I do not want to be like that, because if you can not do it, you'll always lose and you're pretty naked and I'm still sweating in my clothes."

"How do you give me a chance?"

"What can you play? Darts, Billiards, Airhockey?"

"A bit of everything."

"Shall we go play airhockey?"

"Airhockey is with the two puks and the goal you have to defend."

"Right and the puk is floating on an air cushion."

"Do we have to go far?"

"Go."

"But if there are people, then you can not play French."

"Right, if there are people. But it's already 23:32."

"Hey, do you want to torture me?"

"Tension and torture sounds good. But torture meant as a love torture."

"Love torture how are you?"

"I'll tell you later, are you still hungry?"

"Thank you was really delicious, I'm totally well-fed."

"You just clear it off and then it starts."

We get up and cover the table very quickly and I run into the kitchen.

"You're in a hurry, why so fast."

"I'm so curious where we go."

"Oh, curious?"

"Yes and how and again excited."

"Cool! So come on, let's go."
"Do I have to wear something else?"
"Let's see, please turn around completely. Mmm I like what I see, can stay that way!"

He grabs the cupboard and walks along the pool towards the garage door. I follow him and I have to automatically see him on his tight, though hidden by the pants buttocks. Why only but my eyes are simply pulled there or is my heart steering my eyes?

"Well, do you still like them?"
"Do you have eyes at the back?"
"No, but my feeling feels your greedy eyes on it."
"Hahaha! So drive away by car."
"No! No! No! Here we will take the stairs to the left."
"Oh, you want to lead me into the deep catacombs of your house. Is there torture there?"
"Who knows, you always want to be tortured, do you really trust me and would you drop then?"
"I know that I can trust you one hundred percent, but if I can drop I do not know, I have to, no, I'd like to try."

He stops halfway down the stairs and turns to face me. I stand one step behind him and lean forward immediately. My arms wrap around him and my lips cover almost all areas of his face and end up on his mouth. It is flicked and his hands come from my hip, where they have just found support again and again up and then have to climb the two mountains on which they then lie still, now only a little oppressive. And what can I say I can not do anything about it, my left, stiff standing nipple has yet bumbled smoothly between his fingers of the right hand. Yes, he feels it, she wants to be depressed and he does that right away and that's right. Out of mine, through his closed mouth, sounds are coming to our ears.

"Ahhh, yes, yes, yes, yes!"
And he notices my right hand trying to feel his left

nipple through his shirt. Oh, there I have her and imme-diately I squeeze and pull at her violently.

"Auauau, I surrender!"
"I hope so!"
"Ohhh shall I surrender in your opinion?"
"In everything and with me in your destiny."
"Sounds very tempting. Come down."
"How to get down?"
"Well, down the stairs. If we stand here longer and smooch and squeeze, we'll lose the hold soon, if we've gotten wild and that makes ouch, a very violent ouch."
"You are one."
"Come over."

And we take the last steps together because he holds my hand and pulls me downstairs. The light has come on and we come into a room tiled with large floor tiles. My hand rips out his hand. I stopped. He turns around to me and I might make huge, surprised eyes.

"What's up, have you seen a ghost?"
"No, but I would not have expected that here. You keep surprising me!"
"Why is this my party room and there was a small bar down the street, the dance floor with colourful lighting and rotating mirror ball, the sofa corner with a small table and a lot of shell, you can see what's in there?"
"Colourful sweets?"
"Hahaha almost, lots of little colourful condoms!"
"What, you put it that way and your guests use it?"
"Oops, shall I be honest?"
"Well, I'm asking for it."
"I had the house planned and built myself and I moved in just over a year ago and I have not celebrated a party here, just played alone on the devices. You will inaugur-ate the party room with me tonight. Do you do that?"
"This is a virgin party room? Of course I'll consecrate him with you!"
"French or no matter, but strip-hockey!"

"Yes, everything you want and I can add something, right?"

"I do everything with what you add."

"Everything?"

"Yes, everything, I trust you a thousand percent and I know we will have a lot of fun then too. What do you want for music?"

"Ohhh what's that music box? Dreamlike and with water bubbles."

"Yes, that's my dream too. A real Wurlitzer with a hundred CD's inside. Do you like listening to songs from the eighties?"

"Yeah, sounds good, let's go."

Joschua pushes some numbers and the music starts to play. I flinch.

"Oh, maybe I should have warned you first? Here comes the music from all four corners and this gives you the feeling ... ."

"Yes, that's a feeling like being in the middle of it. Madness the sound and not so loud, we can still talk about it as normal."

"Yes this is the latest technology you can hear the music, but the volume is not crazy in the head."

"Wow and what is it now?"

"Well, when the music starts, the mirror ball starts to run and the colourful lighting effects as well. Did I switch this way? Did not always feel like turning everything on every single time."

"Class, top class, lights like a disco."

"In our private disco."

"I've never been alone with a man in a disco."

"Other visitors would only disturb you now!"

"You are so right again."

"Can I offer you something to drink?"

"Yes, what can you offer?"

"Just sit down on the bar stool and I'll check it out. Here is the drinks menu and an orange juice for starters. Study it and you can vote!"

Cold soft drinks

Aloe Vera pur .... 1 x hug
Pure H$_2$0 .... free
Apple juice.. 1 x hug
Apple spritzer.. 2 x hug
Orange juice ....1 x hug
Raspberry juice pur ....1 x take head in your hands
Sprayed raspberry juice.............1 kiss on the left cheek
Red grape juice pur ....1 x through the hair
Splashed red grape juice ....1 kiss on the right cheek
Multivitamin juice ....1 handkiss
Carrot juice ....1 kiss on the forehead
Cow's milk ....1 x smile
Liquid or whipped cream...............................2 x smile
Lemontea.. ....1 x caress hands
Chocolate with + without cream ....1 kiss on the neck
iced coffee...............................2 x kiss on the neck
Ice chocolate... ....3 x kiss on the neck

Cold alcoholic drinks

Cointreau ....1 x nibble the ears
Cherrywater ....1 x caress shoulder
Remy Martin ....1 x kiss navel
Redwine ....1 x tender kiss?!
Rum ....1 x caress the back
Orangenliqueur ....1 x kiss left foot

Terms of payment net immediately on
delivery !!!

305

Warm soft drinks

Cup of coffee..........................1 x caress no matter where
glass of tea...............................1 x kiss no matter where
Mug of chocolate with + without cream.1 x French kiss
Warm milk ....1 x kiss eyes
Warm milk with honey.......................1 x kiss the nipple

Warm alcoholic drinks

Grog ....1 xkiss the left buttock
Russian chocolate ....1 x kiss the right buttock

Specialties

Freshly drawn Ambrosia ....1 night

The waiter is happy to accept more
imaginative payments without
consideration. It can also be ordered
activities of any kind! Test your imagination
and dare to order it !!!

"Well, already elected?"

"No, I'm speechless. I have never seen such a drinks menu. You may have imagination. How I like it and I'm really the first here?"

"Yes, the very first woman in the party cellar and also the first woman I show this drink list. Nice that she arrives so well with you."

"No matter what happens, I will never forget the time since I got the first mail from you, as long as I live and whenever I'm sad, I'll think about it."

"That's very nice of you but there are still many more surprises to come from me, have enough ideas for another fifty years and the power you give me. Is it cheeky of me to tell you, please, please never go away again! You have taken me by storm and I have fallen in love with you since the first mail and now it has become love in the storm. You Mia, I love you!!!"

It is followed by a silence, an audible silence and only our eyes let our eyes meet and in the background the jukebox is playing from the Beatles - all you need is love - and it's like listening to the song and sucking into it. Then I find my voice first and say ...

"You I feel that you have what you just said ... ."

"I love you!!!"

"Yes that's it. I feel that it comes from your heart and I would like to tell you something. I have a week's holiday and if you want, I'll stay with you next week! I love you with all my heart!"

Now I've really done it, he looks a bit baffled and I feel like tears running down his cheeks. I get up from the bar stool, come around the counter, turn to him and I take him in my arms and hold him tight. I feel his body, not just his warmth, but he seems to tremble a bit and I can not find any other words at the moment. It's a moment in my life that I've never, never really experienced, even in my dreams. He is venerable. He is totally touched and I only said the three magical words - I love you - but as he said, these were pure feelings and that into my open heart right inside, because it was so close to being totally open for Joschua and also said those words to him. We are still holding on and I hear his heart beating. I have the feeling that in every place I feel, where my body touches his, which beats loudly and says, never let go of me and my heart responds, never again, never, never again!

After a felt eternity, we loosen our hugs a bit, I look him in the face and take my hands, put them in his face and try to wipe his tears.

"That you have so much heart is impressive, I never thought and that you open it for me and serve it on a gold tray, me!!! I still can not believe that."
"Dito!"
"What happened just now?"
"Probably the most incredible thing in the world, the two of us have found each other and made each other known, from the bottom of our hearts. It's the feelings, I'm still blown away."
"Me too."
"Say, I really heard right, I understood that you love me too, the most beautiful thing ever and then you really said you can stay with me the whole next week? Seriously?"
"Yes, I can and I want, but only if you want."
"And how I want! More than anything else in the world. Thanks for this message. Did not you want to tell me that? No, you wanted to see if it was nice and otherwise you would have left tomorrow. Is it true?"
"Yes, I did not know what to expect and I did not expect you to. I mean with a man like you."
"How come?"
"Sooo heart and feelings, empathy, intelligent, attentive ... ."
"Stop it, I'm going to blush."
"I know that you can, I have already experienced."
"Yes, unfortunately!"

"Not, unfortunately, you have already shown me so many facets of you, all my men have not even managed together."

"Do not always say such nice words to me. No, tell her, they are balm for my wounded soul."

"Why tortured soul?"

"Oh maybe we'll talk about it later, I do not want to destroy this moment now. I'm floating!"

"Well! Then I want to order something!"

"What can I serve the lady for?"

"I'll take a cup of tea."

"Can I serve you lemon or cream for tea? What kind of tea may it be, black, green, vanilla, peppermint, rosehip?"

"Well, if I were honest then I would give up the tea and just want to pay right away. Is that okay?"

"Sure, I'm getting around for payment. And where do you have to kiss me, may I decide on my own?"

"Yes."

"And you do it immediately?"

"Yes."

"You look so questioning. What do you mean, where I want to have a kiss from you."

"Well, on your cock."

"I almost thought that you were thinking that of me. Evil, bad."

"How bad, where should it be?"

"What's the worse?"

"Well, no, I do not know."

"Should I believe that now?"

"Yes, please! Where would you like to have him?"

"Yeah, you know, that's very difficult, because I want to have some everywhere and I just get a kiss. Or do you want to order more teas?"

"Well, that could be talked about, but then I have to invite more women to let all the ordered teas drink."

"No, no, no other women please, only I want to feel you."

"Honestly? Yes! So tell me, where should I kiss you?"

"Mmm I could get it under my right foot, please."

"Under your right foot. You confuse me. Under your right foot, what's your ulterior motive?"

"I never ulterior motive! Well, almost never, but now no ulterior motive. I just imagine how my foot lies on the counter and you nibble under it."

"How to nibble, there's only one kiss."

"Oh, I would have brought you some lemon and cream, if it were not for a snack. Oh, and for your snack I would have put a biscuit to it."

"You can always somehow persuade me, how do you do that?"

"I am quite ... ."

"Yes, you are innocent, but I do not believe so."

"But it is me. It's my heart that influences you that way."

"Ok, I can and want to live with that. Kiss with a light snack."

"But just a light snack, I'm ticklish."

"Really ticklish under your feet?"

"Yes, you could say I could still exchange the snack?"

"How to exchange."

"The snack in a tongue stroke."

"Tongue line? What's this?"

"Well, when your tongue licks from verse to toe once. Slowly press more, sometimes less."

"Oh, that sounds difficult."

"Why hard?"

"Well, first I have to go from back to front and then with changing pressure."

"Oh, you're capable of multitasking, of course."

"Well, if you think that of me, I'll do it too. But you can not move your foot, no matter what I do with my tongue."

"What, what are you doing with your tongue?"

"No movement, you have to promise me that, otherwise I'll have to punish you."

"Oops, I can not guarantee that. You have often surprised me so much and when I move then. No, I can not promise."

"Well, then I will order the tea again."

"No, please, please do not. Is not it enough if I promise

310

to try?"
"Alright, I agree with that."
"Thank you."
"So it goes off, you sit down on the bar stool and I'm sitting here, then you put your foot in his lap like he is now and then you'll be surprised."
"How about shoes and socks?"
"Yeah, you're a smart guy, you got on with me the first time."
"Why am I excited by the thought of what you're up to?"
"Well, how should I know that? Ask him."
"Who?"
"Well your cock, he must know why he gets stiff."
"Good idea. Hey you down there why are you getting stiff? ... he does not answer me ... how did he tell me he just talks to you!"
"You're a rascal. But I will interview him later in more detail."
"You have a super memory."
"I remember the last conversation with him, was delicious."
"And from my point of view it was hot!"
"Let's start, sit down, walk here!"
"Ok, wait until the bar stool adjust, sit on it, the tension rises in me already tremendously and please, here I put you my right foot in your lap to faithful hands."
"Sounds good."

I look at him, start to open the shoelace, while he keeps looking up at me and smiles.

"Well, look, how is your cock."
"But you're mean, you want him so hard, mmm for what?"
"What can I tell you, you are too curious."
"Oh yes, but this time you can not punish me and shut your mouth and nose. You're sitting at my other end."
"Well, I would not be so sure, there are other punishments."
"Which?"

311

"Youuu, do not be so curious. You know, I have imagination."
"Ohh, now I'm scared."
"You can have it, hahaha!"

I look at him all the time, and the corners of my mouth are smiling, but it's not a normal, hearty smile, but rather such a mischievous smile. A smile that should tell him, caution something will happen soon. Watch out! And I grab my heel with his hand and pull him off to the front. Good that he always washes his feet, so he can rest assured he has no cheese feet. Human, that would be embarrassing now. But is not synonymous with the many swimming, because they are always clean again. I would not have dared to do that with many other men in front of him. Now he feels my hand through his black knee highs. I move my hand down from his knee around his entire foot and under him as well. I stroke him and that feels good to me too. Somehow crazy, even that I caress his still stockinged foot, I feel that as wonderful and it spreads a certain peace in my whole body. I even see him relax and just allow it and just enjoy it. Yes, while my hands caress him, I watch his face very closely. His facial muscles have completely relaxed. Oh, I think he could stand that for hours now.

"You seem to like that."
"Yes, it is totally relaxing. I feel your hands radiate a magical warmth and calm."
"You, pay attention to what I tell you now."
"Yes, what should I do?"
"Hold on to the bar with your left hand and rest on the barstool behind you with your right hand."
"Sounds complicated, I'll try it."
"Looks good, you did it. I knew it."
"Now you want to kidnap me at such a later time."
"Not late, early! Hahaha."
"Ok, very early."
"Well, now give me your other foot up but hold on well that you will not slip off the stool."

He also puts the second foot in my lap and I immediately open the shoe laces and take off his shoe. Then I just let him fall to the floor and both his stockinged feet are now side by side in my lap. I hold my hands on both feet as if I wanted to warm her, if he feels that well. Certainly. The warmth will calm him down, because he will be able to feel it throughout his body. Then I go with both hands from the heels to the toes at the same time with my fingernails, medium pressing oppressive.

"Ahhh not that tickles, do you want to throw me off the stool?"
"I told you to hold on."
"I do, but my body twitches when you do something like that."
"Well, something like that! I have to do it again, it's as cool as you react to it."

Said done and I pull again and again and once again my fingernails under his heels. It tingles all over his body, but I will not let him pull his feet away. I've stopped with the sole massage and my two hands each have an ankle and so I hold his feet tight. I watch him closely and see how slow the tingling in his body decreases. He does not shake anymore and his breathing calms down. This is apparently the sign for me to devote to his knee socks. Almost at the same time, I release my fingers from his ankles and slowly drive up his stockings.
Somehow he almost takes his breath away, because he wants to be ready for it when I trigger something with him again. But nothing happens, it just seems to be very comfortable for him and I reach the knee sock cuffs, hook my fingers and pull them down. It will certainly cool him, as I pull the stockings down. I'm effective because in one fell swoop, I pull them over the heels and then it happens. Hahaha, I deliberately did that as I pulled the stockings farther from his feet, I cautiously scratched over his now bare soles and I've just got halfway through my feet. And with both feet at the same time.

"Hahaha stop, hahaha not, hahaha."
"Do not pretend."

And I continue and it tickles Joschua right. He tries to fight back and pull his feet away, but the stockings that still cover his toes prevent him from doing so. But all of a sudden, I pull my fingers out of his stockings and drive my fingernails under the soles back to his heels and on high, almost to his knees.

"I thought I forgot something up there."
"Hahaha, what are you supposed to have forgotten?"
"I do not know that, that's why I look after it."
"And that's why you have to scratch my nose with your fingernails."
"Oh, did I do that? I'm terribly sorry, I really wanted to!"
"Like, I knew it, you did it on purpose. That betrays the tone in your voice."
"Sure, it's so nice to tickle you, you react to it so hard."
"That's mean."
"No, very exciting."
"For whom? To you?"
"Mmm I believe for both of us."
"Well, I think that's great, too. You are also aroused by me. Which man does not want to be able to excite and above all be able to excite the woman he loves and I can do that passively."
"Well, you're just a great pike."
"Wow, thanks for the compliment. Please continue!"
"Do not be impatient."

And I drive down again and up again to then pull back down to get to the stocking over his toes stockings. These touches no longer tickle so much, they trigger a body tingling in his body and his hair seems to be everywhere, as if you are under power. A very nice feeling. In itself crazy, just because I pull his stockings down erotic his body reacts. This has never happened with a man. I can not even remember that I have pulled down a man's stockings. Again the first time. This

314

Joschua lets me do things that I've never done before and that without him telling me that. Just because he's there and the situation is there. Yes, Joschua is something very special. I am his emotional angel who catapult him on cloud seven goddess of love. Oh Mia, what are you thinking? If Joschua knew, I think he would call me crazy. Or maybe he would be happy about what he can do and trigger with me. Apparently I trigger with him so many feelings that he certainly has not known before. It's just great and now Mia is off with the thoughts. Hello heart, please accept.

Here heart I take over and will increase as the first time the heartbeat, because immediately I will take off his stockings completely and see his feet completely naked in front of me. I know he thinks I've thought of something crazy again and he might be right it would be crazy maybe if I took his foot in my mouth and then nibble on his toes. Only at all at the same time. I could lick it around with my tongue and then nibble it in his toe gaps and then every single toe. Mia concluded with the thoughts and approach to the funny work. It makes me really enjoy doing something like that. Joschua, Joschua you poor man must suffer now. So fingers hooked into his stockings and then I pull her slowly over her toes.

"Cold!"
"Yes and more, watch it."

And I just feel like it. I'll blow a strong gust of wind out of my mouth over his feet. A cool shiver runs through his whole body to his head, because he is shaking. It's fun to see him blowing you like he reacts immediately. Oh Mia give him a blow job, but that sounds no not on his cock but over his toes. Hahaha with him you can still have fun thoughts in the thought. Now continue Mia and implement the next idea. I tie the two ends together from his knee socks.

315

"Hey, what are you doing there?"
"A surprise for you."
"Surprise for me?"
"Yes, only for you alone."

And he certainly does not know what I'm up to, so I tie the now long enough stocking around his two ankles and pull the knot tightly together. Hahaha, now I've tied his legs together and he can not run away anymore and I can hold both his legs with one hand. So I have a hand free for other stupidities. Oh, I'm fine. I have to praise myself. Since I have really lame my toy a bit.

"Hey, you tied my feet together. I can not move her that way anymore."
"That's the way it should be, they're mine now, and I'll pay my tea now, even the sugar and lemon you wanted to deliver to me."
"Oh, yes, good."

And my heart and my emotional world is in high alert. I get up now, putting his feet on the bar stool I just got up from.

"Do you have a handkerchief for me?"
"Handkerchief? Yes, in my right pocket. Why do you need that? Are you crying now and want to dry your tears?"
"Hahaha, that was good."

And I I fingered with my hand in his right pocket and push it in so far that my fingers touch his stiff cock.

"Wow, are you hot again? It's amazing, I once had men who did not get so stiff."
"I will not do that with every woman. You are to blame. You are a very special, erotic being and also the actions you make surprise me again and again."
"As my actions surprise you."
"You are not predictable and incredibly spontaneous!"

316

"Oh, I really appreciate that."
"It should be that way."
"Feel what I'm doing now."
"Ohhh you squeeze him tight. You have power in your fingers. No, do not push back and forth, then another bad luck happens."
"Bad luck? Do not you think you're lucky?"
"Yeah, I mean that I just do not want to come now, I'm so curious what you still do to pay for the tea."
"So, you're curious. Okay, then I'll pull my hand out of your bag. But I take the handkerchief out with me."
"Ok, and why do you need that again?"
"Let yourself be surprised."

And already my thoughts are crowding in front of the feelings of my heart and begin to picture the picture of what I can and will do with his handkerchief. Mmm, shall I gag him or blindfold him? But no, something else. I go back to his feet and tie the handkerchief through the riveting stocking that holds his feet together. Well, something that comes to mind when playing with Joschua. Now I tie the other end to the back of the bar stool. I have now positioned his bound feet so they are tied to the back of the bar stool and they look out over the bar stool with the verses. Exactly what I wanted, Joschua now holds with his left hand on the bar and with his right hand on the bar stool behind him, then he can not easily fall down. But that brings him into the position I want, in which he is totally at my mercy, without me having done much.

"You have a lot of responsibility now."
"How so?"
"You have to take good care of me, I will not fall down."
"No, I have to pay my tea debts now. The waiter has to take care of himself. "

And I kneel in front of the bar stool on the ground so that my face is right in front of his soles. Whether he already knows what he has to endure, but it excites him

317

even more. I see his cock getting so stiff. First I lick with my tongue slowly on his left sole of the foot from the verse to the toes and then lick on the right foot from the toes to the verse.

"Wow, what are you doing, it's driving me crazy. Your tongue, she tickles, no tingles, no I do not know, it's so terribly exciting."
"Yes, I feel it, you taste so good."
"What?"
"After Joschua."
"And how does Joschua taste?"
"Well, just like you, just exciting."
"I feel like you're spoiling me again and I can not give you anything back."
"Do not play anything, you give me so much, you do not realize that. It's so wonderful for me to be able to pamper you so much and that you do everything with it is simply indescribable."
"If that's how you feel, then thanks! I'll drop completely now and just enjoy."
"Yes, I fully agree with that."
"Hey, you're laughing so stupid again, what are you up to now?"
"Oh, I would like to see how your excitement increases, every time I do something and also to which you react especially."
"Yes and how?"
"You said I can do anything I want?"
"Yes, everything that is not hurtful."
"I will never hurt you or bring your blood to your skin."
"I know that, that's why I think it's so great what you do. I trust you a thousand percent."
"Thanks and then I will ... ."
"What?"

Without saying anything I get up, come up to him, give him a wet kiss on his lips with a short tongue whisper and then press a kiss on each of his eyes. Then I press my lips firmly together with my lips and lick again with

318

my tongue. Then I lift my head and smile at him and my hands go to work on his zipper. I open it and reach into the slot of his boxer shorts.

"Hey, ohhh, how exciting, what are you doing?"

And I pull his cock out of his pants. He is already very firm and remains outside, even when I take my hands away and go down, kneel down again and start again with the licking.

"Ahhh, you're tickling your tongue."
"Yes, and now I see how that excites you."
"How come?"
"Well, I see your cock responding to my touch as your body pumps blood in and gets stiffer and bigger. Also, the colour of your glans changes. I can see it exactly."
"What you pay attention to."

And I've already taken the toes from his left foot completely in my mouth and press my tongue between the toe spaces. That will certainly drive him crazy. It would me, that's where I'm extremely ticklish, but Joschua will certainly find out at some point. I can not describe the feelings properly. Joschua is between excitement and madness, but I see that he can hardly stand it anymore. If I look up at him and look closely at his glans, it is already a bit damp there. Was certainly a cheeky drop of semen. Hot to be able to see that, otherwise everything is not visible. Playing makes me that way too, I'm getting wet. Yes, Joschua lets me experience everything and that not only can I lick it all over him, but I also have to look at him in every situation, that makes it such an extra sparkling experience for me. Just awesome, so cool.

"Hey stop, no more, please, please, I beg for mercy."
"How so?"
"I can not stand this between toes, you make me crazy."
"Wild is good!"

"No, I can not move freely."

"That's a good thing. Ohhh, now I have neglected the right toes. I can not do that."

"No, please, please, you … ."

"Oh, what must I see there, your glans shines full dark red. I hope it does not burst."

"Wait, I have to recover first."

"Oh, then she will be smaller again."

"Oops, you take me out of breath."

"And that's where I get you."

"Yes, it's not the licking between my toes alone."

"No, what?"

"It's the overall situation. Me with an angel here in the party room. Defenseless delivered to you and you as erotic as you imagine it in the wildest dreams and I may experience now. And then also from you acts that I never thought of."

"Which do you mean?"

"That you use my cock, for example, as an exciter."

"Yeah, I did not think that before, but somehow you lead me to such acts. I act spontaneously and I find it exciting that I may do so with you. It always used to be like this, I never trusted men, they always had the upper hand and did not encourage me. You do that!"

"Oh, thank you, I have to give that back to you, because I only ever had women who wanted to be led. I was never lucky that I met a female being who had her own ideas and wanted to implement them. Unfortunately. And now you have broken into my life, like a rocket and have everything, what I would like from my dream woman."

"Ohhh, you said that again so nice, but you also have everything I would have liked from my dream man."

"Then you are my dream woman!"

"And you my dream man!"

I have to laugh. Then I start to nibble on his toes again. Today, I somehow feel like nibbling. Joschua has so much variety. Fantastic! But only a short rest during these thoughts and then I go wild again with my tongue over his soles and lick and lick and lick.

"Ohhh, yes, thanks. That was the complete payment also for the additional delivery."
"How paid?"
"Yes."
"You just want me to stop."
"How so?"
"You sure want to get out of the situation and I should untie you."
"Mmm."
"No, I still want to pay for the morning tea, the day after tomorrow, and the whole week in advance."
"Oh dear!"
"Nothing, only tea."
"Hahaha."
"Besides, I want you to explode, I want to see how it comes to you and you distribute your semen in the room."
"What do you want?"
"Yes, I want to watch your emotional explosion."
"No one wanted that yet."
"Me though! And now!"

And then it happens, I get up, come upstairs and take his cock in his hand. I give him only a kiss on the mouth and say to him.

"Now you are mine. There is no going back."

And I put my right hand around his cock, that's nice and good and now if I start to move it up and down. Oh, this man seduces me to things, where I always used to be bright red. But experiencing it with him is terribly exciting, but somehow as if it were normal to do such a thing and that makes me feel right. I often used to feel like doing something forbidden. I do not have that feeling with Joschua. Here I always have the feeling to do something new and that is so cool. Oops, what is it? My right hand has picked up the movement and pulls up

321

vigorously, very strongly, and stops there. I pull so hard that he tries to take the pressure out of his pelvis by lifting it up a bit. Of course I notice that immediately.
"No, no, that's not true."
"What do you think?"
"That you want to take the tension out."
"But you also notice everything."
"I'm not feeling poor."

And I'll move him a bit further. Which ensures that I can hold him not only in this tense situation, no, so I can scratch around so well with my fingernails around his glans.

"Oh, what are you doing? What do you do? I'm about to explode."
"Yes, come, come, come!"
"Equal!"

And then I do something quite unexpected for him. I blow over his glans several times quite violently and that tingles him again and again, but that's not it, then I want to very carefully put my fingernail of my left index finger in his mouth on the glans, not deep just a bit and move him there very intense.

"Oh, oh, not, I'll be right over. I explode, not ...!"
"Come honey, come on, let it go, come now!"

And while I still move my fingernail within him, this certain calm before the storm arises again and his breath stops. I say nothing, I look him in the face and immediately back to his glans, because she will certainly spit out something. Oh Mia what thoughts, spit out, but he will be as tight as she already is, glossy. I have the feeling it will happen to him soon. He is already tensing his entire body. Every moment it will happen and I still move my fingernail during this respite and then, he can not do it anymore and he certainly does not want to delay or prevent it any longer. His seeds start and I feel

322

like they're shooting. He has his eyes closed and I feel his seeds leaking out and they jostle past my fingernail.

"Ohhh now!"
"Yes, give it to me, spray me full, yeah, oh, it's so warm and humid and that scent, madness, more, more, more."

And I press with the right hand once or twice firmly, let's see if I can accelerate the remaining seeds. Then I take my fingernail from the seed moist opening on his glans and put my palm on her and embrace her tight. I feel like his warm semen spread all over my hand and on his cock. Ohhh, an unimaginable erotic idea that I can really see. I squeeze his cock once again and the last seeds of this insanely intense ejaculation swell from the opening on his glans. I feel it in my palm exactly. If I leave my hand there and push it, it will soon stick. And while I think about it Joschua begins to smile about his whole face.

"What is?"
"Oh, it's so beautiful."

And now I'm definitely doing something unimaginable for him again. I take my hands away from his cock and put them on his cheeks and press them firmly against his head and then give him a wet, long, intense tongue kiss. He answers him immediately and very violently and I feel like the seeds from my hands stick to his cheeks and become firmer. I do not even know if I wanted that, but when I saw his smile, I had to kiss him spontaneously. Anyway, I find it so exciting. Now he can perceive his own smell, very close and smell as I always perceive him. And he is still kissing me, very wild and wet. There he is again such a moment of pure happiness that seems to give us both so much and that we both want to enjoy for as long as possible.

"Yeah, if you had your hands free now, you want to touch me, right?"

"What, what, have you read my thoughts again?"
"No, I enjoyed it so much, and then that thought hit my head. I think it's great that you can not move, otherwise I could not have tried it with my fingernail. You would have moved."
"Yes, I could never have stopped, but that's the way I had to. Do you know that you have answered to me the most important question from my bondage textbook written by me?"
"Which?"
"Are feelings different or different if you can not move? Now I know, yes, you feel it differently and then, if they are almost overwhelming, they can not move, for example. That's sheer madness. Thanks for this experience."
"I also enjoyed it more than anything, thank you."
"Well, look, I caught you."
"How caught?"
"Well, are not you sticking to my cheeks now?"
"Yes, that's great, I'll stay for a while."
"But only if you keep kissing me so wet."
"Gladly, get your tongue ready, I'll come."

I do not know how long we kissed each other. I've really managed to put my mind off and just enjoy our kiss, tongue, moisture. It's like a little eternity full of happiness and feelings. Then I raise my head, the kiss is over and I take it off smiling, carefully removing my stuck hands from his cheeks. I feel like I pull up his skin with my hands and then return them to the starting position. At the same time, his scent becomes clearly perceptible to his nose. It's crazy. I could never have imagined that I would do something like this and smear his sperm on him. But they are a very hot part of him. Hahaha what I think again. Oh Mia with the right man, with whom one harmonizes one hundred percent, being together is something very special. I am happy.

"Oh, how wonderful!"
"Yes that's it."

"Are you untying me now? You're welcome!"
"Yes, but only if you fulfill your promise tomorrow, now it is too early for that."
"What do you mean, I'm still a bit emotional."
"French Air Hockey."
"Of course, very much, I promise."

And now I have to untie the handkerchief, then his double stocking and his feet are free again and he can try to put them on the ground and does not have to save his hands from the crash.

"Careful, your legs are certainly asleep, set up carefully."

And it's hard to imagine how empathetic Joschua is as a man. I take his feet carefully, slowly down and briefly massage each thigh from him. Then my Joschua sits up and now his two support arms are relieved. Sitting still, he stretches his arms to get feelings again, all the way to the front. I first take his left arm, then his right arm, and massage him, over his shirt, of course. He is still dressed in the upper part, but what do I have to see, his shirt has really wet spots in the lower area. Where they come from. I have to smile about my thoughts for myself inside.

"So you're fit again."
"How did you feel about massaging?"
"Well, it's clear if you kept them quiet and stressed for so long that they were stiff or asleep. I have to help my sweetheart."
"Oh, what luck I have the other men did not see you."
"Do you mean."
"Yes, absolutely! I'm so chubby inside and it's almost three o'clock, you agree, I'm just taking a shower and then we meet in bed."
"No, I do not agree with that."
"What, what do you want?"
"I want to shower with you in the shower and you every-

where and rinse off."
"Ohhh yes, okay. Come along."

And he pulls me on his hand behind him, up, out of the
light, into the bedroom, he puts me down in front of the
bed.

"You stay here now!"
"Why?"
"Stand still!"
"Ok."

He takes a step back and starts undressing naked, in
front of my eyes. Now he comes up to me, unbuttoning
my blouse, pulling it down over my shoulders. I stop
completely. Then he puts himself in front of me and his
right hand goes on my back and makes as always, the
bra closure with a handle. Now he strips the bra straps
off my shoulders and takes off my bra and throws it to
the ground. I stop completely. Now his hands are working on my pants, he opens everything and pushes them
down. I stop quietly. He lifts my feet individually and
takes off my shoes. I stop. Now he takes off my stockings. I stop quietly. Now he strips off my pants. I stop
quietly. Now he pulls down my panties and off. I stop
quietly. He gets up and walks slowly around me, watching everything he sees. I stop quietly. Whether he can
feel like I was smiling inside and I am somehow a little
ashamed. I blush slightly as he walks around, but I stop.
Now he slides his hands over my body as he walks
around me again. I stop quietly. Then he goes to the
bathroom, turns on the lights and turns on the shower
and comes back to me and I stopped dead.

*"You have obeyed me and you have stood still, you will
now be rewarded. Come, I spoil you in the shower."*
"Yes, my master."

He has to laugh out loud when I say master and suddenly we both laugh. It's like a total opening, both of us

completely naked, as if it were the most natural thing in the world. Nice to have a partner with whom you can be so easy. He pulls me into the shower, door closed.

"Is the water warm enough for you?"
"Yes Perfect."
"Good, wet everywhere?"
"Yes!"
"Well, then go on the sapling with you. Please stand still!"
"Again."
"Yes, stand still. If you move, I have to punish you."
"Ok! To start."

He takes the liquid soap, puts a large amount in his hands and starts at my shoulders. I stand still. He stands behind me and soaks my front from the shoulders down and as he probably intended, his hands come to rest on my breasts. I stand still. Then he begins to lick my breasts relish. I try to stand still. But then my nipples have to believe it. I do not know why at all, but they stand out bold and hard. Now he is also soaking her. Probably they stand out so hard because they just want to be soaped. And he lets them slide through his soaped fingers with light pressure and I can not stand still.

"Ohhh what, what, ohhh, yeah! Fixed."
"It does not work, they glide through my fingers, but if you want to keep it up, then."

And he loads again liquid soap and his hands start again where they have stopped, on my breasts and slide down. Oops left hand almost sunk, no, there in the navel, but again freed and now off with his right down. I stand still again, but how much longer? He has knelt sideways from me and his left hand strokes soap over my buttocks and the right is working on the front. To- gether, they glide down the legs. I stand still. But then his fingers get lost with the soap between my toes and I

327

squeal loudly.

"Iiii not, that tickles!"
"Oh no! How so?"
"You lout, you're doing that extra!"

And I'm almost still. I move my feet as if walking while standing. I do not want his fingers between my toes.

"That's not how it works, you should stand still!"
"I do, almost!"
"Yes, but only almost. I'm going to stop, between your toes everything is now lightning."
"Ohh thanks."
"Please happen, belongs to the full service."

And already he moves his hands up to my upper body, to the places where he was not yet.

"Attention, attention, warning, I'm coming now."

And his right hand reaches my clit and immediately begins to circle violently. Circular movements are supposed to clean well, he thinks. Smile and then with his fingers into my den of pleasure. And he lives up to his name, he circles around inside and I can not stand anymore. My thighs start to shake and move. He keeps circling and I start moaning ...

"Ohhh! Ohhh! Ohhh! Ohhh!"

The moans are getting louder and the distances are shortened. His right hand continues the circular cleaning inside and causes even more groaning with me, and my volume swells, because he can no longer keep his left quiet and she apparently decides to clean, sometimes try something inside and slips to the other opening before, feels my muscle around it and his index finger, well lathered, squeezes so vigorously against my sphincter that he opens easily and his index finger can penetrate. This causes a loud scream at my frontal top and the movements of his right and left fingers I can not stand anymore and my quick groan becomes after a very short total silence to a loud cry.

"Yesss!"

And he moves both finders to farewell after a short, slowly some circular laps and then pulls both out again.

"So Mia, the interior cleaning is done."
"And how, I can barely stand. Totally shaky by the emotion explosions. You are really a feeling expert!"
"Can you lie next to me and just relax?"

And then he gets up, takes the shower out of the holder and injects the warm water all over and into my body until his verifying hand can not feel any more soap scum. Then he turns off the water, he dispensed today exceptionally on the cold shower. He opens the cabin door, steps out, takes a towel, dries off quickly. Then leads me to the shower cubicle, takes a dry towel and says to me.

"Stand still!"

I smile at him and he dries me up everywhere, from head to toe. Rubbel, rubbel and I feel visibly comfortable. A hand over from top to bottom makes him feel that I am completely dry.

"Come, the cot is waiting!"
"Do I no longer need to stand still?"
"No, move please and come."

I follow him to bed, he turns off the light and we cuddle together in the middle of the bed.

"You, thank you for everything on this day, for your tenderness, your understanding, your love, thank you,

thank you and have the most beautiful dream of your life. I hope with me. Good night Mia."
"I wish you the same, I'm dead tired and super happy. Good night, dream dear Joschua."

And we immediately sleep happily side by side. It's already 4:36, but we will not get up until we're well rested. It was a busy day, but the happiest in my life.

Sunday 08.09.2013

Sunday morning, I open my eyes cautiously. Hahaha, more Sunday lunchtime, it's 12:16. I blink carefully on the right side of the bed and my Joschua is still asleep, only the head is lying exposed from the blanket. It's like having a smile on his lips. Nice to look at him, somehow there is a very warm feeling, which penetrates into my heart and triggers a slight tingling sensation. Otherwise, when I woke up, everything was empty and cold on the other side. No soul that radiated heat or wanted heat from me. Not to be alone is something very special for me and one should take care of this special. There are people who feel good when another person who touches their own heart is there. You do not feel like you are alone. This is not meant spatially, but seen from the emotional world. I'm one of those people who need a partner to flourish. And now there is such a partner named Joschua next to me and a very special, because he not only gives me the feeling that another person is there, but another person, for whom I also mean something. So lucky. I really seem to have him in my heart so closed that I could say I love him. It was love at first sight and so far everything has been so good. Wow the man is the man I want to grow old with. Mia you have never decided so fast in your life. But when I think, it took me a long time to decide and then it was always bad for me afterwards. Hahaha Mia, now you have

330

decided quickly and then it will work, it is logical. Oh, these thoughts. Anyway, Joschua still has his eyes closed, then I'll close mine a bit and dream.

Oh, he noticed that I moved. Then I want to see, oh he has his eyes a little bit on. Then I'll smile at him. He has to realize that. It's crazy what you think so. Whether he has such thoughts, I can not be the only one. But now I see it, he seems to have his right eye open a small slit. Does he already watch me? Or did he just check if it's already light outside? Softly he whispers, if I'm still sleeping, so as not to wake me.

"Hello my angel, are you still sleeping or are you already awake?"

If I do not answer now, he will let me go to sleep. He thinks maybe I have just the dream of dreams. Stupid only I always wake up before the climax or be awakened by something. But before he even brings words out of his mouth, I strike and say to him.

"Good morning, Joschua."

He is already waking up, but my voice is still sleepy. It certainly does not sound cute and familiar yet.

"Good morning you still sleepy, wonderful Mia!"
"Oh, what beautiful words so early in the morning."
"Early is good, it's almost half past twelve."
"Ohh, I slept like a young goddess."
"And did you dream something, maybe with a young god?"
"I'm not sure, but it could be. In any case, I feel like seventeen inside."
"Then you have to be fine. That pleases me very much."
"And you, what did you dream?"
"I'm not sure, but I was floating, I think it was seven o'clock, all pink, but I can not remember anything, just a nice female voice in the background that made nice

331

things to me."
"Like a strange, female voice?"
"Well, I can not identify the voice, but I had a feeling in my heart like yesterday when we were together. Conclusion, it must have been your voice and that makes me happy."
"How does my voice make you happy?"
"Yes, you have such a special pitch, a relatively high pitch and if you are sexually aroused, then it goes a bit higher. And you do not know and I do not know why, but I love high voices, they just start me. And your voice has a special connotation that totally drives me crazy."
"This triggers my voice with you?"
"Yes, she goes directly into my heart through my ears and I have never experienced it so intensively and directly."
"I think that's really nice and how you describe it again, just wonderful and so emotional and the one where I just wake up. No one ever got me out of my dreams in the day. Never has anyone said such a sweet thing to me."
"Sorry I have to do that. Youuu just animate me. I can not control it, it comes straight from my heart."
"Keep talking so sweet again."
"Now I'm silent, because I still want to pick up words for the next hundred thousand times, you should wake up next to me."
"One hundred thousand times? Do you think we can be that old?"
"Mmm, maybe I exaggerated a bit, that would be 274 years. But it should definitely be 100 years!"
"Sounds good, I agree with that."
"Nice that we have clarified that. And you just want to wake up next to me or fall asleep next to me?"
"What a question, not only wake up next to you and fall asleep, but also sleep with you!"
"When to sleep? Before falling asleep or after waking up?"
"Mmm, let me think. both."
"You, do you know what you just said?"

332

"Yes exactly!"

And he immediately puts his hand under my blanket and immediately hits my thigh. Even without saying any-thing, his right hand tries to put pressure on my back while slightly spreading his thighs. But his cock is not idle and reached in this rotating action my pubic area and pushes to her.

"Ohhh, is he really that stiff!"
"Yeah, it's often the case in the morning, when you've had a nice dream, and today you can do it because you're lying next to me."
"Oh really."
"Something like that, but you're already pretty wet down there."
"Yeah, that's often the case in the morning, when I've had a nice dream. Plus, you're right next to me."
"Oh really!"

And we both move our heads so that our eyes meet and stay that way. My eyes look somehow pleading, as if I wanted to say, yes do it, now, now, take me! This feeling that emanates from my eyes apparently goes straight to his cock in Joschua and he gets up completely stiff and screams back to my heart, I'm ready. Respect I'm coming. So go ahead on all frequencies.

He exchanges his position with my blanket and his body lies completely in full length on my naked, already ex-cited body. Oh that's a great feeling to be woken up in the morning. I put my arms around his body. His arms still resting on my flanks still support his full weight, but my arms are now pulling him down completely on me. I want to feel it. Oh the ninety kilos are to endure. It's ninety kilos for me beloved Joschua. What could be nicer than feeling his wonderful naked body so intense. Without my pressing on me, it would be as if Joschua were doing pushups. I can not do that, I do not want that, so I pulled him all the way. We come together with our lips. His head comes closer to mine immediately and kiss, kiss, kiss again and again and I'm cooking, I think he too and he slowly leads his pelvis a bit up and his hard cock comes very close to my clit. I can already feel it on my clitoris.

"Yes, come in, take me, please, now!"

And he drives his pelvis fast and strong forward, his cock penetrates past my clit into me and it gets hot in me. A short break, but the feeling of immersion was so nice, thank God he wants it again and pulls him back, almost completely out and in and out and in and out and in. Beads of sweat form on his forehead.

"Please carry on, do not stop, go on, on, deeper, deeper, yes, please take me!"

My words do not miss their goal, it becomes sharp and sharper and its thrusts are getting faster and heavier. It certainly has not moved so fast decades and I feel it so clearly and above all I get twitching in my vagina. Wow I did not feel that forever, never with a man, now and then when I played with the vibrator in me. I try to press my labia ever firmer and squeezing his cock more violently. It gets wild and then, I feel I'm about to go, but how far is he? I want to get together with him. Shortly try to stop the feelings and I hear, as if from afar, he is apparently just before the climax, because it enters this calm before the explosion. What is the nice thing to know something intimate about Joschua, so you can experience a lot together and I'm close to it.

"Yes, I'm coming now, I'm coming, come on, come on, come on!!!"

And only a short, violent thrust from him and I feel like his seeds shoot and it gets even moister and warmer in me. At the same time I hear an extremely loud scream, it comes from my Joschua, so I can and now ...

"Yesss, yesss, yesss, ohhh, yesss!"

So many feelings have been solved in me with this action again, with me and also with him. Madness.

"Let yourself fall, you're not too hard for me. I want to feel you completely. You and your sweat everywhere."

And he slowly lets his elbows sag until his supported hands do not carry any weight anymore and I only feel Joschua from top to bottom. Something's slipping, he too sweated a lot, me too, but why only, because only he has moved exclusively. Oh, it must have pleased him so much and he must have been so excited that it drove the sweat out of his pores. He was also fast with his pelvic bumping. I feel like his cock, which still lingers in me, is slowly fed with less blood and starts the retreat. Air comes between him and my pussy, a cool breeze is felt. He slowly gets smaller and leaves my cave totally relaxed. Everything down there feels wet.

"Do you have that warm, wet feeling down there, too?"
"Yes, in the past I used to get up and go to the bathroom, but today with you, it's as if the time to feel you so wet everywhere has always been lacking. But it never felt as good as it did with you now."
"You are mean."
"How, why mean?"
"You have just described the feelings that I just wanted to describe to you. I feel that too for the first time. And that's really amazing. This warm, plump moisture and the scent of your sweat when you started to sweat, that sounded animalistic to me and totally turned me on. What I experience with you, I would not even have dared to dream before I knew you. Please stay for a while."
"Thanks for those nice words that you can smell me so well, because I have a great chance that you want more of it. I am always available for you, but only for you personally. I will not let me pass."
"I am an egoist from today. Only I want to be able to use

335

and feel you!"

"*Agreed! May I demand the same from you?*"

"Promised!"

"*It's a Sunday waking lunch. The most beautiful of my life. I thank you for this!*"

"You, I have never had such conversations with a man. I also did not think that you can have such conversations with a man. I've always had inhibitions, but they're just not there with you. Also that I touched you like this or now that I want you to stay on my moisture, I can not understand myself. Everything is totally different with you."

"*Really, but I just had to do things with you. Yesterday you touched me with your hands full of seeds in face. I used to go crazy there, but yesterday, when you did that, it was exciting and really great. In the short time I've made or admitted so many things with you that I never did before. And all were super beautiful and really erotic. You just drive me crazy.*"

"Me too and I think that's great."

"*How we found each other is like a miracle. The modern technology really has something for itself. Imagine if we had done that with a newspaper ad and then wrote letters, then we would still be in the written part.*"

"Yes you are right."

"*What do you think now of a nice breakfast or just fitness, say swimming?*"

"Oh, may I really vote?"

"*Of course, otherwise I would not ask you. What do you want or do you have another wish. Would I fulfill all of you who are in my power?*"

"Sweet of you. So I would like to take a shower first, warm, then cool down and swim for a while and then fill my stomach hole, but only with you in the vicinity and there."

"*Sounds good, but if we take a shower together and then swim, do you think we'll come for breakfast before the evening?*"

"There you are right, but I order you not to touch me! I just want you to be near me."

336

"Mmm, I'm trying, but I can not guarantee anything."
"Ok, let's try it. But may I just take a quick break?"
"Ok, me too, I'll go to the other bathroom and then come over to shower."
"Sounds good."
"And then we'll try to split up, it'll be a sticky thing."
"You have to go up, should I push you?"
"Ok, hold on only when I go up, you get rid of me."
"Hahaha, I'm not a burdock."

And then he puts his hands next to my upper body again, slowly starts to push his elbows through and our skin starts to separate. It feels like removing honey from the skin. The skin goes up and jumps back when the train is big enough. This gives a funny feeling when you do it slowly and evenly. He looks down at me and sees, now the wave of separation has arrived at my breasts and his eyes are hanging on this dividing line and he stops, just before the separation with my nipples from his skin.

"Oops, what are you doing? Do you want to seduce me again?"
"No, I'm not allowed to touch you, but I'm allowed to solve myself and I do that with relish."
"Yes, I realize that, you rascal. Go on, go up now!"
"How are you in a hurry?"
"Yes, I have to tease."
"Oh, if that's just it, I thought it was important!"

He smiles at me and he pulls our skin further apart until he is sitting on his knees beside my legs.

"It's really cold without your warmth."
"Yes, I miss you too, should I come down again?"
"Down, down from me! See you soon for a shower."

He puts his right foot on the ground, pulls his left and stands in front of me. I look at him briefly and get up very quickly myself, run around him and disappear into

337

bath. Door closed and he off to the other bathroom. Cling, brush your teeth. Then there is a knock on my bathroom door. Joschua comes from the other bathroom and now asks for admission by knocking. He wants to take a shower with me. Well that will be something with him again.

"Mia may your fellow duster back in now?"
"Yes, you can come."

He opens the door and I stand in front of the mirror, putting my toothbrush off. He goes into the shower cubicle and turns on the water and keeps it warm.

"You can come, the water is well tempered."
"I'm coming."
"You come?"
"Not so, just to you in the cabin, but do not think about touching it."
"Yes, I do not touch the cabin."
"Youuu, the cabin can touch, you should not touch me."
"Ohh, and if I'm to lick your back. And you mean?"
"Well, if I'm allowed to lather your own, then you can lather my own."
"Oh how beautiful!"

And we stand face to face and I hug him tightly and stand in the middle of the shower under the oversized shower head. So we both get wet and I can feel it completely.

"You should not touch me."
"Oh, I just wanted to cross the borders, because it's sooo nice to feel your bare skin."
"If you say that beautifully, I forgive you. I like our skin contact too."
"Love how you say that."

I release the hug, he holds out his hands and I give in each palm a large splash of shower gel. Then I take some shower gel in the palm of my hand. He immediately grabs my breasts with it and rubs them with the soap I got.

"Ohhh, yes, it will happen again."
"What?"

And he lets go of my breasts immediately, goes around me and puts his soaped hands on my two buttocks and I ...

"Ohhh, yes, it will happen again."
"What?"

But before I can answer, he kneels sideways from me and his right hand soap my pussy and his left hand my buttock.

"Ohhh, yes, it will happen again."
"What?"
"Well, you broke our rules and touched me where I get feelings. You could only lather my back."
"Ohhh, I'm sorry, your beauty has blinded me so I did not know where to grab it and that's why I searched your back in several places. Where is he?"
"You rascal, ah, I can not be mad at you, it's so wonderful to be soaped by you."
"Really?"
"Yes, it's really fun and you wake up when you take a shower with you."
"And clean!"
"Hahaha, you probably do not think so!"
"That too! And now comes the back. Ready, fully soaped and rubbed."
"And now it's my turn."
"But only my back!"
"Oh, equality for all."
"We had agreed you are not getting enough."
"Hahaha, ok, equality for me poor, female being."
"Oh, if you push on the lacrimal gland now, that does

not matter, in the shower I do not see your tears."
"I knew you were a lout, shut up!"

And he starts to lather my back and then he puts his hands around me and massages my nipples.

"Oh, you're rekindling feelings in me."
"Hahaha, watch what I soap now."

And now I kneel down to the side next to him and my right hand grabs his manhood and my left goes into his popo crack and soap everything vigorously. There are feelings again. Man this man. It's happening again.

"You."
"Yes, what can I do?"
"You, have you ever washed a man's cock?"
"No, I've never been allowed to do that."
"May I tell you, you have to pull back the foreskin and then lather carefully. But your hands are too soapy, that will not work, I can help you."
"Yes please and thanks for the info."

He takes his already soap free hands, holds with his tail and with the other he gently brushes his foreskin back. And already I go and soap, very carefully his glans. He takes his hands away and enjoys my touch with his eyes closed. I notice how he enjoys it and start to massage very quickly his cock with the bare glans. It creates an insane feeling, it moves all muscles. Hopefully he can endure that, is unbelievable his reaction to his glans and that only because of the soap, otherwise he has indeed responded violently, but not so extreme. Will put a little careful hand on. Somehow I feel like it drives him crazy in a wild way. Crazier than usual and the glans is quickly filled with blood.

"Hey Mia, what are you doing?"
"I'm not rubbing, I'm rubbing."
"I'll come soon!"

"How again?"
"Yes, that's an indescribable feeling, it almost only rises in the lower half of my body, but I'm getting wild."
"And I want to experience that."
"You, my feelings are turning over in the glans."
"I can see that, it feels great, you get very stiff in my hand and your glans gets so tight. That can not burst?"
"No, but let me go crazy!"
"Oh, then a handshake."
"Wow, I'll be right, my knees are already weak."

He put his hands on my shoulders and stood on tiptoe. The feeling now seems to shoot like a rocket through his body through the speed of my hand movements and all the muscles want to play along and tense up. He is now standing in front of me and on tiptoe.

"Ohhh now. I'm exploding!"
"I feel like your semen shoot in your cock and your glans is now shiny. There, come the seeds. That may be great to watch. Exciting. Thank you for showing me that. Why did you actually tiptoe?"
"All the muscles are tense to endure that, I walk on tiptoe. As a result of massaging the glans without fore-skin so quickly, most of the feelings have collected in my pelvis and have had almost no room there. That's why it came so fast. That you felt like they came and still pressed your hand around my cock made me explode even more."
"I noticed that at the margin, which came almost faster. Wow."

He goes down again from his toes and his knees seem to feel weak.

"You, I think I'll skip swimming at the moment and we'll go to breakfast soon, or else I'll starve to death."
"Agreed, but shower off earlier, yes!"
"Clear!"

And our bodies writhe in the shower and expel the last remnants of soap from our skin.

"I'm soap free and you?"
"Me too."

So turn off the water, cabin door open and he gives with a new bath towel in the hand.

"You can dry yourself with that."
"No way! I'll rub you off. "
"Ohhh how do I get this great full service?"
"Because I love you!"

And he is silent and enjoys being dry rubbed, even in his sensitive places. I'm very careful there, just pat dry and he has to smile. Is it sooo nice for him?

"So, now you're dry and out, I'm getting ready and then come to you. Where are you then?"
"Well, I get dressed and then prepare breakfast in the kitchen. With oak trees?"
"Oak trees are good. Fried egg, scrambled eggs with bacon or boiled egg?"
"What would you like to eat for breakfast today?"
"Scrambled eggs with bacon would be delicious."
"Yes, with fried bacon. Good will try to fulfill your wish. Take your time. See you soon and thank you for what you have just experienced."
"That was also a great pleasure for me!"

I push Joschua out of the bathroom and close the door behind him. Now he can get dressed in the bedroom in peace and I can dry my hair dry in peace. Anyway, Joschua is faster than me in the kitchen and that's why I attach importance to my appearance, because Joschua will be happy about that. What he probably conjures up on the breakfast table. Oh breakfast it's already 14:46. Oh how time goes by with this man flies by. Oh, fly, with which I always fly to happiness. How is this supposed to continue. Oh, Mia, you know what you're up to. Enjoy, enjoy, enjoy, as long as possible, and I hope it really goes until Christmas 2100. Oh, I've become crazy. No, I am happy. That's what true happiness must feel like. I have never been so happy, so Joschua is the right partner for me. Oh Joschua, I love you so much, please let us stay together forever. Mia does not dream, make up, otherwise he is already finished with all and must wait for you. That does not make a good impression on him. So now finished in the bathroom off to the bedroom and some clothes taken out of the suitcase, which Joschua does not know yet. It's Sunday. Yes, on Sundays we always dressed well at home, just so inside. Oh, I hurry, what is there when he has the table ready for breakfast. Let's see what he could do. Coffee and then rolls, if there are special on Sundays, maybe croissants, then sausage and cheese, jam, honey and oh yes Nutella. Not to forget his raspberries. I like that too. Oh, I'm just surprised, I've always been positively surprised by Joschua. So dressed, make up and happy, off to the kitchen. Is crazy, I'm looking forward to see him again. Just get a kiss and he takes me in the arm. And already I left the bedroom behind me and passed the pool towards the kitchen. The aroma of coffee is already flowing towards me. Delicious.

"Well, I almost thought that again. Everything ready and I hurried so much. Wanted to help."
"Well and me first, I would like to give you a treat. You always make great friends of mine."
"I think great joys are good. I also have great joys."
"Oh, you are really cute. Oops, I just have to take out the rolls and croissants and the stir in the pan. Bacon is already done."
"Hot rolls, is really delicious, what you do for breakfast."
"Hot and stuffed, the rolls and croissants."
"Filled like?"
"Filled with salmon, cheese, ham and chocolate."
"It sounds delicious. Better than at the hotel."
"I only made coffee, that's fine."

343

"Yes, I can use it now."
"Oh, I almost forgot. Will you take the roll basket, please?"
"Ok. Should I take something else?"
"No, I'll bring the rest. Can you take a seat?"

He quickly takes two glasses out of the cupboard and pours O-juice. A glass of breakfast always tastes good. And he's already at the table, glasses on it and finally sit down. Breakfast starts, it is almost 15.10.

"Oh, I'm totally spoiled by you. I'm perfectly happy."
"That's because of reciprocity. You, I have consciously dreamed the night several times, you said last night you stay with me the whole week. Did you really mean that?"
"Yes, if you want me."
"That's a question, of course!!! More than anything else in the world, but I still do not get over the fact that you have taken a vacation. You must have felt it inside of you that I so wished for it."
"Well, to be honest, I thought I'd have to stay longer with my parents and help my father if my mother needed to stay longer in the hospital. When she then knew she was coming out and we all sat together in the hospital room and talked about you, it suddenly flashed through my head, because I have holidays. On the way I thought about it then ... ."
"You were wondering if and when you would tell me."
"Right, first I wanted to see what kind of crazy man you are and if I really like it with you ... ."
"And I know something!"
"So, what do you know?"
"You like it with me and that only because your heart has reported to your mind - you also like it so much that you are here and you do not want to tear it out with the Sunday departure."
"Yes, that's how it really happened to me. When I told you that yesterday, my mind was astonished. The words caused my heart to tell you. When they were out of my

mouth, my heart was beating wildly, whether you agreed with my decision or would have preferred that I leave today."

"Hahaha, your heart knew right away that it would find so much love here, otherwise it would not have said such significant words."

"Hoped it did. Only now!"

"Your heart has given me the greatest joy of my life and your mind is constantly involved in all the crazy things you have already done with me and on me."

The rest of the breakfast is pretty quiet. One after the other bun and croissant disappear in our feed hatches, driven by immense hunger and you can even imagine why he is so big. Slowly, the table empties with the treats and I can not count how often our eyes have met, alternated by recurrent smiles from both of us.

"You, have you already planned something we want to do right now?"

"Not planned directly, but I could give you some suggestions. It's nice weather outside, would you like to take a little walk along the Elbe?"

"Yes. I have never been to Hamburg and the Elbe. Can we go for a walk right on the water?"

"Yeah, well, are we going to cover up and do you still want to change for that?"

"Must I?"

"Not for me, it looks really great, more, but I'm not saying that now."

"That's mean, then I will not stand up here until you say it."

"Hey, you're a little blackmailer."

"Oh, you can not see that, you challenged that."

"Yes you are right. I have that. I just did not want to say anything because ... ."

"I'm curious now."

"Well, because I wanted to say you look absolutely sexy, and if I said that to you in an erotic tone, we probably would not have gotten out today."

"You might be right, but thanks anyway, then I'll stay that way."
"Great, then I can specify with you."
"Specify?"
"Of course, when we go for a walk and I see someone I know, I'm sure he'll have eyes, such an accompaniment at my side."
"You're really fond of me, what should I think?"
"Do not think, just enjoy, it's the truth."
"Thank you, you're a sweetheart."

Let's go. And then he tells me that the river beach is only two hundred meters away from here. He can always see from his study on the Elbe and then when the big pots sail past, then somehow always his thoughts go a piece with the world.

A short time later we are finished and leave the house and the property. We go down a small path to the water and he holds me with his right hand to my left hand. In other words, I go right next to him and the sun is shining on our backs and that makes us so warm and cozy. We chat about God and the world and we are on the water and there is just a big container ship passing by.

"Watch out, the waves will soon be coming from the ship to the beach."
"That's maybe cool. And it has a size, like a skyscraper."
"Yes, he can carry about 4000 containers. And if you think about where it comes from, probably from Asia and what can be in the containers everything. I think it's just great, the whole world is just passing by."
"I have not thought about that yet."

And he stops quickly and goes four steps backwards up the beach and pulls me along. What's going on.

"The waves. Attention, otherwise you have wet feet."

346

"Oh, are you going to dry me off then?"
"Oh, that sounds tempting."
"Bad luck has stayed dry."
"Oh, we can change that."

And he tries to push me forward by putting his hands around my waist, then the waves would hit me. He knows exactly that would be mean, but Joschua has the mischief on the neck or he would like to dry my feet. Only he did the bill without me, because I am also on the line. I turn to him with lightning speed, put my hands around his neck and pull up my legs. With the sudden weight on his neck, though I'm only a flyweight, he has to take two steps forward and one should not believe it, the next wave hits him and floods his shoes. As cheeky as the water is, it hops over its shoe edge and penetrates. His socks are likely to give this message immediately to his cerebrum, feet wet. He certainly has the feeling that I know it no I feel it, although he can not see my face. I pressed my head against his shoulder, laughing inside me. And quickly, he takes two steps back. Not a good idea, because he starts to stumble and he slowly falls backwards and shortly thereafter we both touch the sand completely. However, I am lying on top of him, still holding his neck with my hands. Short rest and then we both start to laugh, I do not know why but I have to laugh out loud. Now I solve my clenched hands, support them next to him in the sand, push me up a bit and we laugh in the faces. We laugh so heartily that my abdominal wall and also Joschua's, I feel it exactly, move violently. We just can not stop laughing. It's a laugh once it's started to turn off very hard. A laugh that comes out of a funny or weird situation, almost automatically triggered and that happens to us both.

"You, how weird that must have looked when we fell over."
"Yeah, and now you're on top of me when people see us, then they think you're wild, hahaha."
"Oh, I'm wild? Hahaha."

347

"Sure, you knocked me over. Hahaha."
"I'm a small, easy person, not me. Hahaha."
"Sososo, too ... ."

But I do not let him finish the sentence, I press my tender lips suddenly and vigorously on his and our lips cuddle quite tenderly together. The automatic laughter has stopped and I have closed my eyes and enjoy these tender lip contacts from him. It's as if we were alone in the world, only the smell of Joschua and the water penetrates my nose. My hands are in the sand and I can feel it between my fingers. Pure nature experience with Joschua. There come thoughts and feelings. Damn, no matter, everything with Joschua is not only beautiful, but always ends in some erotic adventures. When do you lie with a man you love from the heart in the sand on the beach. I loosen my lips from his lips and lift my head.

"Does this always end in erotic situations?"
"Almost the same thing I just thought. You're luring the erotic sides of me into the light."
"Hey, that sounds good, do you have enough of it? I'll stay the whole week!"
"Honestly, that's a lot, a lot, not enough. For years, I hid my sexual desires for those moments and now I have so many of them that last for decades. Think of it through you more and more come to it and by your actions they are always modified and even more erotic."
"Mmm, that's right, we'll have a lot of fun for the next eight days."
"Yes, and experience a lot, very much!"
"Shall I go down from you now?"
"Nope, that's nice."
"Hahaha, what should people think?"
"Oh, if they see us, they are surely just jealous or prude."
"You can see it that way, but you're right. What would I think if I saw people as in our situation?"
"Certainly not that we hurt ourselves, because they also

348

heard how we laughed heartily and saw how you kissed
me youuu!"
"Yes, that's right, I kissed you, but you asked."
"I ask? I'm lying defenseless under you."
"Hahaha, your lips have slightly tipped and shouted,
touch me right now, yes now!"
*"I did not scream loudly but laughed loudly and
heartily."*
"You rascal, you just do not want to understand me, I
can not pass that, I have to punish that immediately."

And already my lips come threateningly close and touch
his lips even so strong that he can not bring words to
my ear. For this my tongue presses from above with
force into him and chats with his violently controversial.
After felt infinite minutes, my lips appear as unexpected
as they come, the retreat. I get on my knees and get up.
He does the same. We stand in front of each other and I
laugh at him. Joschua, did not you hurt yourself when
you fell over? I was still attached to you, but it was so
funny. Boy oh boy. But you also fell slowly and I fucked
soft on you. Joschua looks at me and smiles. Oh, how
can he smile. When Joschua smiles, it always goes
straight to my heart and I have to smile too. Oh,
Joschua, it's beautiful here and, above all, because
you're there.

"Do you know, you look like a sandman in the back,
come knock the sand off."
*"Do not look so hard, I was very nice and must not be
punished."*
"Yes, you wanted to water me."
"Oh, I just stumbled forward."
"Hahaha, I do not believe you."
"Oh, poor man. You do not believe me."
"You're probably to blame yourself."
"How so?"
"You often say words that you can understand differ-
ently than you mean. But I think you want that."
"I, ne, certainly not."

"Yeah, that's what I would say now."

And again you have to take a few steps backwards, the waves from the next ship giant land on. But he takes my hand and we continue along the beach, facing the sun. Waves of wind and sun, plus a man by the hand you love, what more could you want, then the heart is totally happy.

"You, you know, walking along the beach here, smelling the water, feeling the wind and the sunbeams, and holding you by my hand. I'm so happy."
"It's totally crazy, I almost thought the same thing."
"Yes, I've never had that with another person, and certainly not with a man."
"That's what happens to me for the first time."
"You, what am I thinking now?"
"Mmm judging by your mischievous smile, you want something of my body again!"
"What do you mean by your body?"
"Well, what did you think?"
"I just thought how nice it is to walk here with you, what you can always experience with you and what does that have to do with your body?"
"Hahaha, who have you on hand now?"
"Well, you!"
"Yes my body!"
"You are not only body, but also spirit, heart and much more."
"Oh, you are so right. I love you!"

He smiles at me and we walk on.

"You can go on for about an hour now, then we come to a restaurant and we can eat something. Or we turn around and make some food at home. My fridge is sure to make a lot. What do you want?"
"If you can make something to eat, then we do not need to spend any money and I can help you in the kitchen."
"So if you want to help me in the kitchen that would be

really cool. Nobody has helped me in the kitchen for years. Couple in the kitchen with you. Oh yes, immediately."

"Well, that sounds like you're happy about it."

"Yes, I'm happy about it. Now life is finally coming back to my house. When you are alone, it is lonely, especially often in special situations and days."

"You will not believe it, I do not have a house, but I have it in my apartment too. But I work a lot and when you get home, there is the housework and then you're tired."

"And if it's weekend?"

"Yes, it is often very bad, because I often call my parents. You know some people, but at the weekend they are almost all with their families."

"Yes, it's the weekend and we're both with our family. Brand new family."

"Oh that's a good brand new family."

We have already run back to the river beach and now turn into the small path that leads to his house. It's been really 18.51. Such a day is much too short, if you sleep longer. And Joschua tells me while walking that it is so nice for him at night and then he always does not come to bed. He is an absolute night man, although he loves the day and the sun. We have reached the house and go inside. He takes off his wet shoes and stockings on the front door and I do the same with mine, even if they are not wet, but still sandy in the soles. Then he looks at me and says ...

"You, do you want to try the waterslide again before the kitchen service?"

"Oh, yes, a good idea. Does that go completely naked?"

"Yes you can slip completely naked. We can meet at the top of the slide. There is also a chair and a table. I just want to take a shower."

"Okay, see you in a bit."

"You!"

"Yes."

"It's nice that you exist and you're here."

"I agree."

And I go to the bedroom. He quickly turns on the swimming pool lights and the water slide, the house lighting and then goes into the swimming pool. I'm in the bedroom undressing completely naked and just go to the tinker. Mmm so I can not go to the top of the slide, I mean so completely naked and dressed we said yes no. Oh, I can just tie a bath towel. I just think it's great. Joschua has such big white, fluffy towels everywhere. In the baths, by the pool, by the slide. Is just great class at what so thought everything. The house is just a true paradise. So now but up to the slide, no I have an idea, sometimes pass quickly in the kitchen. But then quickly up to the slide. I sit down and wait for my Joschua. You have to see what, Joschua has a towel wrapped around him, a big bath towel. And I see how he laughs when he realizes I also have a towel around. Yes, two doofs a thought.

"Hello, I'm coming!"

And I enjoy watching him walk along the pool and climb the stairs. Level by level until he is with me. He stops and looks at the small table and smiles at me. He enjoys it that I just got from the kitchen two glasses, a piccolo and an orange juice. We just look at each other. He comes near me and we kiss. Oh, I still believe I'm in a dream so beautiful is it near him and I'm just happy. Lets see how it goes on.

"I thought we hit it."
"Yes, I give in. Do you want to be pure or mixed?"
"Please ladies cover."
"Good, I'll take too. What do you want to toast?"
"I want to toast you."
"How to me?"
"On you, because you put your profile with the ad."
"And me for you, because you had the courage to answer."

352

"On you, because you sent so great convincing mails and so totally ignited me."
"On you, because you called me so fast."
"On you, because you had the super idea to invite me."
"On you, because you had the courage to come, to a nearly strange man."
"On you, because you've turned my life upside down in the enormously short time."
"On you, because you want to endure me for a whole week."
"To you, because you are the dearest man in the world."
"Oh, you, because you're the sexiest woman in the world, always having and implementing your own ideas."
"On you, because you animate me crazy things."
"To us!"
"To us!"

We brace ourselves and it is a really nice feeling to have someone else around, not just any other human being, but another person you have closed into your heart. I still do not believe it, love on the first mail. He also seems to have a similar thought, so I would interpret his facial expression.

"What are you thinking of beautiful things now?"
"I just thought what I experience and how it started. And for this beginning, I thought something."
"What did you think was beautiful?"
"Why beautiful, how do you think so?"
"Well, because your face started to smile so hard."
"You, I thought, love on the first mail."
"Is that true of you?"
"Yes, that's how I felt that. And did you already feel something in that direction?"
"I've already told you that after I read your e-mail, I felt like I was responding, then my life changed. And it did more than I had hoped and wished and then in the right direction."
"Wow, so you like this change?"

353

"And how, the most beautiful change in my life."
"As you always put it in heart touching words. Oh is it nice that you are there. Cheers for us!"
"Yes, on us and that it will stay so beautiful."
"No, it will not!"
"How not?"
"Well, I will do everything to make it even more beautiful and, above all, that it will remain so super extreme. I promise to you!"
"Agreed. Cheers on your efforts for super extremely great and stay."
"Yes, cheers!"
"Cheers!"
"Do you want to slip with me now or slip even better in my arms?"
"Yes, how does that work?"
"So I'm going down first and then you come and when you're in the water I'll take you in my arms and kiss you very sweetly."
"Where to kiss?"
"Well, curious?"
"Yeah."
"Well, you'll feel it right away. So watch out, when you enter the slide, the water starts to run, then sit down and lie down if you want to get fast. A small push with your hands and the water will take you. look, I'll show it to you."
"How about the towel?"
"Yes, because you slide faster, you can also start your first."
"Then it will be totally wet."
"Imagine that we have a dryer in the storeroom, it gets the water out of the towel again."
"Well, I believe you."
"And go see how I do it."
"Of course, I can do it, too."
"Playing is good when you're down playing."
"Played? What?"
"Oh, there are many possibilities."
"Which, for example, may I choose?"

"Ok, I make suggestions and you choose."
"Yeah, that sounds good, that's definitely fun."
"What playing or selecting?"
"Well both and the anticipation of playing too, at least until I'm down with you."
"Okay, after the water kiss, we can either play catch ball, throw off the ball, we can do chest or backstroke, or fight a wether towel or ... ."
"We could do some air mattress gymnastics after some ball games?"
"Oh, you mean something like we experienced the adventure in one of our first mails?"
"Yeah that would be great."
"But you will use up a lot of power again."
"Anyway, we cook together after that."
"Hahaha, I already get treats for tasting."
"Yes, and which ones are served very hot. Go on!"
"I'm already gone."

And he sits down on the slide, the water starts, he lies down and lets himself be carried by the water into the depths, until splash, the slide is over and he sinks completely into the pool.

"Mia, you can come now!"
"Should I now?"
"Yes, put on the slide."
"Uiii is that cold."
"It just feels that way, you're just too hot."
"Oh, I'm coming. Danger!"
"I'm waiting. Where are you?"
"Juhuuu, respect Mia in slipping."

Oh, I have never slipped. I hope I do it right. He said lying down. And now I'm getting into the chute too. Immediately I come back down and he is already down in front of the slide and sees me almost completely naked slide. The man is lucky what I do everything for him. Hahaha and I think that is also very cool. Oh cool, the water so just let go and uiii is the cool I slide, you pure madness. And after a full round, I arrive at the bottom and splash just like him just into the water. Juhu I sprayed him wet when he dived into the pool. The water surrounds me and that is really a little adventure. Having such a slide is fun. How crazy is that? I've slid forward with my legs, so I'll come to a standstill on the pool floor right after a short dive. I shoot like a rocket out of the water and shake my head several times violently. My hair spread in mushroom form around the water. I have lost my bath towel in the pool, now I am completely naked again. Crap how he looks at the spectacle again. I am naked and have repelled myself with my feet so strong that I have jumped up to my navel from the water. Then he could see my wobbly breasts or not, because my spray from the head has certainly forced him to shut his eyes. Hahaha then he could not see my breasts shaking. Bad luck for him because now I'm back with them immersed in the water and the water surface is indeed just over my shoulders, so breast look away. Well they are still there just under the water and he can not see them so clearly. Surely the poor will survive that, I hope, otherwise without him the world would go down with me. Mia hello to talk about a man, the world does not go down when he's gone. Well, not with a man but not with my Joschua, because he is more than just a man, that's all I wanted and never got. Until now and he is even more than the wishes that I dreamed of. Oh, it's nice with him here. Oh that was so beautiful, I just dive under it all, and now full elasticity in my leg muscles and jumped out of the water again, well, that's not quite right, but to the navel I can do it again and catch it to shake my head vigorously again. But this Joschua has probably, when I'm immersed again suspected and even before I can dive into the water, he reaches out his arms, under my arms and my armpits come to his arms to stop. Then he pulls me close to him and presses the promised water kiss on my lips. The water runs out of my hair through my face, but the lips are pressed together so tightly that no water can penetrate. So our tongues are completely protected and play separately from the environment. It seems to like Joschua as well, that we hold ourselves under the arms and then the kissing. And when kissing a light turn through the water. I do not have my legs on the ground, but hang with my hands around his neck. The water makes you feel as if you are floating a bit. The hot feelings that arise when kissing and touching the body and the almost naked body that excites. I already lost my towel while immersing and the water envelops our two naked bodies. By the rotation, even if it is not very fast, the water flows past us, in addition, by the countercurrent system, which makes light waves. When I imagine it so figuratively, I'm hanging naked on the neck of a naked man and I can even feel his cock clinging to my body as if he wanted to say hello. That's a feeling, I want to stop time now and just enjoy. How many such moments have I had with Joschua ever since I was together more than in my entire life. It is so beautiful and our lips are still playing together. My first husband never wanted to kiss. What I have not experienced in feelings in these years. Oh Mia stop, you have decided not to pay attention to the past anymore. The present started with the first look you saw Joschua. From then on, life began in a way I could never dream of. Feelings and impressions, all positive and so many new and so many more beautiful than the ones before. Oh Joschua please, please never leave me anymore I love you and I believe that if you can arouse such feelings in me that you also like me, oh please, please something more than just, can not you also develop the feeling of love for me? Oh Mia think about it, he has already said that he loves you. It's beautiful, just beautiful. I'm floating somewhere between earth and sky. Oh nonsense, I'm hanging in Joschua's neck in the water. Also extremely nice. Kiss end.

"I think you've just lost your bath towel."
"Do you believe or do you know?"
"I know."
"Oh, then I'm completely naked. Good that the water covers me."

"Good that the water is very clear."
"Well, that I'm hanging on your neck, you can not quite see me."
"Oh, we have to change that."
"Change how?"

He already ran with me on the neck to the other side and there has pulled the air mattress, which is there inflated on the edge, into the water. He maneuvers the air mattress lengthwise behind my back. Now he leans forward slightly and I take my hands from his neck in shock and come to lie back on the air mattress to lie.

"So now I can look at you well."
"Youuu, you tricked me a lot."
"Nope, not me."
"Oh, and who?"
"I saw being swim behind you the air mattress and since I had hands full, I thought I stop it before it floats away and that was only possible with you."
"Hahaha."
"So and now you let your legs hang down on the side of the air mattress."
"You look right between my thighs do you like that?"
"Mmm what I'm looking at makes me right."
"Really now?"
"Yes, I know how deep it goes through the column into you and how nice and warm and humid it there is and how delicious it tastes and smells."
"Stop it, I get all red and excited."
"I'm glad if my words can excite you, but what happens if my tongue immediately connects directly with you?"
"Then I'll probably explode!"
"Wow this is a feasting!"
"And the air mattress is the table and I'm the treat?"
"Right, now you've got it."
"Have a good appetite then."
"Thank you. Too bad you can not eat anything."
"Oh, the evening is still long."

He pushes the air mattress, with me legs spread wide lying on it just in front of his chest and his mouth can kiss my left knee and stroke his left hand my right knee. Both hand and mouth continue to strive towards me. His hand is faster and moves over my pussy, I moan, on to my ringy button. His mouth follows and finally reaches my magic triangle. It pushes against his mouth again and again, because the light waves in the pool let the air mattress move up and down, of course with me on it and because he keeps his mouth, he is on his feet firmly on the pool floor, always in the same height, comes it to touch and solution again and again. He stretches out his tongue and during the upward movement of the air mattress his tongue touched my clit and his mouth my labia. I moan and he's gone again. He lets the game repeat six or seven times, then squeezes as he moves down, and the pressure on my most sensitive parts increases dramatically as he moves up. But since I can not go further up, he holds the pressure with his head, penetrates his tongue deeper into me and his mouth reaches my clit. It must be a very different taste and fragrance, because my scents now share his mouth with the pool water and that together has not quite as intense a taste as yesterday in bed the pampering. Everything is somehow very exciting, because as he holds the back pressure, the water comes in his nose and eyes. Well, if that turns it on. But he pulls his head up quickly, the air mattress follows and it elicits me again a long, loud moaning. It is so exciting to have fun with Joschua, to be pampered. He presses with his hands the air mattress violently into the water and the water spills all over my body, only my head remains out of the water and he follows with mouth and tongue in me with under the waterline. His tongue increases the beat and his lips on my clitoris begin to excite me by moving up and down. Since he can not hear, he certainly has water in his ears, he also does not notice how loud I already moan and above all how fast. Yesterday, he tasted the change in my moisture, I think he will not be able to feel under water today. The pool water will make him a dash through the taste calculation. I am already terribly far with my excitement. But he does not stop now with the touch of his lips and tongue and he even tries to reach my breasts with his hands. It works and I feel his hands lying on my breasts. No, just do not lie down, he pushes her down and the air mattress comes along. Then he reduces the pressure and his fingers dedicate themselves to my chest nipples, which have already become firm again, and he allows them to slide firmly, very firmly through his fingers. The man makes me crazy. He pushes so hard, I'm going crazy. If I was not so upset that would hurt me, but this Joschua knows how to love a woman. If I am not so excited, then he is always tender. Oh Joschua you can still press more, yes, well and he repeats it again, as if he has heard me, my thoughts. Oh now I feel in me a brief hibernation in my entire body and then several violent twitching that go through my whole body. I have reached my climax and Joschua feels it and he lets go of my nipples, pulls his tongue back, lets go of my labia and emerges with his head again from the water. Immediately I hear a very fast breathing but not from me but from my Joschua. He takes a deep breath again. Since between my legs and again and again in the water, it was probably harder for him. Great that he has held this for my climax. This is such a dear and emotional man. My first husband who also answers me. That's why it makes me so much fun when I'm allowed to be nice to him and he enjoys it fully. Now he did it and I really liked it, because I'm always upset if I'm allowed to pamper Joschua so much. Then he lifted his head so far and stands next to me on the air mattress, looks at me, smiles and looks me in the eyes. I am so happy and my hands are caressing over his head, which he has carefully placed on my stomach. I float not only with the air mattress over the water but with my feelings in the seventh heaven. I never thought that I would experience so much on and in the water. Although I was not afraid of water in the past, I have never experienced any feelings in the water and now such explosions. That's the sky in the water. Oh Mia, you are thinking of a nonsense. No it is not, is really true, I can see Joschua lying on my stomach, at least his head and stroking it with my hands too. It's such an incredibly beautiful familiarity.

"Wow, a thousand times more beautiful than I experienced during your mail. Feeling in reality tops everything."

And he just nods with his head still lying on my stomach, so it takes my ringy true. He will stay like that for a while and lie on top of me with his head. When my tension has subsided, I raise my head and stand in front of the mattress in full size. He looks so mischievous again, he's up to something. Mia watches and he dives under the air mattress and then immediately goes upstairs. As he probably has planned, his head hits the air mattress under my bum and when he straightens I slide down from her into the water. Now he's cool and I'll show up. Well wait what you can I can too, oops where did I suddenly have the courage, no matter. I come up from the water and clap my two palms flat on the water, so that a fountain full of water hits him in the face and he laughs out loud. That puts me in an instant and I too have to laugh.

"There, that's for you and another, you lout."
"Ohhh, I cooled you too fast after the heating period."
"You are crazy."
"Yes, crazy about you."
"Take me in your arms and hold me a little, that's so nice."

And he takes me in his arms and presses me tight. My breasts are completely flat on his stomach. I feel his warmth and I start to shake something.

"But let's get out of here, you're starting to shake. Please go to the bathroom and take a hot shower, then you are fit and you do not catch a cold."

361

"Yes, that's a good idea and then we cook together. Yes?"
"Yes, happy to spoil you makes me somehow always hungry."
"I even enjoy enjoying that hungry! A lot. See you soon."

And I climb the stairs out of the water. He stops before the first step and looks after me. Oh there I have to go the steps a bit more erotic and wiggle my bare buttocks strong. It is not possible to describe what one feels when one has such a being near him and can enjoy with him the joys of life together. What have I missed the last few years without such a being, well, and the twenty years before with the wrong nature, was not the non plus ultra either. No matter, now life is finally beginning to become positive. What use is it if you work and never life begins to enjoy and live alone. It is lonely to go through the empty apartment in the evening or to come back and there is nobody there or nobody comes home. No heat for the heart, that was more than enough. It brings back the power in me that makes life worth living. But now I'm getting very cold. Off in the shower, clothes on, before drying and then in the kitchen. Joschua prepare dinner. What should I eat Joschua right now? In itself wanted to bake pancakes, but I'm so hungry, because he and I would certainly hunger for meat. Let's see if I can persuade Joschua too. Is he still taking a shower? Will he already. From the bedroom and on to the bathroom. I'm barely in the shower when there's a knock on the door. I also think it's great that he does not come in so I could just sit on the clap and so you can feel really safe. What you do not want, he does not. Great, I feel so happy here near him.

"In!"
"You Mia, oops you're still in the shower. Are you hiding with me?"
"Hide? How so?"
"Well you're hiding in the fog."
"Oh, it's so wonderfully warm and the heat goes right

through to the bone."

"Yes, sometimes I stay in the shower until the water gets cold. It's so pretty and I'm dreaming of a female being who's going to take a shower with me."

"Oh no, next time we can shower together again as yesterday."

"Great like. Why I'm coming, I wanted to ask you, I'm hungry and pancakes can not satisfy that hunger. Either we order something, is only 22:03 or we go to a restaurant or we sizzle a steak. What do you want?"

"Oh I'm coming straight to the kitchen, I do not want to leave today, I would like to sizzle with you in the kitchen."

"Sounds good, I would have liked that as well. Do you agree with steak, corn on the cob and baked potato with herb quark? We were on Friday, but I like steaks. How is that with you?"

"I do not eat meat often, but the steak was more than just great and I'd love to eat something like that again. Do you have everything for it?"

"Sure, you woman in the fog. Do I see you in the kitchen right now?"

"Yes, I'm coming out of the shower now."

"Oh, may I give you the bath towel."

"You just want to see me naked, are not you already seeing the sight?"

"I can promise you still in a hundred years I will like to see you so naked!"

"Liar then I have a lot of wrinkles everywhere."

"And beauty comes from within and wrinkles can be attractive and interesting, and I'll get a pair as well."

"Good, I believe you. Attention I emerge from the fog."

"Cool, take the towel quickly so you do not catch a cold, you look so cool, to bite on rrrr."

"Off to the kitchen."

"Go on, see you soon."

Joschua will soon think that I am totally lazy. He is always faster and makes the food and covers the table so nicely. I am so spoiled with him as never before by a man in my entire life. I enjoy it so much, but soon I'll turn the tables and if I have to tie him up so I can get into the kitchen first. Oh Mia on something like that you did not think before. Oh, I have become a different person in the last days. I have discovered there is more than I have experienced between earth and heaven so far. There are the beings, who are also called men, but who are something completely different, namely secret angels on earth, who are only here, so that we women will be spoiled. But it seems to give them so little, that it's like a lottery win, if you get one of them. I got one, so I must have been very nice otherwise. Again, these thoughts. Get out of the shower and quickly dried and just blow dry hair. So now only in the clothes and then the kitchen is stormed. If I come near it will certainly smell again. Whether I sneak my way through the living room and the mountain or no, then I only frighten Joschua and when he gets excited again, we get nothing to eat again and we will then starve to death on the floor in front of the kitchen because we will not be there until then have done more. Attract Mia and do not think. Yes, I'm doing yes, yes, yes and now the last blouse button. Oh no, I better let it, because I get more air. Nonsense Mia you want only Joschua that you look into it or a comment on my breasts. Oh, I'm messed up. No that is really exciting and nice to play with a man like that. And out of the bedroom and along the pool to the kitchen. I knew he had already set the table. Placemats on it, steak knives and forks, cups, a 0.5 litre bottle of light beer, candlesticks on, light dimmed. Oh and there is something in my place. Oh, just a little heart shaped chocolates box. Where did he get that back? An attention that is so small and causes so much in me. But now only once in the kitchen where my private chef Joschua is already whirling again. Oh Joschua has turned on music, I always like to listen in the background. Oh, I can already smell the baked potatoes in the oven, corn for searing even in the pan. Prepared steaks. Oh Joschua what you do everything and I have tasted so delicious so far. As soon as I'm there, Joschua throws the steaks on the contact grill. I go up to him and get me a hungry kiss. Let's take a look but I can not do anything anymore, Joschua is in his element. Joschua is already turning the steaks. And then Joschua puts them, as both sides are sautéed in the oven and then it will soon come to the plate.

If I think so, what I have experienced in the last fifty-two hours, so much warmth and feelings I have not received in my whole life, from all my men before. Sounds good, but it was not that many. Everyone had something about them, where I felt very early, often the first time, something is missing or it does not feel completely right. It often happened that I thought afterwards that I did not need it, but the body demanded it and now I've been with Joschua for more than fifty hours and I have not found the smallest little bit yet because I would change. On the contrary, the longer I spend with him, the more crazy he makes me. This is not only because of his appearance, but mainly because he is a man who takes everything and also accepts my own initiative. He makes it easy for me because he shows me that he enjoys being pampered by me and that also often without me saying something, just out of the situation and he seems to feel my feelings and reacts immediately. Not like other men who often say, oh I do not want to, oh I do not know, ah I can not, ah, yes. He just admitted it, showed emotions and gave me so many beautiful feelings. He simply overwhelmed me with his feelings and his love. I love him.

"Hello, I'll be right there, do not be scared!"
"Juhu here I am, right next to the steaks."
"You are fast, I wanted to do everything."
"Oh you are the guest and you have to spoil."
"That's nice of you, very sweet, not that you do everything, even that you think of everything."
"I bother."
"Yes, you really do."
"That's how it should be, if you love another person

very much."

"To whom do you say that?"

"But now let's get some fat on the grill plate, let it get hot and then put the steaks on it. Let's see how far the baked potatoes are."

"Do you actually cook for yourself?"

"Honestly, when I'm alone, I do not feel like cooking. Almost only what is fast, sometimes pasta, if I'm upset sometimes pancakes. Often I eat when I was somewhere just a burger and chips on the way. At home then a latte macchiatto and something sweet. I'm just lazy, I think you stand in the kitchen for two hours and then you eat it in five minutes and I've never had a visit."

"Do not you have many friends?"

"Oh, you know, the past was not so good, lost a lot, divorce and and and and now I wanted to start again a year ago and finally fulfilled my dream to build a house overlooking the Elbe. But now I'm working alone from home and you do not get too many work colleagues. I have also become very careful when you have already experienced the most impossible things. But now for another topic. I'd like to forget about the past, but it keeps catching you up from time to time. Bad is only when you are alone and too often, then you think and since you have contacted me, I think only of you, us and the future. That's an extra great feeling, a sense of be- ing."

"Do not you have to turn the steaks around?"

"Oh yeah. You should not hang with your thoughts in the past, it's just stupid. Life now plays in the present and wants to the future and my life is currently playing with luck, called Mia."

He turns the steaks over, pulls out the plates and puts them next to the stove. Steaks on it and then pushed into the oven. There they stay for another ten minutes and then they are done.

"Yes, the past was not always rosy for me, but I was often insecure in life and could not decide."

"How not to decide?"

"Well, I have almost always let others decide for me and what comes out is not always what you want in yourself."

"I do not understand, I've never seen such a brave woman as you."

"Like me, why?"

"Well, think about it. It was brave on my mail as you did to answer. Courageous to talk to me and to come here even more courageously. We were alien, just e-mailed and phoned and then brave what you did to me. Since I do not know any other woman who would have done all this and you say you are not brave."

"Yes, I can not understand that either, but somehow my heart said you had to mail and then my heart wanted to hear your voice and that's how we talked on the phone."

"Yeah and then you wanted to see me and just drove on to come here."

"Yes exactly!"

"And then you finally wanted to let the pig out and seduce me ...!"

"Hahaha, you owe at least fifty percent."

"Look, if you had not had the courage, you would have said I was ninety-five percent guilty."

"Mmm, if that's the way you're right."

"One can also say that I have finally taken the good for you out of the depths of your heart and released it."

"Yes, that sounds very good. Hahaha I'm really brave now!"

"Yes, courageous, totally erotic and especially extremely nice."

"Oh and hungry."

"Yes, the steaks are ready and I put everything on the plate. There is no time for the steak rest in the oven. Tastes so delicious too."

"And now it's time to eat, another supper."

"It's not even 11pm."

"Hahaha 22:58!"

"Well, you take it exactly!"

"Sometimes. You turn the night into daylight."

"Yes, that always happens to me and all the people around me have to suffer."

"I do not suffer! Certainly not, or at least I'm starving!"

"Good Appetite. Go ahead, then I can say a lot of things about you. You can not answer with your mouth full."

"But between the bites, I still manage to get words out of my mouth."

"I think I'm great and courageous. Does it taste good?"

"Mmm and mmm as mmm!"

"Hahaha talked with a full mouth and I understood you too. You're just a talent in many areas."

"May I be curious now in which areas?"

"Oh, you want to eat in peace."

"What do you mean?"

"Well, if I enumerate everything in time you can munch in peace."

"Do it!"

"Talent, you dress up horny, sexy. Talent, can speak with his mouth full."

"Hahaha."

"Talent, you are the most sensitive woman I know. Talent, you're smart, you can talk to you for hours without getting bored. Talent, you take a man any fear of doing something with you. Talent, you do erotic things that a man can hardly imagine in the wildest dreams. Talent, you are very modest."

"You have a talent, too."

"What?"

"Let me blush."

"It's great, you look so innocent when you blush."

"Not only do I look innocent, I am too."

"Cough! Cough! Cough!"

"What's that about? I've never done such things as you've ever done in life."

"What things?"

"Well, touch a man's mouth or even take it in his mouth. To get out loud if you make me look at you naked anywhere."

"Then I'm honest, it's so nice when you say that. I've never licked a woman so much or wiped my hands with

seeds on my face."
"As I thought you do with all women."
"What?"
"Well such sexual acts."
"What do you think of me? Do you think I'm a sex man?"
"Well, if I think what you've already done to me, yes!"
"Thanks for the great compliment, but I've never experienced anything like what I did to you or what you did to me in life with another woman. That's probably why never want to leave you out again, you've aroused something in me that I've always wanted but never got, either against money or voluntarily."
"How about money?"
"Well I've thought about it before, maybe you could have found a woman who does exactly what you want, but I never did."
"Why not?"
"Well, because what woman would have done that and honestly, I've never touched a woman so intimately, if not the heart was there. I could not do something with a woman, if I know there are other men besides me. I'm totally old fashioned if I want to be with a woman, then not at all."
"I like that. So never been in the brothel?"
"I was not and never will be."
"I like it."
"But if the ladies did not exist, there would be a lot more rape. I do not want to do their job, it's inconceivable to me."
"Yes you are right. They can do something unimaginable."
"Well, have you satisfied your hunger or may I offer you another dessert?"
"No thanks, I am completely saturated."
"You, are you tired already and do you want to sleep in bed?"
"Go to bed? Together with you?"
"Not with me, but next to me."
"Oh, do not do it."

"Well then I'll give you another suggestion or what do you want?"

"Suggest, but only very carefully."

"Carefully, we cover and then ... ."

"And then I'm interested."

"And then I could offer you french air hockey or a walk on the nocturnal Elbe."

"Well, those are two contrary proposals. You only want me to decide for the french air hockey."

"What do you mean?"

"Now have a walk?"

"You the passing giant ships with lighting very different than during the day."

"Yes, I believe you, wants to see the pots sometimes, but now I'm really hot on you again."

"Hot on me?"

"Yes, I want to play you naked."

"You're cool, what if I'm naked?"

"Do not be so curious. Something will happen!"

"What what what?"

"No, let's play!"

"Okay, I'm just clearing off and you can mentally prepare yourself for the bauble."

"No, I think I'll cover it. Let go and hurry, I'm hot for you."

"You make me!"

And we go into the kitchen with the dishes, packed in the dishwasher, turned on and then we go hand in hand. I pull him behind me along the pool and suddenly I turn around and give him a kiss.

"I love you, you crazy one!"

He just seems to be happy, because he follows me without resistance into the basement and makes there already on the stairs going down the lights and also the jukebox. The guy is easy to love.

"You a glass of sparkling wine or are you even more

turned on?"
"Oh, I do not need alcohol, you're my drug."
"I've never been a drug for anyone. How do you take me in?"
"Swallowed naked."
"Oh, then you have to win in air hockey, too."
"Let's see, seem to have a lucky streak."
"How lucky?"
"Well, I met you and that was like a lottery hit."
"Now you want to embarrass or distract me?"
"No, not me. When does it start?"
"Slow. First, get a coke. May I bring you nothing?"
"Alright, then I'll take a coke."
"Come right away, you can practice."

And he goes behind the bar and gets a litre bottle of coke and two glasses, a pack of nuts and takes them to the air hockey table. There is, as with any game equipment, a storage space for the drinks. I do not practice, I just watch him as he bends behind the counter to take the coke out of the fridge as he stretches to take the glasses off the shelf and grabbing the nuts and grabbing everything then move in my direction. I cast my eyes on his torso and then on his masculinity. I look so provocative that I get hot thoughts again. Arriving at the air hockey he puts everything on the table, opens the nuts and the coke bottle, pours the coke into the two glasses, hands me a glass and ...

"Cheers the luckier one wins."
"Cheers! How do we calculate the points?"
"We always do a game, which consists of three goals. Anyone who has scored three goals is allowed to watch the loser take off a piece of clothing. The loser is allowed to choose which garment."
"Ok."
"But beware, if you're completely naked and then lose again, you have to do everything the winner wants! Ok?"
"Oh that sounds dangerous."

371

"Yes, that's dangerous."
"Ok, I want to play, I agree, you're a nice man."
"What do you mean now? I will not let you win!"
"Ohhh."
"No! No! No!"
"But then I have to really make an effort."
"And I first. Would we like to do some test shots?"
"Yes, good."
"You say how many pieces do you have to take off?"
"Mmm just calculate. Ten pieces and you?"
"Mmm just calculate. I only have eight pieces. Yes, you have more jewelry."
"Well, then I'll take off my watch and the necklace you're getting from now on."
"But you are really a fair opponent."
"That's part of the game. Cheating is no fun, I want to win honestly."
"Me too, but only if we play."
"Okay that's alright, just at our games."
"So can it start?"
"Yes, finally."
"Zero - zero you have offense."

And it gets loud, because the Airhockeypuk bangs quite nicely when you come to the gangs. But only by gangs one often reaches the goal of the opponent.

"Goal! I scored a goal."
"Congratulations. You've probably already played air hockey several times."
"Just watch it. This is the first time."
"Then you are certainly a natural."
"Do not talk so much and continue playing."

He smiles like a little boy and is so hot at the game, you can see his eyes sparkle. Now he just wants to play or just wants to win the prize. Well, see what ...

"Goal! I've scored again. You have to be careful otherwise you'll be naked in front of me."

"Ohhh that would be ... ."
"Goal! I won the first game. Take off, take off a piece."
"Oops, that starts off well. I take off the right shoe. Here please."
"Good on!"
"Now you have even better chances."
"Why?"
"Because I'm wrong now."
"Hahaha just excuses."

And again I pop the disc with him in the gate. I have to praise myself I'm incredibly fast. Now he will certainly take better care.

"Goal what's up, will you let me win?"
"No, you have your lucky day today."
"Maybe, I've had that since I met you!"
"Wow, then I probably have no chance."
"No attention Goal!"
"Mannu"
"Goal! Undress! Undress!"
"Ok the second shoe. Now I'm standing straight again and off we go."

I make the next goal and then Joschua meets twice in a row. I look at him briefly and it happens again.

"Goal this game is up to me!"
"Lucky Strike. Continue."
"Did not you forget something?"
"Yeah well you get the left shoe from me. Satisfied?"
"Okay for now."
"Continue!"

I am unstoppable. It's like a frenzy with me, I have not experienced that yet. In the past I always wanted to win, because when I play for a game, even if it's just a drink, then my ambition is so great that I want to win with all my might, and so far I've taken Joschua by surprise. Or have I just imagined too much what I'll do as a winner

373

with Joschua. This must not distract me from the game because Joschua always smiles at me so mischievously.

"After the next win a sip of Coke and a break?"
"Goal! Continue."
"Are not you thirsty? Goal! Mine! One one."
"Hey you louts want to distract me."
"Goal! Mine!"
"See, it worked again."
"What?"
"The distraction."
"GOAL! Game for me. Move out. Should I guess what you are taking off now?"
"Hahaha wants to stand straight again. Here's the second shoe."
"Heee you have become a little smaller."
"Hahaha but not slower. GOAL."
"Darn. You shoot so fast, sometimes you can not see them."
"Oh what a pity for you! Goal! "
"Youuu! Do you want to totally confuse me?"
"Yeah ... Goal! Move out!"
"Man oh man you can do me! Good you get the left sock from me."
"Ok, throw him in the heap."
"Do you want a sip of break cola now?"
"But only one, just have a run and I want to take advantage of it."
"And I would like to kiss you."
"Well, I agree with that, that gives me new power in playing."
"Ok, then I withdraw my kiss offer."
"Made is made you do not pull back a kiss offer with a lady!"

And already, with an immense power, I approached him with my hands and his lips can not resist the power of my lips. Oh, it's always so exciting to unite with Joschua's lips. I have never had so much fun kissing as with Joschua. He is just so different. Otherwise, a kiss was always limited to the kiss, but with him I have the feeling that a bomb of the emotions strikes and spreads throughout my body and that's just exciting. That's why I can not refuse him a kiss. It's just no, it's a thousand percent right, the right thing for everything in my life. I feel he will change everything, change for the better and happiness will finally come to me after so many years. I feel the warmth of his kiss, she goes right through to my heart. Oh, if only he knew how much I loved him. But now I'll pull my head back and ...

"But your thoughts are loud again."
"What, what thoughts?"
"Just kissing."
"Hahaha you want to know what I thought?"
"How nice it is when we kiss and that it should always stay that way. Is it true?"

He looks at me again quite puzzled. I can not leave it, I have to smile at him and ...

"I'm right and more."
"Please tell me how you know that, you guessed it."
"No, really not, but when we kiss, then I feel it's not just your lips and tongue involved, it's as if your whole body is inflamed."
"You felt that?"
"Yes, for the first time with you, never before. I always go kissing through the whole body. If that were not so nice, do you think I'd just given up my streak of fortune and got so distracted."
"You are sooo ... ."
"If you miss the words, do not worry, your eyes will continue."
"Yes, they then show the feelings right out of my heart."
"Did not know in the past that there is a direct connection between heart and eyes."
"Me neither, but you have discovered her with me and now I want to discover more about you, let's continue to

play."
"Just a sip, so, now I'm fit again. May I give you another kiss of confusion?"
"Yes, please."

And there is still a little kiss, then I go to my side and get ready to start again. Hahaha he looks at me and does not realize how I'm scoring again.

"Hahaha the confusion kiss worked. I'm leading two zero."
"Yes, but now you have brought me back to the bottom of the facts. Danger. Goal!"
"Oops."
"Attention, Goal! Two - two."
"The kiss did give you power instead of taking."
"Yeah. Goal! Three - two! Move out!"
"Here's my second … ."
"Stop, may I take it off you."
"That was not so in the rules of the game."
"But at the bottom of the fine print."

He comes over to me, kneels down with one knee in front of me, takes my leg and puts my left foot on his right thigh. I wiggle and hold on to the table. Then he leads his fingers slowly into my stocking and pulls him over the heel. When pulling forward, he slides his fingers gently over my sole and I pull my foot away jerkily.

"Hey, you know I'm ticklish."
"Well, I know that, but I just wanted to take off your stocking and not tickle you."
"I do not believe you!"
"So, you tell me I want to tickle you."
"Yes."

And already he reaches for my foot again and really tickles me while squeezing my toes.

"Hahaha, do not you, you lout, do not!"

And then I pull my foot away again.

*"Too bad it's so nice to hear your voice with some
despair, then it sounds even more erotic than usual."*
"Sososo now you have the small print but fully ex-
ploited. Go on, I also want to help you undress."
"You in the fine print is only me allowed to do that."
"But I would know, same right for all players, other-
wise … ."
"No, do not punish, I agree, but you can ..."
"But what?"
*"Hahaha, you have to win first, and now I'll pay more
attention, know your ulterior motive."*
"What ulterior motive?"
"Well, that you want to help me undress."
"That's nice, then you have less work."
"Cool answer, you just want to pamper me."
"Could be, I do so much."
"Permission granted. Let's continue playing!"

And the individual games are getting longer, because
we both try not to get a goal in, but it can not be
avoided. Goal for goal and again it is two to two.

*"Well, now the next goal decides if I can kiss your right
foot or not."*
"How kiss?"
*"Goal! I'm sorry, your right stocking needs to go down
and my lips can give your foot a big kiss."*
"Lout, distracted again. Where is that with the
kiss?"
"On your forehead, that wants to be kissed too."
"Hahaha, you do things the way you need them."
"No, I'm just doing what you want right now."
"Hahaha, I would like to hug you."

And already he hurries around the table, takes me in the
arm and kisses my forehead and then my mouth. I like it

because I pick up my left leg again, it's a habit of mine. I always do that when he kisses me and I enjoy it. After the kiss he says ...

"Stocking up, stocking or I'm falling over you!"
"Yes, that almost rhymes. Well, here you have my foot, but if you have taken off the stocking, I want you to kiss him as well."
"How shall I kiss the stocking?"
"No you silly, not the stocking but my foot."
"Oh, that's what I do, of course, immediately and with pleasure."
"How did you not want to kiss my stocking?"
"Ne!"
"Well, that makes me think."

And he has my right foot in my hand, removed the stocking and thrown it away, playing with his lips on my foot. It tingles me and I start to vibrate all over my body. It's as if he chased a shower through my whole body. But before he gives me my foot back, he still tries to get his toes in his mouth quickly to nibble on it. I've seen through Joschua and before he can report success, quickly and easily my foot away.

"No, no, no, no toe sucking. Next games."
"Alright, keep playing."
"Attention a fly on your head."
"Hahaha, do not let me distract you."
"Goal!"
"Mean, now I'm getting very sad."
"Oh, poor girl, I'll comfort you and give you a big kiss. Can you feel it already?"
"Where?"
"Goal!"
"But now man is over. How do you always do that about the gang?"
"Yes, you see, so! Goal! Three zero. Stocking!"
"Ok, you won and I'm stockeless."
"Then it is balanced again, I have no stockings on."

"So now we come to the really interesting winnings."
"Yeah, what would you take off next?"
"I ...?"
"Goal!"
"You!!! Really!!!"
"And Goal!"
"Now you want to know."
"Do not you want to surrender completely?"
"As?"
"Just take off everything at once."
"You would like that?"
"Yeah, then you would not be so frustrated if you always lose now. Goal! Again three - zero. What are you un-dressing now? I'm so excited."
"You're a lucky guy! What should I take off? Shirt or pants?"
"Mmm pants would not be bad, then I could see your boxer shorts and what's hanging around in there, or is it already."
"Partly, partly. If I take off my shirt, maybe you are more distracted?"
"Do as you like, I'll get everything."
"Hahaha. So good the pants."

And we do it very fast, everybody wants to see the other guy naked and keep playing, but now he opens his pants first, but he does not drop them immediately, but takes a step back from the table and turns around, that's his back side to me shows. Then he moves his hips and I inevitably start whistling.

"Go on, keep going, more!"

And he lets his pants slide automatically to the floor during further hip movements, raises his feet one after the other and takes off his pants. Raise the pants, turn them over his head twice to let them fly into the corner. Then he puts his arms on his hips and turns around, his hips circling. That keeps me sharp and that is definitely his intention.

379

"Oh, oh, oh, I like that. But your boxershort already has a considerable inner life, for which I have not even touched it."

"You have such hot thoughts and my cock simply picks them up and saves them."

"Oh that's why the scope. If I send more thoughts, will it eventually pop out of the top again?"

"No, it will not be until you lovingly but surely take it in your hand or in your mouth or rub it on your breasts ... ."

"Or allow him to trade in me."

"Yes, that would be a wonderful opportunity."

"I could also pinch and rub it between my pubs."

"Do you want to make me so hot now that I'm coming?"

"Are you still distracted then?"

"I do not know, but you totally turn me on."

"Well then let's keep playing."

"Attention now comes a direct hit. GOAL! One zero. I lead."

"Not for long!"

"Look, Goal! Two - zero."

"What's going on now, did you let me win?"

"No, we decided that, we really want to play honestly."

"And why are you winning now?"

"Sorry Goal! Three zero. Finally, now you have to undress, I'm so excited. You are very funny. I'm so curious, as if it's the first time that I get to see you naked. Exciting."

"You said that nice, but I'm still not completely naked and not discouraged."

"Ahhh, too, the pants. Pity!"

"What a pity?"

"Well, you could see my excitement with me, I can not do that with you and that's too bad, unless ... ."

"What?"

"Unless I can just come over to you and touch something."

"Touch what."

"Well, you know."

"No, what?"

"Well, I would like to slip my hand into your panties and see if you've gotten wet down there."
"You asked so nice, if you pull my pants over my feet, then you can try it out."

And Joschua rushes around the air hockey table and falls on his knees in front of me. Never before has a man knelt before me in my life. I smile at him and his hands push each leg one at a time, whenever I have lifted my foot over it and now he has two bare legs to the panties in front of his eyes. Now he starts kissing me, from the bottom up.

"That was not agreed. Only a test handle."
"Sorry, but I could not resist your leg. It simply animated me where it was so naked in front of me. And you know what. The second leg will do the same in me."

Said and done. Pants are already taken off and he begins to caress the second leg again from bottom to top. A lot of kisses have to endure it and of course he is not stupid, he kisses from bottom to top and now that the pants are off, his kisses arrive on my panties.

"Oh, you smell like more again. Yes, I can smell it, you are pretty hot."
"Yes, is that surprising? I have never done anything like this with a man and then with you, if I would not be horny, when?"
"Ohhh do not we want ...?"
"No, we are playing to the end. Up and over to your side."
"But I have not been allowed to slip in the panties yet."
"Good, hurry up."

And he pushes, of course, very slowly, his right hand on the panties up to then immediately pull down on reaching the edge and the panties also pulls down, but before I can respond, he pushes my pussy a hot kiss and welcomes my clit with his tongue. I immediately moan, you are the man a trigger of emotions.

"Hey, no, now you know that I'm already excited, so let's keep playing. You're welcome."
"Well, I'm already going back, but first a pussy goodbye kiss. Smacking! That was good. Until the same hot pussy!"
"Now you're talking to my pussy! Crazy guy! Ohhh beloved Joschua!"

And he gets up and not quite by chance he comes close to my head and what else, his lips say hello for a moment and then he goes to his desk. The game continues.

"Is pretty balanced. I'm curious who."
"Goal!"
"Shit again. Oh that's because, I still have your wet scent in my nose and makes me tingle all over my body and therefore ... ."
"Yes, that's why you did not keep the puk."
"Yes, exactly, how do you know that, do you want to give me a quick snoop, then you are distracted too."
"No ... Goal ...! Two - zero!"
"Just wait! GOAL! Only two - one."
"Man, but you have a power, because you can not see the puk at all, but only hear the gate."
"Goal! Two - two. Totally balanced and I wanted that I stay dressed and you are completely naked there. But you also spoil all the fun."
"I'll give you right away, I'm spoiling the fun! Goal! Ace of Three - Two! And take off again!"
"Fine. Good that I turned the heating to 28 degrees earlier, otherwise we would chill ourselves at play."
"Never, how hot do you do me, that's no longer possible. So what do you give me? The boxershort?"
"Yes, you would like that. No, my shirt."
"May I unbutton it? You're welcome!"
"Very much, come here."
"Yes, I do, but first a mouthful of Coke, you too?"
"Yes. Cheers, you heavenly female nature."

"Cheers."

And we met at the side of the bar table and prost ourselves and yet somehow Joschua looks at me from top
to bottom as irritating as if he wanted to and I knew it. I
quickly put my glass on the table. Then I grab with my
right hand just violently in his boxershort and even
before he can say something, I close his mouth with my
already really wet lips. Hahaha not wet from me, still wet
from the coke and his tongue tastes even afterwards.
Oh, this variety of emotions, which I may experience
with this man. Just beautiful and ...

"You, if you pull on, ahhh, then ... ."
"So what?"
*"Well then I can not continue to play sensibly right
now."*
"I do not believe you, you just want me to touch you
even more. Is it true?"
*"Oh, I'm not made of glass. But I almost feel like that
with you."*
"I can feel you right and feel your heart. You, that's
something completely new for me to experience and
incredibly beautiful."
"Okay, but did not you come to remove my shirt?"
"Oh yes, I almost forgot, but what I have here in my
hand is just so soft and cuddly."
"Not for long, then he is extremely stiff."
"Well then I'll let go, we'll pick up for later, do not want
to overload you."
"Hahaha!"
"Well, if I make you crazy now, then maybe you can not
afford enough later."
"Youuu, do you want to destroy my ego?"
"No, absolutely not, just wanted to hear how you react."
*"I know, but it's so nice to you, I'd like to freeze time
now and just hold on and enjoy the feelings that you've
already conjured into me through your hand. You are so
beautiful."*
"You always find so nice words for what I do."

"You just make it so awfully nice and that you touched me was also not planned, just shortly before, when you put away the glass and smiled so mischievously, I had the feeling, now she attacks."
"Oh, you have already guessed that?"
"No. Unaware, almost sensed, your approach with the right hand."
"Somehow I feel like we're dressing magically."
"Yes, one hundred percent felt right!"
"I always wanted to."
"No woman has ever done that, make it!"
"You do not know what I wanted to say."
"Yes, you want to rip my shirt open and all the buttons should fly away."

I look quite puzzled and then start smiling all over my face. As he has described again, exactly my thoughts.

"Yeah!"
"Do it, dare, be courageous, I want it, my feelings will start to rage at the thought of it, do it, please!"

And I grab with both hands at chest height through his shirt button bar. His elbows are pointing outwards and he looks at me intently. I hope I have enough strength to do it with a jerk. I'm so excited.

"Please give me another kiss first."

And after a brief lip whisper, he takes his head back. I feel my strength gathering for my arms and then I tighten my muscles. A jerk, as if an elephant is running and rattling, the buttons just fly through the party room and the shirt with a jerk loses all the buttons and he is almost completely naked. Hahaha, he still has a vest on, but that feeling. I've never torn a man's shirt off a man. I'm messed up. I have something for powers. It's cool.

"Oops, was that really me?"

And I put my head on the now uncovered undershirt of him and cuddle. His breath is very fast.

"Why are you breathing so fast? Because of the effort or the excitement?"
"In which. You do things with me."
"I? You were the tractor."
"Yes, because you wanted it too."
"Yes and that was great. It felt as if you were released in a jerk and the shirt fabric then pressed on the shoulders, they slowed him down otherwise he would be completely gone. An unprecedented feeling."
"I have never done that, but it was really great. Liberating somehow, letting go of so much strength and then exposing another so with it. Erotic."
"We certainly will not be able to cope with the game any more, if we are going to stay that long for each part we have to remove, but it's so nice."
"Yeah, but that's the point of the game, we both like it."
"Exactly."

And he puts his arms around me and his head is on my breasts, again a special moment, I can not describe him so well, but this sense of power just flows through me. We and not me alone, we that's what I've missed so long.

"I have something else left and I can not get rid of it until you win again. Let's go."
"Now we're playing for your blouse."
"It's good, but then you have to win."
"Ok, try me."

But it does not work for him unfortunately. Oh I'm so sad about it. I make the game of my life and score a goal and another goal. One more and he has to give something back. And there it happened. I'm simply unbeatable today. No, the thought of seeing him completely naked immediately inspires me uncannily.

"Goal! I'm really sorry, now is your boxershort's turn."
"No, first my undershirt."

And he grabs his undershirt, touches it down and pulls it over his head very slowly and I start clapping applause.

"Yes! Yes! Go on! Oh I'm not coming to you now and kisses your nipples, I play on and immediately your boxershort falls."
"Let's see."

And he does not start concentrating on me anymore, he just focuses on the puk. And pretty ...

"Goal! Sorry I'm sorry."
"I do not believe you."
"Goal! I'm really sorry. Two - zero for me."
"Now you have a run."
"No, I'm just focusing on the puk."
"Oh, let's change that."

And now I have to subtract the full program. I wobble very strong with my breasts, which unfortunately still held by the bra and covered by the blouse. But he still looks.

"Goal! Hahaha, where did you look again?"
"But that was mean, who can resist such a great wobble and look away?"
"You do not, I know!"
"But you took full advantage of that. Just wait. Goal! Hahaha. Three one. Now your blouse is falling!"
"Why the blouse?"
"How do you want to take off your panties first?"
"Yes, the blouse covers my pussy down there and you can not see it."
"You are mean, but then I will win again immediately and then you just stand there in the bra. This will be a

386

visual treat."
"Try it!"
"I do, but first my profit."

But Joschua wants everything and he plays right away. He wants to win, you can tell. And crap one - zero I lost, oh, it does not matter. I am happy even if he is happy that I am naked. Who else could I enjoy so much with my nakedness? In the past, I even came out of the bathroom naked, and my husband did not even care, and continued to watch TV. Has he just requested his profit? Should he get gambling debts are debt of honor. So I take off my panties and do not throw it on the floor, just take it over to him. He catches my slip and holds it in front of his nose. Take a deep breath. Yes, now he has my hot smell in his nose again. Joschua is really a crazy guy. Oh, it's so heavenly to do such stupid things with him. I feel like a little schoolgirl doing her first sexual experiences. So excited, but also totally free.

"Now you have lost, with your scent power I win the next game."
"There's never been anybody talking to me about it and thinking it was so erotic."
"Yes, the chemistry is totally wrong, but Goal! I'm really sorry."
"Yes, I know, the power scent of me. Give me my panties back."
"No, better to smell it again. Sniffle. Nose full! Power totally."
"You confuse me."
"Goal! Two - zero."
"Slowly, I also believe my scent makes you."
"Not only, he gives me the power to strive for more."
"Well, another little break?"
"No, I want to win your blouse now."
"You want to see me poor woman standing almost naked in front of you?"
"Yesss! Goal! It's time, blouse off, blouse off, blouse off!"

387

"Yes, now I'll be standing naked before you."
"May I also open your buttons, but very slowly, button by button?"
"Yes, come over to me!"
"Alone at the thought, I am already warmer. I can open it."
"I look at your eyes, you're looking forward to opening the buttons and then what?"
"Oh, we'll see that, or rather, you'll feel it and I'll feel it."

And he comes around the table to me and stands right in front of me. I look him in the eye and he smiles back. Then he puts both hands on my breasts. Carefully and very slowly, as in slow motion. He leaves his hands behind and our lips tighten magically and we cuddle with our lips very calmly and tenderly. Now he must feel in his palms like my nipples and push against it. But when he unbutton the blouse, he can feel it even more. And already his left hand takes the first button from the top and opens it. Oh yes, wow, he can do it with one hand. Now he has to do that with seven more buttons, then he is almost there. If he remembers, I have two more buttons on my sleeves. So button, button, button, he has all the buttons on and now he lifts my blouse over my shoulder and he turns me over. I am somehow confused what is he doing now. Oh, now I've seen through this rascal. He wants to pull my blouse down to the still buttoned cuffs and he does not come further be-cause of the buttoned up sleeves. Immediately he turns me around and ...

"So now your nipples are even more cheeky. Really cool."
"You, I can not move my hands anymore, you did that deliberately."
"Yes, now I can finally act on your breasts without resistance."
"Hey, that's unfair."
"No only clever. I'm so hot behind it to be able to touch you undisturbed."

"But we ... !"

Already he has stopped my pending verbiage by delicately but firmly press mouth on mouth and I close my eyes. His hands can now caress undisturbed on my breasts, feel the nipples and take them between his fingers and massage light to moderate. His right hand really slides off my chest and falls down, can only catch again in the nonexistent hair of my pussy. Then stop and slide backwards. Without being able to open his mouth, he can not hear how or if I moan. Cool feeling and immediately it is there, his right hand circles over my clitoris. She is warm, moist and excited. Whether it is fair, if I ask him now to massage me to climax or should he rather break off? I could ask him questions before or after the point of no return. Oh Joschua has it fully in hand. Hahaha, pun. He loosens his gag and ...

"Do you want to continue or stop?"
"What, what do you want to know?"
"Well, whether I may stroke you to climax or stop first."
"Youuu! Youuu!"
"Yes, are you so hot? Oh, women can do it several ' times in a row."

And he starts spinning my clit faster and pressing and pulling my nipple. I want to say something, but his mouth closes my mouth tight again and his tongue bothers me as I speak. I notice how I keep going to the climax and he increases the clitoral touch rate. I want to say something, but his tongue and lips prevent it. Joschua must now feel like I start to breathe much faster and he pushes me easily with my buttocks against the air hockey table. So I can not leave and he can make me happy again. Hahaha, this is a game. He can give me a climax when he wants. It is literally in his hands. A great feeling. But I feel it's nearly time and he pushes more and faster. It is pure madness, how one can feel if one lets a tender man do that. He feels just how far I am, you can feel the whole body when it comes to me. Then the short break before the explosion and then you can trigger me with just a little movement and now it's nearly time for me and I'm totally at his mercy. When and how much he lets me feel it. Complete rest, the whole body tenses, because I have full mouth contact with him, he not only feels it but he notices how my breath stops short and then his triggering movement and everything goes off like a rocket. I breathe like a race car so fast and my body jerks violently in a row. And too quickly comes the decaying phase and the twitching of the body slows down and my breath too. He feels like I relax and sink into his arms. It is also an experience for me to feel something like this directly.

"Thank you, Mia, for letting me experience your climax so directly."
"Ohhh, please, please, but you triggered it."
"I knew I had something to do with it."
"And how. You're a lout, the game has not ended yet."
"Do not worry, we'll keep playing now. We both have one more part."
"Your part hides more."
"You look so extremely sharp."
"Thank you for yourself and your dear words."
"Please, please, it was my pleasure. Would you like to sit down on the sofa and rest before continuing?"
"Yes, like and have a drink."
"A sparkling or orange juice?"
"Ladies place setting."

He leads me by the hand to the sofa, takes the lying, cozy blanket and puts it over me. I put on my legs. Then he brings us a glass of sparkling wine with orange juice to the sofa and hands me one of them.

"To the dearest and most excited woman in the world, to you Mia."
"To you, the hottest man in the world. My dream man!"
"If this is not the greatest initiation of my party room, then I do not know anymore. You are the hottest female I

*can imagine and I have not played or felt the feeling that
everything is so true and honest. You are so natural. A
miracle woman!"*

"WONDERWIFE?"

*"Yes, a beautiful female with intelligence and feeling
and the talent to bring it all across."*

"Oh, you praise me so much, thank you, that does my
soul really well."

*"Yes, in life, people are mostly just saying something
negative, because many people feel better when they
know that others are worse off. That's what they
measure themselves against and say, oh, I'm fine."*

"Yes that is true. You almost only hear negative things
and people talk about bad things. What's wrong with the
woman, has no husband. Nobody wants that. That is
certainly contagious sick. Surely she has ... ."

*"Yes, I know that and it hurts so much when you are the
target of such evil words."*

And I put my head on his shoulder and close my eyes. If
I dream something and if so, what. From my hot climax
or from what I have experienced negative. Well, whether
he thinks it's great that I just lay his head on his
shoulder and fall asleep. There is a bond developed in
this short time. Joschua just keeps quiet and I really
start to dream too. It was an evening, nobody would believe that. One is so familiar and can freely release oneself as one is and feels. Where else can you do that in
the world and with whom? I have the feeling that I will
not regret giving myself the way I really am inside. I
have not been allowed to experience that before, I was
always reprimanded or exploited. Oh, thank you for finding me and trusting me. And now Joschua gets tired,
too. I feel his eyes close for a moment. He certainly has
some thoughts and then he closes his eyes. I think we
are both asleep under the plump blanket. What an evening. So beautiful.

After undetectable time, he decides to change the sleeping place. If we sleep here any longer, Joschua is right,

and tomorrow morning, all 256 bones will definitely hurt me when we wake up. We will not continue to play like that, because the mood is down. Is also understandable after this super beautiful climax experience. Joschua wants to carry me to bed on my hands. Hahaha then he can feel my bare skin while wearing it while lying on his hands and clinging to his naked body. Oh Mia what you probably think again everything. He gets up from the sofa, holding my head he does not fall down. I'm lying on his shoulders, putting my right arm around his shoulder and under his armpit. Then he pushes his left arm under my knees and I'm still half asleep. He raises me slowly and in a half-sleep I whisper ...

"So what's going on?"
"I'll take you to bed, just go back to sleep."
"I'm too heavy."
"Rest your flyweight and close your eyes and keep dreaming. The movements you feel now are of our frenzy, you feel them and paint you the appropriate dream images."

I'm already gone, do not even answer and he goes to the stairs and slowly upwards step by step. So I have never been carried by a man. In the over the threshold wear at the wedding, I was fully dressed. Oh, that thought again. Does Joschua love to put me in bed to sleep? But he will fall right next to it and fall asleep. I am totally of the days, otherwise it would not be so divine. So arrived at the top, was easier than I thought, hahaha does not have to wear me too. Poor Joschua and now into the bedroom and around the bed. Oh, he puts me to sleep on his side today. Oh, how careful he puts me on his pil-low. He does not want me to wake up. You are nice to me. If he knew that I enjoy being so carried away by him and not yet sleep, I think he would be angry with me. So I will not betray myself and keep pretending to sleep. I'm really tired. When he puts me in bed, I roll over to my side and he covers the blanket over me. I really fall asleep in the cuddly warmth. And very softly he whispers in my ear ...

"I love you, dream something beautiful from us."

I only realize that Joschua leaves the bedroom. He will certainly turn off the lights downstairs, but I can not hear him cuddle up to bed anymore. Since I have to be deep and firm in my wonderful dream world.

Monday 09.09.2013

Ring - ring - ring

I hear the phone go in his office. You want something so early in the morning from me. Oops, it's already 10.29. Oh I have, I'm not at home, I'm with Joschua. I slept deeply. As far as I can see, Joschua did not hear the ringing and sleeps even further. Then I will also dream for a very small moment.

"Good morning, my easy angel."
"Good morning, where am I?"
"Well in bed next to me."
"In bed? I can not remember anything at all. How did we get here?"
"You have been hovered on my arms from the party room sofa in my bedside."
"How been floated?"
"Well, I carried you on my own arms and was allowed to feel you very close and almost naked."
"I can remember that, you have not whispered some-thing in my ear."
"Yes, I whispered it's all good, keep dreaming of our cavalry."
"Yes, with cavalry and exercise was something I dreamed about. As I ride on you, completely naked both of us."

"Wow, then you did what I wanted you to do."

"As?"

"When I picked you up, you moved and you asked in your sleep what is and I said the movements come from the struggle."

"Ahhh, you have given me a dream. Worked."

"That's what I call a success."

"Speaking of success, how was it with the Airhockey?"

"Yeah, so I knew when I removed your blouse, you do not have to be angry with me."

"Why evil?"

"Well, because I just could not resist you anymore and I had to fumble my hands on you and when you started to moan so loud, I really wanted to shoot you into seventh heaven."

"You have succeeded completely. You still turned me and pressed with my buttocks against the air hockey."

"Yes, you got that?"

"Yeah, when I felt the edge off the table and could not go farther back, that was a little more exciting."

"Cool."

"I never thought you could enjoy it so much and feel it so intensively, every one of your turns and when you pressed harder on my clit."

"You can only feel that because you just let yourself down and trust me. That's why I enjoy it so much to make you happy and it's crazy, you always drove me so crazy and I was able to drop and did not even have the guilty conscience of the past."

"Why a guilty conscience?"

"Well, I thought, if I get an orgasm, then my partner has to too. I know, really stupid. But that's different with you. I do not think about it I enjoy and I can, because I realize for the first time in life that you, even if only I have fun and I feel it the other way round. That's just heaven. You have really shown me how nice it is to drop. I always used to think about it. Now I have experienced it with you."

"I can only give you back the compliment, it is indescribable. Why are you still wearing my bra?"

"When I put you in bed, you turned immediately to the side and you looked so peaceful, because I did not want you to wake up when you open and therefore I have you with bra on, covered."

"You think of everything! Thanks, it's so nice to you!"

"Youuu, I can take it off to you now, but we still catch up the game, I would like to see how you shoot the puk and your upper body half over the air hockey hangs and then move your breasts. The thought of it already makes me … ."

"How does the thought turn you on again?"

"That's the way to call it."

And I want to look right now and feel his cock with my right hand but ...

"You still have the boxer shorts on."

"Well, you have not won everything yet."

"Do you want to start it now until I win again?"

"Mmm, I have not thought about that yet. But it's a different boxer shorts, I was swimming last night and saw something in the stars and just felt good. Then, of course, I put on a dry."

"Oh, you were swimming without me?"

"Yes, you swam in seventh heaven."

"And you did not want to wake me up. That's kind of you. Here I sleep so deeply and firmly, I'm not used to it anymore."

"I also have a stressful life with me."

"Not exhausting, but exciting. I have not experienced anything so exciting. If I'm honest also not dreamed. I would never have imagined and then you'll get me and I'll find feelings in me that I did not know."

"Well, I have to give that back to you, I feel the same way. You, it's almost 11am and what do you think of a nice breakfast with scrambled eggs and bacon, plus a nice coffee and fresh rolls?"

"That sounds good. I like to smell it when you have fresh coffee."

"Yeah, I always remember my big granny, she always

cooked coffee in the morning and then everything smelled like it. I think of it almost every time I come to the kitchen and smell the freshly brewed coffee."
"Yes, you always have memories when you smell certain scents. Me too."
"And do you want to swim a little before?"
"Then I have to get up from the warm cot."
"That's the way to say that."
"What do you do?"
"I'm just brushing my teeth and then I slide into the water. When the water comes in contact with the cycle fully, then I dry off everywhere ... ."
"Everywhere alone?"
"If you do that, it will be so erotic again."
"Do not you want to be eroticized by me?"
"Yes and how. Do you come with swimming? Are you brave? Then the day starts really fresh."
"All right, I'm just going to the bathroom, then I'm coming."
"Well, I'll wait for you at the top of the slide."

He gets up and walks around the cot and stands in front of my bedside, well on the side of the bed where I'm lying today, otherwise it's his side, but so he could put me down last night better, otherwise my head would have been at the bottom located. I turn around and ...

"Oops, there you are, what are you waiting for?"
"Well, you get up, I want to help you and free you from the rest of the textiles. You know, freedom for the breasts."
"Crazy guy, but not bad, my breasts would be happy. And then you definitely want to test if everything is alright with them."
"Jou."

I get up, push one bare leg out at the other, bare leg under the covers and stand on the floor. Man, here comes my naked pussy again. His position here on the bedside really pays off for him. And then I stand and stretch as hard as I can. Oh that always works so well. I get on tiptoe and stretch everything in the direction of the sky while I turn my back on him. That's the moment for him, where he bravely accesses and opens my bra clasp. He pushes the straps over my shoulders and kisses each spot where they were on each side of the shoulder, his hands playing the spare bra on my breasts. Yeah, he really has nervous hands and they push my breasts a bit. And how can it be different, I like to be freed from my bra and my breasts like it so lovingly cuddel to be.

"Hahaha, I knew that you did that."
"How so?"
"Well, you always squeeze my breasts when you touch them."
"Ohhh, am I doing something wrong, do not you like it?"
"But it's beautiful, just no one else has done it in front of you and it keeps me going."
"Yes, I can feel that, your nipples are already hard again. Hey, youuu, what are you doing?"

I went back to normal from the tip of my toe and put my hands behind my back, then slid inadvertently into his shorts to hold on to his cock.

"Not me, just my fingers hanging out somewhere."
"I realize that and they do not want to leave, as I feel."
"Right and they want to bring something to a halt and then … ."
"Do you want to hear something now?"
"Yes."
"A quickie in the morning dispels sorrow and worry."
"Oh yes we do, worrying. Go on, take off your boxer shorts."

Immediately he wants to take off his boxer shorts, but my fingers are stuck. I have to laugh involuntarily and we fumble my fingers free again, then he lets him slide to the ground and pushes him away with his foot. Oh his cock is already hard again, in full expectation of what is coming now. And I lean forward and support myself with my hands on the bed. Oh, now I've stretched my butt cheeks really lustful. And I shake it up with irritating. So after the motto, penetrate, penetrate, penetrate. He leans forward, gives both buttocks a big kiss and then take his hands on my hips and he pulls me up to her. I feel like his cock touches my buttocks and then slowly penetrates in the slot forward and sinks. I'm really wet and warm again. That just happens in his vicinity, I just need to think, this horny man is the same and it's already happened. I just can not control it. Yes, my body is totally focused on Joschua, my mind is almost power-less. What should become of it?

"Yes, that's it, come move."
"Always slow with the young dogs."
"No, quick, quick, quickie!"

And he begins to penetrate with slight bumps from behind deeper and deeper, until his little eggs hit my buttocks. These strokes increase our tensions enormously and he immediately increases the bumping rhythm. Oh, I'm close to the climax and he seems to be too. Will be a real quickie.

"You're almost there, what are you going to do with me?"
"You with me, it comes to me, further, deeper!"

And he pushes as hard as he can, while he has to hold on with his hands on my hips, otherwise he would fuck me smoothly. Well not me, but if he hits me and I push something back, then he would fall over behind, so violent are our shocks. It is cool. Hard to be taken from behind. He does not hit my clit but the tension is huge and shoots up. My emotions are racing up like a rocket and Joschua is starting to moan faster, like me.

"Yes, on, on, faster, yes ...!"

"I'll be right there."
"Yeah,come ...!"
"Yesss, ohhh, ohhh!"

My feelings explode and it's crazy, its almost at the same time and that's a big emotional mess. Quite different than when you come alone. You feel the twitches of the other so intense and because he has also moved violently, this is transferred to me and the feelings seem to complement each other somehow and extremely high. Also that it happens in such a short time, so a real highlightquicky. So the whole body begins to tingle without being able to fight back. And he hits me hard again, but he does not hold me to my hips anymore and as he probably planned, I fall forward on the bed.

"Hey you lout, now you slipped."
"Yes, the feelings were so extreme that I had to interrupt them, otherwise I would be tingled all over my body."
"As you describe it again. Did you like it so much?"
"Yes, it was an intense explosion and accumulation of emotions in my glans. I could not fight back and the tension was almost unbearable. As if you poured a whole bag of effervescent powder in your mouth."
"Yes, I also had a superquicky. Oh, that's how I've never been woken up."
"Well, you challenged it with your wobbly pastries."
"I succeeded perfectly, right?"
"Yes and how, I'm totally happy."

And he lets himself fall on me. Of course he supports himself with his arms, otherwise I would be flat. But it's so nice to feel his bare skin on mine again.

"Hey, you're sweaty again, I worked."
"The feelings were just too intense."
"Yeah, who do you say that. Indescribable, a real quickie."
"I have never climaxed so fast."
"Neither do I. And then such an extremely violent one."

"Oh, but you radiate a warmth, stay still something lying on me."

"Yes, I feel like you still have some tension in you. I'll wait until you're back down."

"How am I supposed to come down completely when you lie on me?"

"Okay, your're right, I agree with you."

"I feel your hot, tender skin on me. It feels so warm and familiar. Just like we've known each other forever."

"You say such sweet words that go right into my heart. I feel so well in your presence."

"Me too."

And we lie together for some time, then he rolls over and slides down from me. It was nice, really, so in the morning a real quickie, how to start the day even more beautiful.

"But now it's cold, you were a great hot water bottle. Such a cozy warmth."

"Yeah, and your hot water bottle is hungry now, and before that, he has to go swimming again to come down, because my feelings are still turning up there somewhere."

"Good, you persuaded me. I'll follow right away. Did not we want to meet at the top of the slide?"

"Yes, was not that before you seduced me?"

"Yeah, well, you took good care of that."

"Good, then we'll meet right there, I'm looking forward to it."

And Joschua gets up and immediately leaves the bedroom. One can not know if Joschua has such a sharp idea again and I go out again like a rocket. It is a devil and I have come to him, then I'm a devil woman. Thoughts, thoughts, thoughts and I have already arrived in the bathroom and have brushed my teeth and once briefly in the shower and soaped. Now naked to the slide high, not dried. I come out of the bedroom and at the same time Joschua comes out of the other bathroom.

"Is that really true?"
"What?"
"You come swimming naked. I had the same idea. How cool. Otherwise, you'll catch a cold and I'll have to play Uncle Doctor."
"Sounds good, what would you prefer for an uncle doctor?"
"A gynecological examining field doctor."
"Examining stroke doctor"
"Yes, do not you know that?"
"No, never heard."
"Sorry, you've certainly missed something."
"If you're the doctor, but how do I get sick so I can visit the gynecological examining doctor?"
"I can explain that to you at breakfast, now it would be too long, come on!"
"I'll remind you then."
"Well."

And we go to the stairs, I go up in front of him and he can not keep his hand slanted between my thighs and just work against my movements.

"Hey, you again."
"You look so horny when you run naked up the stairs in front of me. I can not help it, I'm just a man."
"And what a."

But when he reaches the top, he should slip in and he gets into the slide and off he goes. I hear only one brrr after dipping it up here that's cold. Then total silence. Now I go into the chute and off the post office. I think the slides are so great I have never experienced and when I could have dreamed that I slide naked and a man watching me. No way. And I'm so excited, right now I'm down and dive into the water. Oh, just before, before I close my eyes to dive, I still see, I almost landed in his arms. Just missed. Too bad. Brrr it's cool, well, probably

401

just because our bodies are so hot from now on. Then I exchange.

"Really cool."
"You have to go underground, jump up and dive in, then it's warm. Try!"

And I do it. I did not want that, but it happens. I dive and jump high out of the water. Now I remember only that I am completely naked and he sees not only my wobbly breasts, but I jump so high that he can even see my pussy. Then I dive again and again. Now I do the typical thing for long haired women again. I shake myself to get the water out of my hair. I meet him again full in the face. He has as I can see just getting his eyes.

"Well hit, do you want to sink me?"
"Yeah, you can swim. Hahaha. You're right, it's warm after the second dive."
"Yes that's the experience."
"Catch me."
"Oh I'll get you and then."
"How and then?"
"Got you, so now I get a kiss."
"Ok, I can live with that."

And while our lips are talking, I put my hands around his neck and then I do something unexpected again. I pull my legs up and put them around his waist. Oh his cock presses immediately on my pussy, but he is not stiff enough yet. Our kisses are getting wilder. After infinitely beautiful feelings and a hot run of the lips, he lets himself fall back into the water and I let go as soon as my head gets into the water. We both turn up again. I came to where I went down and he disappeared under water. He's already at the stairs and I turn around and look for him.

"Huhu here I am."
"How did you get there?"

402

"Just walked under water here."
"Hahaha."
"May I hand you a towel to dry off before I collapse of hunger here?"
"I come, you can also dry my back."
"Hahaha, another extension of the hunger phase."
"Well, then I'll make breakfast very quickly."
"Oh, naked?"
"Mmm no, I just need a moment."
"Is good."

And then I pull myself back in the direction of the bedroom and he follows me. I see how he wants to dry off quickly and I do it too. We are dry almost at the same time and then he starts to get dressed. Everyone stands at his bedside and we look at each other.

"Who is dressed first?"
"When undressing was I faster and now getting dressed?"
"I."
And after the underwear he has a small lead. After the stockings, I'm back in front, he can make up for the pants but unfortunately again. I first button my blouse. He put on his pants first and then his slippers and buttoning his shirt, runs into the kitchen. Hahaha is that a lout, he wants and is there first. And he makes it even before I'm in the kitchen door to put on the coffee and the scent begins to spread. There I stand in full glory, fully clothed and rings in the door frame for air.

"You're a rascal, you cheated."
"No, we did not say we had to get dressed in the bedroom."
"All right, you're right. I'll cover the table."
"Well, I make the croissants and rolls in."
"Nice that I stayed here and I look forward to our week together like a little kid on Christmas."
"Me too! Sausage and cheese or just Nutella and jam?"
"What you take."

403

"Well then the full program."

It is nice in the morning to cover the breakfast table for two people and then if you get from the loved one even help with blankets, then the following breakfast can only be more beautiful. Oh and the water for the eggs still put on.

"Here are the glasses for the juice. If you pour it in now, it's not so cold when it's already on the table for a moment. Egg cups and egg spoons are also here."
"Come."
"How again?"
"But you want to know exactly. Hahaha."
"Yes, everything you do and I like you. Bad?"
"No, just the opposite. But if you learn too much about me, then it increases the likelihood that there is something you do not like about me."
"And with me first, you never want to see me again and I have to give up the hottest sex of my life."
"Hahaha hottest sex, with the women you all had and made happy."
"Well, it's very manageable."

In the meantime, we sit at the breakfast table and begin to prove the rolls and to eat. He likes to add grapes to it. And the aroma of coffee really makes you want more. But now again to my question.

"So many women were not and then you have to distinguish even if it was just a holiday flirting or took longer. The longest and worst relationship was twenty-five years and has produced two children. The woman took one of the most part of my life and also consumed her health. But thank God, that's all behind me and now, for the first time, I am really happy and totally in love, as if I have met the first great love of my life."
"Do you mean me?"
"Yes, Mia I've fallen in love with you that it hurts when I think you're leaving again."

"No man has ever said that to me."
"But you also had longer relationships in your life?"
"Yes, almost eighteen years and there have been nice times. But when you're together for so long, you're living apart. That's just the big danger and we did not have children either. Then he got to know another person on a training course and it had to be. So the divorce came."
"At least you have separated in good."
"Yes, in a sense, but then came a hard time so alone. I went back to my previous job."
"What are you doing?"
"I am a florist. My grandparents used to have their own business and I took over after their death. When I met my husband, he was self employed, I gave up the business and ran the office with him. After the divorce, I stood again, as the saying goes, in the street. There was not enough money for a new self employment and to open a new flower shop today, the market is already quite full."
"You have already had to pay a lot of training money in your life."
"Yes you can say that, but now it pays off."
"What do you mean?"
"Well, I finally had the courage to change my life. Loneliness has often hurt me a lot and you will not get any younger either."
"To whom do you say that, but since you've e-mailed me, since the day I'm getting younger every day and my childhoodideas come through again full."
"Child's head flipping?"
"Yes, that's what you say, when you have only stupid things in your head as a child, just like a fool."
"I did not know that expression yet."
"Do you know what, we forget everything that was before the first mail and just enjoy the fact that we have found each other and I have fallen in love with you and we can experience the hottest sex in the world just together."
"Totally agree."

"Well, may I pour you some more coffee."
"Oh yes, it makes me really lively again."
"Well, I do not want to question that now."
"How to question?"
"Well, why the coffee makes you happy."
"I knew you were asking that."
"I knew you knew it, that I asked that, otherwise you would not have questioned it."
"Hahaha funny pun."
"Yes, it's fun with you. By the way, do you want this morning ... ."
"Tomorrow is good, we have it after twelve."
"Yes're right. But would you like to go on a harbor cruise, the sun is shining and that's fun and in the boat we can sit on a bench next to each other and then I'll put my arm around you and kiss you every now and then."
"Kiss? We are not alone."
"Well, we are big kids and we do not have to give an account."
"Ok, good idea, but now I help cover it."
"Agreed and whenever we meet in the kitchen door, I get a kiss from you."
"Oh, oh, oh, then I carry each part one by one to the kitchen."
"Does that mean you like being kissed by me?"
"And how!"
"Let's go to the kitchen."
"Please wait for me in the doorway."

Said, done and the kitchen doorway kiss starts. We must have looked really funny, because everyone had crockery in both hands and now held it with their hands behind the other's back while kissing.

"Kisses, I can not keep the dishes like that for much longer."
"Next time you just take an eggcup, it's not that hard."
"I can hide it in my hand and then stroke it with it."
"Caressing with the eggcup?"

406

"No, of course with my hand."

And there are still countless kitchen door meetings with kiss attacks.

"Ready, what should I wear?"
"No matter, pants and blouse, we take jacket, on the water it is often windy and cooler."
"Fine, I'll be ready in five minutes."
"But not if I come to the bedroom."
"I would have thought so, but this time I'm staying tough."
"Really hard, not a bit of support in moving."
"No, I'll leave these pants and blouse on."
"Joschua had bad luck. But you, all the buttons are right on to your blouse."
"Hahaha and how, also on my pants."
"How do you have buttons on your pants, where?"
"Hahaha, not like that."
"Ok, I'm good now, see us in the garage on the car."

He goes to the bathroom and takes his jacket, a white leather jacket from the wardrobe and goes into the garage. He opens the gates and lo and behold, I'm already done and come to the car.

"Please come in, madam, may I open the door for them."
"Oh yes, please."
"So watch me close the door."

And already I'm in the car. We leave the garage and land and drive to the harbor. Parking, go down to the Jung-fernsteg, get ticket, go on the boat.

"Do you want to sit inside or outside?"
"Wow in the beautiful sun outside."
"Then let's go all the way back. The bank by the side."
"Well."
"I sit on the water side and you miss, then I can put my arm around your shoulders."

"Feels good, your arm."
"Lying on your shoulders, it's in a good mood. Am I not too heavy?"
"No not at all."

We look at each other and smile, but that's not all, when our eyes meet, our lips feel attracted again and a kiss is the result. Then the tour boat leaves and the captain greets the guests and starts with his explanations mixed with little anecdotes. We do not talk much during the ride, now and then he points to something, just a few words, and we both listen to the sound of the water hitting the boat and the story of the captain. The journey seems to have passed quickly, although such a great harbor cruise takes over two hours, we start again.

"It was very nice and interesting, but the fact that you kept me in the arms all the time was the most beautiful thing for me. I always felt your warmth. Thank you for making the harbor cruise with me."
"Gladly, nice if you liked it too. I would not have driven alone, because I would have certainly stupid thoughts, but with you by my side, I felt really comfortable."
"Did you get hungry too?"
"Yes, that's what the sea air does. What do you want, a fresh fish roll or cake or something bigger?"
"Oh, a fish roll would just fit the sea air."
"In the front of the booth, let's see what the rolls look like."
"They smell good."
"Yes, what do you want on it?"
"Matjes."
"With onions?"
"Yes."
"So a roll with matjes and onions and I'll take the same, also with onions."

We stroll along the quay and plaster our rolls. In itself, coffee time is now at 15.40, but what is still normal with us. Day and night are currently suspended with us and he seems to infect me with it. A totally crazy time but the most beautiful in my life so far. I hope it never ends. What can make a crazy crazy and so wonderful. Measured against today's scale I was never really happy with Joschua. Oh an onion, you are the spicy but delicious.

"Mmm, really delicious a fish roll on the hand."
"Yes, but fish must swim, how about a cappuccino or cocoa?"
"Not bad, where? Maybe at home by the fireplace and then you can also tell me what you meant by a gynecological examining pet doctor."
"Did not you forget that?"
"No, I told you so, but at breakfast it did not turn up and when we get home ... ."
"So what?"
"Then I feel like you're enjoying a cup of warm cocoa ..."
"With or without cream?"
"Youuu distractor, with cream of course. And then ... ."
"You noticed?"
"What?"
"You said home several times. That sounds so beautiful out of your mouth."
"Did I say that? That must have been unconsciously said by my subconscious, because somehow I feel so terribly comfortable with you."
"This is fantastic."
"But now you have distracted again ... ."
"Sorry, I'm calm now."
"I want to experience that!"
"Really?"
"Oh, of course not me ... ."
"I thought so."
"What thought?"
"That you do not want me to be quiet, otherwise it's boring to always talk to a person who does not answer."
"Yes, not only boring, but also outrageous and without education. Anyway, I've learned it the way you answer when asked."

409

"Me too."

And we are already at the car, get in and drive off, of course, in the direction of our home. Man oh man, this thought again, ours. What's going on in my head, I'm not at home here, is it? Yes heart I understood you, you feel like home here. Oh no, even more, I feel more than just at home here. I feel like I'm really happy for the first time in my life. No, I would not be happy. I am very happy.

"You, did not you want to tell me something that could happen?"
"Oh, no, not by itself."
"Do not push it, say."
"Well, if I tell you what I mean by gynecological examining doctor, then maybe it could be that you want to experience it too."
"Oh sure, until now everything was great what you wanted to do with me."
"Well, but also what you did to me."
"Really, did you like it all so much?"
"You're still asking, did not you feel how much I liked it?"
"Yes, I have and that's nice to feel something like this."
"Do not you have a wish that you would like to have fulfilled."
"What wish do you mean?"
"Well, right now we're talking about sexual desires."
"Oh, I'm open to anything that's fun."
"But crazy things you never know if they're fun."
"Well, then you have to try them out and then you can tell afterwards if you liked it or not. You just have to pay attention to a few things, such as the codeword - red."
"Hey, you noticed that. And will you use it even if you do not like something or hurt something. Promised?"
"Promise, definitely."
"And when you say red, the other one stops immediately. Promised!"
"Promised! And now tell me what does a gynecological examining doctor say to you?"

"Watch out, that would distract me from driving too much here."

"Is it such a hot thing?"

"Yeah, that's a fantasy I've never said before, and I've often tried to dream of it, but never experienced it."

"Now you really make me really curious!"

"I tell you, the first other being, when we sit in front of the fireplace with a cocoa and a piece of Donauwelle."

"Good, I'm so excited. I think I want to tell you now, I want to give it a try. "

"You want to drive me crazy already? Now I can already use pictures of you in my dream. Cool."

We smile at each other and sit quietly next to each other for the last few minutes. I'm already thinking about what he wants to experience with me and I'm trying to think about what it can be. We drive into the garage, get out and go into the house.

"I'll do the fireplace and the lights."

"Well, I go to the kitchen and try to make the cocoa."

"With the Tassimo."

"You have to show me that."

"Wait, I'll show it to you right away."

And before that, before he gets into the kitchen, he quickly goes into the living room, firewood and lights it and then he comes to me in the kitchen, where I'm already eagerly waiting for him. I stand in the door to the dining room and when he comes he begins to smile from a distance. He thinks the same as me and then it comes to our door through kiss and he is so tender again and yet so intense, he goes through me again and again. When kissing with Joschua I always like that time stops and we would always kiss. It's just so beautiful, full of cool, no, rather full of romanticism and the moisture that always comes to the exchange ...! Oh, kiss again. Well then, turn around and into the kitchen.

"I always make the cocoa with the Tassimo. Here in the

411

cupboard are all capsules, also for lemon tea, cappuccino and latte macchiato. In the freezer I have Donauwellen, second compartment. Is it enough for you or do you want two?"

"A piece, even if you help me burn calories again."

"How did you get it."

"Ahead of it. It's going to be a hot, super hot emotional evening."

"Oh oh oh that could be if you want to join in too."

"Yes, in any case."

"Once familiar with a woman, I just love it. But then I have a wish too."

"Which?"

"If you have experienced that, whether you like it or not, please let us then swap roles. I really want to try it."

"Wow, if you make it even more exciting, I'll explode right away."

"Please do not, first thaw the Danube waves in the microwave. Two minutes, they are not melted and so creamy."

"Tassimo, can you show me sometime?"

"Quite simple, turn it on, water in, I always make new, before I use the machine again, does not like stale water. Make up here and capsule in and out. Press the yellow button and go."

"It's easy."

"Yes, oh cake already warm, just take out and spread out on two plates. Are you making the second cocoa?"

"Give it a try."

"I put everything on a tray, then we can just take it with us."

"Hahaha, I did it. Second cocoa ready."

"Good, please put it on the tray."

"I do, now I've done something, even if it's just a small thing, but it makes me feel like I'm not just a guest here."

"Cool, now you belong here and can not drive away."

"Do not say such tempting words."

"For me these words are also tempting and I mean them honestly. I'll say the words again shortly before your

departure on Sunday and ask something."
"Ask what?"
"I will not tell you one hundred percent now!"
"You're nasty."
"I can live with this meanness and you have to."

He grabs the tray and goes into the living room. I follow him. He puts it down on the coffee table. The fireplace is already blazing and radiates a cozy warmth.

"It's really cozy here with you by the fire, drinking cocoa and eating cakes."
"Yes, and imagine that at Christmas time or on Christmas Eve with fir tree and lights."
"Does it look different then?"
"Yes, very different atmosphere. I like to decorate for my life, even when I am alone, when I have decorated, then I can really let my soul down and that hurts a round more."
"I know it very well too."
"You, what are you doing for Christmas?"
"I travel to my parents in Rostock every year. Christmas we always have a full house, there come my aunt and nieces. A family party."
"Ohhh, you can not miss it then."
"That sounds sad, why?"
"Oh nothing."
"Hey, do not pinch now."
"Oh, I had just such a lightning thought, but gone with it."
"If you do not tell me right now, I'll tickle you until you can not, and then you'll say it."
"Oh, that sounds tempting, but no thanks."
"Come on, say it."
"Well, I can not destroy such a family idyll. I always wished my children would come with their partners and children on Christmas Eve and we would be a very big and happy family. But nobody likes me anymore."
"I like you, even very doll and a whole lot more."

413

I take his head in my hands, pull him close to me and kiss him a tiny tear that just tried to run over his cheek, just gone.

"Do not be sad, who knows what will happen until then. There are still twelve weeks left."
"Yes. Only this year passed so terribly fast."
"Yes, it was just spring and autumn is coming soon. What did you want to tell me?"
"Oh, if you had been alone too, I would have officially invited you to Christmas Eve, for coffee and cake, turkey with dumplings and red cabbage, and you as a host, and all under it, well, by the tree."
"Are you serious?"
"One hundred percent. When are you celebrating?"
"Well, I always come to my parents on Christmas Eve late in the afternoon and drive late in the afternoon on Christmas Day."
"Well, your parents are lucky that they have such a great daughter."
"You know, they did not always know that, only in the last few years."
"Yes, as they get older, people often become lonelier, and then they enjoy getting in touch with the children."
"Yes it is."
"You, may I think aloud now?"
"Of course, I'm curious."
"There is a possibility that you would visit me directly from your parents on Christmas Day, or you would come to me after the Christmas Eve, without sleeping with your parents, or even better, I would like to see you after the ceremony picking up with your parents in Rostock, then we would have the ride together and I would not worry if you were driving at night."
"How to worry?"
"Well, if you did not drive to your parents until lunch-time, then you have no peace when you celebrate Christmas and then drive to your home."
"Did you just say home after us?"
"Not only said, but meant. It could become your home if

414

you still want me after what I'm about to tell you about me as a gynecological examining doctor."

"So somebody would have told me two weeks ago what we're talking about ... ."

"What do you mean, because I said our home."

"Yes, just ours, then I would have said that is crazy, but as you just said, I felt more than happy in my heart. I can not explain, but it got so hot."

"That's what you said. Crazy, did not you notice, when I said it, my heart beat faster. I would never have dared to say that earlier, but with you it really had to come out and wanted that with pressure."

I lean over to him and look deep into his eyes and our lips approach in slow motion to a very special kiss. A kiss that can change a future, a kiss that can unite two lonely people, a kiss that feels like exactly what we are doing. Is it nice, one is not accountable to any other person, one is grown and still feels like a little girl, excited and yet calm, hard to describe. The kiss has triggered very different feelings than its predecessors. So a kiss tastes like the intention you have with it, sex, love, a life together.

"You want to pick me up, you have to drive far first."

"I like to drive and have over four million kilometers without accidents behind me. Driving has always been in my blood and I can already go to Rostock in the morning and look at the Christmas city, then relax a little. I'm fit when you get in and think, if you were driving alone, this wasted time, but like that, you would sit next to me and ... ."

"How and?"

"Well, let's say, have you experienced an orgasm on the highway with a lovingly guided hand, that would be a Christmas orgasm of Santa Claus personally. Would put on a Santa Claus costume then."

"Hahaha, rarely laughed so heartily, hahaha! You can also persuade one totally with words."

"I do not want to persuade you, just convince you for

the better alternative."

"If I had to decide now I would take the pampering variant, but do you mean the serious, pick me up in Rostock?"

"Yes, it's just a stone's throw. Hamburg - Rostock about 190 kilometers."

"What you all know is true, from house to house, I drove 198 miles Friday."

"And with or without Santa Claus costume?"

"Oh, that goes without, then I see more of you, otherwise everything is so obscured. But I would not want to give up the pampering unit, I have never experienced it."

"Well, then you get as a Christmas gift gift the full hand-pampering program of mine with extras."

"What extras?"

"What do you think is already Christmas?"

"Oh, yes, Christmas rehearsal."

"Test run is good, but it will not be delivered until Christmas Eve."

"Do we want to arrange that already, the Christmas collection?"

"Yes, if you have not shot me in the wind by then."

"My heart says no, I will not shoot you in the wind until then, otherwise I will not get the Christmas pampering program with extras."

"Oh, after receiving the gift you throw me away then?"

"Never, promised."

"What we both talk about is great. And it feels good, so awfully good, just good."

"Yes, you can arouse feelings in me, that's inconceivable, I want it to go on, I'm so happy."

"You also?"

"Yes me too."

And I let my head slide into his lap, pull my legs on the sofa and look at him from below. I slowly bend my mouth and it creates a fantastic smile. He must now perceive a warming warmth from me in his lap. So I have not felt like forever and the fire blazes with big flames in the fireplace. It's already dark outside. As time goes by 21:56. When I was alone at home she was always sneaking, now she is flying.

I still have my head in my lap and I really seem to be dreaming because funny I feel the muscles in my face moving, sometimes they make a smile and again I'm serious, but I always have the feeling I am satisfied and he sees that. How loud a silence can be when a beloved man can look at me and observe me in peace. Oh he will certainly discover many little things about me that are not as they should be or because of the already somewhat advanced life. Often you can not see them in everyday stress, such as the little eye wrinkles that form when smiling, the wrinkles as they form, when my mouth spreads to a smile, as my breasts rise and fall in rhythm with my heartbeat. Oh, what he sees. He will certainly look at me from top to bottom. If that was a good idea to present me in front of him. Anyway, I kinda feel good, he likes me the way I am with all the rough edges. I love him and I mean his love for me is also honest and something very special. I stay a little bit more like that, I just feel good. Rarely have I dropped so much and just felt good. It's something that Joschua radiates, something that attracts me and makes me calm, just something familiar. It feels sooo good. Togetherness!

"Oops no, yes please, do it, yes, I'm coming, ...! Snore, snore!"

Oh man, I think I talked in my sleep. I sleep. I did not fall asleep here on his legs. Oh man who has to get a whole false impression from me I just fall asleep. Oh Mia that can not happen to you. But it was so incredibly comfortable here in his lap and I felt his warmth so clearly, smelled his scent. Mia open her eyes carefully. Joschua looks at me so funny. Oh God, I did not speak in my sleep. Oh, what did I dream? I think that does not exist. I just had a climax or not. Truth or only in a dream. Oh,

417

Joschua did not watch that. His expression, one did not moan in the dream. Oh, must I be ashamed now? I will certainly wake up soon. I really feel like I've had a climax and this one. If I have, unfortunately, very rarely had such hot dreams, then I woke up just before the decisive moment. I think he knows, he looks at me like that. Mia he has heard, oh no, what now. In itself, I would be ashamed. But no, I feel fine. What happens only in me. I throw all the values over the pile. That must be up to Joschua. I feel it now clearly, I've become very wet down between the legs. This climax did not happen in my brain. In itself I slept and dreamed long enough. Oh, what's that, yes, he knows he got it somehow. Mia what is Joschua thinking of you now? He carefully puts his left hand on my pants. Now he feels it how wet and warm I am down there. Uiii it shakes me if he touches me there, even if it is only on my pants. He makes it very tender and slow. He leaves his hand on my pants in the amount of my wet pussy and pushes a little harder. Suddenly I open my eyes completely and he was scared. He is totally surprised.

"What happened?"

And I see and feel his hand down on my pants.

"Ohhh, tell me I fell asleep or did you really make me wet and I had a climax?"
"You, if I tell you that, will I get a big kiss for that, a reward kiss?"
"One hundred pieces."
"Wow, you talked in your sleep and said: Oops no, yes please, do it, yeah, I'm coming ... and I did not know what was going on until I realized it, you had a real orgasm. Since I almost never succeeded and I always woke up at ninety-nine percent, I wanted to know how it was with you and there I put my hand down there carefully and felt that it is quite wet there. So you had a real wet orgasm in the dream. And then I thought, Wow you have to be happy with Mia and maybe I'm to blame. And

418

that really, really felt good."
"I'm embarrassed!"
"Embarrassing, embarrassed to be happy?"
"Yes, and that in front of you in your lap. I have had the last dreamed climax, I think at puberty and now ... !"
"Hahaha you are totally happy and extremely hot for me. It's super cool."
"Really, do not you think that's stupid or disgusting?"
"How stupid or disgusting. On the contrary, it makes me hot and happy. I know why and that you have not gone astray. Or did you dream of another man?"
"No, no, no, I just felt happy in a warm, warm light. I have not seen a person, to be honest."
"I can live well with that, so you're happy with me. Oh, now I know, you've already unpacked your Christmas petting gift in a dream."
"No, I have not, do not want to spoil my surprise."

And I sit up, sit down at the head of the sofa, cross my legs on the seat, put my hand over my mouth and yawn.

"So now I'm fit. Now tell me about your gynecological petting game, please, I'm so excited."
"Are not you tired now?"
"Hahaha, you want to distract. I just slept happily."
"Ok, I have a dream, I want to tie a woman to a gynecologist's chair and then be very tender with her until she explodes."
"Yes, then I spread my legs completely and can not do it anymore. When I think about it, it's already tingling in me."
"Be honest, do not you think that's crazy?"
"You will not believe it, but I've also thought about what it would be like if I was sitting in such a chair and my husband would take me and make me happy. Only with the tie, I have not thought so."
"I thought women always found it silly to sit in such a chair."
"Nonsense, when you go to the gynecologist is often not always pleasant. But has nothing to do with sex

419

games. There you have completely different feelings. You could also lie in bed and you put my legs under the blanket, spread."

"Yes, that would be possible, but if your legs are so high, then the blood gets too much in the head and that could be dangerous. You would have to love that relatively quickly."

"Does it sound reasonable and have you described everything in your book?"

"Yes and much more."

"How long would that take a doctor's game of love."

"Oh that depends on what you do and whether it is fun for both of you, the tied up can break anytime."

"I know, with the codeword - red."

"But you were very careful."

"Yes, I listen to you and save almost everything."

"Oops, I'm not allowed to talk nonsense."

"Oh, some nonsense does not hurt. Now tell me, do you know the one who has such a practice that one may use it?"

"How, do you really want to try this?"

"Yes, if we were all alone and you played the doctor, with a white coat and stuff."

"In a practice, of course, the kick would be extremely erotic."

"What would you do with me there?"

"How do you want to know that before?"

"What do you mean, do you know someone with such a practice?"

"Could be possible."

"Then you can tell me what to expect, if I dare to go with you."

"Well, first you have to go to the locker room, undress yourself and put on a white panties and bra. So the doctor would then pick you up and ask you for the chair. You sit down and your arms are tied to the chair, then your legs, and then the examination starts. On the breasts, the pussy and and and ... ."

"Do not I have the bra on."

"He's being charmed away."

"As?"

"I can not tell you that, you have to experience that."

"And the panties?"

"Experience."

"And if I scream loudly, that's what I'm allowed to call, but not blushing."

"You want to be gagged?"

"Am I never, how does that feel?"

"That's hard to describe, but it's a lot of excitement, because you always have the opportunity to say something and if you do not have that opportunity anymore, that's a bit more that you can not articulate. One is a little more exposed and that excites."

"That sounds good. And then I will explode?"

"I can guarantee you that, I will take care of that. With a lot of feelings and love."

"Yes, I believe you, I would like to try that."

"Do you remember what I said, what I want, when you have experienced it?"

"Yes, you also want to experience that. And I should be your doctor."

"Exactly and will you do that too?"

"I've never tied anyone, but I'll try."

"Then you have only a white coat on, without something underneath."

"Can be done."

"If I make an appointment for tomorrow night, around 9 pm, would you like that?"

"Yes, do you know such a practice?"

"Yes, but you can still pull back until we go."

"No, I do not do it when I have a chance to experience such a thing and then with a man I love ... ."

"How do you love me?"

I look at him and our eyes meet. I smile, take his hands and hold both hands with mine. Then I look at him and say very slowly and firmly.

"I love you, you've taken my heart by storm."

"That makes me sooo happy with what you just said to

me. You did not just say it, you let me feel it. I love you too and I am pleased that you have promised to stay with me until at least Christmas."

"Hahaha, I did not say this Christmas. I meant Christmas 2100."

"Really, you're the coolest female thing I know."

"Will we sit here and talk about everything in twenty years from now?"

"If you have not shot me in the wind because I'm boring you, then I promise you that we'll sit here and talk about everything. I promise you, I'll discuss everything with you if I do not like something, but you have to promise that to me too, if you do not like something I've done."

"Promised."

"Say, it's so late again and I'm hungry. You also?"

"Yes, me too, but I wanted to ask you something else."

"What is my angel?"

"Angel sounds good, thanks for this dear pet name. I wanted to ask you, if you can not practice tying before?"

"Yes, but only after dinner, again it will be a supper."

"What do we want to cook?"

"Cooking at this time? Should not we order something?"

"Do not you have anything left in the fridge?"

"Yes, but if we cook now it will be even later."

"Do you have anything else to do?"

"No, we can do a night cooking, have light and are not accountable. Just have a look in the freezer and in the storage rack. Can use everything."

And then I got up and left for the kitchen. He has to hurry to keep an eye on me. Has worked and in the kitchen he watches as I dig through the freezer and then in the utility room through the storage rack.

"Oh, you can provide a whole army."

"Nonsense, are not many things. I like to go shopping every other day. I do not know what I'm hungry before. We can also make a pizza. The dough is ready and we

422

will fill it as you like. We have the tomato sauce for it, pineapple, cooked ham, tuna, salami and pizza cheese. Or we make toast Hawaii. Or pancakes either sweet or tart with bacon. Or hot rolls and the salmon and cheese."

"I say, you can provide a whole army. Since the decision is difficult. Pizza?"

"No problem, I roll out the dough on the plate and you prove. What would you like to have? Oh no matter, you know what's there, you make a surprise assignment."

"Yes, that's great, I do."

It goes fast, sheet metal from the oven, baking foil on it and the frozen dough rolled out. Then the tomato sauce may be distributed.

"Now it's your turn. I'll cover the table, then we can put the plate in the middle afterwards. Takes about twenty minutes in the oven."

"I already prove."

"Well. ... ready table, with a malt beer or coke or Fanta or milk?"

"I'll put the pizza in the oven. Coke would be good, then I'm still awake afterwards, you know why."

"Please stop a hundred and eighty degrees and look at the clock. Twenty minutes."

"Okay, I have."

"So and I thought after a rich meal we could go to bed and sleep. Since you want to do hot things."

"Yes, very hot games!"

"Then I'll probably have to wake up after the meal."

"I'll turn on the candles. Do you always do that when you're alone?"

"I often turn on candles when it gets autumnal. Then they always give me such a nice, peacefully romantic mood. This in the dining room even if I eat here. But when I'm alone, I go to the office almost every time, to the PC. Whenever it gets dark outside, I always have a candle burning for the autumnal mood. It often happens that the candle has burned down and I immediately

insert a new candle and turn it on."
"But you have a romantic streak."
"Do you never make candles at home?"
"Rarely. Only on special occasions."
"Oh, that's why you're going to start the candles here now. It's a special occasion."
"Well, if that's not a special occasion."
"So, which one?"
"Well, I feed with my new, greatest love of my life!"
"I could hear you for hours, your words hit me directly in the heart and warm it so beautifully. They lie around like a warm blanket."
"Only the truth, only the truth."
"What can the truth be glorious and so many people are lying to one another?"
"They have not experienced that yet."
"I wish all people feel so emotional, which is called love, if they would meet the right partner or partner."
"I do not think that anyone could understand it. Many do not have the antennas, as they say, no heart."
"Unfortunately, I can sing a song of it, too. And people with a lot of heart notice only too late, the other has no heart in the chest, but only a stone. Then it is often too late and the lazy compromises begin."
"Yes, compromises are half the life."
"True, without compromise it is not possible, but you must not be lazy."
"Often there is no way out."
"Now I bring a stupid but true saying. There is always a way out, but often you just can not see it."
"Mmm and outsiders seldom help there, they think it's good if they're worse off than they are."
"Exactly, we already talked about that. It revolves around a lot in life and comes back to the same fact."
"Ohhh the twenty minutes are over."
"I'll take a look at the pizza. Time always flies with you."
"Is she ready, I'm hungry."
"looks good. I'll bring her to the table."
"That's where the tabletop burns."
"No, I have a thick, big, old wooden board underneath.

Since I put the hot stuff always on it. I think we can cut the pizza at the table, whenever we want, and choose the different corners. You occupied differently."

"Sounds good, I'll sit down and pour the drinks."

"I ask Cola."

"Will be done."

"Attention, I'm coming, hot and greasy."

"Do not burn yourself."

"Pay attention. Otherwise you have to play the nurse."

"Oh, not bad, I can connect. Have first aid only a few weeks ago again. I almost forgot everything."

"Wow, but I have wild pictures again in my mind's eye."

"Which pictures?"

"Well, you as a nurse in a white coat ... ."

"Yes, with nothing underneath."

"Oh, yeah, you're right, but you have white socks and canvas shoes on, even in white."

"You can always paint a situation exactly. I can imagine that then figuratively."

"Thanks, but you do not have to imagine the pizza, you can touch it and plaster it. Which piece do you want?"

"Let's see, I've got tuna on it, like boiled ham and there salami."

"If we shared justly, then everyone would get something from everyone."

"Sounds good, you do it."

"I just cut along with the pizza roller. So and now five pieces on each side. Then you can take that way, without a knife and fork in the mouth."

"Animalistic."

"Yes and there ... ."

"Then you immediately come back to a picture."

"Oops, was that as transparent as I wanted to say?"

"Not only your words, but your mischievous smile have betrayed it to me."

"Smile?"

"Well, whenever you want to say something erotic, your face starts to smile so mischievously."

"Oh, really, but you pay attention."

"Yes, I enjoy watching you. It's kind of tingling and

425

exciting."
"Oh, how am I working for you?"
"Yes and still ... ."
"Hahaha, now you have thought something that should become erotic."
"Yes, are you watching me too?"
"Yes, and now I see, if you do not bite into the pizza right now, you're starving."
"Mmm yummy, the bottom."
"And the flooring first. Did you do great."
"Well, everyone can prove that everything is there."
"Then I'll tell you what happened to me earlier. We were hungry for pizza and I go shopping. Buy all the ingredients, think again in the store and go home. There I roll out the dough, put the pizza in the oven, put it in the oven and after twenty minutes I get it out. I think, it looks a bit different than usual, but I notice nothing. Cut off two pieces for each and bring them on a plate to my then. She looks at me, I look at her and she tells me, where is the cheese. When I went shopping, I forgot the pizza cheese, topped the pizza, baked it, cut it, and did not notice that I did not have the cheese over it."
"That's quite obvious. I suppose you were in a dull mood."
"I do not know, but then I had slices of Tilsiter and quickly put over the warm pizza. He also melted and it went. Here everything is on it. Delicious."

It's just nice sitting around a table with Joschua, eating and chatting. You get from one topic to another in the free jump. Joschua can jump and that makes the fun. So we'll push away half of the baking sheet of pizza and rinse with cola. Oh no, I limited myself to Fanta. It's already midnight again. He tells me that the clocks are different with him. I hope I can handle that, because not everyone is like him, crazy about his biorhythm.

"Well, what are you thinking about again?"
"About the biorhythm."
"The biorhythm, how do you get there?"

"I wondered if it would do you good to always eat so late with me and make nonsense. One should be in bed before midnight and then one would be rested in the morning."

"That's nice, you're worried about me."

"Sure, I want to keep you until Christmas 2100 and not break it first."

And we both have to laugh out loud.

"It's really funny with you, because you can laugh a lot and really hearty."

"The praise I give back to you. And got full?"

"Yes and very fit."

"What do you mean by that?"

"Yes, I would like to experience something with you now."

"How should we go out and party?"

"No, do not go out, stay here. You have a paradise here."

"Oh, two in one."

"Like two in one?"

"Well, first you said you'd rather stay here with me. I like that and secondly you said, this is a paradise. You made me praise and make me happy twice in one sentence."

"I am glad."

"So what do you want to do here with me in our paradise."

"Our paradise?"

"Well, what is a paradise without Eve?"

"And am I?"

"Yes, you are my Eve for all lands and eternal."

"Eternally sounds good … ."

"Yes, at least until Christmas 2100."

"Hahaha, very much agree and for what areas?"

"All areas."

"What are all areas?"

"So, the daily life, the hardest area, understanding each other even without words, being there for each other when things are going bad, and the greatest area of all,

427

the hot, voluptuous, sexual erotic."
"And for all these areas do you want me?"
"Yes, I feel for the first time in my life, you can do more than just fill in all areas."
"Thank you, thank you, thank you, thank you!"
"And I leave to you now the free determination possibility for the next hours."
"Mmm, then I want to be tied up, can I then order a climax?"
"Yes, that's booked."
"Only cover up, then I am at your disposal for all kinds of atrocities."
"I cover up and you sure want to go to the bathroom. May I give you a slip, which you please wear."
"Yes."

I'm just going to the bathroom. What I can now experience again for feelings. Definitely again which I do not know. Here it is feeling on feeling. Sonja never believes me when I tell her about it. He says he is already in the lower area, because in the guest room he always has some new women's underwear in different sizes in stock. A simple, black panties in size 38. And he comes up again. I'm still in the kitchen now but when he's back, I'm done too.

"What are you doing in the kitchen?"
"I just covered and put the dishes in the machine. Will you do it?"
"Thanks, I do. Would you, if you go to the bathroom now, put on this panty and do you come back fully dressed?"
"Yes, where do we meet?"
"Down at the bar?"
"Ok, I'll hurry. I'm really excited."
"Me too, I have never experienced it with a woman who is looking forward to it. I'm so curious what you say afterwards."
"And I first, what I feel comfortable. See you soon."

Joschua said he's going into the party room and turned on the light, then into the guest room, turned on the lights, and set the heater to twenty-eight degrees. If you lie still he has explained to me, even if you have a bed underneath, it will be cold and that must not happen, because the active part has full responsibility for the passive part. Normal bondage should also contain no pain, only the pure lust. Oh, he's definitely as happy as I am, that he is allowed to treat me lovingly. Editing does not sound good, pampering sounds better. As I come down the stairs, Joschua sits innocently looking at the bar as if he had done nothing but wait for his great love. It will be a hot game again, I feel it already in me. Slight tingling.

"I think I'm going crazy, what am I seeing? I have to get up quickly, otherwise it will knock me off the stool."
"How was I not?"
"Sure, you look as sharp as a hot pepper."
"Who I?"
"Yes, you! I never thought you would come down like this."
"Did I manage the surprise?"
"Yeah, I was right, a thousand percent."
"By which?"
"So that you are great in all areas!"
"Oh, thank you, my heart is warm."
"Do you need too, you have almost nothing on."
"Oh, something."
"Yes, pumps in black, with the black panties and a black short blouse at the top, half open. Which man does not get stiff and then you are here with me and we are all alone. Strangers would only disturb now. You're a dream."
"You just inspire me and I feel so good around you to do that."
"Come here, let me push you, I want to feel you."
"Oh hug, I'm coming to you."

And he receives me with outstretched arms and I let myself be shut up by them. My arms embrace him as well and we just hug each other gently.

"Ohhh, you put on perfume."
"Do you like it?"
"Yeah, is not that Armani Code?"
"I'm going crazy, yes, how do you know that?"
"Know me with scents a little bit. Oh, you are madness. Men would kill for a woman like that."
"Now do not exaggerate."
"Did not we always promise to tell the truth and I did. Oh, what can I say to play with such a hot woman now and make her happy."
"Thank you!"
"Now I have something to tell you. The way you've come down here now, from the looks, the dress, the surprise, I have to tell you, you've given me a hot, unexpected and super sexy situation again."
"You have tears in your eyes."
"Oops, sorry, but they are tears of happiness, better than any dream."
"Is that nice to have made you happy with it?"
"And now when I think about what I will give you feelings and how you will enjoy them. Huuu, it's shuddering."
"I am so excited. So much."
"First a glass of champagne, that must be now. To you, the crazy hottest woman in my life."
"Cheers and thank you hot man. You know what women want to hear."
"No, not true, I'm just telling the truth about you and your performance."
"You flatterer."
"Are you ready to experience your first bondage experiences?"
"Yes, I'm so excited."
"Ok, I do not know which one of us is more excited now and think of the codeword, you can stop the game immediately and anytime."
"I know, but I also know that I do not need that, you will

never hurt me."
"Never on purpose! Promised. Come on, let's go to the guest room."

As we stand in the door to the guest room, I stop and take in the atmosphere of him and the room.

"Oh, what does it smell like? That's vanilla. And the many candles, full of romantic."
"Yes, the atmosphere is part of it."
"The first plus point for this game, top atmosphere."
"Thank you. May I ask you in."
"Yes you can."

He shakes my hand and leads me into the room. Then he hugs me and whispers in my ear ...

"Do not answer. I love you, please stay with me forever!"

I do not say anything, he knows it's mean what he whispered in my ear, but the words will keep me busy throughout the game. But he certainly had to tell me, they were so dear to him, no matter what happens right now. He releases the hug, steps back, turns my hand 360 degrees around my head.

"Yes Perfect. Please lie on your back in the middle of the bed on the comforters."

Here in the guest room he has a large double bed with a springbox mattress. Before, he has placed both pillows and the down comforters in the middle of each other. I sit on the edge of the bed and then pull myself in the middle and lie down on my back.

"You did well, you'll get a kiss for that."

And already he kneels beside me on the bed and our tongues unite. Very tender. After a short while he takes the separation and, still sitting on the bed, takes my left hand and puts on her a leather cuff about five centimeters wide. It is only made so that you can push a finger under it. Then he takes the rope, which he has previously tied at the end of the bed head and leads it through the eyelet on the leather armchair and tense it so that my arm shows up in one corner from the headboard. Tighten and knot in. The rope has to be quite tense, so have little play. Then he walks around and does the same on my right wrist. Both hands firmly and ...

"Well, now you're mine and I can kiss you, my whole right arm up to my neck and then my mouth."

Said, done and I like it so far what he did. The hand cuffs are very soft and comfortable on the wrist. Joschua goes back to the other side and licks his tongue from the handcuff to my neck and then on to my mouth, giving me a tender kiss at the end of this action.

Now he walks to my feet, letting his right hand glide over my body from top to bottom. Arriving at my left foot, he puts on a leather foot chain. Of course, the restraint is bigger, because the lower leg is thicker than the wrist. Again, he tightens the foot, the pumps I still leave, relatively firmly to the end of the foot. Then over to my right foot and repeat again. So now I lie defenseless before him. How provocative. He stands in front of the foot and begins to blow up from my right foot along the leg. Up to my panties, which he raises something on the leg side and also blows underneath. I start to move something in my hip and moan. Down the left leg he continues with his tongue.

"How are you?"
"Well, I'm excited, I can not move freely anymore and I can not respond to your tender touches. This is amazing, it's as if the feelings go inside."
"They should also and collect there. Now it will be even

more exciting, I will ... ."
"What will you do?"
"I'll just look at you for a while."
"How to just watch?"
"I notice, your breasts are not yet visible. We will change that now."

And he kneels on the bed right next to me. His left hand moves over my forehead and then down to my mouth. There she stays with light pressure on my mouth.

"I will now open the blouse button by button and then your beautiful breasts will be fully in my field of vision. What do you say, I do not understand you."

And his hand presses a little harder on my mouth. I'm very quiet after trying to get words through. Then his right hand begins to open my blouse buttons from top to bottom and I can not articulate myself. He now works my left blouse to the side and there it is, my wonderful, already firm and upstanding nipple of my left breast. He bends his slightly open mouth over it and plays with her lips to her. Curious his tongue pushes to the game. I notice how I start moaning, but it does not penetrate much to his ear. After his lips and his tongue, his right hand also announces himself to play, she has finally uncovered the chest. After she has agreed with the nipple on a later rendezvous, she goes over to also carry the right blouse part to the side. What Joschua can look at again in peace. Whether he likes that. But he would be mean if I would not welcome the right nipple. Immediately, lips and tongue go to great lengths, while his right hand deals with my left breast. These intense activities do not only excite me again, but I also try to move and moan vigorously. But his left hand works vigorously against my mouth against it. Now, for the first time, I realize what it's like to be gagged and unable to articulate. Joschua seems to be listening to my breasts, they are demanding editing and he also takes his left hand from my mouth.

"Okay, did you experience anything unpleasant?"
"Unpleasant? Absolutely not, that was the madness, your warm, firm hand on my mouth and even when I wanted to say nothing and not when you were at my breasts, sometimes very tight, I would not have thought that there were so many Feelings in my breasts. Great."
"Well, I was lucky."
"Why luck?"
"Because I had a lot of fun and I know now, so do you. Do you know how exciting it is to see you lying like this is indescribable and when you smile, like an angel."
"Oh, do not exaggerate so much."
"You dare to contradict me. That has to be punished."

And immediately he puts his left hand back on my mouth and presses against my nose. He feels like I try harder to breathe. His mouth bends to my belly button and his tongue turns round in it. I'm starting to get more and more breath and I'm also trying to somehow push my navel out of his tongue circles. But apart from a few lateral small movements of my stomach, I can not move and he drills pleasurably with his tongue. A short time later, he lifts his head and takes his left hand away from my mouth and partially nose again. I breathe heavily and must start laughing immediately. I'm actually ticklish in the navel, which I learn everything through him.

"It may be unfair to screw me around in the navel with your tongue. Maybe it tickled and I could not leave."
"That's the meaning of bondage. Was it unpleasant?"
"No, only if I had not been tied up, I would not have kept quiet and would have turned away."
"I know. That should also be the meaning, if you are tied up. To be able to move without pain and then to be able to drop and just enjoy."
"And then you put your hand on my mouth and also on the nose. I had to pull very hard to get some air and then it felt like the air I inhaled was very warm. Like on a hot summer day. That turned me on."
"Really, let me feel it."

434

"No!"

I can not get any more because his left hand is already active again. He can only feel the movements of my lips, but he can hardly hear anything anymore. He smiles at me and his right hand slides under my panties. Feedback from the hand - moist and warm, very wet already.

"Sososo, you are already very well upset."

I can not say anything, but blinks a yes with the eyes. And he seems to want to intensify that even more for me, and his right hand begins with some clit rounding. My eyes are getting bigger and bigger and that's why he stops this roundabout immediately and he opens his mouth and whispers.

"There is still no orgasm."
"Sorry, I was ready."
"Well, you have to be patient for a while."
"For how much longer?"
"Oh, that reminds me, I could."

And he gets up and walks out of the room to the bar and gets an ice cube.

"Hello there I am again, now you will suffer."
"How so?"
"Because you just wanted an orgasm so fast."

And he circles with the ice cube over my breasts and I want to scream that it is too cold, but his left hand manages to position itself again on my mouth. Only a faint groan and slight defensive movements are felt.

After the nipples have dealt extensively with the ice cube, he wanders on to the funny belly button. There he puts it down and takes his hand away. Immediately I try to get rid of my sweet, non existent belly by getting in and out of the ice cubes. He has only half of his original

435

power and therefore it is time to bring him down further to cool me down a bit. So the remaining part of the ice cube disappears under my panties, which his right hand now massages with light pressure on the top of the panties. When he looks me in the eye, he finds an excited look and he thought certainly already it hits him a cool look, but no. His right hand can no longer feel the ice cube, only a wet panty. Conversation needs and he leaves my mouth free.

"What are you doing to me, first hot, then cold and in between crazy."
"That's a cool mix, right?"
"Yes, yes, yes, I want more, go on."
"Funny I thought I was the active part and now you're demanding a higher speed? Do you have another appointment? But I promise you, you will not come back today. Hahaha."
"Yes, please continue!"
"And if you continue to make such remarks, then I'll have to gag you."
"Yes, please do that. Now, right now, please."
"Again, you want something from me, that will be your last wish."

And he takes out of the closet a balloon gag with a hole in the ball. That's more pleasant, he says, with a massive ball to start with. He puts the ball on my mouth and ...

"Open your mouth!"

And I shake my head for no. I want to play. Can I have his eyes say to me. With his left hand he holds my nose to me and after a short time I open my mouth and the balloon gag disappears in him. The balloon fastened rib-bons he now leads around my head and closes them on the back of the head. They have a velcro closure that adapts to the size of my head. Then he puts my head down again. So now I belong to him completely and there is no objection from me anymore. He holds his index finger over his lips to the motto calm now. My eyes are blinking yes.

Now, after being silenced, he gets up and walks to my feet and kneels in front of it. He takes off my pumps and takes my toes in his mouth and nibbles on it and his tongue plays in my belly button. I think I can only hear very softly. Even to my ears no loud cry penetrates from me. I only hear it from within myself.

"Not, not, stop!"
"You certainly want to tell me something nice, but your words sound so mombled and quiet, I can not understand them at all."

He goes to my second pump and pulls him off too. Clearly now I have to endure the same procedure on my right foot and toes. Oh no, what is he doing now? Not the same. He takes a brush, a new brush that is otherwise used for baking and paints me between the toes. I'm getting wild, it tickles a lot more like his tongue and it also encourages him to do more. While he continues to give me a brush massage on my left foot, my right foot is the victim of a fingernail massage. I'm starting to breathe more and to wind, but I hardly have a radius. The hand and foot cuffs hold me pretty much in the same position. Only my body in between can move a bit. Now I know what he meant by tying. I'm going crazy right now. I can not fight back, but I thought I would get angry now, but no, I get more and more excited Joschua also predicted. I did not believe him that. Great that he lets me know that now. Very different feelings build up in me, how can I say, more acute feelings, extremely exciting. But he also makes it as if he had already tested and spoiled ten thousand women.

"Oh, I think that's great, a ticklish Mia. I wonder if there are more jobs?"

And from afar you hear dull because of the gag ...

"No, no, not, stop, I can not stand it anymore."

He wants to fulfill my wish now and not be like that. At work, Joschua seems to have got very hot. He takes off his shoes and stockings and gets up on the bed at the level of my stomach, one foot on each side of me and moves the bed down with light knees. Then he starts very slowly, pursued by my eyes, unbuttoning his shirt and taking off. Sure he does that, he throws it over my face and then, without being hit by my eyes, pulls off his undershirt and throws it away. Now he kneels between my legs and begins with the brush to feel the navel and I try to escape again. Then follow the armpits on both sides. I'm sensitive, too. Oh, it's fun to paint with a little more and then less pressure and to be driven crazy. I can enjoy unrestrained, I can not move. This is really nice and I never thought that such acts would excite me sexually. Shortly thereafter, he takes a little break and he pulls off his shirt from my face. I probably look quite exhausted. But he knows no mercy and already this lout plays a little with the brush on my nostrils. I almost sneeze and he stops. It's time to go back to more serious places and he slides a little deeper and kisses my panties. It is very humid, a mixture of my hot excitation moisture and the water of the melted ice cube. As he probably means, how he will get to see my pussy.

"You, I would like to look at your pussy in peace. Watch out."

My eyes ask doubtfully. He brought a bandage scissors, so you can not cut into the flesh, he told me and shows them to me. He holds her in front of my eyes, about eighty centimeters away. Which should now be used, for what? I think so, I also have a lot of imagination and he gave me the panties to wear. Only with it can it have something to do. I'm really excited. Is that all exciting?

438

Now he kneels again between my legs and takes the scissors in his right hand. First he presses on my panties to stimulate my clitoris and I have to groan again because excitement initiation. Then he leads the blunt side of the bandage scissors under the panties, sideways and separates him, but so that I notice it. He pulls up the panties with the scissors and when he is cut, he bounces back on my skin. Then he makes the same cut on the other side. Immediately afterwards, he puts the scissors away and I fold the cut slip down between my thighs to pull it out with a quick jerk under my buttocks.

"Now I can see you and you can not leave. This is a great erotic sight."

He spreads my labia with his fingers and sees for the first time my clit as she lies there unprotected before his eyes naked. He blows violently against it and I react. Then a greeting with his tongue and then a small plucking with his lips. I react with a groan every time I try to move my pelvis away from my clitoris. But I can not do it, the straps on my feet and hands keep me in that position. Since I notice again how the bondage works. She makes me crazy and gets me more and more excited. Joschua gets up again and now puts his feet to the right and left of my neck. My eyes follow each of his movements and he opens his trouser button and then slowly his zipper. Then he moves his legs and lets his pants slide down automatically. She comes to lie on my face, apparently as he has planned. There she stays for some time, so I can breathe in his scent. How does Joschua know that again, that turns me on properly. Then he pulls his right leg out of his pants and then his left leg. Now the pants are completely on my face and he gets off the bed. Since the pants just loosely rests, I get enough air. And his hands seem to have to be pulled back to my breasts like a magnet and work them tenderly.

"Are you still alive? I hope so, because now it goes on."

He takes the pants off my face and smiles at me. He looks at me in the face that I enjoy being so loved. A man who deals so extensively with me, otherwise I always had to take the part in men and they were always short tailed. I enjoy the caresses of Joschua so much and he is also guilty that I can not be nice to him. He tied me up. As soon as the thought is over, things continue. He goes down to the bed. Kneel down and see me right in my pussy. Is not that crazy, I can directly feel his look as he hits my pussy and he goes on through my body up to my face, which turns red and hot. He has to see it, but he does not let it deter him and goes on. His hand grasps the prepared vibrator in cock form and without that I can see what happens now, he pushes it carefully into my cave. Very slowly and I would certainly ask him what that is, but I can not talk. So just let it drop and fully enjoy it. It is getting more beautiful and hotter in me. He certainly feels like I move easily to take him even more into me. As soon as he is inside, turn it on. He vibrates oh man oh and I moan loudly. As loud as you can hear it well with the gag. And now he plays the purely out game, sometimes slowly, sometimes faster and I notice how my excitement increases more and more and then he helps with the hand rubbing my clit strongly. I feel it now he wants me to explode and shortly before, he takes out the vibrator once again and the hand away from the clitoris. If only I could say something now, I would scream, not stop, go on. I would beg him aloud to continue. But my Joschua understood it without a word and continues. In with the vibrator in my cave and with his hand on my clit and with pressure circling. My body is getting more and more wild and almost rears up, because he stops his hand, only the vibrator is still buzzing with full power and then, after my body has lingered in a tense attitude, he circles with his hand several times fast and firmly over my clit and I scream with happiness so loud that the gag it can only mitigate something ...

"Yeah, I'm coming, yeah, help, I'm exploding, yesss!"

And then it is quiet, I only hear the raging heartbeat and the quick breathing of me. Joschua leaves the vibrator inside, but turns it off. Get up and take a blanket, put her all over me and sit down on the bed with me, put his head on the blanket on my stomach and listen to me as I arrived in seventh heaven and he makes it now quite comfortable. My heartbeat and my breath calms down and I seem to fall asleep really short. He allows this, because it seems a second round to come, I guess so, I do not know, but otherwise he would have already untied me. I should definitely get new power through a short deep sleep. In pictures, I am experiencing once again the climax that has just been lived through, incredibly exciting, sexually scratching the limit. I'll tell him about it after the second game, when he's untied me. This will excite him then as I already know him and he will be glad that this game has arrived so well with me. But now a short rest. It is nice when he lies with his head on me and I still feel that he has just made me so terribly happy. I like that so much, he could do that to me quite often, of course not always the same. He certainly has thousands of variants in mind, but as he says he never had a partner who has been through something like this. That's where I come in time for Joschua. If he knew how I enjoy it. So his mind games have brought the hottest success for both of us. What more could you ask for? I can really relax with him and that's just that special kick. Joschua was right when he told me about it. Now I know it from my own experience. But now, Joschua has come into my life and that is a present, better than six right in the lottery, oh well, you need seven numbers now. Well no matter, the main thing Joschua is here and satisfied with me. How these thoughts sound again, just very satisfied. I feel I should be happy, no better overjoyed, then it's my Joschua too. As he said, he loves to make a woman happy, but many have not understood it or he has not reached it in the heart, he has reached me fully. It just has to fit and it

441

does with Joschua and that at least until Christmas 2100. I have to smile about my thoughts and I sleep with Joschua's head on my stomach.

Oops, did I fall asleep? Wow, the clock shows already 3.40 on Tuesday morning. And I'm still sleeping in this shackled position. The padded restraints are really comfortable. And Joschua seems to be sleeping too, because his head is lying quite calm on my stomach. Oh, now he will wake up too. He noticed my stomach movement. He picks up his head, apparently has slight orientation difficulties. Then he must have slept well and dreamed. Definitely something very great. When you fall asleep with such feelings, you often continue to dream such wonderful things. Oh, Joschua woke up and smiled at me. Oh that's that mischievous broad smile again. Joschua, you will free me now, right? He reads my question out of my eyes and just smiles. Well, he will not want to push my emotional world again. I've never had a husband, just like Joschua did not have a wife, he told me, who made a second climax with him. Now he wants to prove to me that I can also experience a second. I will let myself be surprised. He will definitely shorter but hopefully so intense and then off to bed and next to Joschua happy to fall asleep.

"Good morning my angel, it will now be flown again to the seventh heaven."

I look at him doubtfully and I'm not really there yet when he rolls up my blanket from my feet to my stomach and lets it lie under my breasts. Yes my breasts should not freeze. Are they not really involved in this act? Oh, Mia just wait and stay in your dream world. From there you can also start into the seventh heaven of eroticism. If he gives me correct jump start.

He puts his feet back beside my head. I look at him questioningly and he drops his boxer shorts, again with a point landing on my face. Then he puts himself between my legs, throws the vibrator back on and lets him do his work, until I start to moan again and my body moves, then he pulls it out completely. He kneels down, takes the blanket away and plays with my breasts, which are already awake and stiffly stiff. He takes his boxershort off my face. Then he stands over me, at belly height and strokes a condom, with many nubs, over his already hard cock. I'm watching very closely. He strokes him a bit, then kneels between my legs, touches my pussy with his right hand and notes, wet, a new warm moisture. Slowly, his hands resting next to my upper body and looking at my eyes, he pushes his cock up to my pussy. It already feels warm in my lap and with very slight pressure it disappears into my cave and he keeps pushing until he hits my cave wall. Slowly and gently, he makes the purely out play, as before with the vibrator and I like it. The nubs on the condom exert an additional charm. My breath gets louder and faster and my barely audible moan louder. He woke me up and made me hot. Now I get my second climax and the should be nice, only the second peak says it is usually shorter but more violent. It increases the rhythm and pulls out his tail relatively quickly and then pushes him back to the stop. Fast and faster. I see sweat forming on his forehead and elsewhere and his body starting to get pretty violent. I am already so far and Joschua can see that in my eyes. Attention my short rest before the explosion is coming, fits exactly with his and he pushes twice more and I shout out loud, which of course you can absorb very dampened by the gag and I close my eyes. Joschua takes care of me after our climax together and enjoys with me the peace after our climaxes. Both of us float together on cloud nine. A feeling that you would have to freeze in order to enjoy it. It is so beautiful.

Shortly after, Joschua carefully takes the gag from my mouth and kisses me while he is still lying on top of me. His cock is already retreating slowly and leaves my pussy alone.

"Wow, indescribable. I'm absolutely tired."
"I'll untie you and then we'll just lie next to each other and dream. Just go to the bathroom, I'll be right back."

Here at the guest room is a bath for the guests and he goes only briefly on toilet and washes down very short and down to me. He comes back and goes to my feet and first gets rid of my right leg, only the rope of the ankle bracelet. Then he gently massages my right thigh. He was lying quietly for a long time. He pulls him to the middle. Fold and then do the same with my left leg. Now to the poor.

"If I untie you, do not move, I'll massage you slightly first, because they've been lying quietly for so long."
"Ok."

He frees both hand cuffs from the ropes and massaged briefly my upper arms to then gently guide them with his hands down. Works, not asleep. He rolls me onto the right side of the bed, pulling on the blankets below me. He looks at me and puts a pillow under my head and he turns the top down, so the warm side touches my body and I do not feel cold. Then he puts down a pillow and extinguishes the candles. It is 4.25. Now he lies down in bed next to me and covers me.

"See you tomorrow, Joschua sleep well."
"You too my beloved angel, see you soon."
"You're right, it's almost tomorrow. How long can we sleep?"
"Until we get exhausted people awake. Sleep and dream about something beautiful."
"Yes."

I do not hear any more from him. He is sleeping again and seems to be on cloud nine, because he has a wonderful smile on his cheeks. What an adventure and then my thoughts also go limp and recover in your sleep.

444

Tuesday 10.09.2013

Oops, is that a thought? Yes, then the beautiful dream must be over. Hello dear day, I risk to turn a blind eye and the light that comes through the window, tells me it is cloudy today outside and when I hear it rains too. I do not know how, I just opened my eyes carefully and did not move, but I also hear how my Joschua turned to me and opens his eyes ...

"Hi my love how are you? Did you sleep so well?"
"So many questions at once and in the morning. I'm fine and I slept great. How was that with you?"
"Oh, I slept like a little girl, firm and with dreams."
"And can you remember the dreams?"
"Not directly, but I found it terribly positive that could have gone on for hours."
"And they certainly only took a few seconds."
"I want now ... ."
"So what do you want?"
"I want to cuddle and stay a little bit more."
"Cool idea, I'll do it."

As soon as he said that, my hands are already coming out from under my blanket, lifting his and he can hardly believe it, I push my whole naked body over to him and place myself on his naked body. His blanket covers my back now and I lie directly on top of him. I give him a good morning kiss and then slide my body down on his until my head comes to rest on his chest. I spread my legs and he slides with his in between. His cock is now under my belly button. I really seem to be like a fly-weight for him. He says nothing and has no breathing problems. You can not imagine how nice it is to lie so naked on a beloved man and have as much physical contact as never before. My head is now partially covered with his blanket and my right hand is lying on his left nipple and the fingers perform a tender morning welcome ritual of the longer kind.

445

"You, if you stroke my nipple so tenderly, it not only tingles more violently, but ... ."

"I realize it, your best piece is going to be tough. I'm doing almost nothing."

"It's always the way you do it and then the whole body contact zone comes along and it's huge. I've never been able to feel so much body at one time."

"Yes, you are really cuddly, but you can feel your bones in some places. I guess I have to cook so that something can come out of it."

"You are welcome to cook for me, but if I am to take, then only on the stomach. Is inheritance from my father. And I always keep my weight at ninety kilograms."

"Oh, it's nice to lie on you, even if you poke me slowly in the stomach."

"I'm not fucking."

"Well, then you push down there with your pointy thing."

"Lace thing is good, hahaha. It's your fault, you've laid yourself down on him, which is very nice."

"If it's so hard, you should really love it."

"Oh, a morning quiz, then my cock and your pussy will rub hard."

"Yes and I will take care of it!"

"And how?"

And I push myself up with my arms and get on my knees and my pussy presses on his stomach. I already feel my warm, erotic humidity. Oh, what a hot woman I am. I slide so kneeling down and his eyes can not let go of my breasts. What does he think about my breasts now, if he fixes her so, he has to think about it. Of course, what does the woman have for fixed breasts and exactly in the middle she wears her nipples and nipples, which now already firmly stand out. Now he picks up his hands and touches them tenderly. It's always exciting for me, too, when he touches her and pushes and pulls. I like that soooo. But he has already noticed, when he does that, I always start moaning. I can not help it that excites me so. He just touches correctly. But at that moment, I notice how my pussy has reached his tail tip.

"Wow, not bad if my pussy feels it."
"You can say that and those views."
"Can you see me again on my breasts?"
"Yes, and how!"
"Your eyes are fixed on them."
"They are simply a total artwork."
"Artwork is good, they are one hundred percent nature."
"You can see that too, but they are so tight, that's crazy and so symmetrical."
"Nice that you like it, but I also like your cock, especially where I feel it now on my pussy."
"Man, you circle your pelvis so hard, do you want me to come soon?"
"I'm so hot already. I want to feel it inside of me now."
"Please do it if you want to make it explode."
"Thanks, but would I have done without your permission and do you feel like he's just now sliding in?"
"Yes, and how. It's so humid, warm and incredibly punchy on all sides."
"Watch out, now it's really exciting."
"How is that?"
"Well, I just have to lean backwards and that changes the angle of my pussy to him."
"Ohhh, man, that goes off."
"And now some rhythm, back and forth."
"Ohhh, I'm being completely seduced."
"Yes, you can see that, I'll do what I want with you now."

And I rest my hands on his knees and gas my pelvis vigorously. I've only seen it in movies so far. So, as a woman, I can finally specify the rhythm and he has to put up with it. Well, I pay attention to both of us that it's fun, but well it's the time for him, if he wants to totally let himself fall and enjoy. In this position, I have the pants on, um, well, now I have them too, but I determine and I think that's great. Last night he did everything and I enjoyed it. In addition, I myself have great fun sliding back and forth. So poor Joschua, now he can no longer reach my breasts, because I bend my upper body backwards, with my arms on his knees and move only my pelvis on him. Always only so far in one direction that his horny cock stays in me. But Joschua can not stop thinking and his right hand starts to enjoy my clit. I allowed you that.

"Stay flat, that's an order."

I took full command. I think that's really great, nobody has ever let me do that either. Anyway, no one so far. Oh my Joschua is something very special. I move so fast and our eyes are now on each other. I notice how slowly I get out of breath and at the same time begin to groan violently. He closes his eyes. Then he will now let himself fall and fully enjoy. Hurray I can increase the rhythm even further. The madness. His cock slides up and down in me and hits again and again inside. He feels brutally stiff to me and I feel like I'm going to explode to the limit. But I do not get any further thoughts, because Joschua starts to moan powerfully and loudly. Right loud. He reacts so violently to the movement of my pelvis. And I feel like his cock is in me just before the semen delivery. Then, I also had my eyes closed and heard inside me, I open my eyes almost frightened ...

"I explode and yes, yes, yes!!! Ohh, man, ohhh, man!!!"
"Olala, you can groan too loud, that's the madness of a man who is loud in sex, really loud. Louder than usual. Why?"
"You can ask questions, you did not push me into the seventh heaven, but shot you up. The absolute madness. I felt my seeds on the way to you like never."
"And believe me, I felt them when they invaded me and crashed into my pussy wall. Like little cannonballs and each one has a feeling. I've never felt that way, like shotguns. But you have a shooting speed."
"Well, you just cocked him so hard."

And I smile at him and let me sink down on him carefully. Oh that's a wet matter again our bodies are gliding right on each other. An indescribable feeling.

"Let's stay that way, please."
"Oh yeah, it feels kinda mean to walk around so wet."
"Common?"
"Or rather indecent, I think somehow."
"Yes, another feeling, happy and humid and yes, you are right, somehow indecent."
"Yes, it's not great that we are allowed to experience such feelings."
"Yes, without you, that would not have been possible. Thank you!"

And we'll stay like this for a while, I've got my head on his chest again and now and then he moves his whole body under mine and it feels slippery, somehow indecent. A little eternity continues ....

"You want to take a warm shower together and then have breakfast?"
"Yes, where do you want to take a shower?"
"Well, you can choose that. Three bathrooms are available."
"You decide, I have just decided the morning erotic."
"Yes, the best decision of the day."
"Hahaha the day has just begun. It's your turn."
"Okay, then we'll take the guest bath and then I'll dry you and you'll go up the stairs in front of me and then down the stairs again."
"Would you go down the stairs again?"
"Not the same, the stairs to the pool. There we dab something and then there is breakfast completely."
"What is complete breakfast?"
"With everything your heart wants."
"In itself I have only one wish."
"Which?"
"That you sit opposite me at breakfast."
"That's a very nice wish I like you to fulfill, because he pleases me at least as much as you."

"Then we decide then, but first until then."
"Well, you want to go to the bathroom first, and then I'll come to it. Ok?"
"Do not you have to tease?"
"But later, hold something else."
"OK. But I have an idea, which I always wanted to do."
"What?"
"I go to the bathroom first and call you if you can come, then there will be a shower."
"I'm waiting and if I do not come, if you call, then I fell asleep again."
"Well I'll just call louder then."
"Is good."

And I get up.

"It's cold. But you had a warmth, that was just cuddly."
"But you also. See you soon."
"I'm looking forward to seeing the warm water running down your beautiful body and flowing over your breasts. That will be a pleasure again."
"And I can see the water flowing over your cock and your eggs, I'm looking forward to it."
"So I'm waiting, go ahead."

I get up and go to the bathroom. Did my suggestion trigger a fantasy with him? I just go fast on tweezers and the sink, ready ...

"Joschua, can come, I'm waiting for you."
"I'm coming, I'm almost there."

When he comes to the bathroom, I'm already in front of the shower and let the water warm.

"Oh that's a nice sight you're so naked. You have a perfect body and your smile on the face is fantastic."
"Let's see if you'll say that when you're done with the showers."
"What do you mean by that?"

"Now come and stand in the shower cubicle in the middle, facing the wall. You just do what I tell you, understand?"
"Yes, I obey."

He stands in the middle of the shower cubicle facing the wall. I stand behind him, he feels that exactly and I close the cabin door. I hold the shower head over his head and the warm water flows down his body.

"Ohhh, what are you doing?"
"Quiet, I choose. Close your eyes and let them close until I say you can open them again."
"Roger that!"

I have stood next to him. With my left hand I hold the shower head over his head and with his right hand I have grabbed his cock and pull at him.

"Hey, what are you doing?"
"Shut up and I want to see you pee now, go piss."
"What, what should I do?"
"I want you pee now!"
"While you hold my cock?"
"Yes, go now, you have to be very urgent and the running water will help you."
"I can, but I have never done that before."
"There is always a first time for it. Go on, piss."

He has promised to obey me and now he has to let himself fall in the thought. I feel his cock in my hand and he actually does that. He starts to pee. I think I'm going completely red, because it's warm in me, very warm. We do something totally indecent and I move his cock from right to left again and again. That's something I never thought, I feel like it's flowing through his cock and he gets warmer there, too. Then it occurs at the front of his glans with a strong beam of the yes I can steer. And then I discover something else. I have his cock completely in my hand and when I try my hand force-

451

fully to close, then the beam is thinner. I let go then he gets fatter again. And even Joschua responds with a soft moan. But no pleasurable moan more an unpleasant groan. So I immediately put this pressure test back on. What I discover again with a man. Never would I have ever thought in my life a man while peeing the tail to keep. I'm blushing red in the face.

"Go on, more, do not stop!"
"Madness, you ...!"
"Rest, keep injecting, go!"

And I move his cock also up and down, right and left and the water flows from above over everything and in me it cooks, what am I doing there. No matter how dirty my wishes are I see Joschua fills me with anyone who is only possible. He would never have thought he would do that for and with a woman, but it's kind of special. Yes the very first time in my life that I have had such a thing done. I have to smile a lot at this crooked thought. Good that I'm standing next to Joschua and he can not see me. Unfortunately I do not like him either. It feels crazy, but not wrong. You can do anything when both enjoy it and I think Joschua is really enjoying getting over it at the moment. I play with his cock and start rubbing him after the last drops have spurted out of him. I rub more and stronger and press harder. I rub so hard that with each back rub against his eggs and the tail approach firmly. That makes him crazy and he'll be pretty tough in no time. A direct climax after peeing is crazy. If I had never thought of it myself in life, it just turned out that way. But the tension gets bigger and bigger and he has to somehow relax his muscles to keep up. He leans his hands against the wall in front of him and goes on tiptoe. And after a very short break the tension increases again. I feel her so clearly rising in him ...

"Oh man Mia, I'll be right there. Madness, what are you doing with me. Attention, I'm coming!"
"Come on, let's go, I want to see it, go now!"

"Yes, yes, yes ... I'm coming, I'm coming, ohhh!"
"This is a real happiness to watch you and I was allowed to do it today with both actions. Really cool. And now I wash you as a reward."

And I reach for the liquid soap and soap it completely. Everywhere, yes, there again. Then I also soap myself and we take a shower together. Then we leave together again the shower cubicle.

"Come on, we're running to the pool!"

And he takes me by the hand and pulls me still slightly dripping behind him, through the party room, up the stairs and down the pool stairs again.

"It's cold, wait."
"No matter you have to go through it now."

And he pulls me into the water.

"Go up and down now!"

And we both jump up in the water several times, what a sight, because our eyes rest on the partner and what we always get to see when jumping, erosely erotic, our bodies.

"Jump up, I want you to bring your manhood over the waterline, I want to see her wobble!"

And we both laugh heartily and have fun in the pool, swimming, laughing, touching each other. It's like being a kid, totally without any compulsion. I just do what I want and that's what Joschua apparently does too. We have a great time, just like children who play carefree. Then we leave the pool together, dry off. Everyone by themselves, but we both look at it, go into the bedroom and get dressed. But always keep an eye on the others. It's a crazy feeling to watch the other partner in everything.

"You, what I have experienced in the short time with you everything is just fantastic. And above all, what I experienced, what I had never experienced before, and now with you for the first time."

"And I first, I have not even thought of such things until I visited you here, then it went in my head and I had requests, what I would like to do with you, I did not know. Thank you for participating and I think it's so exciting. Many new experiences. Please give me a kiss and push me once."

"Clear. You know, you radiate such calm and happiness, I just want to look at you. It totally turns me on."

"Can you see that I am the happiest woman in the world?"

"Yes, your eyes sparkle like stars, with such a depth and then your cheeks, they are somehow reddish in colour, as if you were fresh from the cold and then your mouth. The corners of your mouth are raised and make your lips a radiant smile. You just shine out of yourself. I have not seen it that way either. You have created an aura around you that shines for me in all colours and brings joy to my heart. Mia, I love you!"

"Wow!"

"I think there comes a little tear from your beaming eye?"

"Tear of joy! Only tears of joy! Because I found you!"

He comes over to me on the other side of the bed, takes me without a word in his arms and presses me to his heart and whispers in my ear ...

"Mia, I love you! I love you so much, more than I have ever felt in a woman!"

And he puts his head on my shoulder and just enjoys this overwhelming situation. There is something very special in the air. Joschua puts his arms around my waist and stops very quietly. It has become so calm at the moment that we hear our hearts beat. Such an incredibly positive silence and tranquility, just the special thing I always sought and never found. I will not leave him from my side, not from my life and never from my heart. He now has it!

We stand like that for a while and it seems like a break that's too short. But that's the break in which you can recharge your life batteries. They were almost exhausted with me and the hope of new cargo, as good as extinguished and now that. I want to be one hundred years old on Joschua's side and only there. What he thinks right now, because he is also in a quiet there. Thoughts must go through his mind, I feel it, but which one?

"You Mia, I interrupt this silence. What kind of thoughts did you have?"
"Your thoughts first, please."
"I thought that before you came into my life, I almost had my life batteries down to zero and saw no hope to recharge them. And now the batteries are fully charged by you so I want to be one hundred years old, but only with you by my side or me by your side, as you want to see it."
"Only a hundred, then we can not do Christmas 2100 anymore."
"Well, I also like to live next to you until Christmas 2100, but Christmas has to go until the morning of the Twenty-eighth Twelfth."
"Oh, you want to fully enjoy Christmas 2100?"
"Of course, if we have not starved before, it's already 16.00 clock."
"Yes, I completely forget the time with you. I just enjoy our togetherness. I've never experienced anything so beautiful and crazy."
"Believe me, me neither!"
"Good, then I allow you to have breakfast with me now."
"Thanks, are you coming?"
"May I have a quick bath?"

455

"Do you want to make yourself more beautiful?"
"Only the hair blow dry otherwise they will be so curly."
"I would just have to go to the office and since yester-
day I was not on the PC just to see if something
important has come in."
"Great, then I go to the kitchen and make breakfast.
Finally, let me do it. May I?"
"I'm glad to accept your offer. When I'm done, when
you're done, call me."
"Cool that I may make breakfast, then I feel a bit more at
home again."
"Oh home, that's really great as you say. See you soon."

And Joschua is just going to the office and I, as I'm getting ready in the kitchen and start the automatic breakfast preparation at top speed. Coffee, rolls, croissants,
eggs, dishes, orange juice, fruit, sausage and cheese,
jams, peanut cream and Nutella. Outside is such a rainy
day, I make candles and very important music. He has a
radio in the kitchen and I turned that on. Just listen to a
good music station. You can also turn on the lights in
the weather. He has two five-branched silver candlesticks, one I place on the dining table, the second on a
small table in the corner and I have all set fire. This is
how it looks more comfortable. Although it is only
September, today it feels like it's an autumn day. But he
has given the perfect atmosphere for the event so far.
No sun outside, but all the more in here in our hearts.
Almost everything ready and I hear the office door.
Joschua comes and I stand in the kitchen door, there he
comes over on the way to the dining room. I can already
see it from a distance, he is holding something in his
hand again, a small praline greeting in the shape of a
heart. He comes closer and when he is with me he says
immediately before I can say something ...

"A heart from my heart for your heart!"
"Oh you are sweet. You spoil me totally. Thank you. For
that you get a hearty kiss."

We take a seat at the breakfast table and the coffee smells and the hot rolls and croissants spread an even more starving fragrance.

"I am really amazed at the speed with which you have conjured up everything so perfectly here. You really know your way around."
"I've always watched you closely and noticed that the rest I just looked in the closets with us."

And we have to look at each other and laugh, then we embrace each other and push and lovingly.

"Nice that you took candles. The silver candlesticks also give the right mood light."
"Yes, it's so nice to you! I thought they fit the mood of today and it's romantic, breakfast by candlelight."
"For what mood?"
"Well first time for the feeding ceremony and then they will certainly trigger romantic connection feelings."
"But that sounds attractive again."
"Yes, that's the weather for indoor romance."
"We can also stand outside in the rain and ... ."
"No, it's too cold for me, then we would catch a cold and we would not be fit for ... ."
"Fit for what?"
"Fit for, oh your phone rings."
"Let it ring, who wants what can later call again or talk to the answering machine. I'm not leaving now, it's just nice to have breakfast sitting opposite you."
"Yes, I can only confirm that."
"So, fit for what?"
"Well, you're too curious again."
"You, that's not intentional, I'm so curious by nature. Always been. Curiosity also makes you smart and keeps on training. If I had not been curious what happened to my ad, then I would not have put her at all. And then?"
"That would have been terrible, then we would not have met and loved each other."
"You see, my curiosity brought us together."

"Well, if you rewrite that, you may of course be curious."

"Well, the curious wants to know what we should be fit for."

"Well, for what will happen to you at our next erotic session."

"Happen to me? Must I be scared?"

"Well, who knows, if I have the upper hand."

"Oh, if that's you, then I do not need to be scared. You will never hurt me."

"Do you think?"

"Yes, one hundred percent!"

"Why do you believe that?"

"Because two who really love each other would never hurt."

"But you have formulated that great again."

"I bother. But do you know what you should do?"

"No?"

"You should give your parents a sign of life from you. They're probably worried about whether you're still alive."

"Thanks, good idea, since I've been with you, I have not thought of anything else. Only to us, what we do, how beautiful it is, how great we have found each other and how brave I was to visit you. And it was really worth it. I am happier than ever in life and I owe that to you."

"Oh, I believe you, but thanks for so much praise, I'll blush again."

"As red as in the shower?"

"Well, that was probably the absolute hardship of which I would not even have dared to dream. I had dreamed of it before, but I would never have dared to talk to a woman, let alone suggest it to her."

"Yes, I just had the urge to try it at very short notice. I do not know how I got that. "

"Yes, and then the orgasm afterwards. Madness, I was like in a different world."

"That you liked it too, is not it great? We have the same ideas and wishes. The fact that I should experience a partner who does something with this was simply unimaginable for me."

"I have often had stupid erotic fantasies, but could never realize them and alone it does not work. But I'll talk about it with a female, we did not talk about it before, you just did it and I enjoyed it so much. Only afterwards did I really realize what happened to me."

"You could have finished with - red - anytime anything."

"Hahaha you were really careful what I told you about bondage and stuff."

"You also explained it to me well, and I have to say that when you first explained it, I did not perceive the meaning that way. That she can be so important and extensive. I think you should always have a codeword in a partnership, even in everyday life, then you can really tell your partner, if something goes wrong, without screaming or beating for example."

"Anyone who beats is not worth a partner anyway. Beating is the stupidest thing you can do."

"Yes, you're right, but you always do not know that before you enter into a relationship. In the beginning everything is often rosy and then it changes after years."

"To whom do you say that, I have also had more than enough bad experiences. But I'll promise you that, whatever you do, I'll never raise a hand against you. No way!"

"I know that, but do not ask where from, I have it in the feeling, my heart says he will never do it, he loves you!"

"Yes, your heart has a great attitude, I like it. If you did not have it so deep inside of you, then I would be very hard pressed."

"Can you press me on behalf of my heart?"

"Good idea, come here to the big press."

And after we pressed and talked with our lips together, well kissed my, he looks at me again and says ...

"That's a good idea, from now on we have a codeword for everything we do not want and the other one knows immediately, stop."

"Great, agree!"
"So now go to the office and make your life sign call, I'll cover it off."
"I want to help you first."
"No, thank you, I can just do it and when you're done, I'll suggest what we do."
"Can not you already tell him?"
"No surprise, see you soon."
"I hurry, you know I'm curious."
"Take your time, I will not forget the suggestion."

And he watches me go to the office and disappear into the office door. Of course, I do not do that without turning around for a second and throwing him a hand kiss. I think he thought that I also have eyes in the back, because he has returned a little surprised the hand kiss. It's really cool that I can still do it, that looks me a man behind. Should I wiggle more with the buttocks next time, maybe he will make a sound and betrays himself thus. Am I not awesome? And I have already chosen. You will be home at six o'clock. Then the listener is picked up at the other end. I first tell my dad how well I am and then mom comes to the phone and also there I seem to sound as if the pure happiness bubbles out of my heart. She immediately notices and I tell her how Joschua received and received me. Clearly no sexual details, that would be impossible for my parents, but the overall work of art I present Joschua so. I can literally hear how mom at the other end of the line, a stone from the heart, everything went well. If I think about it, then it was really a risk to drive a stranger home, that's what they told me once again. And then they were both happy for me. I have such lovely parents, they have to live a very long time. I also promised them that I would visit them soon with Joschua and then show him off. Performing sounds good on a leash. This is my Joschua. Oh Mia now come to me while telephoning such crazy pictures in the head. No, it is clear, not to show off the dog leash but as a man. What is Joschua my partner or my friend or my husband. Anyway, I'll talk to him even more if we go to them. Oh you even mom noticed that I'm really excited on the phone where I talked about him. Sure, then my heart beats faster and faster when I think of Joschua or talk about him. And my mom is also happy when I say Joschua has said that I can call and thought of you what you think if I do not sign up. His parents are both dead long ago and he is very sad about that when he talks about his mom. But we both do not talk about the past. We both set a time for ourselves with the first mail, what was before is everyone's own past and you talk about it but it does not affect our current relationship and maybe our future. When mom hears the future, the question immediately comes, of course, you want to marry and I explain to her that it is probably too early for that and that you probably do not always have to marry immediately. My parents are still a bit old fashioned in this regard, but only a little bit. Oh, it's nice to talk to them on the phone, childhood memories always come back to me, they have a nice youth and they have always been there for me and will be there as long as they live. They always say that to me and that gives me a certain security in my life. I think you will like him too, he is a very different man than my ex. In a word, he is just a big heart with some flesh around it. Oh and a lot of spirit. I think I could feed my parents for hours from Joschua, but then Joschua would surely fall asleep somewhere in a corner of boredom. I hear my parents, mom put on loudspeakers and dad sure has his ear on it, we have just had breakfast and his comment was yes the youth. If that happened to you before. Well my daily routine is, no with us there is no daily routine at the moment. With us only the wild sex and new experiences reign, just everything that makes you happy. Oh these days have been the most beautiful in my life so far and my parents are very happy with it. Then I say goodbye to my parents. As soon as I hang up the phone, I notice how it pulls me to my Joschua quickly again. It can not be, you can be so crazy about a man. Yes Mia you can and I have the handle of the office door back in my hand and open it. Out into the hall and where could my

Joschua be right now? Oh, it's so beautiful, it's raining and you can hear raindrops on the glass roof. Oh that's so cuddly romantic and Joschua has the palm and the underwater lights on. That's just not to describe, it's just like a fairy tale, just wonderful. Oh, I see light in the kitchen, then Joschua has to be there. Oh my poor, I just left him alone with everything. When I think this way I have to dig deep, that a man in my life has spoiled me so much and I can not find anything in depth. Well I will spoil him, not only with my sex but also in everyday life. Yes, as Joschua always says, as it always sounds, how can I always say after a few days? Yes, it seems to me as if I knew him for ages and my love for him would become more by the day. With these thoughts, I'm already almost past the pool, because I already hear his male voice taunt me ...

"I am in the kitchen."
"I come to you, do not run away."
"Well, your parents were happy that you still exist?"
"Yeah, nice that I called. They have really thought, if something happened and now they are calm again."
"I know how parents are happy to hear from their children."
"Now tell me, what do you want to do with me now?"
"No, not something like that."
"Like that?"
"Well, what you just thought."
"I did not think anything."
"Well, if you say that. Ok. I would like to admire many lights with you."
"Lights?"
"Yes, many colourful lights."
"Oh, do not make it so exciting, I'm still bursting here."
"You must not burst, think of Christmas 2100."
"Hahaha, tell me where are we going?"
"Well, I thought the rain stopped and it's sixteen degrees warm. We go to the Hamburg Cathedral."
"Oh, you mean the fair?"
"Yes, his name is Dom. Then we can see a lot of colour-

ful lights and absorb the scent of many goodies."
"Do you want to go with the carousels?"
"If I'm honest, not so much. My stomach is not always there."
"That's good, because I do not like driving fast attractions."
"Well then we look at everything and feed ourselves."
"How to feed?"
"Well, maybe a pizza, then pancakes and bratwurst, champions and then for dessert something sweet, crêpes or waffles. And we can share everything, otherwise it's too much."
"Sounds good, but do you want to roll me home afterwards?"
"No, if we share it, it's not too much. Besides, we do not need to buy everything."
"Fine, but definitely colourful candyfloss."
"Oh yes, it sticks so well."
"And it tastes so delicious."
"Do you have a thin jacket to wear?"
"Yes, I'll be right back."

I still have to get my jacket out of my suitcase and put on my shoes, then into the garage. Joschua is waiting for me in front of the garage door and I am already rushed there. A smile from him welcomes me.

"I'm looking forward, may I take you while strolling in the arm or holding by the hand."
"I ask for it! And you can kiss me anytime. "
"That sounds good, I'll definitely use that."

And we sit in the car and drive to the cathedral. Once there we park and before he can get out, I lean back over to him and I give Joschua his first cathedralkiss.

"Mmm the kiss tastes like more!"
"Later my darling, later."
"But not too late, hopefully."
"Wait. Yes, you are right, many, many colorful lights and

463

this scent of ... ."
"After roasted almonds."
"Oh, let's get some."
"Clear."

And we steer directly from the parking lot, hand in hand to the stand with the freshly roasted almonds. I was no longer on a fair and now on the famous Hamburg Cathedral. With Joschua I always experience new things. Well, if we are together in one year and then go back to the cathedral, then I can say, do you still remember our first time. Mia now stops all thoughts and starts to enjoy. You can think later, besides, you're just thinking nonsense right now. Just be happy.

"A bag of almonds."
"May I already suck one as a starter?"
"Of course, wait, I'll put it in your mouth."

And while he frees the almond from the bag, I stand with his mouth slightly open in front of him and waiting for the almond. But before it reaches my mouth, his lips meet there ... and then the almond penetrates through my still open feed hatch. I smile with relish and chewing on her while he also throws in an almond, then takes my hand and we continue to stroll over the cathedral.

"Look at the merry go round, if I went in there, believe me, then you'd have to doctor me."
"Nice thought, but I'd rather play a different kind of doctor with you."
"Oh, that reminds me, I have a practice appointment for a gynecological examination."
"Great, you want to drive me crazy again?"
"No, I do not, just fuel something."
"When do we have the appointment?"
"When do you want him?"
"As fast as possible, I have such a strange pull down there."
"Okay, then we'll see if the doctor has time to complete

a complete examination today."
"Sounds very good, then I'll be well down there after the visit."
"Mmm, hungry or hungry again?"
"Do I have to bunk calories for the night?"
"No, I can fill it up at home, if you need it."
"Oh, a shooting gallery."
"Do you want to shoot?"
"No I can not."
"Oh, then you want me to shoot you something?"
"Can you do that?"
"Let's see what should it be? Oh the big teddy bear."
"How did you get it?"
"Because you looked like that."
"Just look, you can not shoot it."
"But I'll ask. Hello, how can you shoot the teddy?"

And the shooting gallery owner tells him that he has to hit the red three times on each of the three targets and then he takes a rifle, the shopkeeper loads the Diabolo ball and he launches. Peng, retension, peng, retension, peng ... and after several shots he scored the first two times three hits. Peng, retighten peng, retighten and ...

"Yeah, all you have to do is hit again and then you'll get the big, brown teddy."
"Yes, let's try."

The shooting gallery owner looks a bit desperate. Yes, then he has bad luck, because peng and hit, then he has to part with his teddy. And he does it. He hands the teddy directly to me and not to Joschua. Well, because I'm right next to him and we talked. Wow a giant teddy, bigger than a baby. For that I have to press Joschua immediately, no, I give him a kiss and he shines on his whole face.

"I've always wanted to be a teddy but never had a guy by my side who could shoot like that."

465

"Oh, pure coincidence."
"Well, do not understate, you fired very quickly and safely one after the other."
"Well, I just doped myself."
"Yourself doped?"
"Yeah, I thought if I could meet and give the teddy to you, then you give me a kiss and smile at me."
"Yes, it worked just fine."
"Yes, the teddy is almost as tall as you, can not I get another kiss for it?"
"Yes, very much."

And I put my free hand around his neck and give him a very tender kiss, although my tongue has also spoken a word.

"Ahhh, that was nice."
"Now I'm hungry for a gyros bun."
"look, there are some over there. They smell good too. Come let us eat Gyros."
"Do we share a Gyros?"
"Well, we bite alternately."

At a bar table, we then bite alternately into the gyros roll while the teddy lies over the table next to us.

"You - mom - that would be it, but if you were like the teddy now here on the table would be and your hot buttocks backwards, then I could ... ."
"Yes, I can almost feel it pushing in, very slowly and over and over again, ohhh, until ... ."
"Stop, we're in the fairground and the people are."
"Hahaha, but I'm horny for you again."
"I'll tell the doctor afterwards, Diagnosis Horniness."
"And what will the doctor do about it?"
"He'll just denigrate."
"Sounds good, how does he do that?"
"Curious? You have to wait until after."
"Come on let us go."
"I'll make a suggestion for you, there's a ticket over

466

there and we're going to buy ten lots for each one of us and whoever has the most winnings who will do what we do right now."
"Well, what do you want when you win?"
"Mmm then we'll go fifty-seven minutes over the hype and if you win we'll go play Uncle Doctor right now."
"Agreed."
"Twice ten lots, please."

Everyone pulls ten pieces out of the bucket. Joschua and I pull out ten tickets each, and then we face the ticket booth, where it's a bit quieter and take turns lot by lot.

"I want to win!"
"Ok."
"Hey, I want to win, not win."
"Ok."
"Youuu!"
"Yes, my angel, what is there?"
"You make me even hotter, careful, otherwise I'll nip you here behind the trailer."
"Madness, I've always wanted that."
"Now you also take me in my arms."
"Oh."
"Let's open the lots."
"Ok."

And we open one lot after another. No one shows the other if he has a profit or not. Only when we have opened all the lots, we will show them.

"Hahaha. Did you open them all?"
"Hey, why are you laughing?"
"I'll show you right away."
"Ok, I opened all the lots, how many winnings do you have?"
"You've certainly won. You know, I've never won anything in my life."
"That's not true!"
"How so?"

467

"You have won my heart and my love."
"Oh and I thought I had conquered you and your love."
"Well, you can see it that way. And how many profits do you have?"
"Only two pieces, but you'll be astonished and how many do you have?"
"I have six proud pieces! And so I won and we're going to play Uncle Doctor right now."
"Good, but first we get the profits."
"Yeah, good idea, do not want to leave her here."
"Are you getting the profits. Here you have a lot from me."
"I thought you had two profits?"
"More on that later."
"I do not understand that now, but I'll pick up the seven."

And I go to the ticket booth and give my profits. My and of course from Joschua too. The employee accepts the lots and calculates the sum together and shows me from which profits I may choose. I want to look at Joschua, but Joschua is already next to me. Did not notice, was really so absorbed in what I may choose with Joschua right now.

"Take what you want."
"It's going to be difficult. Mmm the tricycle?"
"Do you have any cousins or cousins?"
"Yes, he is three years old."
"Then take that, I think well, then you have a present."
"Well, I take the tricycle. Thank you. Now let's go to the doctor."
"Wait a minute, I have to pick up my present for you. Please this lot number."

And the shop clerk sees the lot, goes to the bell and growls loudly. I look a bit puzzled and Joschua looks at me smiling.

"I'll take that big tan up there."

And the salesman climbs on the steps and reaches for a huge teddy and gives it to Joschua, then he turns around to me.

"See, I have the brother of your shooting teddy. He is just as tall. Now you have a teddy family."

And we look at each other and both have to laugh heartily.

"Man, that's insane. I had never gotten anything at the carnival, I can hardly go with you, then I have a huge teddy family and a tricycle. This is another experience that I will never forget. But I still had more tickets and that's why I'm allowed to decide now."
"Yes you can, but first I have to go next door to the shack."
"What's that nice thing about it?"
"I would like to have the heart up there."

And he pays and the seller gives him a gingerbread heart with the inscription - I love you.

"I just want to tell you something."

And he holds out my heart with the inscription - I love you - and I beam it. He hangs it around my neck and I'm still shining. I feel like I'm struggling for words. I am so, I do not know exactly, but everything this man does for me and what he thinks. Yes, I miss the words. I'm still beaming at him. And he strokes my right cheek with my right cheek and shines back. I am unspeakably happy.

"Thanks, that's just missing the words. It does not matter what we have done so far has always become a highlight in my life. Thank you for everything."
"It's great to see how happy you are, that's really fun for me. Are we going to the car slowly?"
"Yes."
"I take a teddy under my left arm and the tricycle in my

469

left hand, you take the teddy under your right arm."
"Great, do not crush it. Otherwise you'll hurt him."
"Oh, we can then heal again from the uncle doctor."
"Good as well."
"But do not bother me to hurt him. Now we have to keep over there."
"We wanted to go to the car."
"I mean the place up front, that's on our way to the car."
"Ok. Oh, you mean the place where the colourful cotton candy is!"
"Exactly the place. As you have guessed again."
"Oh, you also think of everything, very dear of you, I'm looking forward to it."

Now he also buys me a pink cotton candy and gives it to me in my left hand.

"How am I supposed to touch you now?"
"Not anymore, you have to go alone now, completely independently, on your own responsibility. You can do it. I'm going close to you."
"Promised?"
"Promised."

And we go to the car. I still plucking at my cotton candy. How do I look? I already have everything stuck around my mouth, because I do not have the right hand to always push it into my mouth. You could say I have a sweet mouth now. If someone sees me who thinks, the old one has a bird. But I feel in my heart just as if I was a little kid who goes crazy with his parents and is amazed everywhere. In the vicinity of Joschua or better by his side I'm really back to teenagers. In any case, I feel that way and Joschua obviously has his full fun with it. Yes we are a crazy couple, but so terribly happy. I did not know that you can be so happy.

"You put our Teddy family on the back seats and the tricycle in the trunk."

Said, done and he opens the door for me and then it happens, before I can get in the car, I come very close to him and he presses me a violently moved kiss on the mouth. Our tongues make the mutual sugar test and when we want to separate our lips, there is a rude retreat, because the cotton candy sticks us almost tight. But we pull it together with our combined efforts and our lips shoot back into our faces after the breakup. We look at each other and both have to laugh out loud. It's a batty Joschua, just nonsense in his head, but that makes him so sympathetic and adorable. We get in and he starts the car.

"And is it still far to the doctor's room?"
"Nope, only about twenty minutes. Do you really want to go there now?"
"Yes, in any case. I'm really excited."
"You remember what you promised me?"
"What do you mean, that I'm always nice to you?"
"No, I'm really happy about that, but it was not. Forget it, that's the way it always is."
"Say what you mean."
"Well, you promised me that you would try the same with me. I also wanted to try, if I can experience such feelings as you, for example, in our guest bedfetter adventure. But … ."
"Oh, do not be angry. We have so much time for each other and that's what I wanted to save for later."
"Yeah, that's the excuse I thought you would use."
"Oh Joschua, do not be sad, I'll do it to you so often that you always go out of my way, because you think, oye, now I have to serve again."
"Hahaha, you can not do that. I have a lot of catching up to do for decades and then you leave on Sunday. Or I'll tie you on Sunday night, then you'll have to stick to something else."
"You would like that."
"If you knew what I would like, then … ."
"Tell me, what would you like to have?"
"No, I can not just say that in between while driving?"

"Why not?"
"Because it's the most important wish I've got in my life right now."
"Oh please, please tell me."
"Oh, you're not a bit stubborn."
"Oh, I ask you dearly, tell me!"
"Oh, maybe tomorrow."
"Ah, by then I have died of curiosity,"
"Really, that's not possible, I still need you!"
"For what?"
"Well, to tell you my greatest wish."
"Well then tell me, otherwise I'll hold my breath until you tell him."
"No, not."
"Attention at three I hold my breath. One, two, three and ... ."
"Please, little angel, breathe again, I'll tell him too."
"Say him, say him!"

He drives on the right side of the shoulder, good that he is expelled as a parking area and free, stops, turns off the engine, turns to me and sees me with his blue eyes in my wonderful brown eyes and ...

"I tell you now what my heart wants to tell you."
"Only your heart or your mind too?"
"Of course both!"
"Then I listen."
"Well, it's 10.30pm Tuesday and I can not stop thinking if you leave on Sunday night. I think then as a man I will be more than sad and compete with the Elbe."
"I do not just believe you."
"And I wanted to ask you something, which occurred to me quite spontaneously. Do you think you could possibly imagine living longer with me?"
"Mmm what do you mean by longer? Another week's holiday more?"
"No, not vacation. You, I thought our hearts are so well together, they speak the same language and it would be almost inhumane if they were torn apart."

472

"Yes, but what do you mean really?"

"Well, you're so awfully smart, can not you think that?"

"What?"

"Oh, you know, I'm so shy."

"What did you need the wrong word now?"

"Why wrong word?"

"Instead of shy, totally determined and purposeful. You and shy, that I do not laugh as I have experienced you, you are confident up to the hair tips."

"I?"

"Yes you, but as I do not know you now."

"Oh, do you want to meet me more?"

"Yeah, I would not be averse to that."

"Cool, then it would be good to get used to each other even more, if you would spend much, much more time together."

"Yes, and how? Do you have any idea?"

"Yes."

"Well, do not let every word get out of your nose."

"Well, I'm scared."

"Fear of what?"

"Afraid that you will say no."

"Try it once."

"It's harder than when I'm going to uncle doctor with you to make you happy there."

"Do not bother, I'm not biting."

"Is good. Youuu, me, that means my heart and also my mind have become so terribly accustomed to you in the very short time that we have spent together until now, that they will not be able to survive without you. I know you think I'm crazy and please, please do not be angry if you do not feel that way, but I want you to stay with me forever. Love on the first mail and then the phone calls and you came was great. But the time we've spent to-gether has topped everything in my life. Please, please stay with me. I love you from the heart."

"No man has ever said that to me. I'm speechless."

And without saying anything, but that's not quite true, because I've turned bright red and a tear trickles down my cheek, followed by more wet drops and my face starts to radiate. These are really happy tears and I put my arms around his neck. Then I pull myself up and I come very close to him, but stop. He looks at me expectantly with gleaming eyes. This look makes it possible for my whole body to feel a warmth and begin to tingle. I just have to shake a little and he laughs, because he seems to be just like me at this moment, a moment I can not describe, you have to experience it.

"What's that?"
"You sent me a load of emotions with your gaze and tears, and they triggered a total tingling sensation in my body."

I smile and come even closer to his face that our lips must simply unite and also the tongues come back to their full commitment. It's feelings when our tongue tips touch so tenderly, I've never had that with any other man. You have to imagine that, you used to test the voltage of nine volt battery blocks, with the tongue, and when they were full, there was always a small punch in the tip of the tongue. This also happens with Joschua's tongue touches. An insane feeling and today after the situation before that, which was full of emotions, the emotions are so strong that I even feel them into my pussy. I let my right arm slide down from his neck to his pants and stroke a little harder, so that he can notice it through the pants. I hold on for a short time and then notice the tension in me and especially in his pants ...

"Mia, where is this supposed to end?"
"In my mouth."
"What do you mean by that?"

But I do not answer him anymore, but my right hand has been kind to his zipper and pulled him down.

"Good that you have a boxer shorts on."
"How so?"

"Because I can open it up front now."

Said and done. I opened the boxershort button and brought his cock to the light, oh nightlight. What should I do now, I'm really crazy about the role right now. Torn by feelings that flow in on me and the intellect, which, although only very quietly announces itself, says caution. Careful, we are in town and it is already 23.00 but there are still people on the street. But I'm no longer really interested, because I have opened my mouth and put over his hard cock and massage with my tongue the glans opening and the approach of the foreskin alternately. Joschua has finally cleared his mind, because he slips into the seat a bit. Mind to heart, please take over. Heart, I am already fully involved. Tongue, me too. What should I do now? Keep him in the mouth or pull out before his semen leak? I have a man for the first time in my life, where I really enjoy putting it in my mouth. Oh Mia on the couch in the living room already. But now with Joschua, where my heart is full of feelings for him, it is something very special and in my mind's eye pictures are playing as his seeds shoot into my mouth and spread out. I can see it in my mind's eye and feel each of Joschua's cock movements closely. My tongue deals only with his glans, which would have the feelings with him almost to the climax. Had also a great starting position, because the feelings about what he has told me are already dodged throughout my body and with him that has expressed by the size and hardness of his cock. Good that I can always see it immediately. Yes, we women have a slight advantage. Men can not see our moisture from the outside. Now it will happen soon. I catch my lips to press his cock and move my head back and forth. The extra pressure of my lips around his cock manages to push him over the threshold of madness in a matter of seconds.

"Yes, yes, yes, Mia, I come!!! Now!"

But he does not need to tell me that. I feel his semen penetrate my oral cavity and spread it with my tongue all over his cock. The absolute madness and I quickly turn a blind eye to see if maybe people are standing around the car and watching. No, thank god, no one because I can continue to enjoy. And shortly thereafter, I release his retreating tail into the cold and my head comes up to him. I give him something with his lips and the then emerging tongue from his taste. A long, very long kiss follows and intensively, always alternating with violently rotating tongue inside and then again with very tender tongue touches. And I feel his taste, I have never made it that way and mmm not at all blatant. But even the most beautiful and longest kiss comes to an end and I sit back pretty chubby on the passenger seat and look at him.

"Do you understand it?"
"What?"
"Well my answer!"
"Like your answer?"
"Well my answer to your question."
"It could not be clearer and more soulful. You have not answered a woman like that yet. It's really funny."
"What's funny?"
"Well, when I think that way, you've said and done so much that I've never heard or felt of a woman in my life. You are the number ONE. And you will always be, because I will not give you any more and there is no room for another woman in my life. Only you! You! You! Promised."
"But that's big words. If a hot, twenty-one year old blonde ever comes across you in the hotel lobby and looks at you and waves her room key, then ... ."
"Hahaha, that does not work."
"How so?"
"Because you're walking on my hand on this hotel aisle. Oops or do you want with the blonde?"
"Hahaha, no, not really!"
"You see, then you have to make do with me."

"Yes, I want that! Say, should I drive?"
"Why?"
"Well, you give me the impression that you are some-where on cloud nine."
"Yes, but that can not hurt driving. Besides, do you mean to say that you're not in high spirits emotionally?"
"Yes and how. Never before has a man asked me such a great thing and underpinned it with feelings."
"Well, you have triggered the emotion with me."
"You too with me with your projectiles."
"Really?"
"Of course, it makes me feel good, I love you very much, and it's so nice to feel you. I used to never feel that way when I was with a guy."
"Oh, you, if two people can feel the same at the same time, then that's what you're looking for, and if you want to hold on to it, that's right, is not it?"
"Yes!"
"So you want to stay with me until Christmas 2100."

I look at him and it does not take two seconds and then I say to him, in a very soft, soulful voice ...

"Yes I will."
"Millions of thanks, those are the most beautiful words from your mouth!"
"Yes, what did I say and then after a short time I told you. I still can not believe it."
"Yes, that's how I feel, but my heart has triumphed over my mind. No, no, my mind is screaming right now I'm lying, he wants you to stay here too. So you have it now. We all want you! Stay with us!"
"You are the best guy I have ever met. I remain!"

And he holds my left hand with his right, looks at me and there is a very warm, exciting feeling through me. How can it be that words of a person can hit you in the heart and cause so many different feelings. He lets go of my hand only briefly to close his zipper to prevent colds on my withdrawn tail. Then he takes her again and holds her, while we now the rest of the way, a few minutes drive home. That's fine, because he drives automatic and we both are silent, but our feelings inside seem to be somersaults. I believe in him, too. His expression is, if you look at him from the side, somehow enchanted questioning. He certainly wonders how he got those words out of his mouth. I'm just as touched by myself, I said such serious words and they came easy to me over the lips. My heart was fully behind it and I am really happy that a male person has managed to elicit these words from me. That's just great and while my thoughts still entwine around these words, we have already arrived at home. Open gates, drive in and gates closed.

"You, emerge from your thoughts, we have arrived at home."
"Yes, I somehow lost time. There were so many thoughts in my head that I could not think many of them anymore."
"That's how it was with me, the car drove here automatically."
"What all this can do."
"Yes, it supports our love!"
"Yes."
"May I ask you to your new home?"
"Are you really serious?"
"Yes, one hundred percent!"
"Thanks, I have to get used to it."
"What?"
"That there will be a man in my life, or better, I will be with him."
"Not with him, with me."
"I mean that, with you."
"Not with you, with me."
"Dumbass. Hahaha! "
"Welcome to your new home!"
"Thanks, I feel very comfortable here with you Joschua!"
"Hahaha, now you've taken every pun. Come on in,

please. We do not want to mind a piccolo on this life changing decision and we can welcome the new day right away. It's already Wednesday!"
"Yes and sit by the fireplace."
"Cool, I'll start the fire."
"I'll get the glasses and the champagne."

Good that Joschua always has firewood by the fireplace. So he can always feed the fire quickly and light. When I came out of the kitchen with the glasses, piccolo and orange juice, he dimmed the lights and turned on soft music. Oh, I love it so much when the water breaks the lights and the waterfall rushes through the light waves. This time, however, he has placed a dozen tealights on the coffee table in chord time and he is about to light them. Here I come slowly, taking in the atmosphere again and watching him light the tealights.

"Oh already the full cozy atmosphere, that's nice to you."
"With us!"
"I still can not believe my luck. One week ago I was alone and had so many wishes to find a man, just my dream man. I think everyone who is alone wishes for a partner whom he puts together in his mind the way he would like him to."
"Right, but not a man but a woman."
"Hahaha, I would have thought so too."

And we sit, knees bent, facing each other on the sofa, each holding our glass of orange juice with a few drops of champagne in our hands and looking at each other. It is a reputation without words, just a feeling of well-being, which is a person whom one has found and will never give up, and who has almost all the interests one would have wished for oneself, as well as one's own ideas. Just fantastic. We sip on our glasses and are both immersed in such beautiful thoughts. I do not know when I once experienced it, just sitting in silence and enjoying it, enjoying it a lot.

"Is not that nice to sit next to someone you love?"
"Yes wonderful. And then to be able to look at you like that, the eyes are happy too."
"Sycophant."
"No you are wonderful. You are a harmony in yourself and you radiate something from inside, a warmth and a familiarity, as if we were together forever."
"And still remain until Christmas 2100."

And we both have to laugh out loud and prost ourselves without our eyes separating.

"The fire gives off such a particularly cozy warmth."
"Yes, I have often sat here in the evening, as we do now, but I was alone and that also felt my heart and was lonely and sad. You can still have it so beautiful, but if you can not share it with anyone, it's only half as nice."
"Two hearts are better than one heart."
"And from now on we are two."
"Unimaginable, history does not believe us."
"Life writes the craziest stories."
"Yeah, you say you actually have the docot room ordeer for another time."
"Yes, we can go there tomorrow night if you want."
"Class, I'm really hot on it."
"But now it's already 2:00. What do you think if we both go to bed and sleep?"
"Together or next to each other?"
"What do you want?"
"Honestly, I'm pretty skulker from the last days, especially the night shifts. I was never used to it and then the feeling experience was with you today ... ."
"What?"
"Well your promising words, they really blew me away and I have to process them first. They were so extreme, so special and never have words like that ever reached me. I'm still completely exhausted now, because they are still spinning around in my mind."
"Yes, I know, I feel it and then, above all, the answer you gave me, an answer without words, just indescribable."

"Yes, it just came over me. I thought it was so nice and then in the car and in the dark where other people could have seen us. Just so erotic."

"Yes, you can say that! I've never felt that way either."

"Do you still want to swim?"

"No, I do not think so, just take a shower and then off to bed."

"Oh, a warm shower would be great."

"Well then we meet in bed. Tell me, do you come out of the bathroom naked and crawl into bed?"

"Would you like that?"

"Yes, I like to see you when you're naked. No matter what you do, you just look great."

"Well, are not you exaggerating a bit?"

"No, you are beautiful, a pure natural beauty."

"Thanks for those kind words."

"You're welcome, but we did not want to lie to you and that's what I have to say, if that's the case."

"Are you going to take a shower with me?"

"No, I'm just taking a shower in the other bathroom. Then wait for me in bed."

"But also without textiles."

"Sososo, I should be naked too. Do you want to attack me tomorrow morning or better tomorrow morning?"

"Oh, who knows, such a daytime adventure with you is great and I'm looking forward to it during the whole sleep phase."

"Really, that's so nice of you, it tilts me again."

"Youuu. I take the glasses and the bottle with me and go to the bathroom via the kitchen."

"Oh, do you want to spoil me now?"

"How so?"

"Because you touch."

"That's probably clear, you've spoiled me until now after line and thread and if I should live with you, then I'll do something or do you think I'm just sitting around here lazy?"

"Oh that's fine, my women have never bothered so much. I've always done that on the side or our house-keeper or nanny."

"Well then, poor man, you have to endure another kind of woman, me!"
"Oh, I'll get used to that, but you're not going to make me a pasha?"
"No, that's not how it works. Just spoil something."
"Fine, I agree with that."
"Take me in the arms and give me a kiss on the way."
"But something like that!"

We get up from the sofa, he puts his arms around us and we give ourselves a tender kiss. A kiss in which I lift my left foot back. Oh, as he already knows me and certainly knows when he realizes I've lifted my foot, that I'm so absorbed in the kiss, he just triggers happy feelings with me. How I look forward to the time to get to know him more intensively. After the kiss separation I go as I said with the glasses and bottle in the kitchen and then the other wheel of the pool along the bedroom. He watches me until I disappear in the tunnel under the slide and whistles to me afterwards. I turn around, laugh and no I can not throw a kiss back on him, but have my hands full. Good that I thought of it, otherwise I would have produced a bad luck here. Then I disappeared and he disappears in the direction of swimming pool, but waits before I went from the kitchen to our bedroom and then turn off the lights and the water system. Otherwise I would have had to go in the dark. He really thinks of everything. Not only am I comfortable with him, but I'm sure. For the first time in my life, I have no doubt I caught the right man. I quickly undress, take a warm shower and brush my teeth. Then dry and as I am, completely naked, over to the bedroom and crawled under the covers. When I enter the bedroom, Joschua is already back and is already in bed and smiles at me and I thought I can look forward to his beautiful sight when he comes out of the bathroom to crawl into bed. Now he has taken all the joy from me, he is already in bed. He has dimmed the bedside lamps and is waiting for me. The words he said to me today, those wonderful words have somehow made me dream in the shower and forget about time. It is the man who has taken my heart from now on and he will stay forever. I hope, no I believe, no I feel it, it is forever! And now I stand naked in the bathroom door and behind me is still the bathroom light, so he can see me exactly when I come to the bed. Oh, but before that light and then I go to his bedside and ...

"Ohh, you come to my side?"
"Oh, I've messed up there, then I'll have to crawl over you."
"Well, I'll just hit my comforter down so you do not have to climb that high."
"Hahaha just want us to have skin contact while climbing over."
"Oh, am I so transparent?"
"No, only very tender and kind."
"Yes, that's the way it should be forever. You should always feel good with me, always!"
"I will, certainly, where you are so nice to me."

And I climb over him so that my knees kneel at his right upper body and my hands already arise in front of his left upper body. My elbows give way and my breasts accidentally touch his upper body. He can not leave it and his right hand gives me a pat on my left buttock.

"Auauau, you scared me. That's not what a man does."
"Yes, a man does not do that, but I'm your beloved Joschua!"
"And who is allowed to do that?"
"Yes, if you ask me to do so."
"How did I ask you?"
"Well, first of all, you pressed your breasts to me and then jerked off your beautiful tight buttocks so I should just do it, right?"
"You are a word acrobat. If you clap again, then ... ."

And he lets his hand hit with a double slap on my right and then left buttock and I put all my weight on him fully on it.

"So you are flat."
"But my right hand is still free and that can ... ."

And again he successfully lands a double hit, but then I lift myself up quickly. I'll take away his gossip pad and turn around so quickly that his hands are lying on his left and right next to his head and I'm about to break my elbows again. Now our lips meet and my breasts are pressed flat on his upper body. Darn, I pressed down his cock. He wanted to sleep, but at the touch of my body and the gossips of him on my bum, he wants to know it again and now I flatten him. It tastes so good of tooth-paste and its body smells of vanilla. Yes, his shower gel. And we are still kissing, and I'm just starting to push my body back onto its superbody and move. He thinks now determined, I'll probably turn him a good night fuck. But all of a sudden I take off, give myself a push and roll over to the other side of the cot.

"Brrr, that's a cold shock. I'm totally frozen."
"Come on, I'll pull your blanket over your body again and sleep well tail, I'm not going to bother you anymore."

And then I pull the blanket over him all the way up to his neck. Then I take my hands and tap on the blanket care-fully everywhere, so that it is close to him on all sides.

"So now you will be thawed again very quickly, so you can have a warm, beautiful dream with me, of course, as a leading actress. Good night my dream man."

And I've already disappeared, pull my blanket under me and cover my nakedness. Quickly I turn off the bedside lamps and it comes to silence.

"Good night Mia, my angel."
"Good night Joschua, see you later."

484

Wednesday 11.09.2013

I somehow realize that I have awakened from my dreams. A careful look to Joschua. He still floats in his dream world and the alarm clock says it is 9:46. Oh the day yesterday was so exhausting for us. Oh, I find it so cuddly in my cot and Joschua next to me, I'll just close my eyes again and sleep. Here with Joschua since I am here anyway for me the day - night split for normal people lifted. We just always do what we feel like doing and I have to say that at home I would always have been tired early, even if I had some free time, that's just like going to work regularly and I did not have a man of my body as confused as Joschua. Well confused, I mean predominantly sexually. It is the sheer madness of what I have experienced in the few days. Having met and felt a person. Discovering a person in the sexual field. Found a man who thinks like me. Experiencing a person who is happy as I about the same things. Found a person with whom I can laugh heartily. Found a man who more than satisfied my most daring fantasies. A person who shows me there are even more feelings in me than I knew until now. A person whom I can fully trust. A person who carries me on hands and whom I love with all my heart. Oh Mia it's nicer than all the Christmas I've experienced together. It is absolute madness, I just miss the thoughts, because it is much bigger than that. I am inside as if changed. In the past, there were often negative thoughts and feelings. Now I only believe and feel positive vibrations. I always have to smile when I see him. I always want to touch him when I see him. I always want to kiss and embrace him when I see him and I - oh I love him so much and the greatest thing is he feels the same way, otherwise he would not have wished for me to stay with him always. It was not crazy when he asked me in the car last night. Mia how could you give him a blow as a positive answer. In the past, I would never have come up with such a craze. It often just animates me beyond my limits, but only in a

485

positive sense. And he does not force me to do that. I always have the feeling that I can decide freely and if I say no he would immediately accept it without ifs and buts. That's what I've always missed, because I often had no say in decisions and if I wanted something different and not my ex, then I always got a bad feeling and gave in, even if I did not want. Funny I have never had that feeling with Joschua. He also asks very differently. He formulates so softly and emotionally and explains his decisions. I want and that really makes me feel for the first time in my life, by the side of a man, I am equal and not under him. Wow, that's a nice feeling. I have experienced so many beautiful feelings with and through Joschua and all together gives my heart the absolute security. I love Joschua and the beautiful is my mind also says yes. We both agree and that has not happened that often. Yes I think so, yes Joschua you are the man for eternity. Yes, Christmas is 2100. Oh, even my thoughts have to smile. I loved him in the storm and will always be nice to him. Funny I've never even thought it's wrong or he's an ass. No, my thoughts are always positive. Oh, even in my dreams and thoughts, it's all about this handsome, wonderfully fragrant and always funny and good humored man, Joschua. My Joschua, that sounds like it. But I just do not give it anymore. Done deal. He has it now. But I think he would be happy about these thoughts of me. Yes he would. Oh man, now I'm asleep again with thoughts. Los Mia risk an eye and oops, Joschua is not in his bed anymore. One is then again something for us to do. Start at Mia get up and quickly into the bathroom, brushing your teeth, tweezers, take a shower and after drying quickly into the bedroom and put on. So that was now at full speed. I can be fast. Oops what's that, I open the bedroom door and what must my eyes already watch quite awake. My Joschua swims around in the pool and I have not heard him and dressed. In itself I had suspected him in the kitchen. And now I am standing by the pool stairs and look to him. He swims on his back and is completely naked and his cock is quite small and limp on him. You can not take Mia so easily, the poor tail, so small and lonely. I think I have to change something and button up my blouse and let it slide over my shoulders to the floor. My shoes fly to the right and left. Then I finger around on my waistband and this also slides down. I bend down briefly, well that I am so agile and then I have my stockings in my hand, which I demonstratively slowly, on the lying on the floor blouse, drop. This is accompanied by really greedy looking looks from Joschua. He can hardly wait, that I stand naked in front of him and then storm into the water to him. He stays in the middle of the pool where he was lying on his back. He is really interested as always, the more skin is exposed by me. He thinks it's hot. I can see his cock exactly, he also finds my exposure very stimulating. Yes, he really gets bigger. I've never seen so accurately and may, as a tail to the tail. So I want to enlarge it once more. Let's see if I succeed. Now I'm only in bra and panties there. But soon he will see how my hands reach backwards and make a clasp on the bra. He was right, the bra opens and I pat the straps over my shoulders and let him fall. Tease him a bit more. My hands lay down very fast, probably too fast for his taste, protecting my now bare breasts. Too bad, that would have been such a refreshing morning sight for my Joschua, but it would not be me if I did not feel his thoughts and suddenly pull my hands to the side and ohhh offer him a hopefully erotic sight. I stand with outstretched arms and I enjoy his intense lustful looks with relish. But I have to say, to see Joschua drifting on the water, still in the supine position but no longer swimming, but playing dead man is really animating. He is a wonderful sight for me and in the morning, we agree, my brain, my heart and my erotic feelings in my pussy, which, as I realize, is getting very wet, even though I'm not in the water. Wow Mia you are a funny woman. I have to smile about such thoughts, which I never had before. So it must be up to Joschua. Now I turn slowly with outstretched arms at three hundred and sixty degrees. Joschua looks at me but he says nothing. He seems to enjoy it. And after the turn my hands quickly create a textile free zone in my lower area. I can not help it, because I see how his eyes are on me and I again extend my arms to the side and turn around slightly bouncing around my own axis again. That was too much for Joschua or better for his cock, because he is really curious again and firmly up. Man oh man this cock and this man who is hanging on it. What is it that makes him so hot from a distance and to be allowed to. There are supposed to be marriages where this is no longer the case. I know that from experience. But I can do it with Joschua and that is very good and it has turned me on now, oh wait my poor Joschua you have to endure much before breakfast. But before I start storming I burn this picture into my mind's eye, I want to keep it forever, a dream sight, this lying man with a standing tail.

"Ohhh that is a divine sight, which I have just taken in my mental image collection forever."
"You're welcome. Please, I like to play photo model for you, because I have to see, too, the photographer gets a little excited. Certainly because of my pose."
"You can say that out loud and not only outwardly something is stirring."
"Sososo and the early morning."

I should not have said that, which stirs even more in me, because Joschua laughs out loud, stands in the water and goes straight to me. Immediately I go down step by step and on the last step, I do not believe, I make a potter in the water, dive and swift like an arrow in his direction. Immediately before Joschua I shoot out of the water again. In doing so, I shake my mane around so as not to have the drop of water and water running over my face for long, and when I slide back into the water I quickly put my arms on his shoulders and my legs cling tightly around his hips. He is rigid with fright, what a performance, the bright madness, the dream of every man. Hahaha. Unfortunately I have so much forward momentum when jumping out and clinging to him that we both fall backwards into the water and go down. I'll probably take a deep breath instinctively, because then I do not need to let go of my beloved Joschua under water. Okay, then he has to bring us back to the surface and he tries to find ground under his feet. Fails and we emerge again as we have submerged. I cling to him like a burdock and hardly he stands again and even before he can say something, because my hair is already running a lot of water over his face, but that does not bother me to press my lips to his. No more water can penetrate, because he opens his mouth and not the lips move, but my tongue goes joyfully to the morning greeting over to his and licked. Here I am, hello awake already. And while we talk intensively, sometimes tenderly, I slide down a little lower. I've been stopped now by his stiff cock, the outside has hit my pussy and is now pressed down strongly, because I'm sitting on it. What would he like to have disappeared in my damp cave? Oh, I do not want to be like that, because I am so happy and already he penetrates my hip movement help. Now there's a morning welcome ritual down there too. I pull my neck tight with my left hand towards me, so that our lips can not separate and put my legs back on the pool floor. Oh no, the other position is also possible under water and certainly durable for him. Tough, oh my thoughts have been funny since I'm with Joschua. Now he feels a pressure on his neck that pulls him down a little, because I have put my legs into the old leg position that wraps around his hips. Now my tongue is getting faster and wilder, and I'm starting to move my pelvis back and forth. But lo and behold Joschua's cock has slipped out. Am I so slippery or have the wrong pelvic position? Well that's not possible. I can feel it bumping in front of my cave entrance and I easily change the entry angle by lifting my pelvis. Hey presto he immediately took the situation and shifted into my inner life. Hahaha, I guided him like a funnel and pulled him into the depths of my pleasure center. My tongue tells him by a violent attack, he is fully inside. Now I start, for him I have to be through the

489

water like a barely perceptible flyweight, to move slowly with my hip up and down and the water around us makes these movements immediately and reinforces them even more. In me it starts to cook. Not so, but my erotic feelings have been awakened and begin, I do not know how he always does it, but to get into ecstasy very quickly and I strengthen my hip movements, but suddenly leave his tongue and lips in peace, loosen my hands from his neck and bend me backwards to the water. He can hold me, it is easily possible for him. I press at an angle on his cock, which presses down in me, and so hits a direct hit on my G-spot.

"Ohhh that's nice, go on, please move on."

And I'm starting to slowly but slowly amplify my hip movements, as I and he are surrounded by the water, it is an extra slight resistance that you have to overcome, but the waves are coming back and the water is starting to spurt up on both of us. Cool, uiii and my excitement rises and rises. We're getting wilder, that's only me, because Joschua tries to keep his balance in my bump-ing and then my excitement increases immeasurably and my whole body seems to burn, although I am sur-rounded by water. He gets hotter and hotter and my and his screams do another ...

"Go on, you go on you horny goat, come on, let me go, take me, push, harder, harder, yes, yes, yes, even more, ohhh, push to, deeper, you stallion can do it. Come on!"

And his hands are under my buttocks to support me while holding and he pinches into it, since I also lean back and so unfortunately can not reach my breasts, several times vigorously in my buttocks.

"Yes, give it to me, you stallion, pinch me more, go, you wild goat. Come on."

And the water around us does not know how to react

490

anymore, it ripples more and more wildly and our movements get a bit faster. The water reacts and sprays
already over my breasts. My eyes start slowly to see
everything in a light fog and it will not be long before ...

"I explode you stallion, come now."

There was a scream too much and it explodes like a
rifle, shooting its seeds into me ...

"Yeah, more, I can feel it again, wonderful as you come
in me. Ohhh it's real madness!"

And he still has some energy and squeezes again with
the last twitch in his cock the remaining seeds with high
pressure and into me.

"Yes, ohhh, how divine. Youuu ...!"

She threw my arms forward and clinging to me, just as
everything started at his neck and with my head resting
on his shoulders, breathing heavily, lie down.

I notice his legs starting to shake a bit. The tension
decreases. Wow, no doublev wow! It is indescribable.
The water around us begins slowly to relax again and
there is a calm everywhere, a warm, plump, so happy
feeling calm, as when the world embraces one. As if you
are wrapped in warm, golden light, completely
enveloped and never want to let go. I breathe again
slowly and evenly and one somehow has the feeling that
the water wants to tell you to wake up hello, because it
feels suddenly much colder than before. I raise my
head.

"Good morning darling, did you sleep well and dream?
Auauau! What are you doing, why are you pinching my
buttock?"
*"I have to see if I'm still dreaming or if what I've just
experienced is really true, because I did not know that*

there really is something so beautiful."
"What do you mean, our water sex experience?"
"No you! You can not exist, you are an angel on earth."
"Yeah, hahaha, I just came down from cloud nine for you."
"Yes, I believe so and now you always take me to your house on cloud nine."
"Yes, that's the way to say it, but it's the other way around."
"How, it was not heavenly for you?"
"But!"
"Then it was at least devilishly good."
"Hahaha, pun! No, I mean, you're the angel who flew into my life and turned it upside down."
"I am not an angel."
"Yes, because who else could have given me wings and let me fly on cloud nine. But only an angel."
"You always say such nice words to me. May your angel carry you out of the water under a warm shower?"
"Yes."

And he walks, as we together or still in each other hanging out of the water with me and in the pool shower.

"You can release a hand, please turn on the shower."
"Oops ice cold!"

And in fright I drop my legs to the ground, let go of his neck and take a step back. Now he is alone under the still cold shower. And I look at him from bottom to top.

"Well you look, really tasty."
"You want to embarrass me again and make you red, you rascal."
"No, I'm serious, please turn around."
"Are you so, do you like my back?"

And without saying anything I come back into the shower, put my hands around him at belly height and

492

press myself firmly from behind him. The water is now chubby and warm and flows over the two of us from above and down to us. I just hold him tight and it's wonderful. Such a nice feeling triggered only because I stand naked behind him and me to him. So I could stop for hours.

"You, do you think that's so nice?"
"Yes, just as if we were one."
"I will never let you go again."
"Oh ha, that's nice, I agree."
"But I'm hungry and I have to let you go, otherwise I'll be lying dead behind you soon and then I can not spoil you anymore."

He turns to me and smiles so wonderfully at me with very bright eyes.

"I love you, may I ask you to have breakfast in twelve minutes?"
"Oh, my Joschua very much."

And we part from each other, slowly because the heart does not want to be torn apart and Joschua is drying himself off, while I still enjoy the warm water, which flows over my beautiful body and makes me slowly disappear into the shower clouds. In the meantime, he has dried himself off and goes to get dressed in the bedroom. Joschua comes to me dressed out of the bedroom, as I dried but naked from the swimming pool come. His hands stretch out immediately after me and his mouth just needs to briefly greet my breasts. Lip contact on my breasts and then he immediately goes on and my eyes accompany him in the direction of the kitchen, where he turns around in front of the kitchen door again and sees how I looked it up. I pick up my clothes pulled out by the pool, wave to him and disappear quickly in the bedroom. What a Wednesday morning, what a morning! Sure, when I'm dressed and come to the kitchen Joschua is almost finished with everything.

This man is a genius in fast magic. Oh yes he spoiled me after line and thread. So I have also put the overdrive on and off to the kitchen to my Joschua, oh that's nice I could always think it, Joschua and then I stand in the kitchen door and just look at him.

"Hello, who is there? This is the angel Mia! You are fast today. Oh, you did not blow your hair. Not that you catch a cold now."
"No, it's warm with you."
"With us."
"I'll probably get used to it a bit harder, a man never said that to me."
"What said ours?"
"Yeah, it just belonged to my husband and I was just allowed to be there and use it, but he always said his own."
"Yes, I know that enough, but when you live together and love each other, it's not just me or you, it's us. We will share everything and if you can give the most intimate thing you can, sharing your heart and body, then it's logical to share everything else."
"Yes, but men often see it differently."
"I do not, I want you to feel well here too and if only I would say it's mine and you're only allowed to be here because I let you, what's that, nothing half and nothing whole."
"You're right. But that's as beautiful as you say, I can feel it right."
"Me too, and my stomach feels hungry too. What do you think of scrambled eggs with salmon this morning?"
"But you really want to pamper me."
"Yes and no!"
"Like, yes and no."
"Yes, I want to pamper you, no it will not stop if you have said yes. I always have breakfast like that. Probably also because I go to bed late in the evening and then have breakfast later. Mostly I skip lunch and just drink coffee ... ."
"Made with cake."

"Yes, can you see clairvoyance?"

And quickly everything is brought to the table. Oh, to-gether it is really faster and then still the smooching, when we pass each other.

"Do we have everything on it?"
"I think so."
"Alright then, oh no, there's something missing."
"What?"
"Press once and kiss once and pet once."
"How is that for dinner?"
"No, as an appetizer, come here, I want you pkc."
"What? Pkc, what's that?"
"You still have a lot to learn, pkc means pushing, kissing, caressing."
"Hahaha come here, you child's head."

We hug each other and slowly our mouths approach to kiss while their and my hands caress each other's backs and buttocks.

"Well, now we can have breakfast, may I ask."
"Thank you, my darling!"

And we sit down, today without candlelight, because the sun casts its rays through the window and thus also fills our hearts.

"Can I ask you something between sandwiches, scrambled eggs and salmon?"
"You can always ask me anything you want."
"You, have you ever thought about how it could be, that I would not need to leave you here any longer."
"No, you have not left me any time yet."
"Imagine that you would get four weeks leave from your boss and then we could do everything together in peace and you'll be sure if you want to enjoy life by my side."
"Sounds good."
"It may well be that after two and a half weeks you

would rather live alone again."

"Could be, but will not happen, strangely, I am one hundred percent sure."

"Man, that sounds good. But if we experience our gyno adventure tonight, maybe."

"Tonight, I'm so curious what I can discover in your treatment for new feelings in me."

"Did not you experience something of that in the water?"

"And how, when I leaned back, I do not know why, it just came over me, the feelings were fantastic and I could feel you so intensely."

"Cool, a woman who is looking forward to experiencing something with me."

"Yes, and I'm so curious, incredibly curious and excited."

"You will not believe me too. It's the first time I'm going to have such a role play with a real woman."

"Real woman, probably played with a doll before?"

"No, you're stupid? But not with a doll. Only in the thought and you can not touch so great as you, your thighs, your stomach, your breasts."

"Stop it, or I'll jump you in the lap right away."

"Oh, that would not be unfortunate and then you lean back and show me your wonderful breasts in a highly erotic situation. Yes, if you slowly dribble honey over it in this position and then it flows very slowly over your breasts to your navel. Oh, if I put you on your back then ... ."

"Lay down?"

"Yes, so that I could then bend over you to be able to lick the running honey with my tongue."

"The navel is not working."

"I know, there you are ticklish. But that brings me an idea."

"Which?"

"No, no comment, the buns are getting cold."

"Hahaha, you're distracting, that's not true."

"In this case, yes?"

"How so?"

"Because otherwise I'm starving and you do not want to, then I can not fight our role playing game with you tonight."

"All right, but will you tell me later."

"Yes, tomorrow at breakfast."

"How about tomorrow?"

"Yes, it just can not be done before. The honey sticks my lips together."

"Hahaha well then I will not jump on your lap now."

"A pity, but I have to accept that too."

"Yes you have to."

"So you want to apply for a vacation? What would your parents say if you told them about it?"

"Well, I can try that and tell you then."

"Do you want to call her after breakfast?"

"No, I prefer to go there and tell them alone when we sit opposite each other."

"That's a good idea. You see, you already deal with it. Thank you! I'm so happy."

"You're a rascal."

"Oh no, no, I'm just saying what my heart dictates to me."

"Then thank you, dear heart, I like you and always advise Joschua so well and never stop."

"Well then, I'll always listen to my little heart in regards to you."

"Well, it looks like you're full."

"Yes, I am too."

"When I cleared ... ."

"We! We!"

"Thanks, when we cleared up, did you plan something?"

"Would you like to see how I earn my money?"

"Yes gladly. You have never told me that."

"What do you mean what I do?"

"You are by no means employed anywhere."

"Why not?"

"You're too dominant for that and you would not let a boss stand next to you."

"Ok, I've never been employed in life. Stop, I worked as an employee during my studies. Right, never again."

"Then you are a boss."

"Hahaha I used to be with a lot of employees, but not anymore."

"Help me, do you drive far to your work?"

"Mmm, not far and I do not drive either."

"Can you reach your workplace on foot?"

"Yes, I can do that!"

"Far away?"

"Nope, relatively close."

"Oh, here at home?"

"The candidate has a hundred points."

"Oh, do not make it so exciting."

"Fine, I'm photographing naked women."

"Hahaha, now you want to hug me, right?"

"Yes and no. After all, I wrote a book, a bondage text-book, and I needed two hundred shots to explain the book better, and I'm still missing shots."

"Then you can take a picture of me."

"With pleasure, but never for the public, only for us private. What you do not know about me yet, I can be very jealous."

"How do you mean?"

"I do not want to share a woman I love with another man. She should be completely alone for me. Not that I lock her up, she can go away on her own, but do not smooch with another or more."

"You're right, I did not want you to kiss or touch another woman."

"You said - you - that meant me, that's what I like about you. One thing I can promise you, I'll never kiss another woman, let alone touch her. I would have to be crazy, I have the dearest and sexiest woman in the world by my side and that I should break me? I'm not that stupid. Besides, I love you and would never cheat on you. I can promise you that."

"You are really nice, that you said, you love me. I am pleased with the compliment with the erotic woman."

"Yes, if you are not hot, who else is it? Just think how you have shown you naked by the pool, without any shyness, just bare headed with your arms spread open.

498

More eroticism is not possible."

"Did you like that. I also do not know what rode me there, but when I saw you lying there so naked in the water, your tail so tired, my heart said, you have to help him to wake up and then it happened."

"I never dared dream that and then when you sat down and covered it. Uuu it still tingles me, something in-describable."

"Yes, that was it for me too."

"Come with me to the office, then I'll show it to you and because I work from home, I barely have any contacts outside and that alone. That was the reason for my ad, which you already know."

"Have many women reported that?"

"Many not, I immediately noticed in the spelling, who was a professional and only wanted something for money, of which I think it was three pieces and one, since the spark has not jumped, even on her first mail. I immediately canceled and then there was a hot mail from such a crazy chicken from Schwerin."

"Hahaha chicken are you calling me?"

"The dearest and best chicken in the world, and when I first met the chicken, it was one of the most erotic women in the world called Mia."

"Yeah I like it."

"Sit down next to me on the second office chair. I drive up all three PCs, it takes a moment and then I have to open the corresponding pages. What I want to show you I daytrading, so from home or on the go to buy and sell the stock."

"You can live on that."

"Yes you can."

And he explains how I could make my money on the stock market and he also does some regular trades as he always does. We spent almost two hours at the PCs buying and winning four times, having fun and laughing. Even trading makes with Joschua at the side of a huge fun.

"So now we stop for today, it's already 13.00."
"And what have we won now?"
"Let's see, four times eighty euros equal to three hundred and twenty, of which one loss, one hundred euros deduct, gain two hundred and twenty by two."
"How about two?"
"When doing daytrading, you have to put away fifty percent for the tax, so by two. If you put away half of it immediately, you will not have any problems afterwards when the taxes are due. And if you have to pay less, then you have a nice additional income."
"I've heard of it, but how it worked was a book with seven seals. Thank you for explaining that to me so well."
"No problem. You also have to know what you are getting into with me."
"Cool, do you have any other exciting secrets?"
"Well, you'll know that over time. But we could go shopping together now?"
"Shopping and then tonight what delicious things cook together."
"Sounds good. I've already written a grocery list and then if we see what we're hungry for, we can take it with us."
"But that's a life with you."
"What do you mean?"
"Well, it's all so easy and straightforward with you."
"Well, it used to be different. But let's just get the grocery list and the basket, let's go."
"Can I just go to the bathroom?"
"Yes, then we meet in the car on the doorstep."

And when I get to the front door Joschua is still in front of the car and enjoys the last rays of sunshine. Oh there he is, you Mia barely I see him is going on with me directly the blasting on my face and also inside me. Just a man to fall in love with and now he's off the market. Oh you poor other women if I knew what you missed. Just fine, because now you have no chance, I will not give up without a fight.

"Hello, hope you have not waited too long."
"No, just wanted to enjoy the last rays of sunshine."
"Oh, may I stand next to you?"
"Before me, too, the sunbeams fall on both faces and your body is pressed back against mine."
"Oh, and you're warming me from behind. Yes, that feels good."
"We did not want to go shopping."
"Oh, let's just enjoy the sun a little bit, the rays are so nice and warm, and you're behind it, you can not get better."
"If you say that so sweet, I'll go right away."

And we stop something like that. Me in front of him and his cock feels my buttock slit. What is he thinking again? He probably wants to knock again and feel good inside. No, you down there will only be shopped.

"Ohh does he want it again?"
"Tell me, do you have eyes down below?"
"No, but my pubs have nerves and can feel it."
"Oops, I'm going to turn red."
"Oh well, that gives you such an innocent touch."
"Oh, just touch, I'm almost always innocent."
"Hahaha, that's what I would have said, but let's go out or something else will happen."
"Yes, go shopping."
"How do you want to experience anything with me?"
"Hahaha shopping with you is an experience."
"I can tell you afterwards. Believe it but now almost."
"Let yourself be surprised."
"I will."
"Please get in my angel, buckle up, we'll start soon."
"Very well my pilot."

And we go to the supermarket. A journey of about ten minutes. Find a parking space, get out and take your shopping basket.

"I place the shopping basket in the shopping cart, then I

501

can clear it at the checkout. Otherwise, you will always be around at the car for clearing and when it rains, you will also get wet. Yes one operation saved."
"You like to organize and everything has to fit, no hand-shake or walk free."
"Oops, is that so conspicuous?"
"You can tell, you never want to go empty handed."
"Bad?"
"No, very effective. Surely you have the shopping list synonymous to the market where you buy coordinated."
"Oops, how long have we known each other?"
"Hahaha, I do that sometimes too, otherwise I forget something."
"Likewise. What do you think about fresh raspberries? Anyone who eats raspberries often sells the cancer."
"How do you know that again?"
"I spent some time on nutrition and supplementation, read a lot and attended classes."
"What did not you learn?"
"You, I have a lot of interests but I had to learn a lot with learning by doing. For example with the right partner and love."
"Yes me too, but now I have found the right one."
"Do you mean me, oh many, many thanks, that's so good. What would you like to eat tonight, meat or fish?"
"Oh, dear you."
"You get me for dessert."
"Oh yes, are you lying naked on my plate?"
"Rather on a wooden board, I do not have such a big plate."
"Wooden board is fine too."
"Good and what are we going to eat tonight? Remember, you will burn a lot of calories during the examination."
"Yes, I am already looking forward to it. Let's eat fish, if you agree."
"Yes, what fish, smoked mackerel, roll up pugs, herring in cream sauce, coalfish with herbed crust in aluminum form, fish fingers, red rake unbranched or which one do

you want."

"You can make it hard for one, what would you take?"

"What do you think of cod on ginger pan vegetables?"

"Boa sounds tempting, that would be great. I have never eaten. Does not that take a long time to prepare?"

"No, about half an hour and you can set the table in time and watch me from behind."

"And touch or you're just cooking in apron."

"If you touch me then I certainly can not work properly and it takes longer."

"Then maybe we should practice that."

"Oh yes, that would be great. Well then we need for that, a bag of frozen cod, a bunch of carrots, a bunch of spring onions, a red chopped pepper, a lime, fresh ginger a root, parsley. The rest I should have there. I hope I have not forgotten anything."

"You certainly will not. I'm hungry now. "

"But you have to wait a while, but when we get home, we can start right away."

"No, you have to change first."

"Move?"

"Yes, nude and only an apron."

"Are you serious, do you want that?"

"Yes, and how!"

"And now the leftovers on the shopping list."

"I push the cart and you load."

"Kiss .... It's really fun with you, even shopping."

And we make the purchase in record time, go to check-out, pay and get everything in the car. He also puts me in the car carefully, nonsense he keeps the door open like a gentleman and home. Go into the garage, gate to, unload Joschua and the shopping, off to the kitchen.

"I'll pack it. The stuff we do not need then I put away, you have to ... ."

"Yes, I know, I have to practice controlling myself, but when I think about it, you look at me like this ... ."

"But you can also remember, I'll touch you."

"Ohhh, really. Then not only the fish gets hot."

"No definitely not."
"Ok, hurry up, you're hungry."
"And you want to be spiced."
"Yes. see you soon."

Joschua disappears into the bathroom. Sure, he does a short lingerie in the genital area, that's so, if you know, you get along with a woman. I already feel like Joschua .... . Then he's sure to put on a bib apron and Crooks, he has a stone floor all over the place and that would be too cold for his bare feet. Oh I hear the bedroom door and I can see him coming past the pool in my direction. Hahaha, I was right, can not believe it. He comes in a blue bib apron and it looks like he's naked underneath. I dimmed the light in the kitchen and put the two five armed silver chandeliers out of the dining room into the kitchen, lit candles and filled two glasses, with champagne and orange juice, and now receive them with these in my hand.

"Well, where have you been for so long? I'm waiting for you for ages."
"I was satisfied soon."
"Whaaaat?"
"Hahaha, I would never do that if I'm in for an adventure with you."
"That's what I mean."
"Oh, can I get a glass too?"
"Yes, but first the sharp looking chef has to turn around very slowly. Cool and wobble now with the buttocks."
"Right?"
"Yes, but everything is tight, nothing wobbles. looks really hot. I have to do the touchtest."

And already I put my cook with his white cook dungarees both hands on his buttocks and they start to knead this and to end this inspection with a strong double stroke.

"I do not think such words and test grips have been

504

said or done to me at fifty. Hahaha, those words are good."
"Tell me, what are you wearing for an apron?"
"How so? Apron with bib."
"And what's that down there, did you put something in the front pocket?"
"I am, oh that, that's the new Mia mood thermometer."
"That what?"
"The Mia mood thermometer, that shows me how close and hot Mia is."
"How does he down there know how hot I am?"
"He smells your excitement!"
"Ah, that's good and it's not wrong either. I'm already warm."
"How warm, I love when you're hot."
"Do not worry, I will. Where you look and stay close to me. Yes, I can only get hot."
"Cheers to our sweetness!"
"Cheers on your Mia mood thermometer."

He starts snipping the vegetables, seasoning the cod, and before he puts the fish in the pan, I ask him ...

"Can I take a picture of you?"
"How, as I look now, hot and greasy."
"Yes, it's totally erotic."
"Good if I can take a picture of you during the RPG."
"And what are you going to do with the photos?"
"They are archived on my PC and then when we sit to-gether in thirty years in the evening and it does not work with the sex, then we look at the pictures. You never get those memories again and you get older and older."
"Oh, archive. Do you already have any of you?"
"Let's just say, when I wrote the bondage book in 2000, I did some test shots and instead of an expensive model, I tried it on myself."
"And who photographed you there?"
"My then wife, but all the pictures I have on my PC."
"Youuu, if I'm very good, may I take a look at it?"

"Well, I'm still young and pretty. And when you see that, you do not like me anymore."

"Silly man, now you are absolutely interesting and sexy."

"Thank you! Well, yes, if you agree, we'll save ours for later, too."

"Otherwise, but no one is allowed to see."

"You are private and the most intimate. Nobody is allowed to see them, they only belong to us."

"Okay, if you think so, then you can take pictures of me. Let's see if we look at the later times."

"Me too, in pictures one often acts quite differently than one believes oneself to see oneself. I have to prepare the food now, you're hungry and so are I. If you go to the office, in front of the right screen is a small, blue digicam. We can use them and while I continue to fry, you can take pictures."

"Sounds good, I'm already gone, but please stay so stiff."

"I can not guarantee that. If you come back, then you must certainly help."

"And are you looking forward to it?"

"Yes and how, I'm just curious how you do it."

"Let yourself be surprised, then I'll be gone."

"See you soon. Eat in ten minutes."

And he gently takes out the fish, which he has sautéed on both sides for four to five minutes, and puts the cut vegetables in the pan for a short searing. As a result of the fish sizzling in the pan, the vegetables now also take on some of it. Then he hears, I'm on the move and when he turns around, a flash from the doorway hits him. I shot the first picture of him. A really hot photo but his naked botty is not on it, so still quite youth free.

"But you've become really small, no bump in the apron. What should I do there?"

"You're a specialist for that, but there's something to eat in five minutes."

"Ohh, then stop."

I go to Joschua, give him a kiss and grab it with my right hand from the side under his apron. He'll think right now, she'll touch me, but I do not. But then, it flashes. I took a picture under the apron. After the first shock he has to laugh.

"Hey, what are you doing?"
"Hahaha, of course, a before after photo."
"Oh sooo! But then I'm calmed down."

And already I reach with his right hand for his cock and I squeeze his small, but already easily filling tail, firmly between my fingers and start pushing him very fast back and forth.

"Oh, take another three minutes to eat."
"I can do it!"
"Who can do that for you or me?"
"We!"

But something unexpected happens. He is already so stiff that he is about to come and his breath begins to race and there, I notice how stiff and hard he has become in my hand and then I'm really mean, I stop suddenly and it does not take long and already it flashes again under his apron.

"If we look at those pictures that are one hundred per-cent cool, then you'll probably always be tough, but I think the three minutes are up and the food is ready."
"What, what, now?"
"Oh, you did not think the dessert would be served by me before the main course. This is not right."
"But I ... ."
"Should I help you to distribute the food on the plates?"

And he turns around to get the plates, but before that he gets two violent gossips from me on his bare buttocks.

"Hey, they really feel great."

And laughing, I get the plates, put them next to him, he is probably still completely baffled and ...

"Go aside, I suggest you're somewhere else. It would be a pity for the delicious food, at least it smells great."

And without talking, I push him with my elbow to the side and it flashes from the front. Oh, I'm fine. I become a photographer.

"We take the picture directly behind the other two, because I can not describe the expression now. He is unique."
"I believe you about that. So what, you are ... ."
"The coolest woman in the world for you, but only because I love you."

And I give him a kiss on the cheek, fill the plates and go with them into the dining room.

"Where are you? Come on, the food is getting cold."
"Yes I come, just make the stove."
"You can come like that, you do not need to change your clothes."
"Ok, hahaha!"

And we sit down at the dining room table opposite and enjoy the sauteed cod on ginger pan vegetables. And it tastes wonderful to me, this compilation, it seems Joschua also to mouth and we talk about the photos and the upcoming role play at the gynecologist. Then ...

"You, we did not have anything to drink. I thought after the meal we need a little sweet dessert. You can choose between a latte macchiato with the first gingerbread and printen or a yoghurt with greek honey. Of course you can have both."
"Even at the risk that you think I'm a glutton, I'll take everything."
"That's good, me, too. You can sit quietly, I'll serve it to

you."

"No, I'm coming to the kitchen with you."

"Why did I know that? Good, then please take your plate and cutlery and follow me unobtrusively."

"Sure and I will enjoy the way to the kitchen behind you."

"I knew it. But have fun and a good view."

And off in single file. Arrived in the kitchen, dishwasher filled, Tassimo hired and a plate of biscuits, when filling he tells me how he loves it, when the first Printen and gingerbread in September in the markets. In his youth, they always came in the middle of November. However, he also says Christmas, he is no longer hungry for gingerbread, speculoos and co. Christmas must be then homemade cookies and butter cream cake or stollen, but homemade with marzipan. Oh soon he will bake again only about eight weeks. But my Joschua will not bake alone this time, but with me. That will be a great big baking shaft. Let's see how much flour we need then. Now I ever tear him out of his thoughts, because a kiss on his mouth wakes him up again with fresh wind of my tongue.

"Hey, dreamer, you already dream with your eyes open. What?"

"I just imagined how we'll bake together in eight weeks here in the kitchen."

"Oh, this is going to be a baking adventure."

"How so?"

"Well, who knows what's going on."

"Almost the same thing I thought."

"The crossbar is finished twice."

"Yes, the gingerbread plate is also full and I also take the Greek yogurt with honey."

"Think of two spoons for it."

"I already have it in my hand. What's up, you went to the dining room in front of me. Behind with is probably even uninteresting?"

"Nonsense, but I wanted to shoot a photo with the full

509

gingerbread and of course with you on it from scratch. Please stop and cheese!"
"Cheese!"
"Cool, now you can uncover."
"Do you always feel hungry for something sweet after dinner?"
"Very often. Did you also see, in the morning is the last roll half always with Nutella or jam."
"Yes, I noticed already, just like me. We fit in an awful lot of things."
"And in what not?"
"Ohhh, now you want to embarrass me. I do not know anything at the moment."
"I think that's just great, I feel the same way."

And we continue to chat about God and the world, letting the latte and pastry alternate with a teaspoon of Greek yogurt with honey. He keeps looking at me and it's so warm around my heart. I am no longer alone and more, I have finally found a male being for whom I feel the great love. Finally.

"It's already 19:25, do we want to go to role play?"
"What should I wear?"
"Just stay that way."
"Then I have to take a shower in advance and dress up everywhere."
"Take good time, I'm still dreaming a bit."
"What?"
"Well of course, other thoughts have in my head but no more space."
"That sounds good. I hurry up."
"All right, I just go down and play some pool. I just feel like it. When you're done, just come down."
"Billiards ok, I do not have to understand that now. I'll come down when I'm done."
"See you soon. I love you."
"And me too, and I'm really happy. This is my first RPG of this kind. What I'm going to feel good."
"I hope as much as I have in the dream for you."

"That sounds like a lot, a lot and a lot of fun."

I disappeared in the bedroom, but now fast. But Joschua wanted everything from the dining room table to the kitchen on his own. He finds it terrible, like me, when you come back or wake up in the morning and then everything is still standing around somewhere. If you keep everything reasonably tidy, then unexpected visitors can come. Yes we have so many same settings. Oh, I'm as excited as the first time. So far, I have rediscovered so many feelings through him in me and now he wants to do something I've never done, not even in my mind, I can imagine what it is. But I know I can say our codeword - red - at any time and I'm one hundred percent sure he will stop immediately. Would I even if he would say so. I have this man in my heart closed. Now I'm looking forward to it, when he ties me and plays with me. Yes, he is really right, trust is the basis for doing something like this and I can feel so many emotions. Oh Mia did not think so much, I cleaned everything on me, clearly and now only the bathrobe and the white bra and panties he gave me. Why should not I wear my own lingerie underneath. He certainly has something specific in mind again. I can not understand how a man who plans such things in his head can be so tender and has never experienced anything like this before. Everything just in his mind's eye that's really impressive. But now everything dressed and bathrobe over it, then I should meet him downstairs at the bar in the party room. So and from now on it goes to the next experience level of crazy feelings with Joschua. Oh, I'm already wet in my pussy. The man already makes me so hot in thought. Leave bedroom and take the direct path to the basement. Oh Joschua is already down, because I see light up the stairs seem and music penetrates from below. I am already on the first steps down and it tingles already all over my body. But now down to the party room. And I'm downstairs and what must my eyes see there is Joschua the doctor at the pool table. How cool is that because it is getting crazier. This will be a role play with full reality. Joschua put on a white doctor's coat and probably nothing like the kitchen apron. Hot. And like a doctor, white doctor's socks and white doctor's gossips. Oh and then a name tag with Dr. ...

"Hallooo, I'm coming to you Joschua."
"I'm at the bar and wait with a glass of champagne."
"Sparkling wine and then driving?"
"No, of course not, we stay in the house doctor's office."

How close first to go closer otherwise I can not see the nameplate and I go to him and my head bends slightly to the sign. Ah, tonight I'm being examined. Joschua is a gynecologist and he also wears the stethoscope around his neck. Am probably in a private doctor's office today, because it is already 21.06 and all other practices have been closed at this time already. Hahaha how cool is that?

"Like right now? Oh the sign is cute, Dr. Joschua gynecologist. And you are dressed like that too. Will you feel the pulse now and listen to my heart?"
"Yes, but I can tell you already, pulse and heart rate increased very much with you."
"Yeah, you know, if you're the doctor."
"Just because I'm the doctor?"
"No, because I do not know what you're going to do to me crazy."
"Do you have your health insurance card with you?"

I look a bit surprised and confused, smile at him and then I give him a beautiful romantic kiss on the mouth. My tingling and excitement is already enormously high. That's the madness, so beautiful so incredibly beautiful.

"Yes, this health insurance card is valid, please take a drink, that calms something before the doctor visit."
"I can not drink that much to calm down. Honestly, I do not want to. I want to be totally excited and experience

something with my private doctor."
"Well, may I take you to practice then?"
"Yes gladly. Oops, I'm shivering a bit."

He goes to a shelf, pushes it aside and there's a door behind it. Now it gets even scarier and scary, but Joschua opens the door, turns to me, smiles and reaches out to me his right hand. I grab her and he pulls me close. Then I get a kiss. After the kiss, I see a small vestibule and two doors. Joschua sees that I stand there with a smiling mouth open and he explains that he has set up his photo studio here for the recordings for his bondage book. Now it is just a doctor's office. Here everything can be rebuilt as needed. I have not experienced anything like that. It's exciting. I think I can already hear my excitement, because my heart beats to the neck. What's happening now. Funny is only I'm not afraid it's a joyous excitement on what is coming now. With other thoughts, I'm sharp as a scoundrel on what awaits me now ...

"Please go into the cabin, make yourself completely free and put on the black bra and panties. They would have to fit you. Are unworn, brand new. When you're done, you can knock, then I'll get you out."
"Yes, that's good."

I go to the cabin. He closes the door behind me. Do not finish just lean on. And in the cabin hangs a bra and panties in black. What he wants now. Oh, I will not ask questions, take off my white two parts and put the blacks on. I just seem to work as Joschua says. Did he hypnotize me? Mine I'm just excited and happy, and it will be definitely erotic, no more determined. You can get my head cinema moving that's unimaginable. I did not even know that I had such a mental cinema and how I could turn it on. He must have gone through the other door into the practice room. So now I'm dressed as my doctor wanted it. Then I should knock on the cabin door. So tap in rhythm. What, a song, no dear SOS three times short, three times long, three times short. It's also an emergency situation. Will finally get to my Joschua's arms and be examined. I feel it already will be the most erotic and crazy at the same time investigation of my whole life. Otherwise I never liked to go to the gynecologist and now I'm looking forward to it. Boy oh boy.

Shortly after my rescue knock the door opens and I stand like in a gynecologist's room with everything that goes with it. I can not shut my mouth anymore and look around slowly. Oh, what do I have to see, the doctor's desk with its super armchair and two chairs in front of where the patients are being questioned, a dipstick on the wall and a scale and then a big leather couch and the notorious examination chair. In addition various cabinets with many drawers and it's warm, he probably turned up the heating for this room so that if I'm going to be naked and I'm sure I will not freeze. Oh that's nice and so realistic. Some lamps and a camera on tripod is also there. I can not believe it, the sheer madness of this man. A true woman seducer. No, no, if he was just until last Friday, now he's mine.

"Wow, that looks like a practice room. Everything is there."
"Yes, my photo studio with practice equipment, but now to you, only a few questions. Please sit here on the chair at the table."
"Yes ok."
"Do you have any pain?"
"Yes, it itches me so much between my thighs."
"Have you had that longer?"
"For a few minutes and now it's getting stronger."
"Do you take any medications or drugs?"
"Yes, since the Joschuadrug."
"Hahaha, nothing else?"
"No?"
"Any man stories lately?"
"Yes, sexual intercourse has increased since last Friday."

514

"Well, do you know how tall you are?"
"Not exactly."
"Then I ask her to stand here against the wall in front of the dipstick. Please barefoot. Well. Height 180 centimeters."
"Why are you taking a picture of it now?"
"Photo of proof for the proportions. Please turn right ninety degrees once. Yes, just fine and lightning, turn on and flash and one last time turn please please and flashes."
"Do I look good in the photos?"
"We'll look at each other after the investigation. But please wait. We do the same poses again, but now with these black pumps."
"How do you know my shoe size?"
"Size thirty-eight. I checked, if I'm honest and I had these in stock."
"Now I'm dressed in black."
"Yes, erotic. Please see me again head on."
"Well, may I smile?"
"Yes, everything you want and flashes, please continue to turn, flashes, turn on, flashes, turn on, flashes. Finished. Do you know their current weight?"
"No, what are we going to do now?"
"Please go over to the Libra, but take the pumps off, the rest you can keep on."
"Oh, does not that spoil the weight?"
"The two parts are negligible."
"Pity."
"Well, you're not one of those women who want to give the doctor a pretty look around him ...?"
"Hahaha, yes, to wrap him around the finger and fill in the smock down there properly."
"Well, they are such a patient. I have to be careful that nothing happens to me."
"Hahaha, I would advise them."
"Well, weight seventy-two point five. Is ok for her size."
"Oh, how good that pleases you."
"I did not say I like it, I just said the proportions are great. So now we measure the chest circumference."

515

"But touch it carefully."

"How so? Otherwise they'll break."

"No, not that, but if you knead it like that, I'll always get so excited and then I can not rule out rape of the doctor."

"Ohohoh, then I'm very careful."

"Yes, now you do it."

"What?"

"Excite me when measuring your chest."

"How's that?"

"Well, now you drive so tenderly over my breasts, ohohoh, tender doctor."

"Done, you survived. Breast circumference one hundred and ten inches."

"Ohohoh, what do you want to know now?"

"The waist circumference."

"But do not tickle in the navel!"

"No, just measure it carefully. So good, sixty-nine."

"Satisfied?"

"Yes, note and now the hip circumference."

"Ohohoh, again touches and this time on my panties."

"I did it very fast. So hip circumference ninety nine centimeters. I can only tell you, really great proportions, really great."

"Thanks, also do a lot of sports."

"Yes, I realized that, you can swim and have a lot of stamina."

"How do you know about my stamina?"

"By birding, you last longer than other women, if I may compare."

"Thank you, the comparison is allowed."

"And now stop it, I'll do the humidity test."

"What?"

Something unexpectedly he pushes his hand briefly in my panties and notes very sober, the woman is already quite wet and even groans in this test. Yes, it could happen that I am about to fall for this delicious doctor. Oh Mia rules you, behaving like that in a doctor's office. I have to smile really loud inside.

"So all preliminary examinations with perfection survived. So far, they are perfectly healthy and their moisture production is perfect. Now to the internal investigations. Please sit here on the chair. Feet on the pads. No, let her thighs hang over the upholstery and forward. That's good."

"Should not I undress?"

"No, I do not want to be seduced."

"Oops, I can not guarantee anything."

"This is not how it works, I have to rest a little during the investigation and wild whirl around with his hands just bothers. Please put your hands on the side pads here, right and left."

"Then I'm lying there like a cross. The arms bent at ninety degrees."

"Yes."

"The arm guides on the upper and lower arm are well shaped and padded."

"You have to, because the investigations take a little longer. And are the cushions on the thigh and lower leg from comfortably adjusted, otherwise I have to change the supports."

"No, they are perfect for me. Who has been rehearsing here?"

"Oh, oh, ..."

"Tell me, but honest."

"I'm always honest, we promised ourselves."

"So answer my question, who has sat here and been doctored by you?"

"Mmm ... ."

"Go tell it or I'll go."

"So the device is just new. You are the first. I have only dreamed of other women here at the investigation, but there was still none there. You are the first and honest, I am more than happy about that. I still have to practice the examinations and they are so wonderfully honest and so incredibly soulful."

"Flatterer, but I like to be your first object of investigation, but only under one condition."

"Which one?"

"I am the first and after me no other woman comes to these investigations led by you."
"Oh, not one?"
"No! You have to promise me that?"
"Promised."

And now he puts on my wrists, attached to the support tapes with Velcro straps. On both sides. In addition, a further hamper around the upper arms, which are also moored to the pads. Good that the chains are eight inches wide, so they can be tightened and do not cut. They are black and that looks good. It's a feeling, somehow not scary but exciting. Now I can say I am in his power and fully at his mercy. Well, except for our codeword, that will end everything and I know that one hundred percent. And because I'm so sure, I can now drop and enjoy. I can do nothing more to drive him crazy. Oh yes, I can, I can drop, enjoy and show him what he does to me now I really like it and then I know it will make him really hot too. Besides, I have promised him that I will do it with him and he is looking forward to it too.

"Doctor, is that right, I can not move my arms anymore."
"Yes, that brings some peace to her. Now we do the same with the upper and lower legs. They look very erotic, just have to push apart the legs for the legs and snap them into place. So now they are sitting wide legged and you can get to all exam relevant places comfortably. They look like a turtle lying on their backs. This again a sharp souvenir photo."
"Mr. Doctor, but I have not experienced any investigation, is that really correct?"
"Well, now they will not be presumptuous, after all, I have studied and am on the latest examination level."
"But what did you study? Happy woman shackles?"
"This is too much for me now, they are begging for punishment."
"How punishment, what are you going to do?"

He goes to the cupboard that stands behind me and

518

opens a drawer. What is he getting out now? This uncertainty turns me on, I would not have thought. To the sexual excitement comes a joyful excitement on what is coming now. I see that he stands behind me and holds something in his hand. Pure excitement.

"Please open your mouth."
"No."

I do not open my mouth when talking, I'm smart and want to play. He now presses me a balloon gag with light pressure on my mouth or lips. I still do not even see what he thinks out to break my resistance. That's really fun. I can still determine, oh oops, he has a plan B. Now he's pinching my nose with two fingers of his free hand. This lout I have to give up and open my mouth and he has squeezed the balloon gag and with the strap with velcro fastened at the back of the head. Oh the gag has holes, I can also breathe through. Try something to say if it still works, but it comes out of my now gagged mouth only stammering out. He walks around me and gives me a kiss on the now only slightly open mouth. But our tongues can not touch anymore and it just becomes a whisper of the lips. Also very beautiful and above all erotic, because his tongue touches my gag and feels my oral moisture. After the separation, his lips look past my nostrils again and push them together lovingly. I can breathe through the open mouth, because the gag is provided with holes.

"So now I finally have the rest to begin my investigations. Let's see if they react perfectly and thus determine their full health."

He walks around me once and takes a picture of each side. You become the memories for eternity. Later, when we are old, we will sit together by the fireplace and look at these pictures and think about what it was lucky to find ourselves and what we were both happy about when creating these pictures. I have never done such pictures. Another premiere. Oh Joschua, I'm sooo happy, you know that. Yes, I think you feel that.

"The doctor is starting now with the first full body reaction test. The brush test."

Brush test what is that? He always makes it exciting. If he continues to do so with my excitement, then I'll come right away without him touching me down there. He looks into my eyes, oh what he probably reads from them, my full lasciviousness.

"We will talk about their eyes now and so they will answer my other questions, if they understand me, they'll blink once with their beautiful eyes."

I blink once and he smiles at me. Now he grabs a drawer again and takes out a brush, the famous pastry brush, and keeps it visibly in front of my eyes. Oh, I already suspect what's coming up to me. I can already almost feel what the brush will do to me right away. Joschua, no Mr. Doctor steps behind me and makes short, tender brushstrokes on my face. I turn my head to the side. Over and over again.

"Good reactions and now we brush around at her nostrils."

You're crazy, it sure tickles. What kind of a test, that's certainly pure torture. And this lout seems to enjoy it. First he says what he wants to do and then he waits with relish something that I can really look forward to it. Hahaha not my dear Mr. Doctor, so not. But already the brush dances over and something in my nose. I try to move my arms to avoid this brush or to push it out of my hand and I tug at my arm and leg cuffs, but I have no chance. Then Mr. Doctor already sets the brush strokes in my face and closes my mouth with his lips. During this action, he unexpectedly began to paint under my right armpit and I tried to withdraw his lips, which want to massage my lips by twists. One tickles the brush? And how, please Joschua stop I have to explode with laughter. And then he leaves with his lips my mouth and goes down with the brush on my body. Now he puts his left hand on my right breast and pushes it a little flat. I'm so curious what happens, at least my eyes ask what now and he really seems to read it there. He walks with his fingers under my bra. Then he raises the bra up and pulls him down until the nipple is exposed and already his brush, the brush, of course, begins to dance on her back and forth. I cringe violently and as the arms and legs can not, I raise my stomach and want to shake my breasts.

"That is not so, they disturb my investigations."

Oh he stops, how is the game finished? Oh no, it would have been a pity too. What does he take there, oh a very wide strap, which is attached to the chair on one side and pulls it over my stomach to fasten it on the other side. Hahaha well that all are provided with velcro. What all thought in advance. He can tighten continuously and he does that, so I can not lift my stomach out of the chair.

"Well, now they can not slip out anymore. Hahaha."

Oh it will be, I knew he could not leave it, now he makes a first visit to my brief to greet him with his lips and play around with it, which lures me a muffled moan. But he did not forget the brush inserts. He also has the right areas in his sights. They are my feet. Good that I always care for my feet. Not only care but I always paint them with red nail polish. He looks at her closely, which apparently turns him on. Oje he plays with his brush and he goes so slowly and with a bit of pressure through each and every toe space on both feet. I struggle with my feelings, he realizes that very clearly. He could now paint the rest of the body, but then the killer effect would be overdone and he is so sensitive.

He puts the brush on the cabinet in the bowl for used examination toys.

What would a doctor be without his stethoscope? I know from personal experience that when it comes to the skin is always very cold. I feel he will use it, he already takes it away from his neck.

"Her brushwork reactions have passed her body with grade one. Now I'll check her heart."

And he takes the stethoscope from his neck, puts the two ends in his ears and holds the scanner in his right hand. Now he looks me in the eye and smiles at me, then his scanner falls on my skin over my heart. As he observes my eyes intensely with his, he sees exactly how I react when the cold scanner touches my warm, hot skin. Shock and once again a feeling aroused. He now holds the scanner briefly on my lips and then goes deeper over my navel, the reactions are less, because the scanner has already absorbed my heat. But he also keeps it on my panties. He will not hear anything, then he shoves it underneath. He can not hear my excitement, only my faster beating heart. Now he pulls the stethoscope out of the panties and puts it away.

"You, I have heard everything and the result is worrying, you are very excited."

I have to smile and he sees it on my whole face, involved in the laughter. From this he suggests that I like his investigations, and he starts further investigations.

What is he doing now, he leaves the practice. One thinks there already practice, we are with him in the house in the photo studio. Oh, it's so realistic. Oh my doctor comes back, but what does he have in his hands now? I look at him questioningly. I can not see what he has in his hand, he hides it. Then he picks up my bra on my right breast and places an ice cube there so that it lies on my nipple. He releases the bra and holds the ice cube to the nipple. I sob, at least he should interpret it that way. It is awfully cold and the cold is pouring into me. But that does not stop him from placing the second ice cube on my left nipple as well. Then he goes down and sits down between my legs on a small wheelchair. He now walks with his left hand along my left thigh until he comes under my panties. He does the same thing with his right hand. Now his two hands are under my panties, where it is hot and humid. I feel my excitement rising and I am torn between his hot hands and the cooling ice cubes on my nipples. He calls it the so called hot cold test. You have the ideas.

"I know, it's a difficult test and they soon made it brilliant, so I want to free them from the ice cubes."

I'm breathing heavily and he feels my excitement. If he continues to upset me or let me down again. Ahhh he takes the ice cubes out of my bra and throws them in the trash. They are almost half melted and my bra is wet now. That makes him really wild and he kisses my wet breasts through the bra and pulls with his lips holding the nipples, fiercely around. Oops my excitement continues to rise. He looks at my bra, the wet patches seem to be very exciting for him and he takes some pictures. But it goes on, he has probably planned some more investigations, but before he really asks me ...

"Mia can I continue with the examinations or should I stop. So please blink once for yes. Should I continue?"

I open my eyes wide and blink once. He should not stop, I am discovering new feelings. The ice cube test I knew but the feelings are different in that I can not move and he is totally at the mercy.

My eyes ask again, what's up now. He reaches into a drawer again and conjures a hairdryer. Inserted and off you go, heat level medium and already a warm wind blows through my hair and then directly on my wet breasts. The hair dryer always move back and forth that it is not too hot and you can see how the nipples slowly warm up and curious to stretch. Also with the slip his hair dryer looks over, after he made a short stop over my navel. The drying moisture in my panties now exudes the typical, erotic Miascent. He turns it on properly and he puts the hair dryer away again. Oh what he has already made me feel. I had not thought of such things. I thought he was just playing around in my pussy, but he's a lot crazier and my feelings start to climb a huge mountain. With each test he makes me hotter or better he puts me closer to cloud seven test by test. This hot doctor, hahaha, my private doctor.

His hand now grabs a bandage scissors and cuts carefully but determinedly through my two bra straps. That's why I should not wear my bra. Now let both breast cappers fold down, hahaha. Oh, what a Mr Doctor, another daring cut between the two bra front pieces and the bra is almost gone. He pulls him on the left side of me completely out and my breasts are open. They literally scream for photos and he fulfills their wish immediately. The breasts are so hot, he has to do something and he does it, he pulls out of the drawer two, are the breast pressing. Oh now it will hurt to see if and how long I can stand it. Did not he say he does not stand on SM. Let's see what he does. He puts one chest clamp on my right breast and carefully turns something tight. The platelets press my nipple together and the firmer he turns the more I start moaning. He repeats it on my left nipple. My excitement continues to rise, I would not have thought that. He does it very carefully and only a little bit. He just wants to flirt with my navel, tongue technically and already she is dancing in my belly button. It drills and lashes wildly in it. I try to escape her with strong inhaling and exhaling. But the wide strap holds me tight and exhale so much that his tongue can not reach him anymore I can not. I have to endure it.

"That will not work, her navel already has to pass my tongue test."

And then he sits down again on his swivel chair between my legs, but on the way there makes his tongue a little trip over my five right toes, which thoroughly scans his tongue under the protection of his mouth, down to the interstices. It tickles and he has fun again. Doctors should have such fun at the patient examinations. Oh man how that tickles. That's certainly his tickling test. Ha, I know how he thinks. I'm fine. Oh, tickle that. Hahaha. Oh, Mr. Doctor please grace. I did not know how much a tongue can tickle in the right place.

If I now imagine how he looks at me, sitting from the perspective between my legs and looking up, that is a full erotic sight of the extra class for him and turns me on. Crap that I can not move. That's not what I imagined in my wildest dreams. I smell down there where he sits already determined violently, as wet as I am already. How he already seems to love this fragrance. The chemistry is right, as they say so proverbially, he can smell me good. My scent makes it easy, I feel it. Oh Mia quit your mind games the next unit of investigation continues. Oh he starts kissing me on my right foot and then he licks from there to my right thigh. Goes over my panties all the way to my left foot goes. Kissing and licking and gently following the hand on the underside, so a light erotic tickling unit. I breathe faster and faster, and I feel his touch make me tremble. He presses his mouth firmly on my panties on my pussy and my clit gives this contact to my brain. Attention to generate even more excitement. He gets up again and goes to the cupboard behind my head and takes out two doctor's gloves. She holds it over my face and then slowly pulls her there. Now he wants to make me totally crazy with the gloves. Oh the feelings are very different than his bare hands. How exciting also the fragrance, because he puts a glove covered hand on my gagged mouth and closes him almost completely and the second hand he arches over my nose and counts to five. Then he lets go and I breathe heavily. The excitement is almost at its peak.

"Everything ok?"

And I blink once. So he may continue to investigate, which makes me totally fun and increases my excitement a bit further. Man until now he does with everything he has made me incredibly hot. He is extremely sensitive. And as a man, I would never have thought that.

"Again the gloves on the face?"

And I blink again. I also like that and get excited. As we talked about it, I just thought, yes, and did not think it possible that he really does that to upset me so much, but doctor Joschua has taught me a better one again. He starts, but first he gives me a kiss on the forehead and both my eyes and whispers in my ear ...

"I love you and I'll drive you mad."

And then he holds both my mouth and nose again for five seconds and apparently it's the gloves on my skin that excite me as well. More than the first time he only did it with his hands. There was the scent of his skin and now it's this rubber glove fragrance. I did not know that it would be interesting to get other material on the skin. Arouses other exciting emotions. After five seconds, I regain sole control over my air supply and he now walks past me, between my legs. He has taken some parts in passing from the closet. A cream tube which he now puts on my left thigh and now he has one of the bandage scissors in his hand and cuts right and left my panties to then fold down to the front. The cutting and feeling of the blunt wing of the scissors on my skin makes me feel right. It's like everything here today wicked and that's how it feels. I do not think he knows how excited I am and he can still do it, but I'm really over ninety percent excited on my hundredth scale. Oh no sooner did he pull the panties forward, why not pull him out with a jerk? He picks up the cream tube, opens it and puts the lubricant on his left glove covered index finger. Then he puts the tube away and he takes with his right hand circular movements on my clitoris and I feel, I'm very close to the explosion and in that moment he presses his left index finger against my anal sphincter and opens it a little. His rubber gloved index finger slips in about two to three inches and in that moment, I hardly believe it, I reach the hundredth point. No, I reach it, but the excitement does not trigger, but seems to continue to rise. Oh Joschua, where should I go now with my feelings. I can not move and my feelings are getting more and more. Joschua, I can not explode any more, Joschua and now I'm passing the peak because I feel all the muscles in my body tense and stay tense for a while. Then the lights go out. I've closed my eyes and it's getting dark and then, I think I'm standing in the middle of a fireworks, dancing in front of my inner eye bright colours that run into each other, explode like rockets, just like the feelings in me, they seem to individual to burst like rockets and everywhere in my body also in the arms and legs, in the stomach and these lights are getting brighter and more violent. Oh Joschua me, me, I ohhh and very slowly it is as if the lights are dimmed in front of my eyes and dimmed until it is dark again. Then my body slowly begins to lose tension, piece by piece. He is so loving and tender and it is as if he makes right touches to me at the right moment and even now, he did not stop right away and like others rolled over and over, no, he continues to work on my clit cautiously and slowly Very slowly, he pulls out his right finger again. Another groan as this leaves my anus again. There has never been one inside. Also, I have to moan once again as he rounds my clit even firmer and then picking up the clitoris touch. Now my muscles are finally starting to relax. Oh how beautiful he gives me

527

now actually an intense kiss on my tongue pussy, but then hits my clit with his tongue and I react violently again. Then he completely leaves me and gets up to look into my eyes, which are still closed. He gently blows wind over her and I understand his desire and I open it and we look each other in the eyes. Only my racing heart is felt. He smiles all over his face. It must have been a lot of fun to him, but certainly not as much fun as he made me feel. Man Joschua what you have done with me is simply indescribable. He raises his hands so that I can see them and takes off his gloves and throws them in the trash. Then he loosens my chest braces slightly and I moan again. Never had my nipples been caught and I never thought that the constant pressure on them was so exciting. Where Joschua knows it all. I'm still smiling at him, but it's a totally happy smile of the whole kind. Some beads of sweat have accumulated on my forehead and increased to such an extent that they begin to run down the temples.

"Is my patient okay?"

I answer with a wink, a nod and a smile all over my face.

"Well, I have to say after the first examinations, they are in top form. Let's see if the check ups confirm this."

My gaze changes into a questioning, something more. But I can not shake the feeling, doctor Joschua has had fun and wants to do more research on me. But what else for which. Is there any that I have not thought of yet? Well no matter until now it was the hottest and most exciting and crazy and also dearest investigation of my life I would like to continue it. Oh Mia, are you curious about what he will do to you? No, he will only investigate me. Hahaha and how. He just wants to be thorough and then say how healthy I am.

"Now they come down from their excitement and then I can examine them further. I'll cover them up so they do

not cool down. "

He reaches into the cupboard and takes out a small package. Then he holds it in front of my face, I should see it first and then he opens it. The result is a gold coloured thermal film that he puts over me, down between his legs, he pushes her to stop something under my smallpox and above the shoulders and behind something pushed into it, even on the sides. Now my upper body is covered with the thermal foil. He leaves the room. Where does he want to go now, maybe even just to satisfy or to tease. Oh Mia you and your thoughts. They are getting worse. Oh, where does that come from? It is cuddly warm under the gold foil. Since I can sleep well after this terribly difficult effort for me. Oh, I can still feel the excitement dancing through all my muscles. Is that a beautiful feeling.

Then he returns to practice and thus back to me. He has a glass, oh with champagne in his hand. He takes a sip of champagne and moisten his lips. I watch him closely and I'm curious what happens now. He leans over me and squeezes his champagne drenched lips on mine and cuddles with them. Now my lips have accepted the sparkling taste, but it does not give more or does it. He puts the glass on the cabinet behind me and takes a dis- posable syringe, 5 ml out of a drawer. He makes it so that I can see it exactly and I watch him what he has probably thought up again. Then he pulls them with the champagne from the glass and holds them over my face. Since the balloon gag has holes, he puts the syringe on a hole and carefully pushes the champagne through the hole in my mouth. Since the balloon has many holes, the champagne drips through several holes in my mouth and I notice how I take the champagne with my tongue on the gag.

Now he takes some photos from different angles and with different lights, bright, dimmed and dark. This is how some time passes. Candlelight would fit in with the gold coloured thermal foil, yes, he has the same opinion as me, because he brings down the two five armed candlesticks from the dining room and puts them behind my head and he turns on the candles. Now a shot from below, then the candlesticks are visible next to my head and it makes some wind and the candle flames wobble and the light looks very bizarre. That will be pictures again. If we look at Joschua, what will we feel good about. This keeps the memory of such beautiful hours awake. Maybe then you get back there then like to try other crazy things together. I have the feeling that I am dreaming or have I fallen asleep. Well, it's nearly midnight again. But I have the feeling, I'm still something ahead. So Joschua will not stop. I already know him pretty well.

I look at Joschua. Oh yes I see his lustful eyes, it's time for the next investigation. Funny he does not take the thermal foil away from me. If he did that I would be really cold. It's chilly and warm underneath, and that's why I got so tired. As I judge him, he thought of that as well, after all he did the heat foil to me and for the same reason the heating was turned so high in the room at the beginning. He is just nice and indulging in him is not only a sexual experience, he also takes care of everything else that I feel so comfortable with him. He tries to quietly walk around me and reaches into the drawer behind me and brings out a soft, opaque cloth. Then he stands behind my head and blindfolds me. Now I am awake. Oh he releases the velcro from my gag, he wants to ask me now for my feelings. Oh man, this Joschua, hardly he has carefully pulled the gag out of my mouth and I want to tell him something, my mouth is already busy again and this time not with another gag, but his head has approached mine and his lips open my lips and tongue licked wildly in my mouth. He deals intensively with my counterpart and brings it back into life. He still tastes a bit like sparkling wine.

"Hello, rested well and have you survived all investi-

gations well?"
"No, not good, very good! And is it going on now?"
"You are insatiable, I would not have thought that now, but we will talk later in the evaluation of the investigations. Now it goes on."
"Oh yes, Mr. Doctor, please do it, please continue."
"Well, they'll still curse me, so to challenge me."
"Yes, empty promises."
"But you are a naughty patient, I think I have to gag her again."
"Oh, yes, go ahead."
"They seem to please you really well."
"Yes. Is very exciting."
"If they beg so, then they get the gag in again. Mouth open, otherwise a punishment will follow."

I do not react and he does the same game as before. Press balloon gag on lips and hold nose. Shortly thereafter, I open my mouth and with the gag. Cilisted behind the head again. This time he probably wants to do it differently. He takes a roll of tape from the drawer. Tapeband is a special tape, which has no adhesive surface and therefore does not stick to the skin or hair. It just keeps, as he told me yesterday, when you put tape on tape, then it holds rock solid. Now he wraps the ribbon around my head and headgear several times over my gagged mouth. Thus, I'm from the chin up to under the nose and wound up there can not get more air.

"Well, now you can not give any more stupid comments and just have to breathe through your nose. Oh, that reminds me you'll get another five seconds punishment."

And he holds his hand arched over my nose and counts again to five. He feels like I try to breathe, because he feels the train and the blowing out of the air directly in his resting hand.

"Well, the punishment is done, now we can proceed

with the investigations again."

And I blink my eyes once. Now he takes a roll of tape, three inches wide, and sticks a stiffener glued from one side to the chair, directly over my upper breast attachments, and reattaches it to the other side of the chair. He does the same with a strip below my breasts. Then another strip below my belly button. So the heat film is fixed and I get a little less movement.

He takes the bandage scissors and now cuts a hole in the film, where he will then pull my nipples. Only the right breast of mine. He feels my nipple, squeezes it and pulls it up a bit, it flashes my nipple back and he only has the foil in his hand between two fingers. Now he cuts off the film under his fingers and so creates a round hole. Through this hole he pulls my nipple and I feel that very clearly. In this man, even a little erotic touch from him can excite me sexually. The man is just pure madness. He does the same procedure on the other breast. Now I lie in front of him, covered with the gold foil but now my two nipples are out. Photo, lightning. Oh, now he has some braces in his hand again. This time but other breast clips, apparently with different pressure levels. He takes braces with a very light compression, very comfortable and puts them on me. Again I try to make moan like sounds, but no sound comes out of my mouth. I only hear it in me. For this, a slight tremor spreads on my body. Oh dear, it starts again, my excitement begins to emerge.

Oh you always put that handle in the drawer behind me, there he always brings out such erotic toys. No, not erotic toys, he uses normal things and does erotic things with them. Now he has grabbed something again, but I can not move my head with the tape around my mouth, because he has also wrapped it around the headrest. So I can not see everything he does anymore and I am only partly dependent on my emotional experiences when he touches something on me. Now I feel like he pulls the film under my buttocks and folds it up. I really liked what he did with his right index finger at the last examination. How do I get there now? Oh yes, because he puts on new disposable gloves. Oh, what a noise and then I see it, he holds it up and smiles. It's a giant vibrator, now it makes me hot again just because he lets him go and that without him touching me with it. I can now guess what will happen. The humming stops and then after a few photos, it starts. First he greets my clitoris with his tongue and brings her something in the mood, then he kisses me on the slightly exposed belly approach. Then he turns the vibrator back on, small step. It's a big headed vibrator, that is, the head is so big that you can not insert it. So he is only pressed on my pussy, in particular on my clitoris and the pressure strength, he can bring me either slowly or quickly or alternately to climax. Now he pushes the vibrator very carefully on my clit and it's like a small excitement thrust. I jumped tremendously. Yeah let's see how fast it is and already I have the feeling, I'm already at the upper limit. He stops the treatment with the vibrator just before my climax and gives on his left index finger again lubricating cream, but he has to wait until it is almost up to me, the explosion.

So now he penetrates with his index and middle finger of the right hand into my cave and massaged carefully my G-spot. My feelings rise and he pulls out both fingers again, waits a moment and he notices how I feverish that he goes on and he fulfills my wish. He has changed the vibrator rhythm to an alternating rhythm. Slow for five seconds, then full power for five seconds. This is a difficult shot, because when the full power is running and then comes the climax, he can quickly roll over, that is, he triggers and then falls off very fast by the additional power. Now he gently presses the vibrating vibrator on my clit and he watches carefully. It's my second peak, it will come faster, also because of the vibrator and I realize that I will lay down a rocket launch. Shortly before my climax and the short stop phase, he pushes his left index finger again, this time to the stop on the hand, in my anus. At the same time he presses the vibrator vigorously on my clitoris and it may take four to five seconds and my whole Mia body tries to fully regenerate against all holding units. Immediately he reduces the pressure of the vibrator on my clitoris, but lets him continue to vibrate there. Then he pulls out his index finger again and presses his flat hand fully against my buttock bottom. By while continuing to vibrate and his pressure on my butt flattens the climax not quite off. He holds this position for about a minute and then presses once again the vibrator with the change setting firmly on my clitoris. Does he want to test my climax ability, does he really manage to catapult me to climax for the third time in a row? He takes off his left glove and takes the vibrator in this hand and tries past the vibrator to reach my G-spot with two fingers of his right hand. It succeeds and now he massages, without further break, my G-spot and the vibrator works at full speed on my clitoris. It does not take long and I try to get more air. I'm on my way back to an emotional rocket launch. And then it's the third time, I breathe so much and suddenly I stop, a short while. My body starts to shake and I start to breathe heavily again. Now full tension in each of my muscles and then I can not stop it, I explode. Immediately he stops the vibrator and pulls out his fingers. He folds down the thermal foil and leaves me to myself. He just sits down between my legs and watches as my third climax abates. It is total insanity, what do I have there only for a doctor, sex is not better. He is absolutely amazing and then he loves me too. I'm so happy. Why did not he press his cock into me. That he has renounced, has not done any harm, because I had more fun than ever since. Nonsense never. I can only confirm that often the reality, if one is allowed to experience it, is a thousand times more beautiful than any dream. Oh, it feels so fantastic. Now he lets me down a bit and then he will certainly untie me. The clock on the wall shows already 1.23.

He gets up, takes a few more pictures. Then he goes up to me and gives me a big kiss on the bound mouth. Then he takes off my blindfold after dimming the light. My eyes were now in the dark for some time through the bandage and there they are sensitive to light. Oh Joschua also thinks of everything, because if you get a light shock now, the beautiful feelings that are still in me are immediately gone. Now he wraps the bondage tape around my mouth again. Goes easily and then he loosens the velcro on the gag and pulls me out of my mouth very carefully. A small kiss on the mouth completes the liberation action. I'm still far away, but I see him smiling at me.

"Thank you, many, many, many thanks!"
"I have to thank you, you were better than in any of my dreams just awesome. I'm going to slowly release you and massage your arms and legs a bit. Would you like to sit by the fireplace afterwards or go to bed at the bar or just go to bed or sleep?"
"Oh, just like I'm in bed and dreaming."
"Okay, when you're standing again, I'll put the robe on you and you'll go straight to bed. I'm just doing everything and I'll follow right away, if I may."
"I even ask for it, I still want to snuggle up to you while falling asleep."
"Super."

Then he walks down to my legs, loosening the two straps on both sides and massaging my thighs before releasing the supports and carefully placing my legs on the floor. He also proceeds in the same way with both arms. Now the breasts are removed and the breasts brought back to reality with very tender kisses. Then he removes the tapes from the chair and the abdominal belt. Unbelievable, I am free again and he helps me to stand on my feet again and holds me for a moment in his arms. He looks at me, smiles, puts his arms around me and kisses me completely, very tenderly and his tongue can deal with my tongue again, without a gag in between. Then he lets me stand for a moment and reaches for the robe to kill him.

"Can you stand and walk again?"
"Still shaky, I'm still so happy inside."
"Good, then I'll go up with you. Come with me to the door."
"Yes."

At the door he turns off the lights and he asks me to wait, then he returns to the practice and blows out the candles. I'm waiting at the door and we both go upstairs to the bedroom.

"I'm really tired, are you still snuggling up to me? Completely naked?"
"Yes, I can do it. Come on, I'll take your robe and off under the covers."

We stand at my bedside, he takes my bathrobe and I immediately crawl under the covers. He goes to his side, takes off his doctor's coat and crawls under his blanket. He wants to slip over to me, but then he realizes that I've already fallen asleep. I have the feeling that the third climax has made me totally tired. What I'm going to dream now. Good night, dear thoughts, until after.

Hello, this is Mia!

You have just that first book of my new book series read and there are some more to follow with many new, erotic ones experiences.
Do you have so much reading?
Having fun, how do I write?

Oh, I want to tell you, too, the book you read was from mine view written. If you like it want to read Joschua's view, that is also available on the book market and ebook and also here will follow a few more.

The title: crazy about you

unrestrained desire
told by Joschua
So you're spoiled for choice, though
you fall on book 2 + 3 + 4 + ... want.
I would be glad if you gave me times a
response would mail, what you felt
while reading the book and have
experienced.

E-mail:
hoffmannosnabrueck@gmx.de

Impressum

Bibliografische Information der Deutschen
Nationalbibliothek: Die Deutsche Nationalbibliothek
verzeichnet diese Publikation in der Deutschen
Nationalbibliografie; detaillierte bibliografische Daten
sind im Internet über dnb.dnb.de abrufbar.

© 2020 Hartmut Hoffmann
Herstellung und Verlag: BoD – Books on Demand,
Norderstedt
ISBN: 978-3-7519-6966-6